I0831186

RIMEWINTER

Cover design and illustration by Janette Ramos

Library of Congress Control Number: 2022902817

ISBN 978-0-9885082-7-9

Printed in the United States of America

Published by Giraffix Media

THE SWORDSPEAKER SAGA

RIMEWINTER

DJ EDWARDSON

GIRRAFIX

KNOXVILLE

For my daughter Sky

S.D.G

Contents

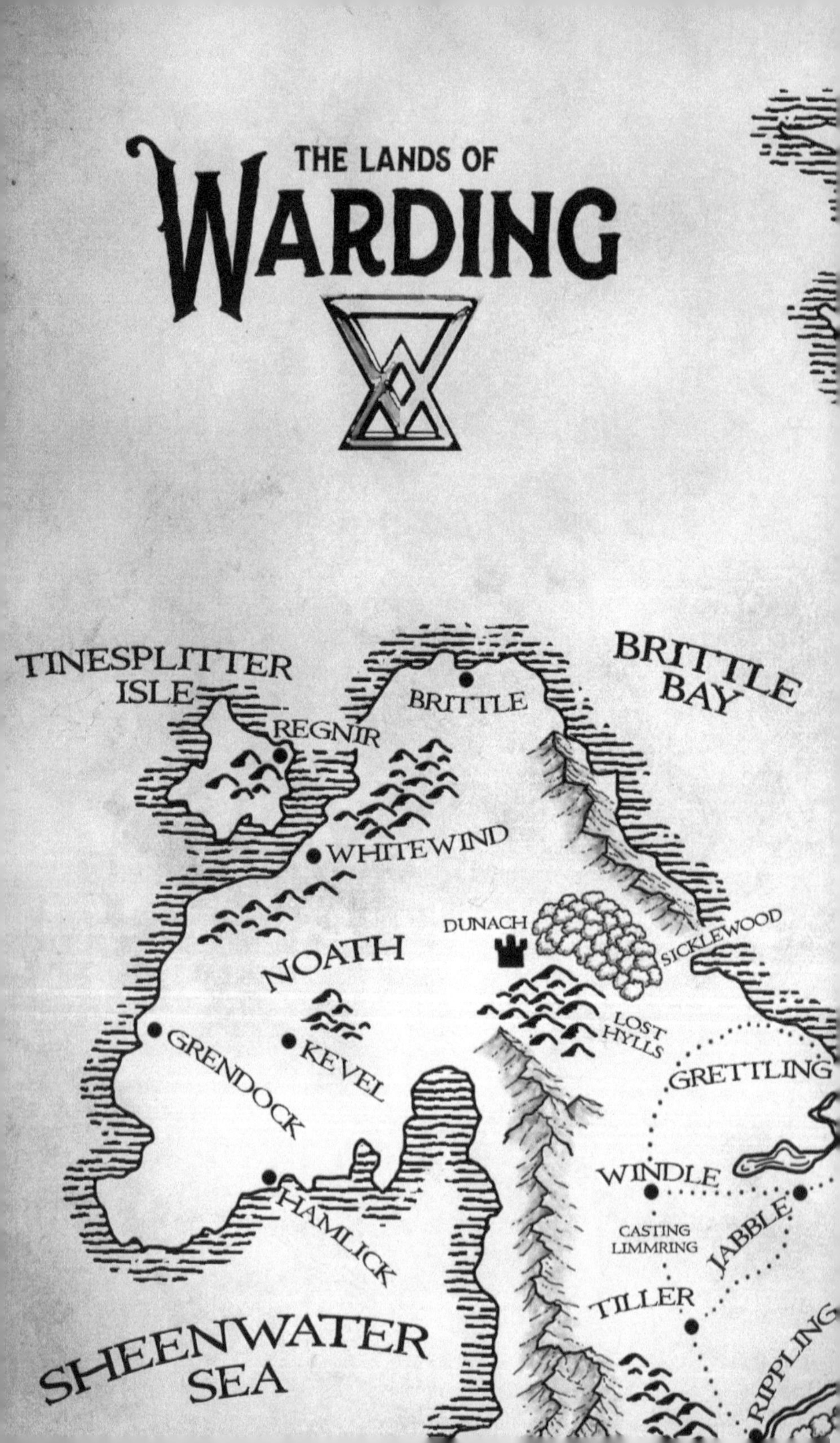

TINESPLITTER ISLE
BRITTLE
BRITTLE BAY
REGNIR
WHITEWIND
DUNACH
SICKLEWOOD
NOATH
LOST HYLLS
GRENDOCK
KEVEL
GRETTLING
WINDLE
HAMLICK
CASTING LIMMRING
JABBLE
TILLER
SHEENWATER SEA
RIPPLING

MORSHORN
CLAVHORN
HAUKMARN
DIREROC
MARRED WASTES
AVAR
GAVEL
CHOR
LATHETHICKET
DIRING SEA
ROVING
THE CLEFTS
FENNIGAR
FURROW
SEABRIM
WINDSTERN
INRIS
CASTING SELVEDGE
CASTING URLISH
QUELLING
HEMMING HYLLS
CHARRING
DUNSKEIN
NICKLING
MAVRIM'S GAZE
CASTING ALDRIC
MERRILING RIVER
MADRIGAL
FATHOMWOOD

Chapter 1

THE PEDDLER'S WAGON

A hail storm in summer is an unsettling thing. Hail is odd and unexpected enough even on chilly days. The crashing pellets remind us that the world is not as safe as we thought, that it is, in some sense, "out to get us." But when that same assault of nature comes amidst sunlight, as it did on this day for Kion, it is all the more disturbing. He hardly thought this journey would be free of trouble, but this was not at all the sort of trouble he'd been expecting. If this was the beginning, it made him wonder what surprises lay ahead. As the pounding squall clattered on, his thoughts turned inevitably to that singular thing that he had been thinking about for six days straight: finding his mother. Everything else—the war, the living sword he carried at his side, and even the discomfort from his still-healing arrow wound—paled in significance to this one truth: his mother was missing and it was his fault.

It was almost certain that she'd been captured by the haukmarn when she left Charring to return to their farm in Furrow. Kion had thought that sending a messenger to tell her he was leaving on a short trip to Roving would reassure her, but instead it had sent her hurrying back to find out what had become of her wayward son. And now she was gone. The trackers Aunt Lizet hired to search for her came back without any trace of her either on the road to Furrow or in the Hemming Hylls. She had headed north just as the haukmar army swept in to attack Charring and they must have taken her as they marched south. Kion had to find her, and find her quickly. Haukmar captives did not last long. Hopeful news had come recently that a group of prisoners had been freed on the road to the seaside town of Fennigar. The report was that Warding soldiers had ambushed their haukmarn captors and rescued several dozen captives. Most of the freed prisoners had already been sent home, but several of the sick and wounded had been brought on to Fennigar until they were well enough to travel.

Kion, along with his sister Tiryn and Zinder the nyn, his best friend in all the world, had set out to see if his mother was among those recovering in Fennigar. The haukmar armies appeared to be in retreat. Warding's enemies had been defeated at both Charring and Fennigar and no word of any new battles had come over the last eight-mark. It was believed that the haukmar leader, Vayd Mokán, had succumbed to the wounds he'd suffered in Charring by Kion's hand. Without his leadership, it was doubtful the war would continue. Though the haukmarn still held the Fortress of the Clefts at Roving, the main roads of Casting Selvedge had been quiet ever since his defeat. But there was no assurance that the land would stay at peace.

These thoughts rattled around in his head as noisome and relentless as the hail crashing onto the rocky outcropping under which they'd taken shelter. They were two days northwest of Charring. Aunt Lizet had loaded Zinder's cart with supplies and provisions for a long journey, but even as well-stocked as they were, and with Tiryn riding in the back, Zinder's mule, Crusty, handled the burdens with little complaint. There was little the beast objected to, provided he was allowed regular breaks for grass, though Zinder usually had to resort to a significant amount of coaxing to get him going again once they stopped.

The buffeting winds from the storm blew sharp and strangely cool into the shelter, but as strong as they were, they could not abolish Crusty's pungent odor in the tight quarters. Beyond the shadow of their protective rock, the hail clashed and skittered and settled into a pebbled carpet on the short, grassy slope between their refuge and the road to Fennigar.

In the midst of Kion's ponderings, Zinder slapped his forehead so hard, the crack of it sounded over the hail. "It was the Scribe!" he said, breaking the long, wordless wait for the hail to end. Zinder rarely stayed quiet for long.

"The Scribe?" Kion said. "Why in the Four Wards are you bringing him up again?"

"It was him! He was the one who sold me that old rusty blade at Roving—the one that turned out to be Truesilver!"

Kion fingered the hilt of his sword. The round citrine set in the middle of the guard glittered enigmatically in the dark, as only a stone set in a living weapon could. Kion had come almost to think of it as Truesilver's eye, though the blade had other means of seeing which Kion did not fully understand. Two smaller gems were set at either ends of the cross-guard.

"Is that true, Kithian?" Kion addressed his sword. "Do you know the man who sold you to Zinder? Was it this mysterious Scribe Zinder keeps going on about? I, for one, have my doubts that he even exists."

Zinder adjusted his wide-brimmed hat. "Ah, lad, now don't start that again. The Scribe may have done a disappearing act in Roving, but you've read *The Lay of the Glaives.* Parchments and poems don't just appear out of thin air, I'll have you know."

Tiryn's eyes twinkled in the shadowy light beneath the overhang. Though she did not talk much, she was clearly enjoying the nyn's reaction to Kion's teasing.

"If it was the Scribe, he did not reveal himself to me. The Scribe rarely makes his presence and purposes known. He prefers to walk in mystery," Kithian said, in an ancient, elemental voice that only Kion could hear, though he passed on the sword's words to the others, as he was in the habit of doing.

"So Truesilver knows the Scribe? There's more proof for you, lad, that old Zinder hasn't gone completely daft."

"How did the Scribe come by *The Lay of the Glaives* in the first place?" Tiryn's curiosity drew her out of her silence. She and Zinder shared the same love of poems and books and legends and all things inkish and papery. "And where are the other parts of the poem? You said he only gave you the first part, right?"

"Good questions, but I'm afraid the answers are as elusive as the Scribe himself. Perhaps some scholar in Gilding knows where the rest of the *Lay* is, but as I'm no more than a poor, poetry-loving blacksmith, I couldn't say. This much I can promise you, though. I'll shake that scribe so hard the next time I see him that the answers will tumble out of his fancy gold-plumed hat!" He stood up from his seat in the front of the cart and beat the air with his fists, throttling the imaginary scribe.

"Tell Zinder that he is fortunate to have seen the Scribe at all. To have spoken with him face-to-face is a rare honor."

"Just who is the Scribe, then? What do you know about him?" Kion said.

"The most important thing I know is that he seeks, as do I, to serve and protect the people of the Four Wards, and that he does so with the blessing of the Mastersmith upon him. His comings and goings, however, are his own. Perhaps none but the Mastersmith truly know his purposes."

The Mastersmith. Fitting that the Scribe should have some connection to him. For he was an even greater enigma than the Scribe. The Mastersmith had made the glaives of old, but Kithian spoke of him as if he still lived. When Kion asked where that might be, Kithian would only say that it was beside his forge, where no man could come, save at his own peril.

The hail at last began to subside, and Kion, whose thoughts had turned briefly away from his mother, did not bother passing on Kithian's words this time. His mind turned, along with his eyes, onto the mist-shrouded road before them. It cut through the small valley and then sharply around a mossy hill. Hopefully, his mother lay at the end of that rutted path. And if so, then neither hail nor haukmarn would keep him from her.

The wheels of the cart had ceased to crunch over the hailstones some hours ago. A bright northern sun re-emerged to restore order to the northern plains. All was back as it should be. Three hawks drifted above in wide circles, patrolling a serene sky, the recent storm all but forgotten. Before them, the well-worn road snaked around one of the few hillocks that remained within the rolling fields between Charring and Fennigar. The land flattened and grew more open the farther north—and thus the closer to the coast—they went. From the wagon to the distant horizon, supple, bluish grass, dotted with copses of bushy heartwood trees, waved them on. The great wide landscape revealed a world so much grander than the sheltered confines of Kion and Tiryn's home in the Tors. A month ago, neither of them had ever traveled more than a few miles from the familiar haunts surrounding their tiny cottage. And now here they were, setting off into what seemed like an endless trove of unknown wonder and beauty.

And yet, Kion could hardly find peace in his surroundings while his mother was in chains. At best, she was lying sick in some bed in Fennigar, but there were far worse fates that darkened his imagination. He tugged at the wrappings around his shoulder where his wound still itched.

"What if the reports turn out not to be true?" he said to Zinder, who sat beside him in the front of the wagon. Tiryn rode back with the food, bedding, tents, a box of tools, and, in a crate filled with straw—heaviest of all—eight casks of flax oil. The oil was as important as their food, for without it Truesilver could not make its crimson fire. "What if not all of the prisoners escaped when the Warding outriders ambushed the haukmarn? Or what if she wasn't even on the road to Fennigar? What if she was taken to Roving?"

"Now, lad, what is it that sword of yours says? 'We can only fight the battle in front of us.' We know at least some escaped.

Fennigar is not a long journey. We'll know the truth soon enough. For now, this is the best chance we have at finding your dear sweet mother. Let's not even think about her going to Roving. Because we both know the haukmarn wouldn't leave her there. They would take her all the way to the Marred Wastes if they were northward bound and that's a fate we could not save her from, not with a dozen Truesilvers and every man a fanewarden." The Marred Wastes. Home of the haukmarn. It was said no man could tarry long amidst its fetid airs and his mind remain whole.

Zinder had barely finished speaking when a pea-sized chunk of ice pattered against his leather boot. Another followed, bouncing against the floorboards of the front seat. More and more came, quickly filling the pleasant midday air with a troublesome din. Zinder stuck his pointy white beard at the sky and squinted angrily.

"Has summer lost all sense? Hail on the sixth of Lockwin! Twice! Shar's dome, this is the maddest weather I've seen since the sideways blizzard of '99."

"Fire and ice, another delay."

"Let's hope we can find shelter before it gets worse."

Zinder swatted Crusty with the reins and the mule darted off toward the hillock. By the time they reached it, the hail was coming down as big as acorns.

"Ahh!" Tiryn squealed as she scrambled under a heavy wool blanket. Kion extended his cloak over Zinder. It was made of good, thick wool also, but he could still feel some of the larger bits of ice slapping him through the fabric. Poor Crusty had no relief from the pounding assault and he let his misery be known with a chorus of woeful squeals.

Their race to the hillock proved to be in vain, for it offered no real protection from the storm. The wind blew straight out of the north and the hillock was on the south side of the road. They could try to go around to the back of it, but the rocky ground surrounding it was no place to bring a cart. They'd break a wheel for certain.

"What's that?" Zinder said, pointing beyond the hillock. It took a few moments before Kion spotted it through the curtains of hail—a large, dark shape off to the side of the road.

"Is it a house? It's big, whatever it is," Kion said.

"Ah, I can make it out now. It's a wagon, a covered one. Whoever it belongs to might let us shelter inside or beside it—if you mind your manners and let me do the talking."

"I'll listen to you jabber on for a week if I have to—anything to get us out of this storm."

They hurried down the road and brought the cart off the hail-encrusted path and into soft grass. Hail littered the floorboards of the front seat and the back of the cart. An ice chunk the size of one of Truesilver's citrines smashed into Kion's good shoulder. He felt it even through his cloak. That one was sure to leave a welt.

"This storm's a real moatengator," Zinder yelled over the battering, clattering barrage. "If the owners of this wagon don't take pity on us, our bodies may end up buried under all this wintry nonsense."

Their cart ground to a stop on the south side of the massive wagon. Immediately, much of the storm's fury fell away, blunted by the towering, fifteen-foot structure. It had a large awning of thick black canvas which would shield them even further, if they were allowed to dismount and come beneath it. All manner of pots, tools, pouches, bags, and knickknacks in various states of shoddiness hung from the wagon's sides, making the racket that much worse. Merchant wagons like this sometimes came through Furrow, but they were rarely this large, nor did they carry such an extensive array of goods.

Tiryn peeked out from under her blanket, but Kion motioned for her to stay hidden in the back of the cart. They still did not know if the owners of the wagon would turn out to be friendly.

Kion had never wanted to bring his sister along in the first place. She was timid and slight and had come close to dying of the wistering fever little more than a four-mark past. He dreaded the thought that some misfortune might befall her before the end of the journey. But he had been overruled by Zinder and Kithian, and so he'd been forced to bring her along. He hoped he did not regret his decision.

The merchant wagon was pulled by a team of four horses, all of them fine, huge creatures, with chestnut coats and sable manes. As stout as they were, they stood exposed to the hail and they huddled and scampered at the front of the wagon, doing their best to avoid the icy deluge. The three men sheltering beneath the wagon's awning fared far better. Not only were they entirely safe from the hail, but judging by their dress and appearance, the business of this particular merchant had been doing quite well. Though the shortest and the oldest of them leaned on a thin, reedy-looking staff, his cloak was new and finely stitched and his boots were fashioned from quality, well-oiled leather. The hood of his cloak shrouded most of his face, allowing only the barest tip of a pale, needle-like nose to escape the darkness within. The other two men sported rough, bearded faces, but their lamellar armor had been kept in fine condition. The sheathed short swords at their belts confirmed them as caravan guards, and the suspicious eyes they turned on the newcomers showed that they were more than ready to use them. Kion sensed their chances of taking shelter under the wagon's awning would be slim to none if those two had anything to say about it.

"Master," one of them said. "What should we do with this rabble?"

The man in the cloak shuffled stiffly forward and tipped his slender staff toward Zinder's cart. His movements were so brittle Kion imagined he could have heard his bones cracking if there'd been no hail.

"Hold, strangers." The old fellow's voice rasped inside his chest in an unhealthy fashion. "What do you mean, swooping in here like a flight of hawks after a pack of conies? Be off, or my men will make you wish you'd done otherwise." His voice was thin, like its owner, but it had a piercing quality that caused it to rise above the storm.

Kion wasn't looking for a fight, but instinctively he reached behind his back for where Truesilver lay on the floorboards. The voice of his blade came swift in warning.

"It would be best to let the nyn speak. I do not believe these men will attack us unless provoked."

Zinder raised his hands in a show of peace. The hail thundered against the backside of the merchant wagon and thumped against the cloth awning overhead, forcing him to raise his voice. "We mean no harm, my friend, nyn's honor. We seek nothing more than shelter from the storm. All we request are a few passing moments to share this good ground with fellow travelers away from the ravages of a summer day that doesn't know what to do with itself."

The old man pushed back his cowl so that the rest of his wrinkled face and his two sunken eyes slid into the hazy light beneath the awning. His skin stretched so tightly over his cheeks that it looked as though his skull ought to have been poking through in places. His lips and eyebrows were almost non-existent, and his ears might have been made from sheets of paper. The two toughs put their hands to their swords, but the raised hand of the old man, which appeared to be mostly knuckle, kept them at bay.

"Ah, a nyn. My old eyes took you for a child and that boy there for your master or guardian." The stranger paused, glancing briefly towards his covered wagon. Two shuttered windows and an oversized door guarded the interior against prying eyes. "I suppose you have tools with you, then—tools suitable for fixing a wagon?"

A grape-sized pellet whacked one of Kion's fingers. He tugged his sleeves over his hands and hunched forward, trying to make himself as small as possible. If only this fellow would get past the formalities and agree to grant them shelter. Kion had little patience for petty talk like this when it was obvious what needed to be done—which was why Kithian had asked him to let Zinder do the talking.

"I'm a nyn. I can fix almost anything." A hopeful warmth trickled into Zinder's reply. He could smell a business proposition from half a league away. "I see you've got two wheels there in need of fixing. I'd be more than happy to help you get that fine wagon of yours back on the road again in exchange for a few brief moments of shelter."

"You ask no more than that?" The old man let out a satisfied snort, the kind that told he had done his share of bartering. "Then we have a deal. I'm sure you can't fail to be an improvement over my two men here. I hired them for their swords. Their wainwright skills are sorely lacking."

The coldness in his men's eyes only deepened at this remark, but Zinder ignored their frosty looks.

"Zinder Hamryn, at your service." He hopped down and bowed in practically the same motion.

"And you may call me Toft, Meander Toft," the old man said. "Come, the replacement wheel is right over there as you can see. We've been stranded for several hours. I was none too keen to see you come trampling your way toward our shelter, but I never imagined a nyn would come galloping along. Odd to see one of your kindred in this backwoods northern country. Might I inquire where you've come from? Charring, I presume?"

"The very same," Zinder said. "And yourselves?"

"I have a small estate halfway between here and Charring. We were on our way from there to Fennigar when the wheel shattered."

Meander Toft's tone had brightened considerably after his initial greeting, and yet Kion kept his right hand gripped around

Truesilver's hilt. A faint, acrid smell crept through the air which could only mean one thing. Haukmarn, or at least the glowing white wanstones that gave them unnatural endurance and strength, were somewhere nearby.

"Be watchful, swordspeaker," Kithian said. *"There is more to this merchant than a broken-down wagon."*

Chapter 2

ALL DISTANCE DRAWS NEAR

The hail ceased not long after Zinder began work on the wheel. The replacement, framed and spoked in dark oak, was well-crafted and ready to mount, but Meander's guards had not been able to get it to stay on. It kept slipping off every few miles. For that reason, Meander had been more or less stuck, halfway between Charring and Fennigar, for the better part of two days, only managing to go short distances at a time before they were forced to stop and fasten it back on.

"And no haukmar assaulted you during that time?" Kion said. The word in Charring had been that the haukmarn had retreated back to Roving, but that could change at any moment. Even before the war, haukmar raids were not unheard of along the major roads. And that scent of wanstones had to be coming from somewhere.

"Have you not heard? They got scared away back north when some brash boy set fire to Charring. I suppose that's one way to drive them out. Destroy everything you have so there's nothing left for them to conquer. It's far too early to be sure that the war is over, but the attack at Fennigar failed too. All that is wanting is to sweep away the remnant holding out at Roving."

Tiryn had come out from hiding. Meander and his men, however gruff and suspicious they might appear, did not pose any immediate threat as far as Kion could see. The old peddler even took down a few stools from amongst the odds and ends hanging on the sides of his wagon and offered them to Tiryn and Kion while Zinder and the guards performed their work.

He offered them tea, but Kion declined, warning Tiryn with his eyes to do the same. It was likely harmless, but that wanstone scent had him wary, and he thought it best not to risk it. Tiryn, as she so often did, missed his silent warning and took the merchant up on his offer. She had a soft spot for old folk and probably couldn't imagine one of them wanting to do her any harm.

"That is good news," Kion said absently. He kept glancing at Zinder, ostensibly to check on his progress, but mostly as a way of studying the wagon. Was the wanstone scent coming from there? The smell was faint, more like a tickle or a twitch in his nose than the overpowering acidic air he remembered from his fight with Vayd. Perhaps it only meant that haukmarn had passed this way recently. "But I wouldn't be too sure the haukmarn will be defeated so easily. Strom is dead and some rumors say that the haukmar leader, Vayd Mokán, survived the fires at Charring and will soon rally his harriers."

Meander interrupted his sip of tea. "Well, I heard the boy also wounded him terribly somehow. Can you believe it? A mere boy? Supposedly he had some sort of enchanted sword. It cut through Vayd's armor, straight to the heart, if you believe the monstrous yarns the talesingers are spinning."

Not exactly true, but Meander was not far off. Kion didn't say anything. No need to tell Meander that he was the boy from the tales. If there were haukmar lurking nearby, there was no need to go around announcing his presence.

Zinder finished pounding out the dents in the boxing on the first wheel. After applying some grease to the axle to ensure a better fit, the guards helped him slip it on. Zinder worked up more of a sweat correcting and directing the men than he had in readying the wheel, but they got it right eventually. He brought out a U-shaped wrench from his tool chest to tighten it in place.

"So, Tiryn, how do you like your tea?" Meander continued. The good-natured way he addressed her made Kion shift on his stool. It sounded false as fool's gold. "You haven't said a word since you sat down. I hope you're not finding it disagreeable. Don't worry, I shan't be offended if it's not to your liking."

Tiryn reluctantly pulled her face out of the large cup she'd been hiding in. "It's delightful, thank you. Just like the kind my aunt makes, only with less honey." Her words came out just above a whisper and straightaway she went back to hiding in her tea.

"Yes, well, I prefer it bitter myself."

"Have you ever seen a haukmar, Mr. Toft?" Kion attempted to work the conversation back around to where he could ask about the wanstone scent.

"Oh, most definitely. I'm much older than you, remember. If you've lived as long as I have and wandered as much, you've seen just about everything."

"Well then, you must know they're awfully hard to bring down. I would say it's more likely Vayd survived than not."

"I see. And your many years of experience with the haukmarn tell you this, I presume?" Meander's voice dripped with condescension. He was at least shrewd enough to know that Kion would not fall for his feigned kindness.

Kion wanted to blurt out, "I know because I was the one who cut Vayd down," but he checked the impulse. "It's just a hunch. What do you know about the haukmarn, then? I'm particularly curious about their wanstones. Do you know much about them?"

The question startled the merchant, but only for a moment. He looked about and leaned in close, lowering his voice. "More than most. You see, I'm not a peddler only. I'm something of an amateur scholar. I've read what little has been written on them, which is mostly just speculation, but I've recently come into possession of a few of the actual stones. I'm keeping them for study. They're the reason I'm headed to Fennigar, you see. To find out if I can sell what I've learned to the leader of the Warding forces there. I believe my knowledge will be worth a good deal to the right person."

Meander's shrewdness and pride lit up his pale face. Kion could almost see gold coins floating in his eyes.

"You're bringing the stones with you? You have them in that wagon?"

"Well, yes, if you want to know. Though what's it to you?" Meander raised a suspicious eyebrow.

So there weren't any haukmarn after all. But the news that this peddler had some of the stones was suspicious all the same. How had he come by them?

"I heard the wanstones can drive a person mad."

"Oh, that's pure moonshine. People only say that out of ignorance. They're perfectly harmless when you know how to handle them."

"So what are their secrets then?"

Tiryn peeked out from behind her cup, two curious eyes hovering over the rim.

Meander set his own cup down in the grass, having drained it dry. "That is why it's called a secret, boy. If I told you, it wouldn't be worth much to the fane's men, now would it? Unless you've got a few hundred or so gold rounds in that cart of yours, you'll just have to wonder what secrets old Meander has locked away in that mind of his."

Given Truesilver's ability to sense lies, if Kion had a few moments alone with this peddler and his blade, Toft's secrets might not be so safe, but there was little chance of that happening.

A loud whistle from Zinder interrupted the conversation. "There you go, sir, you're ready and righted for another romp through the upside-down weather of Casting Limmring." He wiped his hands on a rag and slipped the last of his tools back into his metal box. The two guards kicked out the logs propping up the wagon and it settled, heavy and ponderous as some great wooden beast, onto its newly restored wheels.

"You've exceeded my expectations," Meander said, rising

from his stool with audible creaks that did not come from the wood.

"I'm a nyn," Zinder said with an exaggerated bow. "What did you expect?"

Tiryn stared back at Meander's wagon as Crusty pulled them around the bend.

"Well, it certainly was good fortune we ran into that peddler —for him as well as us," she said. "I think I'll have to write a song about him someday. I might call it 'The Meandering Peddler.'"

"'The Shifty Peddler' would be more like it," Kion said. "Something wasn't right about that man."

"Oh, Kion, you don't trust anyone, that's all. You act like the whole world's against us. I'll admit he was a bit rough around the edges, but he did save us from that storm."

Zinder cast a backward glance down the road as well and tugged on the rim of his dull gray traveling cap. He had a dozen or so others packed in his bags somewhere, but this was one of several he favored when on the road. The drab color and style were well suited to nondescript travel and Zinder was nothing if not practical. Once they reached the safety of Fennigar where bandits and haukmarn were less of a concern, his more flamboyant offerings would burst forth from where they were packed away.

"I fear Kion might be right on this one, lass. That wagon reeked of wanstones. I don't trust anyone who treats with that sort of thing. He's up to no good or I'm a fire-breathing fish."

"Zinder, did you actually say I was right about something?" Kion said in open-mouthed astonishment.

"There's a first time for everything." Zinder's eyebrows rolled in a sinuous wave.

Tiryn nestled further down into the baggage. "Well, you two

may be right, but I'll choose to go on thinking the best of people until they prove me otherwise. It might not be the smartest thing to do, but I can't bear to live life the other way around."

"I wish everyone had your heart, lass. But I've known too many peddlers in my day. And another odd thing. I asked him about what he did with the old wheel since it wasn't around. He said he used it for firewood. A bit suspicious for a peddler. I'm sure he could have gotten something for it from a wainwright."

"Yes, that does seem odd. What does Kithian think about him?" Tiryn said. She was far more prone to seek Kithian's counsel than Zinder was. She'd taken it for a certainty that the sword was more than just a mere blade from the very start, though she'd never seen the weapon make fire or fly through the air to Kion's hand or do anything beyond glow softly in the dark.

"He was certainly hiding something, but what I cannot say," Kithian said.

"Was he lying about the wanstones? Had he really studied them?" Kion said.

"Again, I cannot say. His mind was wrapped in knots and the truth was riddled within."

"I thought Kithian could tell whether people were telling the truth or not," Tiryn said.

"Some people are harder to judge than others. The learned or the clever require the direct touch of a swordspeaker."

"That man was certainly a scholar of some sort. That much is true."

There was not much more to say about the mysterious Meander Toft and so, as the road drifted on, their talk fell gradually back to the fate of Tiryn and Kion's mother, as it always did. Fennigar was still the better part of three days away, and though the hail and the encounter with Toft had in truth cost them little time, Kion counted every moment precious.

The warmth of summer returned with the passing of the hail. It was only the first eight-mark of the season, so the air was still brisk for the most part, despite the diligent efforts of the glaring orb above to search out all the dim places that still clung to the memory of spring. But the strange storms had passed now and the great green majesty of Inris lay before them.

Kion fingered Truesilver's hilt again where it lay just behind the back of the seat. If only he could vanquish the foe which now dogged him in the same way he'd struck down Vayd. Yes, that first battle had been full of terror, and Kion had no real hope he would survive it. But long drawn-out fear is the slow killer of dreams. And his fears grew with each mile, swelling into a foe far greater than any haukmar. Flesh he could fight with steel and fire, but not knowing when or where or if he would find his mother was something he had no way to defeat.

As the sun shrank into whatever distant troubles lay beyond the western horizon, Zinder tapped the side of Kion's foot.

"We may have to turn in early tonight. Crusty looks to be hobbling a bit."

Kion turned his eyes on the mule for the first time in miles, and noticed the irregular gait. Another setback. Another small defeat. Why couldn't they have a great charger like the soldiers he'd seen in Charring and Roving? Maybe even one like Strom Glyre's great steed, Torrent, which he'd read about in the Bladewarden's journal, which had come into Kion's possession just before Strom's death.

Kion stared down at his knees for a long time without answering.

"If you're not careful, you'll think a hole in the ground big enough to swallow up the three of us," Zinder said.

"I can't help it, Zinder. What if she's not in Fennigar? What if we're wasting our time? Inris spreads out forever in every direction. How can I find her in all of this? Wouldn't you feel overwhelmed if it was your mother?"

"Well, now, nynnian mothers are rather different than their human counterparts. My mother had me working at the mill by the time I was able to touch a doorknob and doing half the cooking and cleaning around the house before that. Nynnian mothers are more like taskmasters than anything else. 'You can't waste time, Zin. You've only got so many years under the withering sun. You've got to take advantage. Now hurry up, you're late.' That's the sort of thing they say. But that's beside the point. Remember that passage from Strom's journal you told me about the other day, the one about his first battle—at Nickling I believe it was? He didn't know what he was doing. He doubted his training, doubted his battle plan, worried his men wouldn't trust him. But he fought through all that and held his own against a far greater force."

"You're forgetting one thing. He lost that battle and had to flee in the end," Kion said.

"But he stayed true to his duty, didn't he? And his courage helped save a good part of the army—the same soldiers who later regrouped and won the war. Sometimes the battle before you is just something you need to get through until you can fight the final one. War is just a series of little battles you fight to get to the one that really counts."

"He speaks the truth," Kithian said. *"The journey to find your mother has only begun. It may be that the road to find her will stretch long before you come to the end of it."*

Kion saw the wisdom in his companions' words, but even so, he resented Crusty's wobble, though the mule certainly couldn't be blamed for it. He might have taken the delays better if this hadn't all been his fault. If only he could take back the message he had sent. If only his mother had stayed in Charring.

"You're saying you don't think she is in Fennigar?"

"No, only that patience is seldom wanted, but often required."

"Fine." He swallowed a grumble. "We'll stop early if you think it best. I wouldn't want Crusty to get injured."

"There's a good lad. Don't you worry. Old Crusty will be right as radishes in the morning."

Kion certainly hoped so. Still, he couldn't help wishing again that he had one of those magnificent chargers.

That night, Zinder went straight to sleep after they'd made camp and he'd seen to Crusty's leg. As a nyn, he slept less than most men, but every now and then he seemed to need to make up for it. And in truth they had kept up a blistering pace for the first two days of the journey.

But Kion and Tiryn, who had managed to catch short winks now and then during the day, stayed up gazing at the streaking sparks overhead, which stitched the sky with glittering patterns. How many nights had Kion sat out with his sheep doing the very same? The shifting trails of light above the Four Wards had a way of sweeping away his troubles in some grander mystery, the hidden language of the night that not even the wisest understood. Oh, to return to the life of the Tors, when his troubles had been small and his life so very simple and his mother safe in their cottage.

"I know what you're thinking. Because I've been thinking the same thing," Tiryn said, pulling her gaze away from the great dance of shimmering lights. She had a knack for guessing Kion's thoughts, though she rarely came out and said so. It used to bother Kion, who preferred to keep his thoughts to himself, but after nearly losing her to the wistering fever, he'd had a change of heart about that, as well as many other things. He was too grateful just having her there to get angry over petty desires. "What happens if we don't find her? What will we do then?"

"We can't lose her. We won't lose her. I will find her if I have to spend my last breath looking."

"Don't say that, Kion. Not that way. I need both of you. If we're ever going to get back to the way life was, we have to get through this together."

"I know, but I keep asking myself, what would Father do? How long and hard would he search? And I can't bring myself to give anything less than that." The words of his father's letter before he had gone off to war, the one he kept in his pack even now, came back to him as they so often did.

> *...Wait patiently for my return, or, should I fail to come home, do honor to my memory and protect your mother and sister with all that is in you.*

Tiryn placed her hand on his knee. In that small touch a thousand words passed between them. The memory of the long nights they'd endured together, unable to sleep, trying to stay awake, thinking somehow that they needed to be up in case Father returned. Every night they'd sing the song of Seven Fires together—back when Kion used to sing—staring into the window candle, wishing as hard as hope itself that he would return. And now they were living that dark memory all over again. Only this time there was no candle, and no mother to hold them as they cried themselves to sleep. The wound of their father's death ten years ago was only just healing and this fresh pain made all the old heartache come rushing back again, stronger and more piercing than ever.

"Do you remember the song Mother used to sing when she went walking in the woods at night?" Tiryn said. "She didn't think we heard it, but somehow it always gave me strength. I thought that if she was out there singing Father might hear and find his way home. She was like another candle in the window."

"Yes, I remember it. 'All Distance Draws Near.' And I thought the same thing, that maybe she could even see Father somehow when she was singing, or that he could see her, though it was nighttime and he was a world away."

"I don't think you were far off. Music has the power to erase distance and time. It draws us out of ourselves and into something greater. Would it be all right if I sang the song now?"

Kion never used to like to hear Tiryn sing either. It was too painful. It brought back too many memories of Father, who was the most gifted musician in the world as far as Kion was concerned. But that was another thing that he did not mind anymore. Music was Tiryn's sword. It was the way she fought against her enemies, the way she struck at despair and fear and hopelessness. And perhaps at this moment, a song would prove even more potent than his own extraordinary blade in battling the emotions that warred inside him.

A lass through the hills went strolling
Over wind-woven grass and beyond
Out over the heath mist is rising
Graying the paths that she trod
Lost in the moonlight she wanders
Declaring her love on the moors
To the horizon she gazes and wonders
When she'll see the one she adores
How lovely the heights of the highlands
For upon them all distance draws near
And the hope of her love's swift returning
Brings his voice echoing back to her ear

With Tiryn's own voice undulating into the night, Kion put his arm around his sister, held her close, and wiped the tears from her eyes. The song had given him strength. The strength would fade by morning most likely, but for now, it was enough at least to bring him through the night.

"We'll find her, Tiryn. I promise. We will find her."

Chapter 3

THE GRIZZLY GRIDDLE

Squawking gulls strutted across the silt-colored battlements surrounding Fennigar, a swamp port dug in by the sea. Though helmeted soldiers stood guard here and there, the legions of gulls outnumbered them by far. The sky above reflected the dull greenish-gray of the weathered town below. Broomy marshes spread out to the west as if they were a fungus kept at bay by the dark stone walls encircling the town on three sides. A mist-veiled harbor lurked to the north. Some terrible odor drifted from that direction, brought in by a sticky wind, rank and oily and repugnant. The stench came from, as Kion would soon learn, the smell of fish. The inhabitants of the town had grown quite used to it, but for someone who had lived all his life on the windswept Tors of Casting Selvedge, it reeked of slimy, wriggling, nasty heaps of things dead or dying. To his nose, even sheep smelled better than this.

When they got close enough, a number of run-down sections in the walls revealed themselves. Three were under repair, but in many spots, work had yet to begin. The breaches varied in size from a few stones missing from the crenellations to holes large enough for a small troop of haukmarn to march through.

A long line of bedraggled travelers waited at the gates. By the time Zinder's cart rolled up to the entrance to the town it was well beyond sundown. The gulls had flown away and tiny, near-invisible, biting gnats swarmed in to relieve them of their post as the chief nuisances of Fennigar. The pests feasted on poor Tiryn, and buzzed in thick clouds around Zinder's head, but for some odd reason they left Kion alone.

"Shoo!" Zinder scattered a cloud of them with a fierce buffet of wind from his hat, only to see them re-form again moments later.

Tiryn huddled under a blanket for protection, but her tormentors kept managing to find chinks in her woolen armor. The stink only got worse the nearer they drew to the city, and the few buildings which could be seen through the gate were as drab as driftwood. Several looked as though they might have been cobbled together from the remnants of some shipwreck.

"Well, well, a nyn." The guard at the gate addressed them. His emerald livery marked him as being in the service of the margrave, who, along with the fane, shared in the defense of Inris. Sweat and grime ran down his stubbled face, and his tunic and once fine tabard were soaked clean through, but he seemed less bothered by the state of his uniform than he was by the tediousness of having to wait on all of the many travelers who sought entrance to the town.

"Zinder Hamryn, at your service." Zinder stood and gave as eloquent a bow as possible while being beset on all sides by armies of gnats.

"What business have you in Fennigar?" the guard said, momentarily stirred from his weariness by the unusual appearance of a nyn.

"Food and shelter, and in that order. What's the best inn for such things that might still have some room at this hour?"

The guard scratched his forehead and looked Zinder up and down, which didn't take long.

"You look like the Grizzly Griddle sort. Not too rich, not too poor. If you take the third left onto Barnacle Road from this, the main thoroughfare, you can't miss it."

Except for his large green hat, which he'd donned to combat the gnats, Zinder was still dressed in his drab gray-and-brown traveling outfit. Had he been dressed in his usual, ostentatious manner, the guard might have assessed him otherwise. That was just as well. No need to waste their coin on lodging. Kion had slept with his sheep out under the sparklight on many a night. A bare stretch of ground was as good to him as the fane's own bed. What he *was* looking forward to, though, was a well-cooked meal.

"Many thanks. Now, might I trouble you with one last question, before we take our leave? Have you any news of the war?" Zinder said.

The guard perked up even more at Zinder's question. "War's over. Leastways, far as I'm concerned. We beat 'em back from the walls six days ago. Took our lumps to be sure, but we sent 'em packing. We'd have drowned in our own boots, though, if Roardin and his men hadn't 'caught 'em in the casting,' as they say. His soldiers swept in out of the fog like spirits of vengeance and fell upon the haukmarn from the rear. Saved the day, they did, mark it in the books."

Kion leaned forward and broke in. "Roardin? Strom's swordswain? He's the one who saved Fennigar?" Roardin's name was mentioned in Strom's journal dozens of times. And from everything he'd read, Kion was certain that this man was the swordswain he had talked to after the Bladewarden's death in Roving.

"The very same. He's set up a garrison here in Fennigar until the walls are repaired, to make sure the haukmarn don't stir up the courage for another assault. But I doubt they'll be back. Far as I'm concerned, any that didn't die here fled back to their holes in the Marred Wastes. And good riddance, I say!"

"Please, if I may," Kion said. "One more question. We heard a group of prisoners was freed on their way to Fennigar. Did any of them find their way here?"

"Ah yes, that was Roardin's doing as well. Freed the prisoners on his way here. There's a half-dozen or so of the poor folk in a makeshift camp down by the docks. Most of 'em are sore off, but at least they're alive."

"More good tidings!" Zinder clapped his hands. "We've come here looking for someone who may have been among the prisoners. Is the camp open to visitors at this hour?"

"You're a bit late, I'm afraid. It's all closed off now. Check in with them tomorrow morning, though. You're sure to find your friend or family if he's there. Roardin's men are in charge of the camp, nursing them back to health until they're strong enough to return home."

"We thank you for this bounty of news." Zinder shared a twinkling glance with his friends and flicked the guard a silver nick for his troubles. "We're off to the Grizzly Griddle. A good evening to you, sir."

At that moment, Kion didn't mind the stink or the wretched atmosphere of Fennigar one bit. If his mother was here, all that was foul would become sweet.

"And to you, Master Nyn." The guard bobbed his head in friendly salutation, his mood considerably improved after the coin and the talk of the war.

"Did you hear that, Tiryn? The war's over and Mother could be only a few streets away," Kion said as the cart rolled through the gate. He was not ready to give himself over fully to hope, but the guard's tidings quickened his heart in a way he had not known since he'd rescued Tiryn from the haukmarn in Charring.

Tiryn made no effort to rein in her emotions. She popped out from under the blanket—defying the gnats—her lips turning upwards into a smile as bright as the moon.

"Oh, Kion! What news! Mother's only one night's sleep away, though I doubt I'll be able to sleep after this."

As much as Kion wanted to echo her excitement, the old nagging fears seeped back in, even amidst this promising turn.

"We haven't found her yet, Tiryn. We have to wait and see what tomorrow brings."

"Oh, you sour sod." Zinder swatted Kion on the arm. "You've a clean bed and a good meal awaiting you after a long road. The war's over and your mother may be a wink away. You can at least allow that things are looking up for a change."

"Take what blessings the day brings, swordspeaker," Kithian said. *"For none are assured beyond the setting of the sun."*

Kion allowed himself a smile for the benefit of the others, though he doubted it fooled either of them.

"Well, it does sound promising, I have to admit."

Behind that smile, he clenched a fistful of doubts. He could not let go of them, not until he saw his mother with his own eyes. Tiryn might not sleep from anticipation, but Kion would drain the night away in worry. For both of them, the morning could not come quickly enough.

The delighted little company, lifted by the news of the prisoners on the docks, wound its way through the sand-covered roads of Fennigar. Within the walls, it was impossible to tell exactly how big the settlement was. Every house they could see had but a single floor and there was not a hill in sight. No street ran straight for more than a few dozen yards. Some odd twist or change presented itself at nearly every intersection. Curved roads, winding roads, roundabouts, and dead ends lurked around every corner. And darkness made the town all the more indecipherable. Whatever Fennigar looked like during the day, in the evening it was half-locked in a dream. The low buildings seemed to spring out of the streets like rickety planks that had landed there after a tumultuous storm. Few buildings had windows and even fewer had chimneys. Most were brittle-looking huts that made Kion's cottage seem like the fane's own palace.

And yet, for all its twisted streets, shabby architecture, and awful stench, the city was not without charm. Vines blanketed the sides of many houses, their waxy leaves glowing subtly in the moonlight. Strange, ethereal flowers grew at irregular intervals along the sides of the streets as well. Their stalks lifted them nearly as high as the rooftops. Even a haukmar would have had a hard time reaching the thin, off-white petals which rimmed their wide, circular faces. Oddest of all, those petals gave off a greenish-white glow and filled the streets with a robust, grassy fragrance, which blunted the rankling air.

"They're the most beautiful flowers I've ever seen," Tiryn said, her eyes hardly daring to blink.

"They're called fenlights," Zinder said. "And they only grow in marshlands like this. Lovely, aren't they?"

"I wish we could have a garden of them," Tiryn said.

"They are pretty. And the smell is even better. It masks the stench when you get close enough," Kion said.

The cart ambled on. Crusty's trot slackened by the moment, as if the poor animal were being lulled to sleep by the heavy air and sleepy quiet of the nocturnal streets. Hungry as he was, Zinder let his faithful beast go at its own pace. Four days of hard riding, carrying three people—in addition to all their assorted baggage—had sapped the poor mule's strength. Soon enough, though, they turned onto Barnacle Road and found their way to the Grizzly Griddle.

Rising above the surrounding neighborhood by a full story, the inn was hard to miss. In contrast to the soft glow of the streets, the Griddle beamed like a fragment of the sun, fallen to the ground and still smoldering. A muffled hum exuded into the street from within. A substantial wooden sign hung above the double doors. It featured a burly, friendly-looking bear brandishing a hefty-looking pan in one paw.

A pair of stout boys came and stabled Crusty while Zinder ushered his friends inside the large common room. Griddles of various sizes lined the walls, black ones, gray ones, thick ones, and thin. All had dents and battered signs of age. A great hearth blazed off to one side, crackling with embers and energy. A long bar at the back served as a barrier between the customers and the kitchen. The Griddle was full of life, if not of patrons. Of the twenty or so tables in the common room, two-thirds were filled with the kind of folk who probably had dirt under their nails and holes in their shoes. They looked to be hardy, friendly folk. A group of ten or so sat around the hearth, clapping and capering to the fiddle of a spry old fellow wearing spectacles and tattered clothes. A frayed rope served as his belt and he wore an apron checkered with stains both muted and fresh. Smoke-colored hair ran down his jowls, but it faded near his chin and halfway up the side of his head. Whoever he was, he was thoroughly enjoying himself.

Tiryn came immediately under the spell of the music, gazing in silent amazement at the merry assembly sitting before the hearth.

"Go on, lass," Zinder said, gesturing. "Take out your pipes and join them."

"Oh, no, I couldn't." Tiryn's eyes fluttered as she came back to herself. "I don't know them."

"Well, after you've met them you will. Kion will order something for us and I'll take you over and introduce you."

Kion cast his eyes about the room. Two dark-haired girls with corkscrew curls moved among the tables, porting trays laden with food and drink. A puffy-faced fellow behind the bar went brightly about his business, filling glasses and popping in and out of the kitchen with plates of steaming goodness for the girls to deliver. The room was friendly enough, but the thought of tossing his sister into a crowd of strangers did not sit well with Kion, however cheery they might appear. Tiryn was sensitive and shy and it was his job to protect her. And the last time he'd been at an inn, things hadn't turned out so well.

But hunger made his decision for him. They were all famished, and the buttery, salty scents wafting about the room came with a mysterious tang that piqued his curiosity. He supposed he could keep an eye on Tiryn from the bar while he ordered.

"Very well, what would you like?" Kion said.

"Whatever you're having—only double," Zinder said.

"And I'll have half," Tiryn said.

"Of course. Just be careful." Kion strode towards the long bar, determined to unravel the secret behind that mysterious smell and put in an order for whatever it turned out to be, but he glanced back often toward his sister as he went.

Tiryn straightened, trying to look confident and independent, but as Kion left, she said to Zinder, "Are you sure about this? How are you going to introduce me to people you've never met?" She stuck the end of one of her braids in her mouth, a nervous habit.

"Didn't you say you liked to think the best of people? Don't you worry. Everyone's either a friend or an enemy in this world. And the only way to find out is to meet them. But these look like the friendly sort."

It took another minute for Zinder to fully convince her, but eventually Tiryn drew out her wood pipes as the folk around the fire finished up a rousing rendition of "Fare Well, Dear Nell." Two of them were girls younger than Tiryn, which was a promising sign. Nothing too rough could happen with them around.

"Greetings, merry balladeers," Zinder said with a fantastic flourish of his rakish, red-plumed hat. "Allow me to introduce myself. I am Zinder Hamryn, blacksmith of Casting Selvedge and maker of things both ingenious and grand, but of late given to wrangling of children and saving of cities. And this is my lovely ward, Tiryn of the Tors, a maid endowed with such gift of song it would be a tragedy if she did not join you in your musical festivities."

The fiddler with the glasses bowed gracefully and spread his arms in welcome. "Well met. A nyn and a minstrel, no less. It would be an honor to share this fine evening and this blazing hearth with two such fair folk as yourselves. I am Baradoc, owner and proprietor of this venerable establishment, and these are a few of my fellows, old friends and new. Besides providing food and lodging, I am also the resident talesinger of this place." He strung together a bright musical signature on his fiddle. "There's always a warm welcome and stirring song awaiting at the Grizzly Griddle. And tonight, we have much to celebrate. The haukmarn are driven back from our city and were turned back at Charring as well. Come, join us. And you, my dear lady, raise those pipes and let us hear them sing."

At a nudge from Zinder, Tiryn eased sheepishly into the center of the gathering, her cheeks flaming hot as the hearth fire.

"Hello," she said, her voice whisper-quiet. "What would you like me to play?"

"Well, since you're new and perhaps a bit unsure of this playing before a ficklety crowd, how about we start with a duet? Do you know 'The Rafters Song'?"

Several folk clapped and cheered at Baradoc's choice, particularly the two young girls, who gave little leaps in anticipation of hearing the tune.

"I do not, I'm afraid...but I do enjoy learning new songs and I suppose I could follow along and try to pick it up."

Kion cocked an eyebrow from afar. That was a braver answer than he expected.

Zinder gave Tiryn a nod of encouragement. "Oh, you'll like this one, lass."

"All right, then, let's give it a go," Baradoc said.

"Hoi, mates," said one of the men. "Come on over, we're singing 'The Rafters.'"

The news quickly spread around the room. Several parties left off their meals and pressed in around the fire. Nearby tables had to be pushed back to accommodate the inrush of people.

Tiryn's pipes quivered like a leaf, but once the music began, a calm settled upon her and the music took hold. By the second verse, she didn't miss a note. The song rang out fast and furious about the inn, with people dancing and prancing and shouting the words at the top of their voices. And this is what they sang.

Lift your voice to the rafters
Slap your mate in the afters
Sing so loud that you'll wake 'em
Shudder, shiver, and shake 'em
Let your song ring the halls
Till it brings down the walls
And it bursts down the door
Then you sing one verse more!

Sing and shout, here we go
Heigh ho yo to the rafters!
Up and down, high and low
Heigh ho yo to the rafters!

Stomp the toes of your friend
Give a knee to his end
Feel the floor, feel it quake
How much noise can you make?
Let your song ring the halls
Till it brings down the walls
And it bursts down the door
Then you sing one verse more!

Sing and shout, here we go
Tally ho to the rafters!
Up and down, high and low
Tally ho to the rafters!

Bash and bowl through the table
Crash and roll all you're able
Say, how loud can you sing?
'Tis a marvelous thing
When our song rings the halls
Till it brings down the walls
And it bursts down the door

Then we sing one verse more!

Sing and shout, here we go
Heigh ho yo to the rafters!
Up and down, high and low
Tally ho to the rafters!

The dancing was a raucous, tumbledown affair. If there had not been music, an observer might have taken it for a brawl. As the whirling and slapping and jostling song came to an end, the glow from the fire had leapt into the hearts of those gathered around it. Zinder was laughing and joking with several new friends who'd been bumping, kneeing, and stomping along with him.

Tiryn's face no longer shone red from embarrassment but had settled into a contented rosy shade.

Though he had not joined the dance, Kion stood in the back of the room with his head turned thoughtfully to the side. Another sort of contentment welled within him, not from the music, laughter, and high spirits which had overtaken the room, but from seeing his sister happy again after so many days of doubt and worry.

"Your sister is quite talented," Kithian said.

In that moment, Kion's own troubles and concerns about tomorrow dimmed. His only thought was of how proud both his mother and father would be if they could see their daughter now, playing so well and so boldly before all these strangers.

"Yes, she is. And she grew a little braver today, I think," he said, nodding to himself, the only silent figure in all that rowdy scene.

Chapter 4

STREETS OF FISH

Perhaps the scent of fenlight flowers weakened during the day—the flowers were just as tall and lithe as the night before, but had lost their otherworldly glow—or perhaps it was that the stench of fish overpowered other smells closer to the docks. Whatever the case, Kion did his best not to breathe through his nose as he wandered the cramped and curvy streets of Fennigar alongside Tiryn and Zinder early the next morning. But even if he could have stopped the smell of fish entirely, the sight of them could not be avoided. Their glassy-eyed bodies hung from poles, ropes, and boards. Sellers hawked them from buckets, crates, and bags. There were long, silver fish with feathery fins, small lime green ones with round bodies, and lots of medium-sized varieties in hues of gray and blue. Kion, who had never eaten sea fish until last night, marveled at how something that tasted so good could smell so awful. The merchants sold other things as well, vegetables, bread, pots and pans, candles, clothes, and sundry items typical of other markets, but fish were the main offering by a wide margin.

Though the fish claimed dominion over the city by sheer numbers, their rule was not uncontested. Everywhere, gray-white gulls flapped and swooped or perched on roofs and sign-posts, as if waiting for the proper moment to rise up and seize control of Fennigar. Their discordant litany noised down every street. But their bothersome racket was nothing compared to the worrisome doubts that refused to stay silent in Kion's mind. While he had managed a few fretful hours of sleep the night before, he could not shake the suspicion that his mother was still in the power of the cruel haukmarn in some filthy camp far away from here and that their morning errand would turn out to be in vain.

"Are we still heading in the right direction? With the sun behind the clouds, I can't tell up from down. I never thought the sea would be such a dismal, smelly place," Kion said.

"If the docks are to the north, then we have certainly gotten off course. But with the unpredictable nature of these streets, it is hard to say which path will take us there." Kion wore Truesilver strapped to his back where it would cause less trouble as he navigated the well-traveled streets. Even early in the morning, the subdued atmosphere of the town from last night had given way to a strong current of people that grew thicker by the moment.

"This isn't how I pictured a seaside town either," Tiryn said. "In all the stories, they're said to be such enchanting places. I'm sure the docks will be different, though. The stories must be right about those. I hope we find Mother. It would be so wonderful to see the crashing waves together."

"Somehow I doubt there'll be much to see," Kion said.

"It's not always this gloomy," Zinder said. "You should see it during the Treadwater festival. It's even more colorful than Seven Fires, though it still smells about this bad." He was the one bright spot in all the street. Though a steady flow of people ambled by, none could match his enormous yellow hat with its blue feather and smart white band, which so perfectly complemented his grass-green tunic and pants trimmed with flaxen stitching. So bright was his attire, it was as if he had his own personal sunbeam breaking through the clouds.

"Well, I don't suppose there'll ever be another Seven Fires," Kion said woodenly. The flames of his village still smoldered in his memory. Though only a month ago, the entertainers, booths, music, and laughter of that festival now seemed little more than a distant legend.

"No, I don't suppose there will," Zinder said.

Tiryn, who had not seen the scorched aftermath of Furrow and ever sought to brighten the mood if she could, patted Zinder on the back.

"I imagine they sell very nice hats somewhere hereabouts. Perhaps we can go looking for one after we find Mother."

"Now there's an idea. No town worth putting on the map is without a good hattery. I believe I bought a fancy purple one here years ago. It was one of my favorites. Wore it for years until the downpour of '22. A sloshy whirlwind filched it right off my head. Probably ended up as the nest of some storm crow if I had to guess."

"I'm sure she'd thank you for it if she could," Tiryn said.

"Ha! As if a crow ever deserved anything so fine."

Kion stopped in the middle of an intersection to stare down each winding way as far as he could. There was no sign of the docks in any direction. Baradoc had given them what seemed to be straightforward directions, but somewhere they'd gone wrong.

"Hats can wait. Do either of you have any idea which path leads to the docks?"

"I'm afraid not. Perhaps we should stop and ask," Zinder said.

"Mr. Baradoc said it was a good distance," Tiryn said. "I know these streets never stay straight for long, but this one is the only one heading north at the moment. Why don't we travel a little farther and at least see what's around the bend."

"Right. Let's keep moving for now. If we can't see Sackheap Street by the time we get around that corner, we'll stop and ask," Kion said.

They plowed through the huffing crowd of errand runners and street peddlers. The people here wore the same plain, hard-lined faces as the villagers from Furrow. Only the presence of fishing poles and a preference for sandals over boots, and sleeveless vests over cloth tunics, differentiated them from their easterly neighbors.

They had just reached the bend when Zinder blurted out, "There he is!"

"There's who?" Kion said. "Roardin?"

"The Scribe! The one who sold me the sword and the poem and sent us on that false errand to Roving! Look! He's the one with the big golden feather in his hat and the frilly collar! Oh, horn toads, he turned the corner. Quick! If we hurry we just might catch him!"

"Fire and ice, Zinder, we're here to find my mother, not some poem peddler." Kion tried to pull his friend back, but Zinder had already launched himself after whoever he thought he'd seen.

Tiryn and Kion shared a helpless look and set off after their fleet-footed friend. Zinder was easy enough to spot. His unmistakable hat was a bright yellow splash weaving amongst the muddy-hued crowds. Dodging the fishmongers, their patrons, and the rest of the hodgepodge of street drifters, they bowled their way down street after street, never quite catching up to Zinder before a merchant or a cart or a twist in the road stalled their breathless pursuit. Each obstacle forced them to slow, skitter to the side, and pound down the sandy streets once more. When at last they caught up to the wayward nyn, he was stopped in the middle of an intersection, his access to the cross-street blocked by a herd of pigs bobbing along without a care in the world.

"What happened to your quarry?" Kion said, rushing up with Tiryn as the last of the slovenly animals passed by, their tails jiggling as they went.

Zinder's head hung low and he held his hat in his hands. Whenever his hat came off it meant trouble.

"Gone. I turned the corner and for a moment I thought I saw him, but then those pigs came and it was like he simply vanished. Either that or he was trampled to death. Though I don't see any signs of a body. Oh dear, I hope my eyes aren't starting to go, are they? When that happens to a nyn, the end isn't far away."

Tiryn gave his shoulder a gentle touch. "I'm sure your eyes are just fine, Zinder. The man was probably just...very fast."

"Or worse, perhaps I'm going mad. What if I'm seeing things?" Zinder donned his hat with none of his usual flair. He looked, in fact, quite defeated.

"Maybe that hat is just too tight for your head," Kion said. "Tight hats and madness are known to go hand in hand, or so I've heard."

"Shar's dome, lad, you certainly know how to a kick a fellow when he's down. But if I've gone mad, it's only to keep you company." The old gleam flashed in Zinder's eye and he laughed off Kion's remark.

A great chorus of squealing and howling, squawking and screaming drowned out their conversation. Down the street a small handcart had overturned, spilling mounds of fish onto the grit and grime of the road. Three or four pigs scampered about, eluding the irate swats of their pursuer, a fierce-eyed man whose straw hat had been converted into an instrument of vengeance. Meanwhile, a much older pig herder waved his cudgel, wading his way back through his herd, shouting at both the man and the pigs to stop. A few gulls flapped about, their eyes on the fallen fish.

Onlookers stood by either laughing or frowning, mostly depending on their age, with the older folk muttering and shaking their heads and the younger ones given to smirks.

"Pigs. They're always trouble," Zinder said.

"I suppose we should help that man get his fish back in the cart," Tiryn said.

Kion was loath to suffer another delay, but no one in the crowd was moving to help.

"I suppose so. It's still early. I'm sure we have plenty of time left to reach the docks—if we ever find the right street."

"Well, it will take my mind off that scoundrel of a scribe at least," Zinder said.

By the time they reached the whirlwind of commotion, the

fish seller and the pig herder had nearly come to blows. Pigs ran about, circling the cart like so many bloated vultures. More nosy folk had joined the onlooking crowd, blocking the street entirely. And more gulls swooped in by the moment.

"Those pigs of yours have trampled half a dozen of my fish!" shouted the fish seller. "You've no business being on this street with a herd that size!"

"As if you couldn't see us coming!" the pig herder shouted back. "But like the dunderwit you are, you thought you could just plow right through, didn't you? You nearly ran over my animals!"

Half the crowd muttered their agreement with one side and half with the other. From the looks on their faces, a few from either camp were ready to join in the moment a brawl broke out.

Kithian spoke to the pigs calmly, using the animal speech which Kion could not yet fully understand, despite his glaive's efforts to teach him as they traveled. But the pigs understood. In little time at all, they ceased their cavorting and stood uncannily still.

"The animals will not trouble you, swordspeaker, but be mindful of the people, for they are acting more like beasts than men. It might not be wise to stay here."

Kion leaned over to Zinder. "I'm not sure we can be of any help here. Things seem to have gone too far for us to save."

"Leave it to me, lad. A calm voice cures calamity. Just give me a moment and I'm sure I can—" He stepped forward, but was cut short by the arrival of four armored soldiers wearing the white livery of the fane.

The sound of their clinking mail and thudding boots blew a cold wind over the heated scene.

"What trouble stirs these streets?" The man who spoke had keen blue eyes and dark hair fringed in gray at the edges of his beard and temples. His cool demeanor was the mirror opposite of the two quarreling men, though their rage dwindled considerably with the soldiers' arrival. The pig herder's face, especially, shone now with pale fear.

"A minor disagreement, Swordswain," the old man said. "We just had a little bump—an accident. Nothing to trouble someone as important as you."

"His pigs bungled my cart," said the fish seller. "And he won't reimburse me for the ones they trampled."

The two men went back and forth, speaking softly, but forcefully, each insisting they had done no wrong, but Kion gave little heed to what they said. His eyes had locked on the swordswain from the moment he arrived. Kion knew him from Strom's duel with Vayd. This was the man who had spoken words of comfort to him after the bladewarden's death, words that echoed with the strength and wisdom of one who had endured much sorrow and yet had not surrendered to it.

"That's Roardin," Kion whispered to Tiryn and Zinder.

"Yes, I do believe you're right, lad. I remember him now from the Fortress of the Clefts."

"He has understanding in his eyes," Tiryn said.

Roardin had heard enough from the two quarrelers. He raised his hand and spoke clearly so that all might hear.

"I can see that neither man is innocent here. Each of you ought to have shouldered your own part of the blame, but as you seem incapable of doing so, my judgment shall fall on you both. I command you, Morlin, to pay this man six nicks for the trampling of his fish. As for you, Tingal, you shall deliver six fresh fish in good order to the barracks for your foolhardy attempt to barrel through this man's herd. And, Morlin, do use Gristle Street or Beam's Way for bringing your herd to market next time."

Neither man seemed overly pleased with the judgment. Seeing this, Roardin added, "Come now, this is no time for resentment and strife. Are we not friends here? Is not your city safe this day from the threat of war? Has the joy of victory been so swiftly forgotten? Let your hearts consider what this city would be like had it fallen and be glad. Now, I must take my leave. I've business to attend to elsewhere."

He and his men started off in Kion's direction and would have passed him by, but he stepped directly in front of them.

"Stand aside," said a soldier on Roardin's right. "The swordswain has urgent matters to attend to."

Kion offered a clumsy bow. He wasn't well-versed in such things, but for a shepherd, it wasn't awful.

"Please, sir, I only ask for a moment. We're looking for someone who may be among the rescued prisoners at the docks. May I please have permission to speak with Swordswain Roardin?"

The soldier gave his leader an impatient glance.

"It's fine, glinthelm," Roardin said. He gestured down the street. The gathered crowds were quickly dispersing and heading on their way. A few remained to help get the spilled fish back into the cart, fending off the gulls who grew more bold as the people left. "We can speak as we walk. How may I be of aid?"

"It's my mother. She disappeared more than an eight-mark ago. I think she may be among the prisoners you rescued."

Roardin nodded in a way that showed his mind was occupied by other things, but his answer was cordial enough.

"One of the prisoners, you say? I'm afraid I can't help you just this moment. Some of them have taken ill, so we're not allowing anyone in the camp. But you're welcome to put in a request with—" He paused and gave Kion an intense look. "Wait. You're that boy who challenged Vayd at the Clefts, aren't you? I should have recognized you at once had I ever thought to see you again."

Something caught in Kion's throat. With an embarrassing cough, he cleared it. He could not believe this great warrior remembered him. It was almost like he was speaking with Strom Glyre, for something of the bladewarden's noble gaze and calm command lived in Roardin's face. Perhaps it was not surprising that the one who knew the bladewarden best would carry himself in like manner.

"Yes, that was me."

"It warms my heart to see you again. I've seen many acts of bravery in my day, but none surpassing what you did in Roving. These are your friends, I presume?"

Kion's embarrassment only deepened at these words. Perhaps what he had done looked brave on the outside, but his courage had come too late to save Strom, so what good had it done?

"This is my sister, Tiryn."

Tiryn managed a much more pleasant bow, though she'd had no more practice than Kion. Perhaps practice wasn't the only requirement.

"And this is Zinder, my good friend and the finest blacksmith in Inris."

Zinder's bow topped them all.

"Pleased to make your acquaintance, Swordswain. If I may be direct, that armor of yours is long overdue for repair. It's a shame I do not have the time or I would offer to fix it myself, but I imagine you've your own smiths who could serve you just as well."

"Hardly. They are skilled enough at their trade, but none have the skill of a nyn. But as you say, it seems as though we're both short on time. It's quite a stroke of luck you caught me just now. I'm headed to the barracks to saddle up for a scouting mission, but I suppose I can put that off a bit longer. Your act at the Clefts merits that much at least, and far more, in truth. Would you like me to take you to the docks myself? I can't promise that your mother is there, but I believe we should be able to resolve the matter quickly."

"I would be ever so grateful." Kion was tempted to salute, but he would probably bungle that as well, or perhaps it would seem out of place. Something of Strom's air of courage and character marked this man. Strom had written much of him in his journal, but the real Roardin far outdistanced even the bladewarden's lofty praise, as much as flesh and blood surpassed the written page.

A small drop of hope fell into Kion's parched wilderness and for once he allowed it to bring comfort to that dry, desolate land. Roardin must have had a hundred men at his command. And yet, there was Kion, a simple shepherd boy, walking side-by-side with the swordswain. If anyone could help him find his mother, this was the man. Kion could imagine no better ending to the dark chapter of these recent days than this: that Roardin the Swordswain had saved his mother and that even now she was but a short distance away.

The splintered boards of the docks creaked and wobbled with every step. Several of the sad, sun-baked beams looked like they wanted to give way, but Roardin strode unconcerned upon them. They walked past the shops, stalls, and warehouses lining the ramshackle walkway. Even more so than in the town proper, the fish were everywhere. Perhaps the groaning planks were in fact just complaining about having to endure the endless heaps and barrels brimming with scaly stink. But Roardin gave no sign the odor bothered him either and Kion did his best to follow his example. The smell was a small thing to endure to find his mother.

A mere handful of boats clung to the sides of the many piers. Most must have been out to sea. Of the few that remained, the largest barely passed the length of Meander Toft's wagon. Graveyard fog rolled around them, so thick it appeared as if the mists alone kept them moored. Though the chalk blanket covering the waters withered to smoke as it hit the wood of Fennigar's pier, it swallowed up any trace of the sea. A gentle lapping was the only hint that a vast and trackless body of water lay close at hand. Though Tiryn had often dreamed of seeing the ocean, her face was too bright with anticipation over her mother to show any disappointment over the hidden sea.

Kion's eyes were drawn ever and always past the end of the docks where twenty gray half-tents huddled together on the sandy clay. Aside from the prisoners and soldiers there, that part of the harbor was deserted. Four men in the white tabards of Verisward stood guard at the edge of the camp while other soldiers attended the people milling inside or lying on tattered bedrolls. A makeshift barrier of slender sticks shoved into the sand marked the camp's boundaries, but the temporary fence stood barely taller than Zinder and the gaps allowed anyone to see in or out. The soldiers in the heart of the camp filled bowls with something steamy from a large iron pot. Dingy bandages and newly-fashioned crutches contributed to the miserable attire of those being fed. A few of those confined to cots had a greenish tinge to their lips—the tell-tale sign of the sprull. As Kion drew closer, a low moaning sounded from several places. Though Zinder chatted on with Roardin, trading stories of battles and swords and armor, the sorrowful scene ate away at Kion's hopes. He thought about what he would do if his mother was here, but was too sick to leave. Or what would happen if she never recovered. It was possible that her time with the haukmarn had broken her the way it had broken their neighbor, Rike. He had never been the same after his imprisonment. Kion's mind ran through all the dark and wicked cruelties the haukmarn might inflict upon their captives. With some effort, he forced the thoughts away. Whatever condition he found her in, if she was here, he would face the consequences when they came. He scanned the camp intently, but the arrangement of the tents made it impossible to see everyone.

As Roardin arrived outside the entrance to the camp, he caught the eye of one of his soldiers and motioned him over. The man approached, grit and chunks of clay leeching onto his boots and slowing his arrival.

"This is Glinthelm Winst," Roardin said as the man gave him

a cross-armed salute. "He has the official roll of the camp. If your mother is here, he'll be the one to know."

"Swordswain Roardin, we're almost finished with breakfast. We've got two who are well enough to be released. As you ordered, we—"

"You can give your report later. These folk have come all the way from Furrow. They are looking for their mother. Her name is Annira Bray. Does that name appear on the roll? Either among those still here or those who've left?"

The slight shake of the glinthelm's head had all the force of an axe stroke.

"I don't believe we've had anyone by that name."

"Please, check the roll to be sure." Roardin kept his eyes trained on the glinthelm as he went to a little metal box atop a wooden stand near the fire pit. The swordswain was kind not to give up hope, but Kion already knew what the outcome would be.

"Whatever the answer, remember that I will be here with you on the other side of that answer, Kion." Kithian's voice lent him strength as Kion braced himself against the expected pronouncement.

The glinthelm's eyes revealed the answer before he said a word.

"I'm sorry," he said, handing Roardin the paper he'd retrieved from the box. "You can see for yourself, Swordswain. She's not on the list."

Not on the list. Who knew that a scrap of paper could hold such power? All it would take was a few charcoal scratchings to bring his mother back. Was that too much to ask? A few lines on a piece of paper. Annira Bray. Such a simple name. It would only take a moment to write.

"She looks just like me, only—only older." Tiryn stepped forward. She clutched the glinthelm's arm, her shyness dissipating in the face of her mother's fate.

Roardin gave the two siblings a grave but steady look. It was the look of eyes that had known a great many hard truths in their lifetime. The eyes of a man who had delivered grave tidings before.

"I am so very sorry. I truly am."

Tiryn retreated, covering her face in her hands and shivering in silent tears. The color fled from Zinder's face. They'd come all this way for nothing. They were no closer to finding Mother than when they left Charring. Perhaps they were even more distant.

Zinder yanked off his hat, scrunching it between his hands. "You're sure your list is complete? You couldn't have missed her?"

"The list is very thorough. You're welcome to wander around the outside of the camp and look over the fence, but we can't let you come in for fear you might catch the sprull that's broken out."

Truesilver warmed on Kion's back, offering comfort to his glaivebond, but a cold emptiness swept through Kion. For a moment, he stood frozen in the miry clay. He did not know what to feel. Rage? Sorrow? Fear? None of these were sufficient to hold the depth of his pain. Far better not to feel anything at all.

"No. She's not here. Thank you for your time," he said.

Roardin gave Kion and Tiryn a cross-armed salute. Kion ought to have been awash with pride that a warrior of Roardin's quality had shown him such respect, but the gesture barely registered. Kion should have saluted him back but found he could not. His arms would not work that way right now. All they could do was reach around and hold his sister and endure her shuddering tears.

He had seen so much suffering since he had left home. The death of Strom, the burning of his village, the men who gave their lives to save his in Charring. Why had he let himself dare to hope? He should have known he wouldn't find his mother in this camp. What a fool to think it would be that easy. They would have to start all over now. The journey must begin anew. Only this time, the way would head down a far darker path. For if his mother had not been with the prisoners heading toward

Fennigar, she must have been taken to Roving. But she would not have stayed there. Would Kion be forced to brave the deadly desolation of the Marred Wastes? Was there any hope his mother was even still alive if that was where she'd been taken? And yet there was no other path that he could see. This trail had gone cold. If only he could find another sign that she had been taken somewhere else, anywhere but the land of the haukmarn. For even a swordspeaker dared not travel down that road and expect to come back alive.

Chapter 5

AN UNEXPECTED OFFER

Muffled sounds of merriment and spirited talk pressed through the plaster-coated walls. Down below, in the Griddle's common room, Zinder and Tiryn were no doubt chatting and enjoying their meal, though how they could do so after the morning's news, Kion did not understand. At first, Tiryn hadn't wanted to go either, but she was impressionable and eventually succumbed to Zinder's entreaties. He said it would do them good to take their minds off their mother, but Kion refused. To enjoy good food and cheer on a day like today felt like a betrayal. If his mother could not enjoy such things, how could he? Every laughing, smiling face would only serve as a reminder of what she could not have.

So he sat in his room that evening hungry—he'd skipped lunch as well—but a hunger far greater burned inside of him. He had to find her. If that meant going to the Marred Wastes, then so be it.

The room's lantern sat lifeless and cold on the bedside table. Only Kithian's gentle warm glow and the dismal light from the clouded window offered any resistance to the encroaching darkness.

"What should I do, Kithian?" He stared out into the murky drizzle through the blurry window. Truesilver lay on the bed behind him. "The other prisoners must have been taken to Roving, but I fear death awaits down that road—not only Mother's but my own."

Kithian's voice came to him with the same clarity as always, as if he spoke close to Kion's ear.

"Though I have never visited that land, from all that you and Zinder have told me of it, to go alone there would accomplish nothing but to throw your life away. It would take an army of the strongest warriors on the fastest steeds to enter that place and come back before madness overtook them. And you have no such army to command. Nor would it be right for you to ask so many to risk their lives to save one person, even one as dear to you as your mother."

"I must go alone, then," Kion said, for a kind of madness driven by fear stood ready to overtake him unless he found some other way.

"Do not make your decision in haste. You must think this through. How would you know where to look, even if you could survive the journey? No, you must act upon what you know, not upon what you feel. Those are hard words for you to hear, I know. But I must tell you the truth, even when the truth is hard."

"I know you are wiser than I am, Kithian, but you don't know what it's like to have a mother. She is the strongest, kindest, most precious woman that I know. Everything I have, everything I am, is because of her and Father. The Mastersmith is your maker, but the relationship between a smith and his creations is not the same as a mother and her son, even if that smith can create living weapons capable of speech and thought."

Kithian's light waned, and for a moment Kion wondered if he had spoken too harshly, but the steady voice of his glaive told him that this was not so.

"It may be that I do not fully understand your love for your mother, but the Mastersmith has a claim on you as well as me, one greater than you know. For your mother did not make or create you. Only one has that power, who may craft flesh as well as steel. But in a way you speak rightly. For if the Mastersmith has given a special place in his creation to his glaives, he has given an even greater place to the sons of men, for they are most like unto him of all that he has made. Yet, however deep

your love for your mother may be, a heart unguided by the mind is a perilous thing. You speak now out of fear. I can hear it in your voice. But you must arm yourself now with knowledge before you choose the next step. You must act upon wisdom, not upon emotion. To run off and face the dangers of the Marred Wastes may be brave, but in the end, it will be of no help to your mother if she is not where you choose to go. You must be certain she is there before you risk attempting a journey to a place such as that."

The Mastersmith. Kion had given little thought to his purposes in all of this. Was he truly the maker of men and not just the glaives themselves? If so, then why had Kion never heard this before? And yet, he had never known of the existence of glaives until a short time ago, either. There was so much that he did not understand. It was far too great for a simple shepherd from Furrow to grasp, but there was something both wonderful and terrifying in Kithian's words.

Kion stared hard into the mist of rain brushing the rooftops. Rain always made him wish he was home—sitting and absorbing the warmth of the hearth, a bowl of his mother's potato soup cradled in his lap, the thatched roof and dirt walls protecting him from the damp and the drench. To be home. Now more than ever, he longed for that. But without his mother, the old cottage would be nothing more than a cold, hollowed-out memory.

"But how can I know for certain where she is? She could be anywhere. We'd have to be able to fly to search all the places she might be. How I wish Nar-vel-lis were here. If we could just have him—wait—that's it. Kithian, couldn't we get the birds to look for her the way Nar-vel-lis did in Charring? If we talked to enough of them, we could get them to spread out all over Inris. Surely there'd be a chance one of them would find her." He turned from the gray window with a sudden rush of feelings: joy, fear, and surprise all at once. It was as if a shaft of light had pierced the cloudy sky and landed at his feet, shining a way forward.

"It is well thought. But scouting Charring is one thing. We would need a thousand birds, and some willing to brave the Marred Wastes, to look for her all across the North, and even a bird may only fly so far and see so much. No, I fear that it falls upon us alone to find your mother. We must find someone who has seen her and knows for certain the path that she took."

The shaft of light melted and sank through his fingers as quickly as it had come. Kion collapsed beside Truesilver on the bed. The citrines embedded in the hilt and cross-guard flickered in the gloom. Such a singular weapon. A sword that could make fire, see through lies, glow in the night, and fly to his hand when he called it. Kion possessed the greatest sword in the land, yet he was powerless to do the one thing that really mattered: save his mother.

"Why did they have to take her, Kithian? If only I hadn't sent that messenger, or run off to Roving. She'd still be here with us and we'd all be safe and…"

"And you would have fled from your village with her and your sister, but what would you have done then? Have you ever asked yourself that question? What would you do if your mother was here with you now? The enemies of the Four Wards would still be threatening her and Tiryn and the rest of your homeland. Have you ever stopped to think about why the Mastersmith sent me to you? I have slept for hundreds of years. Have you thought about why I was awakened now —at just such a time? Have you considered why you were given the gift of swordspeaking? There is a larger world beyond you, Kion, and as much as you love your mother, it has need of you. The haukmarn have fallen back for now, but talk of the war ending comes too soon. No army ten thousand strong would come to naught after the loss of two battles unless they were arrayed against a force far stronger than what the Four Wards possess. We shall never abandon the search for your mother, but it may be that she is beyond your power to save. If that is so, what will you do then? You must learn to see the greater story unfolding around you, and you must take your place in it, not follow the path of your heart only. You must fulfill the Mastersmith's purpose

first and above all. For you are a swordspeaker and this is your calling."

Kithian's words singed his heart. They were kindly spoken, but it was a hard kindness. There were no doubt many things the Mastersmith intended for them to do, but Kion could not bring himself to face such things now. Not until he knew the truth of his mother's fate. Perhaps it was not the wisest decision, but it was the only one he could bring himself to make.

"I know you've been given to me for a purpose, but—" His words were interrupted by a rustling at the door.

Tiryn's face popped in as the door opened just enough for Truesilver's soft light to catch her face.

"It's good that you're awake. Hurry, put on your boots and come down with me," she said, slipping inside.

"I already told you, I'm not going down there with you."

"No, Kion, listen." Tiryn stared at him, barely able to contain her excitement. "That peddler—the one we met on the road—he's downstairs in the common room."

"Meander Toft?" Kion's suspicions rose at once. "Wait—what? What's he doing here?"

"He said he was coming here on business, remember? He told us that he was heading to Fennigar."

"But him showing up at the same inn as us, that sounds a bit suspicious, doesn't it?"

"However he found us, that's not important. What matters is that he says he has news about Mother! He says he knows where she is!"

"What? How does he know that? Where is she? I have to talk to him." Kion leapt to his feet, bounding forward, but Tiryn stood before the door and motioned for him to stay.

"Wait, it's not that simple. He says he'll only tell us if we pay him. And he's asking a lot. Zinder's trying to talk him down, but it's not looking good. Zinder said to come get you, that you were a *true* bargainer. And he winked at me when he said the word 'true.' I wasn't quite sure what he meant, but I figured you might know."

A true bargainer. Kion knew exactly what he meant. He squeezed on his boots and scooped Truesilver up off the bed.

"He means that he trusts Meander about as far as he can throw his own fingers. He wants me to use Kithian to see if he's telling the truth, if he really does know where Mother is. Come on. Let's test this peddler and see what game he's playing."

The two sped from the room, scurrying along the balcony. They had the full view of the commons as they went. Kion spotted the dark, hunched figure of the peddler at once. His two guards sat on either side of him. Zinder sat opposite, fairly hopping up and down in his chair, his nose red as a welt. Not a good sign. His hat was also off. An even worse sign.

"Oh my, here we go," Kion muttered.

"Be watchful. For this man to have found us here means that his greed may spread beyond a mere desire for coin."

"I know. But if he really does know where Mother is, we may be able to turn his greed to our advantage."

"Perhaps. But greed may wound more than simply those who feel it."

The room was not even half-crowded. Night had only just fallen and most folk were still coming back from the docks and other business about town. Baradoc's fiddle sat silent beside the hearth. He was busy stoking the fire. Zinder and Meander's haggling clouded the peaceful room like a thunderstorm in a quiet valley.

"Robbery! Shame-faced robbery!" Zinder bellowed. "You know I could never afford such a price. Do I look to you like the fane's own blacksmith? Is my hat made of gold?"

Meander Toft, who had his hood down but wore a leather cap with large flaps down the sides, unbent his crooked spine and let out a grating, saw-like chuckle.

"My fine fellow, you are quite the spirited haggler. But I've already come down a hundred and you've yet to adjust your offer a single coin."

Their boisterous negotiations drew considerable stares from those around them, but Zinder paid no attention. He raised his voice even louder.

"Because I can't pay more than I have, you nick-pincher! You'll just as soon get gold squeezing it from a rock."

Meander touched the points of his fingers together and hunched forward. "But rocks don't have mothers, do they, my friend? Think of the boy and the girl."

Kion swept in and slapped one hand on the table, thrusting his face between Zinder and the peddler.

"Yes, think of the boy. Well, here I am, Mr. Toft. Now, where is my mother?"

Meander recoiled and one of his guards grabbed Kion by the sleeve. He looked like he might pull Kion right out of his shirt, but at a wave from his master, he eased off and allowed Kion to take a chair beside Zinder. Kion leaned Truesilver against the edge of the table beside him, which drew looks of intense interest from both Meander and his guards and several of the patrons nearby.

"Watch your men, Toft," Zinder said, stroking his mustache. The pink flush in his face grew deeper by the moment. Tiryn slid noiselessly into the chair on Zinder's left.

"My sister says you claim to know where my mother is," Kion said. "So I'll ask you again—where is she?"

Meander brushed some non-existent crumbs from his cloak.

"Kion, is it? Perhaps you're too young to understand how these sorts of arrangements work. You see, we exchange goods once the deal is complete. And we have yet to come to that part."

"My mother is not a good! She's not up for sale. Now tell me where she is or I'll make you tell me."

Zinder placed a hand on Kion's shoulder. "Calm down, lad. It'll do no good to threaten the fellow. Though he certainly deserves a good beating for trying to sell your dear sweet mother for a few gold rounds, he'll tell us nothing if it comes to blows."

"We don't even know if he's telling the truth. Are you telling the truth, peddler? Or do you just intend to send us off on a wild goose chase?"

"I assure you, I know how to find her."

"This is the difficulty with double-minded men such as this one. I cannot know for certain if he is lying or not. Only by your touch. And yet, keep pressing. He may let something slip."

"How do we know we can trust you?" Kion said.

"I give you my word as a peddler," Meander said with such sincerity that he almost sounded believable.

Zinder's eyes would have rolled up into the rafters if they could have.

"As if that meant anything. Peddlers are about as honest as those thimbleriggers who show up at fairs with their shell games. The more you talk, the less I believe you."

"Well then, if my oath is not enough, I don't see how we can continue. But mark my words, I know where she is. And if we do not strike a deal here, you will never see her again."

The cur. The filthy, good-for-nothing cur. It was all Kion could do to keep from unsheathing Truesilver and forcing the truth out of him at sword-point.

"I am sorry, swordspeaker. His thoughts are guarded by clever locks. You will need to find a way to touch him for me to uncover the truth."

Kion eyed the burly guards. They had their eyes locked fast upon him. Wonderful. As if they would ever let him get close to the peddler.

"Please, sir." Tiryn surprised everyone by grasping Meander's hand. "We'll pay anything, down to the clothes off our backs. Just tell us where she is."

The surrounding patrons were all but leaning in by this point, to see who came out atop this heated contest.

Meander patted her hand, then promptly withdrew his own.

And now he was farther than ever from Kion's reach. Why hadn't he been bold like Tiryn? But the guards didn't have their eye on her the way they did him.

"Well, I see that at least one of you understands the true value of my offer," Meander said. "And yet, I'm afraid it stands at five hundred gold rounds—down from six, I remind you—and yet all the nyn has offered me is one-fifth of that."

Zinder threw up his hands, his cheeks puffing like a bellows. "Oh, bother it all. I've told you that's all we have—selling my cart, my swords, my tools, and even dear old Crusty. If you gave me a year, maybe—maybe—I could double it, but we don't have that kind of time and neither does she and you know it." Zinder was in danger of becoming a living furnace. If his face turned any redder, his hair might start smoldering. Between the shade of his forehead and his stark white hair, it half looked like that already.

A sickly sigh escaped Meander's barely visible lips.

"You're sure that is all you have?"

"Nyn's honor. We're two shepherds and a blacksmith. We're as poor as three ship-wrecked mice."

A long breath rattled from inside Meander's feeble lungs. He clasped his hands together, his fingers moving in a rippling weave. Long he stared at them until his eyes strayed towards Truesilver, its bright gems and golden pommel resting gently against the table.

"What about that sword you've got there?" Meander studied the blade, measuring its worth with a practiced eye. "That doesn't look like anything a shepherd would carry."

"This?" Kion's throat closed tight. "This was a…it was a gift given to me by…well, by the Bladewarden himself, if you want to know." That was almost true. The sword had been carried by Strom for many years before coming into Kion's hands, though it had not appeared in its true form back then.

"The Bladewarden himself, you say?" Meander turned to his

guards. "You see, boys, I told you he was more than he seemed. It's a pity Strom died at Roving. I'm sure he would have helped you find your mother if he was indeed your friend and if he were still here. But perhaps in a way he still can. The gems in that sword must be worth five hundred gold rounds alone. So this is the bargain I propose: if you give me the sword, I'll tell you where your mother is. An even trade. Your sword for the life of your mother; what do you say?"

The shock of the offer left Kion in a daze. Instinctively, his hand grasped the handle of his sword. He would never have dreamed when he marched down the stairs that Toft would ever offer such a trade. His mother meant more to him than all the swords and armor and castles in the Four Wards. And yet, Truesilver was no common sword. It was a living being, a being with a name—Kithian. And Kithian was more than a creation of metal and gems. Kithian was his friend, more than his friend, in truth; for, ever since the bonding that took place when Kion first held his glaive, Kithian had become an extension of Kion himself, a part of him that he could no more sell or give away than he could his own thoughts and memories.

Tiryn slid her arm into Kion's. She did not fully understand Kithian's true nature. Zinder had seen the blade's fire, had seen it speak with birds, had been there at the bonding. He had at least some idea of what Meander was asking, but Tiryn did not. And there was no way Kion could explain it to her now. She looked at him with expectant eyes, eyes ready to burst into either tears of joy or despair depending on his answer.

"This peddler knows more than he is letting on," Kithian said, so intent on studying Meander that he did not sense the battle raging inside his glaivebond. *"He did not come here by accident. You must find a way to touch him if I am to penetrate his thoughts."* There was no fear, no worry in his voice, not even a hint that he believed Kion would ever trade him away to a common peddler, even for the life of his mother. But if Kithian only knew how

strongly Kion was tempted to do just that, would he have spoken with such confidence?

Zinder leaned halfway across the table, shaking his fist. "I was wrong. You're worse than a thimblerigger. You're a bald-faced swindler! You don't know what you're asking. And this is the thanks we get for repairing your wagon. If I ever see that contraption again I'll turn it into toothpicks!"

"Enough. You have my offer," Meander said triumphantly. "Give me the sword if you ever want to see your mother again."

Kion stretched out his hand. "Please—"

Meander was quicker than he looked, and his guards even quicker. One of them grabbed Kion's hand and pinned it to the table while Meander scooted his chair away, a look of trepidation in his eyes, as if he had just avoided an attempt on his life.

And yet they were not quick enough. Just before Meander pulled his hands away, Kion's fingers had grazed the peddler's skin with the barest touch. But would it be enough?

"He is telling the truth. He knows where your mother is. But there is something else. Some darker secret he is hiding. We need to know more. You must touch him again, with more than a mere brush this time. A little longer and perhaps the full truth will become clear."

But looking at Meander now, sitting well back from the table, his guards hovering protectively over him, Kion saw how impossible that would be.

"Your decision, shepherd boy?" Meander's lips twitched in a sneer, his confidence reasserting itself.

Tiryn squeezed Kion's arm, pleading with her eyes on behalf of their mother.

"Oh, Kion…" she said.

How could he choose between the woman he most loved in all the world and Kithian, who was as close to him as his own life? And yet, looking into his sister's eyes, he saw the sacrifice that was required of him, saw it like that sunbeam he'd imagined earlier, parting the clouds once more. In a way, Kithian's own words had doomed him. Meander knew the truth and that was exactly what Kithian had said that Kion must discover before setting out to find his mother again. Kithian was immortal. No peddler could do him any harm. His mother had no such protection.

"I'm sorry, Kithian…" Kion whispered so that no one else could hear—only himself and the sword he was about to betray.

Chapter 6

TRUTH AND LIES

In the same moment that Kion placed his hand on Truesilver's hilt to trade his glaive for the location of his mother, the double doors to the Grizzly Griddle burst open wide. A dozen soldiers rushed in, Roardin at their head. He thrust a gauntleted finger toward Meander Toft and announced in a booming voice:

"Daysman Ilk, you are under arrest for betraying the city of Charring into the hands of our enemies. Seize him."

Meander Toft, who apparently was in truth Daysman Ilk, the former leader of Charring, rose with surprising swiftness, lunging for Kion's sword. But Kion, who mere moments before had been prepared to surrender the blade, sprang back and flourished Truesilver from its sheath.

"Fool!" Ilk spat out the word as patrons leapt from their seats, fumbling over themselves to get away from Kion's table. Chairs clattered and plates clinked and everyone moved at the same time.

"Watch yourself, Ilk. Or would you buy this sword with your own blood?" Kion said.

Roardin's men swept in, but Ilk's guards leapt across the table, straining to reach Zinder and Tiryn. Zinder was too quick, but Tiryn was caught unawares. Before anyone knew what was happening, a long knife flashed at her throat.

"Back, you dogs, or the girl's life is over," said the guard.

Shouts and cries rang out across the room. The patrons froze or shrank back from the threatening steel, fearing for the life of the terrified girl. But Baradoc kept his wits, snatching a burning brand from the fire in one hand, his fiddle held in the other.

"Hands off the girl if you know what's good for you," he said.

Kion made a brand of his own with a single word. "Glaivefire."

Thick red fire erupted along Truesilver's blade and an awed silence fell upon the room as all eyes were drawn to the otherworldly flames.

"Release my sister," Kion said, advancing on the guard.

The guard stepped back, still gripping Tiryn, never taking his eyes off the flaming sword.

"Y-you stay back," he said, his voice surprisingly small for a man so large and strong.

"I told you to let her go." Kion slashed the air and a thin jet of flame shot from the blade onto the guard's exposed hand. The man screamed and his knife dropped to the floor. Tiryn wrenched herself free, the guard too astounded and in too much pain to maintain his hold.

"I knew it. I knew it was a real glaive," Ilk said. A soldier had seized him, yanking off his hat in the process. His exposed head was almost entirely bald, with only small tufts above his paper-thin ears. Ilk's eyes stared hungrily at the blade. "Just like the legends said."

Roardin's men rapidly overwhelmed Ilk's guards. They wrenched the hands of the traitors behind them, a dozen soldiers subduing the three false-hearted men.

"That is quite a sword, my friend," Roardin said, approaching Kion, but stopping before the heat of the flames grew too great.

"Perhaps the matter is now in hand," Kithian said. *"Shall I quench my fire?"*

"Yes," Kion said softly, glancing awkwardly at the many patrons staring at him. Tiryn collided against him, wrapping her arms around his chest.

"Thank you, Kion. Thank you." Her breath came fast and uneven.

The flames had vanished, but a reddish light still clung to the naked metal of Truesilver's blade.

"There is even more to you than I had thought," Roardin said. "How did you acquire such a marvelous weapon?"

Ilk cut Kion off before he could answer. Though he'd been cowed physically, the old bluster was still there. "He got it from your former bladewarden, who was too much of a fool to unlock its secrets."

"Hold your tongue, traitor. Speak ill again of Strom Glyre and I shall see that you lose it. I'll have words with you when I please."

"He's right, though," Kion said. "You never found Strom's blade after his duel with Vayd because somehow it found its way into my friend's cart."

"But that is not Verisguard. It looks nothing like it."

"Indeed. But I assure you that they are one and the same. Only, the sword's actual name is Truesilver."

The patrons drew close, surveying the blade with wonder tinged by disbelief. The eyes of Roardin's men sparkled with a different light, one of admiration at the exotic blade and the one who wielded it. One of the inn-folk, a young boy barely taller than Zinder, pointed and said, "He must be the Sword of the North, the one who freed Charring all by himself. It has to be. Did you see that fire?" He pulled on the skirts of a dumbstruck woman who could only have been his mother. Murmurs ran through the crowd, with several people echoing the boy's words.

Zinder hopped up onto one of the chairs. "Now, ladies and gentlemen. Please, please, stay calm. You've guessed right. This is indeed the Sword of the North. But listen here—listen up. You've only heard half the story. He didn't beat the whole army back all by himself, you see. Oh, no. Who do you think sprung the locks and sawed the bars to get him into the city? Who do you think guided him every step of the way? Who do you think charged in with his crossbow when the fat sizzled hottest in the pan? Why, Zinder Hamryn, his faithful friend, of course. Yours truly! And I've been thinking of a name for myself as well. You can call me the Hammer of the North. Not that I fight with a hammer, but it has a nice ring to it, don't you think? I'm a blacksmith by trade, you see, but I'm no feather when it comes to a fight. I can hold my own there too, you know! Yes, indeed!"

The whole time Zinder was talking, the patrons, especially the younger ones, pressed even closer. Some of them reached out to touch Kion's clothes. A few of the more precocious ones even touched Truesilver's blade.

"Back, now. Step back, step back," Kion said, sheathing the blade. "I don't want anyone getting hurt." Thankfully, they obeyed, more out of astonishment than any real fear.

The affair with Ilk was all but forgotten by the crowd, who peppered Kion with questions about the sword's strange fire, the battle with Vayd Mokàn, how he had defeated the rest of the haukmarn, and what great battles he would fight next. Was he headed to Roving to send the last of the haukmarn howling back to their horrid homeland? Was he going to invade the Marred Wastes and defeat their enemies once and for all? Much to Zinder's dismay, none of the questions seemed to be addressed to the Hammer of the North, except from one old lady who asked if he could fashion her some pots.

"Excuse me." Roardin spoke into Kion's ear to ensure that his voice was heard over the clamor. "I need to see these prisoners to the lock-house, but might I have a word with you outside first?"

"Yes, of course. Only before you take Ilk away, I have a few questions of my own for him. Would that be all right?"

"As you will. Innkeeper Baradoc, I'd like to speak to the boy and his friends privately. I request the use of your stables."

"Whatever you wish, Swordswain." Baradoc tossed his brand back in the fire and wiped his hands on his apron. "Now, my faithful Griddlers, in honor of the Sword of the North and his great victory, free drinks for everyone for the rest of the night!"

The announcement was met with a roar of approval.

"However, I'm afraid we will have to let the great swordsman alone for the moment. He has battles to plan and haukmarn to slay. So, off—off with you now—back to your seats, and Misty and Meg will be out to serve you shortly."

These words were met with considerably less enthusiasm, but the people shuffled obediently back to their tables all the same.

"Ungrateful pack of snoops," Zinder mumbled, falling in line with Roardin's train as they left the inn. "They've no appreciation for all that goes into a battle. All they see is the clashing swords and the shining armor. They don't stop to think about who *made* the weapons and armor and who *got* them to the battle. As far as they know, heroes just fall from the sky, strike down the enemy, and ride off on a whirlwind to fight the next villain."

"Well, I appreciate you," Tiryn said.

"I'm sure they didn't mean any disrespect," Kion said. "You do make a good point. There's more to great victories than feats of arms. I'm the first to admit I'd never have made it this far without your help. You were there for me when the night was darkest, Zinder. I'll never forget that."

Zinder blinked several times. For a brief moment, the loquacious nyn was at a loss for words. He patted Kion from behind and there came a little extra lift to his step as Kion's acknowledgment of his friend's worth took hold.

"You deserve all the cheers and the titles they can throw at you, lad. I'm just along for the ride. Honestly, I'm not sure what got into me back there. Got a bit carried away, I suppose. But thank you for saying that, all the same."

A steady drizzle gave their clothes a dewy sheen as they passed into the large stable next to the inn. The strong odor of hay and manure did not make for a pleasant atmosphere, but Kion had far too many things on his mind to notice. Now was his chance to find out what Ilk really knew about his mother. The horses and hay, the tack and carts, faded away as the soldiers ushered Ilk into an empty stall and sat him on a rough-cut stool. His two henchmen, along with the bulk of the soldiers, remained on the other side of the swinging gate as Roardin, Zinder, Tiryn, and Kion packed inside.

"The prisoner is all yours, Kion." Roardin gestured towards the disgraced daysman.

Kion knelt before his adversary, the man who had given his own people to the haukmarn, and for what? No doubt a hefty sum of coin. Was it any wonder he'd been willing to sell Kion's mother as well? What a fool Kion had been to try bargaining with such a man. And to think that he had almost lost his glaive to this schemer. He wondered if Kithian would ever forgive him —if Kithian even knew what he had almost done. Could Kion even forgive himself? But there would be time to wrestle with that later. Now was the time for answers. Now was the time for truth.

"So, your real name's Ilk, then? Well, Mr. Ilk, it's time you tell us what you truly know. But first, I'll give you some information of my own. This sword at my side can tell me whenever a lie is spoken by the person I am touching." He placed one hand on Ilk's shoulder and kept the other on Truesilver's hilt. "So, tell me, Mr. Ilk, where is my mother?"

Ilk eyed Kion's hand with a mixture of revulsion and spite. He squirmed in his stool like a child who resented the punishment he was about to receive. No longer covered by his cap, Ilk's barren head and stretched skin made him look exposed and shriveled and pitiful.

"Do you really have to touch me? Or is that something you just made up to make me feel uncomfortable?" Ilk said in a woeful tone. The arrogance and self-assurance he'd displayed while disguised as a peddler had all but vanished.

"I do. Now answer my question. And remember, I will know if you are lying."

"Well, could you at least loosen your grip?"

"If you'll stop squirming."

"Fine."

Ilk settled down and Kion eased his hold.

"Well, now. In point of fact, I'm not sure that even if I did tell you it would do you any good."

"He is lying. He wants to test me, to see if I can truly see through his deceit."

Kion gripped Ilk tighter. "Try again. I told you I would know when you were lying."

"Was the sword talking to you, just now? Tell me that it was," Ilk said eagerly.

"Yes. Now tell me the truth."

"Fascinating. What's it like, hearing its voice? Does it sound human, or is it more like a thought in your head?"

"I will ask the questions, Ilk. How do I find her?"

"If I tell you, will you let me go?"

Roardin answered for him. "Of course not. You are a traitor to your people. You shall suffer the fate all traitors are due."

The old slyness of Meander slipped back in. "Then I don't see why I should tell you anything. What's in it for me?"

Roardin stepped up beside Kion. "Why did you do it, Ilk? Why did you betray the fane and your own people? Don't you know the haukmarn are monsters?"

"They may be monsters. But they are monsters who appreciate my skills and worth. Something the fane never did."

"They're savages who will cut your throat the moment you cease to be of use to them." Roardin's composed visage cracked, letting his contempt for Ilk show through. "Tell me what you know of them since you've sold your honor and your humanity. Vayd's still alive, isn't he? Where is he? And where do the haukmarn intend to strike next?"

"How should I know?" Ilk said.

A quiver ran through Truesilver's hilt. *"He's lying again. He knows exactly when the next attack will come,"* Kithian said.

Kion dug his fingers in a little more. Ilk gave out a little squeal, but Kion did not loosen his grip.

"You lie. Tell us the truth. When and where is the next attack coming?"

"Blast! I should have known the war wasn't over," Zinder said. "Tell him to stick out his tongue. I'll bet it's forked."

Ilk gave a petulant snort. "You really think I would be foolish enough to tell you what I know?"

Kion yanked Ilk forward. Information about the haukmarn was important, but he had not forgotten why he was here.

"Enough of this. You will tell us where the attack is coming from—but first, tell me how to find my mother. I swear to you, if we have to sit here until the end of days, you will tell me where she is. I'm not leaving until you do."

Ilk's eyes roved about the stall, avoiding the gaze of everyone there, as if he could win this contest of will simply through silence. Perhaps he could.

"Tell me the truth." Kion gave Ilk's shoulder a shake.

Ilk threw up his hands, as if to ward off an impending attack.

"You're stalling, old one," Roardin said. "Tell the boy what he wants to know. He may not have the authority to force an answer out of you, but I am more than willing to do so on his behalf."

Ilk squirmed again feebly, making several pathetic noises. The steel-hearted tone in the swordswain's voice had gotten his attention.

"You're not going to hurt him, are you?" Tiryn asked.

"Would you like us to step outside?" Zinder said.

Roardin adjusted his sword belt meaningfully and stepped forward.

"Kion, I'll take over from—"

"Fine, fine, fine. I'll talk." Ilk searched the space beyond the stall, his dark, pebbled eyes flitting between there and the looming swordswain before him. "I'll tell you what I know. But it won't help you." Ilk grumbled and clicked his tongue a dozen times, delaying the truth as long as he could. "Your mother was taken by ship to Tinesplitter Isle. There. Now you know." He stared anxiously at Roardin, pleading silently for him to step away.

Roardin instead took half a step closer.

"They've renewed their alliance with the Noathryn?"

Ilk ground his teeth together. "Yes. I suppose it doesn't matter if you know that. You'd have found out for yourself soon enough."

Kion broke in. "But my mother—you're sure she's there? On this island?"

"Yes, yes, if she survived the journey by sea. I can't promise you she did, of course."

"The man speaks true." Kithian's voice was filled with such happiness for his glaivebond that Kion was sorry he'd ever questioned Kithian's understanding of what his mother meant to him.

"They're paying the Noathryn with Inrisian slaves, aren't they?" Roardin said.

"I never said they were honorable masters, only appreciative ones." Ilk risked a smug chuckle. "But as for the boy, I don't see that my news will do him much good. Tinesplitter is on the far side of Noath and you'll be hard-pressed to find a captain foolish enough to sail you into Noathryn waters now. But if you do intend to seek her, then every moment you stay here speaking to me, your hope of saving her diminishes."

"That may be, and yet I doubt that he has told us the full truth. We must find out all that he knows."

Zinder stepped up beside Kion, and by the way he stroked his mustache, it was obvious that the wheels of his mind were spinning at full tilt.

"Oh, we'll be off soon enough. But not soon enough for your liking, I imagine," Zinder said, his eyes flashing beneath the brim of his hat. "And we owe it to the good swordswain here to find out as much as you can tell us, not just about Tinesplitter and the children's mother, but also about your relationship with your haukmarn friends. You betrayed Charring for coin or power or both, that much is clear. But why did you hunt us down in Fennigar? Why chase after a few wandering travelers you met along the road?"

A genuine smile—or as much a one as he was capable of—drew itself across Ilk's withered skin.

"Leave it to a nyn to discern the central question of the matter. It is too bad you're so short. The blade would do far better with you wielding its magic. But yes, why am I here? That is a very curious thing, is it not? You see, I wasn't lying when I told you on the road that I was a scholar. I've studied the glaives. I've read the legends in the Grand Archive of Gilding."

"You've been to the Grand Archive?" Zinder bristled at the reference to his height, but the mention of the great library of Gilding momentarily banished his animosity toward the traitorous daysman.

"Oh, yes, many times…in my younger years, before the fane banished me to this cursed country." Ilk's bitterness returned and with it, Zinder's awareness of the true nature of the man before him.

"So you knew about Kion's blade all along? Why didn't you take it from him when we met you on the road, then?"

"I should think the answer was obvious. I didn't know you had it. How was I to know this tattered shepherd boy was the same warrior who vanquished Vayd and put his army to flight?"

"He speaks the truth again. It makes me wonder what he has read about the glaives."

There would be time for that later. "Who told you I had the sword?" Kion said.

Ilk raised a scraggly eyebrow, enjoying his place as the most knowledgeable person in the room.

"Someone who wants it very much."

Kion's mind went back to Charring. The only ones there who'd seen Truesilver in its full power had been the haukmarn.

None of the people of Charring actually saw the sword aflame. The fire had gone out by the time the militia arrived to rescue him from Vayd's personal guard. So only the haukmarn truly knew of Truesilver's nature. And only one of them would have had the audacity to send Ilk to take the weapon from him.

"Vayd. He sent you to try to trick me into giving you the sword. He tried to take it from me when I was wounded by the arrow. He wants it for himself, doesn't he?"

Ilk paused, eyeing Kion with predatory cunning. The twisted longing for power and acclaim that festered in his eyes was both disturbing and dangerous.

"It would make a powerful weapon in the war, would it not?"

"Though Ilk speaks the truth, he misunderstands the nature of the glaives and their bonds with their swordspeakers. A weapon's gifts cannot be used without the weapon's consent."

For the first time since the questioning began, Kion withdrew his hand from Ilk's shoulder. This new revelation rippled through his mind, telling him far more than the mere words themselves ever could. For he now knew that Vayd was definitely alive. And not only had he survived, but he would hunt Kion down until Truesilver was his, though the blade would be powerless in his hands.

"A few more questions." Zinder placed Kion's hand back on Ilk's shoulder. "Answer me this. What was inside your wagon when we met on the road from Charring?"

"From the look in your eye, Master Nyn, I'd say you've already guessed."

"Vayd Mokán himself or I'm made out of butter," Zinder said, his voice almost breathless. "It was you that got him out of Charring!"

Ilk inclined his head in agreement. "I may have had some hand in it."

"Your treachery knows no bounds, Ilk," Roardin said. "You shall go down in the history of the Four Wards as the vilest traitor of this age. Your name shall be a curse to all men of honor. A swift and deadly justice awaits you."

"This soldier could not have spoken more truly," Kithian said.

"But I still don't understand. Why didn't Vayd attack us and take the weapon?" Kion said. "If he was in your wagon, why let us ride on?"

"As I said. I did not know at the time who you were. I only told him of our encounter afterward. I can assure you that he was none too pleased when he found out. But it could not be helped. Vayd was asleep when you arrived, under the effects of some restorative herbs I had given him. I could not have wakened him if I tried. You forget that he was wounded near to death. Even with the restorative powers of the wanstones, he might not have survived were it not for my knowledge of the healing arts. But he is doing quite well now. His recovery surprised even me—truly remarkable."

Roardin clenched his fists at his side. Ilk's brazen treachery strained the patience of even this noble warrior.

"You are to be pitied. You gave up the truth for a lie, life for death, and honor for shame. I may be a mere soldier, but I shall see to it that your deeds are given their proper place in the histories and annals you hold so dear."

Vayd was alive. But Kion had to lay that aside for the moment. His path now lay to the west, toward Tinesplitter. He knew where to find his mother at last.

Before he could press Ilk with another question, the sounds of thudding feet broke into the stable. The guards outside shuffled and gave way. A soldier ran up to the stall, winded and pale. Kion rose with the others to face him.

"Swordswain Roardin," he said after a brisk salute. "Someone lit the signal fire in the south tower. We put it out, but it looks like it was done by traitors from the inside—some sort of sign to the haukmarn. They're massing to the south and east—twice what we faced last time, from what our scouts say. The fog gave them cover, but they will be here within the hour. And

Noathryn ships have been spotted by several fishermen, bearing down upon the harbor."

Ilk's lipless smile glimmered once more in the weak light of the stall. He had known the attack was coming all along. He had only drawn out the interrogation long enough for the haukmarn to be alerted.

"So much for justice," Ilk said.

Roardin gave him a scathing glare, but his anger soon passed. A cold clarity settled in his eyes.

"Kion, we must leave this place. I know you said that you wish to travel to Tinesplitter, but that may no longer be possible, at least not from Fennigar. If you must delay your journey, then I would ask you in the fane's name to stay and fight. You seemed but a boy in Roving, but today I have seen what you and your sword can do. I believe with Truesilver, you could do more in this battle than a whole host of my best men. Will you stay and fight with us? Will you lend us your sword as you did the people of Charring?"

Kion shuddered in disbelief. How could this noble warrior think of him this way? Kion was an insignificant shepherd, an unknown and powerless commoner without a silver nick to his name. But setting Roardin's praise aside, a more unsettling question arose. Should Kion stay and fight? Was he duty-bound to honor Roardin's request? He had not gone to Charring to save it. He had gone there to rescue his mother and sister. And he had not come to Fennigar to fight in a battle either. But this city was as much a part of Inris and the Four Wards as his own village. Could he, should he, fight for them? Would he be able to save them even if he did? He was only one warrior, however magnificent his blade. And what about his mother? That question, above all, weighed heaviest upon his heart.

"I am ready and willing to help the people of this city, Kion. It is my purpose to serve all who stand against tyranny and to take up whatever challenge may come, no matter how desperate. If Vayd is with this army, this may be our chance to finish him and end this war as we

failed to do at Charring. There is no telling when we might get that chance again, or how many might suffer and die if we pass over that chance now. And yet, faithless would I be in counsel, swordspeaker, if I did not remind you that not all battles go as swiftly as they did at Roving and Charring. You may be delayed many days or many an eight-mark, ere the battle is won. Even then, there is no assurance of victory. Make your choice, glaivebond, and make it swiftly. Many lives hang upon your decision."

Kion turned from the swordswain, from Ilk, from Zinder and Tiryn, from everyone. It seemed that battle was once again upon him, but the first battle to fight was the one within his own heart. How could he abandon these people to the haukmarn hordes? And yet how could he abandon his mother when he finally had a clear path to find her?

Some choices bring sorrow on either side.

Chapter 7

THE GLOOMING BOG

In the end for Kion, the choice before him was no choice at all. His love for his mother could not be denied. It was stronger than his love for Inris and the Four Wards, stronger even than his bond with Kithian, stronger than anything. He could not fail her. He could not abandon her to a life of slavery and suffering in distant lands. As terrible and cowardly as it felt to deny Roardin's request, he could not fight this battle.

Kion faced the swordswain's penetrating gaze. "I am sorry. I cannot aid you in this fight. The battle could last for many days and I must find my mother before it is too late. Perhaps it is already too late, but still, I must try. To do any less would be to fail her as a son."

Roardin acknowledged Kion with an impassive nod, taking the news like the seasoned soldier that he was.

"I understand. I wish that you would stay, but I will not compel you, though as a swordswain of the fane, I would have the power to do so. Wisdom tells me that your blade's fire is no one's to command but your own. And yet, if you do find your mother and the war has not ended, we would welcome your sword to our cause."

"I will gladly fight for the Four Wards when that time comes."

Kion at last managed to give Roardin the salute he deserved.

Kithian's voice was subdued. *"Only time will tell if you have made the right choice, swordspeaker. But there is one thing that might keep you from following through on your decision. The messenger said that the haukmarn have the city surrounded and the Noathryn are bearing down upon the harbor. How, then, do you propose to leave this place?"*

Zinder and Tiryn gazed at him expectantly. Whatever he had decided, they would stand with him, that much he knew, but he also knew that he had made the choice they were hoping he would make.

"I suppose we're off again, then," Zinder said.

"And I am needed elsewhere." Roardin strode ahead of them out of the stall.

"Swordswain—" Kion hurried up beside him. "If I may. Is there any safe way to leave the city before the haukmarn attack?"

Roardin gave orders for Ilk to be secured in the barracks and motioned for Kion and the others to follow as they rushed from the stable. Kion met Ilk's eyes one last time. The venomous light there was cause for warning. Ilk still thought he would come out on top of this all somehow, even as the guards forced him roughly to his feet.

"There is a way," Roardin said, the speed of his speech increasing apace with his quickening stride. "Though it is by no means certain. The haukmarn cannot fully encircle the city, for the Glooming Bog guards our flank to the west and they would be foolish to invade from that way. At best, they will send a few scattered bands of scouts to watch over it. If you move quickly, you may escape through the marsh and into the Billows, the gentle hills that stretch between here and Grettling." Roardin spat out orders to the soldiers in the train behind him. "Head to the west gate and await me there, except you two. You hurry on and tell the Swamp Dog we have need of his services. Ready two horses with provisions and wait for me at the barracks. Kion, you and your friends gather your things from the inn and I'll wait for you outside. Hurry, we haven't much time."

"Right, come on, lad. You and Tiryn bring down our things and I'll ready Crusty. I believe they keep the carts out back." Zinder started off behind the inn, but Roardin called him back.

"I'm sorry, Master Nyn, but unless your Crusty is a stallion with experience navigating dense marshland, you'll have to leave him. And you won't be able to bring a cart with you, either."

Zinder stared right through Roardin. It took a moment for the swordswain's words to settle in. "No, we can't—not Crusty. He's been with me for years, ever since I came to Furrow."

Kion wavered in the well-trod dirt between the stable and the inn. Shouts and marching feet stirred throughout the city. The sky was thick with gulls. Eyes flashed white with terror in the faces of those who poured out from the inn. The dread of war hung in the air.

"I wish it didn't have to be this way, Zinder," Kion said. Crusty was only a mule, but he'd proven himself time and again and gotten them through some tight spots. And Zinder was uncommonly fond of his animal.

Zinder took off his hat and, for the first time in his life, he threw it in the dirt.

"Horn toads. Sometimes life's just hard."

"Oh, Zinder. I'll miss him too," Tiryn said, her voice wistful and low.

"I'll see to it the animal is properly looked after," Roardin said.

Kion knelt and picked up the hat. He would miss Crusty, too, but in this they had no choice. If the swamp was the only road to Mother, they had to take it.

"Zinder, why don't you go say your good-byes to Crusty. Tiryn and I will gather our things."

Zinder gave a dejected nod, then turned and shuffled off back toward the stables, surely that day the most miserable nyn in all the Four Wards.

Two men led a pair of towering stallions from the stables near the barracks. Their coats glistened from the light drizzle. The animals had the chiseled forms of regal statues, worthy of display in any town square. Their sharp hooves and rippled legs looked strong enough to trample the strongest enemies underfoot. One was dark as pitch. A white diamond on its forehead was the only mark in the steed's obsidian mantle. The other horse was a deep bay, with a mane of coal and brushes of ebony about its nose and hooves. The second one was the smaller of the two, but only just.

Tiryn stared up at them with such wonder and reverence they might as well have been royalty.

"You're actually going to let us ride them?" she said.

"Yes, young lady, I am," Roardin said, speaking quickly. "These fine beasts are your best hope of escaping the city."

Of the two men leading the horses, one wore the white tabard of a Verisian soldier, while the other, a stubby fellow in scraggledown leather, was the furthest thing from a soldier imaginable. His frayed clothing, matted hair, and mud-splotched face showed that he had little regard for the trappings and conventions of the civilized world.

"Kion, Tiryn, Zinder, this is Leanoch or, as he's more commonly called, Swamp Dog. He'll be your guide through the Glooming Bog," Roardin said.

"A pleasure," Leanoch said in a frog-like voice. His lips barely seemed to move but his eyes spoke far more than his mouth. He was sizing them up and from his unconvinced expression, they had failed to meet his standards.

Kion and Zinder exchanged questioning glances. Leanoch did not look like he would be the most congenial traveling companion, but if he knew the swamp, that was all they needed.

"Pleased to meet you, Mr. Leanoch," Tiryn said, mustering

up the courage to offer her hand. Leanoch looked at her as if she were offering him a dead fish that was long past due.

"You can call me Swamp Dog," he said in his croaking voice. "And these are our horses, Cyprian and Smokewind. So, who's riding with me?" He pulled Smokewind, the great black horse, forward. Kion could not help but be reminded of Torrent, Strom's magnificent black steed, which he'd not only read about in his journal but also seen at Roving.

Zinder raised his hands as if he'd been caught in a crime. "I suppose that would be me. It seems like the best way to keep the weight as even as possible, and so that Tiryn doesn't have to, well…as I said, I'll be riding with you." Zinder stared up at the horses as from the foot of a mountain before the climb. "Though you should know I've only ever ridden a mule."

"Fair enough," Leanoch said. "I'll be doing the directing as long as we're in the swamps. Hopefully by the time you get out you'll have learned enough to keep from getting bucked to the four winds."

Leanoch picked up Zinder—quite without warning—and tossed him into the saddle atop the dark horse. Zinder gave a little cry, but managed to hold onto his hat.

"Time is short, we must move quickly," Roardin said. He and the other soldier helped Tiryn onto the bay, though she was so enraptured with the animal, she barely noticed the men at all.

"Cyprian. Your name is as beautiful and elegant as you are." She fingered the horse's mane with a light touch, relishing her place atop the majestic creature.

"None of us have ever ridden before," Kion said as he was assisted into the saddle behind Tiryn. "You're sure we can do this?"

"You will be fine," Roardin said. "These beasts know the swamp like they were born to it. Such fine steeds are hard to come by and Leanoch only parts with them on my orders. Be mindful of his sacrifice on your journey. He may be rough and ignorant when it comes to social graces, but he is the best guide I have."

Zinder gave Roardin a queasy look. He had one hand over his mouth and nose and was doing his best to keep as much distance as possible between himself and his riding companion.

"I wish I'd chosen another coat for this journey," he muttered. "...And a scarf would certainly have come in handy..."

The rain pattered down like gentle applause. Carts and townsfolk rushed past them on the street. A company of soldiers poured out of the barracks. Roardin and the other soldier hastily loaded their gear and provisions into the saddle bags and onto the backs of the horses.

"Here, take this." Roardin handed Kion a satchel. "This belonged to Ilk. Some of his papers. My men have already taken the ones that might be of use to us, but perhaps there is something in them that can aid you in your journey to find your mother. The Glooming Bog is not large. With Leanoch guiding you, you should be out of it by tomorrow. After that, I suggest you make for Grettling and see about hiring a ship."

"Thank you, Swordswain," Kion said. "I don't see how we can ever repay you, but after I find my mother, I promise that I will return and offer my sword in the service of the fane. I give you my word as a swordspeaker."

"I will hold you to that promise, young Kion. Go swiftly now, and may we both achieve victory in what we seek."

"May it be so. By your leave."

"Good-bye, Roardin," Tiryn said. "Thank you for the horses and your help with Ilk, and for everything. You are a great and noble man."

"My thanks as well, Swordswain," Zinder said, his voice muffled under his hand. "And please see to it that Crusty's well-treated. He likes a carrot now and then if it can be spared."

"Of course. May your strength remain until journey's end." Roardin waved and gave the traditional Warding benediction.

With a nod from Roardin and a clicking sound from Leanoch, the horses pranced away from the stables, out through the gates, and into the fog-choked swamps to the northwest, the last safe passage out of Fennigar.

Or so they hoped.

Chapter 8

SWAMP DOG

They had not been long in the marshes when the fog and rain swelled to obscure the last trace of Fennigar's walls. The land beyond reeked of decay. Tall reeds rose out of still waters and wide-leafed plants and moss blanketed the rest. The trees, gnarled weavings of bark and foliage, were dotted with fuzzy growths. Their branches hung, weary and bent, as if the trees longed to be toppled and know no more. Dismal clouds sapped what little color there was from the water-logged forest. It was impossible to find anything that wasn't some shade of black or greenish-gray.

Setting aside their dreary surroundings, horse travel was at first a thrill. Kion enjoyed the swaying rhythm of the vast bulk beneath him. The animal was as sure-footed as Roardin had promised, but Cyprian did slip once while crossing a deep bog and water sloshed onto the saddle. A small amount of moisture dribbled between Kion's legs and the leather, making it difficult to stay well-seated for some time after. He kept sliding one direction or another and had to work his way back to the center. Even Tiryn, who had been murmuring expressions of delight at the marvels of travel on horseback, grew subdued as the journey wore on. The dampness and the gloom and the fetid air were too much even for her bright nature to overcome completely.

With Zinder seated in front of the Swamp Dog, and Smokewind in the lead, Kion couldn't get a sense for how his friend fared, but knowing Zinder's penchant for cleanliness and his aversion to foul smells, he was probably worse off than Kion and Tiryn. As for Leanoch, he rested as naturally in the saddle as if he and Smokewind were a single creature. He led them on through the damp gray landscape of the Glooming Bog as easily as Kion might have led his sheep through the Tors.

Though the waters rose at times high enough to brush the soles of their boots, mostly the way was little more than a muddy slog. There was no actual trail that Kion could make out. Thankfully, Leanoch knew where the safe paths were, though from time to time he would halt them, sniff at the air, listen, and turn in a different direction.

They had been traveling for almost three hours when the first sounds of pursuit came. It was a faint splashing and the telltale squelch of boots in the slimy mire, followed by grunts and heavy breathing. It was difficult to know which direction the noises came from, for sound carried deceptively across the standing water and through the soggy trees. But their guide took no chances and quickened their pace, making it harder than ever to stay in the saddle. Twice Kion had to pull Tiryn from sliding off into the swamp.

The sounds drew closer. Guttural commands carried through the marsh, revealing the identity of their pursuers. The haukmarn moved brashly, cursing and crashing through the terrain. But the Swamp Dog led the horses steadily away until the land grew still again.

"Perhaps the haukmarn have lost the trail," Leanoch said, startling everyone with his gravelly voice. "Among their kind, only the wulfmasters have much skill in tracking, but their dreadwulfs have no taste for the swamp. They are useless in the marshlands."

"Let us hope so," Kion said.

They ate and drank in the saddle, never stopping, except once when they passed under a great, hoary tree and a sudden cascade of dark water came down atop Leanoch and Zinder. The Swamp Dog didn't seem to notice, but Zinder was beside himself.

"Confounded tree drool! Uck!" Zinder blurted out in a shrill voice. "It smells like moldy sandals—and the taste—oh dear, it's making my tongue swell like a sponge. It's poisonous or I'm ten feet tall."

"Shh," Kion said. "You don't want to give us away. There could still be haukmarn about."

"Easy for you to say. Your tongue isn't soaked in swamp rot," Zinder hissed back, though he did lower his voice. "I'm sure you'll feel a wave of regret come over you when I fall over dead in the mud a mile from here. It figures I'd go out in some embarrassing way like this. 'How did the poor fellow go?' 'Well, he was attacked by a tree, you see.' 'Ah, you don't say? How humiliating.' 'Yes, it wasn't really his fault, though. If only his friend had listened to him and done something about the poison instead of telling him to clamp his mouth shut.'"

Zinder would have gone on, but Leanoch dismounted and abruptly pulled him off the horse. He plopped him down on the driest bit of mud he could find and shoved a rag in his face. This was followed by a waterskin tossed in his lap.

"Here, dry yourself and rinse your mouth. And keep quiet."

"Well, I—" Zinder reacted indignantly over Leanoch's utter lack of manners, but the sound of another distant splash halted his complaint.

"What was that?" Tiryn asked. It had stopped raining, but the canopy was thick enough that it would not have made much difference. Though there should have been a half-moon to guide them, the dark sky was shut against all light from above. Not even spark trails could pierce the steel-gray cloak of clouds.

Swamp Dog raised a hand to his ear, his nose twitching. After several long minutes, his eyes darted back towards the direction they had come.

"The haukmarn have picked up our trail."

He tossed Zinder back up and sprang into the saddle behind him. Cyprian, over whom Kion had no real control, lurched forward, tipping him against the bags fastened behind him, but he righted himself in time to avoid a fall.

The Swamp Dog urged the horses on even faster than before. The ground was more solid here and though it was too overgrown to reach anything close to a gallop, Kion felt the air rushing past his face for the first time. Between the awareness that the haukmarn were still after them and the terror of trying to stay in the saddle while Cyprian barreled through the trees, Kion scarcely blinked. His life, and his mother's as well, was now in the hands of a man he'd only just met. If Leanoch couldn't get them safely away from the haukmarn, they would have to stand and fight. And the prospects of surviving a clash in this muck were doubtful at best. One slip would be all it would take to send him to a swampy grave.

Trees and ferns rushed by in a shadowy cascade. All the while, new sounds cropped up from every corner of the swamp. They were more definite now and it was clear that more than one group pursued them. It seemed impossible that Leanoch could find a path to avoid all of them, Swamp Dog or not, and yet his knowledge of the land and his cunning ways kept them free. Time fled with the miles and still the Swamp Dog evaded the haukmar net. At points, the sounds would die away altogether, only to reappear some time later from another direction. And yet, as the darkest hours of night approached, for all of Swamp Dog's craftiness, the haukmarn appeared at last.

Large, dark figures hacked their way through the tangled undergrowth to the south. They were still a good ways away and would have been hard to make out but for the specks of white light glimmering from the wanstones in their armor. On open ground, the horses could have outrun them, even as weary as they were, but in the choked morass of Glooming Bog, it was only a matter of time before their pursuers caught them.

"How many do you see? It's too dark for me to tell," Kion said. There was no sense in keeping quiet now.

"Too many," Zinder said. "Leanoch, how good are you with a sword?"

"I can hold my own, but haukmarn fight like rabid wolves. If it comes to a fight, this may be your first and last night in the Bog."

"Kion, I hope we don't have to fight," Tiryn said, twisting back to look at him. "I don't want you to get hurt—I don't want anyone to get hurt."

"I'll be fine. I've got Truesilver, remember?"

"We will fight if we must, but not until our guide's swampcraft fails. He may yet free us from this net."

Leanoch cast a look over his shoulder while the horses again wound their way through the trees. "You do not fight a haukmar on the hunt. You outsmart him. That is the only way to survive."

"Well, I hope you're one smart fellow, then," Zinder said.

"They do not have their axes at our throats yet. When their axes are at our throats, that is the time to worry. For now, they are still behind us. And I know some secrets of the marsh that they do not."

The horses, spurred on by the Swamp Dog, surged forward. He led them into a steep depression. The presence of the hollow was unusual, for most of the marsh was quite flat. Down inside, they finally lost sight of the haukmarn, but the clamor of pursuit refused to fade.

The Swamp Dog halted the horses and leapt from the saddle. The base of the depression was filled with rotted leaves and logs and sandy sludge.

"Why have we stopped?" Kion said.

"I will tell you once we reach the other side."

Swamp Dog led Smokewind through the muck in a snaking path. Cyprian followed just behind. Mercifully, the moon glimmered through a break in the clouds, helping them find their way, but by the way he moved, Kion guessed Swamp Dog could have found the path with his eyes closed. When they reached the opposite side of the little basin, he hurried over to Kion. The heavy tread and careless speech of the haukmarn were close now. Swamp Dog motioned for Kion to dismount and he slid awkwardly onto the damp turf.

"The soldiers told me that you are the Sword of the North, that you can make fire."

"Yes. Only I'm not so sure how well it will work in a place like this," Kion said.

"Let us hope we do not have to find out. You see the path we came across? That is the most obvious way to cross this hollow, the most direct. That is the way they will come. And if they do, the swamp will claim them. But if they take the longer way around, you must stop them with your fire. Can you do this?" Leanoch made a circular motion, indicating the rim of the depression they had just passed through.

"I will try. And if I fail?"

Leanoch pulled open his coat where a row of four daggers was strapped across his chest. "We fight until the axe is at our throats."

Tiryn reached down to touch Kion's shoulder. "Kion, isn't there some other way?"

He wished now more than ever that Tiryn had listened to him and stayed in Charring. This was no place for her to be. But it was no use saying that now.

"The haukmarn don't know this land like Leanoch does. And I will protect you if it comes to a fight. Nothing bad will happen to you—to any of us." Kion stepped away from the horse, his feet padding gingerly across the slippery ground. The terrain was even more treacherous than he thought. This was no place for close quarters fighting.

Zinder unpacked his coalwood crossbow from the rest of his gear and loaded a thick bolt.

"Well, I'm sure getting chopped in two by a haukmar axe is a more heroic way to die than death by tree drool so I can't complain. Still, I wish—"

The haukmarn roared into the edge of the bowl and whatever Zinder meant to say was forgotten.

Spotting their quarry after the long chase, the rambling horde of gray-skinned giants bellowed in savage triumph. "Kill! Kill! Kill!" hollered the one in the lead. Harriers came hurtling into the hollow in ragged ranks, a thundering, ashen wall pouring into the moonlit hollow, axes raised, eyes flashing with hate. The only armor they wore was upon their shoulders—padded leather embedded with smoldering white wanstones.

"Kithian, will your fire work here?"

"Yes. My fire can burn green wood or even travel across standing water. It is glaivefire, born of the Spark. Nothing can quench it but the will of my glaivebond or my own. I will not allow you and your friends to meet your end here, if it is within my power. Only direct the fire where you will."

As always, Kithian's voice lent him a deep confidence. Kion knew that as long as he listened to Kithian's words he need not fear any foe.

Red flames licked Truesilver's blade and Swamp Dog's face showed that it was capable of surprise.

The haukmarn howled in twisted delight. Unlike at Charring, they did not fear the fire this time. They had found the one their master sought, and the blade's fire would soon belong to him. They surged forward, but when the troop reached the bottom of the hollow, their charge stalled. Whole ranks began to fall. At first, Kion thought they must have stumbled into some hidden quagmire, but the flurry of slime and sticks that rose in the air and the tortured cries of the fallen told him that they had met a far deadlier fate. Yet so wild and fierce was their charge that more than a dozen disappeared into the hidden pits of the hollow before they realized the nature of the trap. Their cries turned from murderous to horrified. Some attempted to skirt around the pits, to find the Swamp Dog's hidden path, but soon those fell as well.

Half of the harriers disappeared, never to rise again, but

twenty or so remained, for they had lagged behind the others and retreated back to the edge of the basin in time to avoid the peril of the mire. Grunting orders, one of the survivors divided those that remained into two bands, each setting off on opposite sides of the ridge, just as Swamp Dog had warned.

"It is time," Kithian said.

A shiver of fear ran through Kion's hand. Though he had beaten them at Charring, it was still no less terrible to watch these lumbering monsters come at him. Kion sucked in a deep breath and sliced the air to his left and right in quick succession, sending two small jets of flame flying off in either direction. They landed some twenty paces away, two short lines of fire in the muck. Ordinary fire would have fizzled instantly on the soaked ground, but Truesilver's fire held fast. Not only that, within moments it began to grow. The hungry flames surged across the hollow, making their way toward the outer rim.

The haukmarn wavered at the sight of the fire. It was one thing to see it on the blade. Now it was coming toward them. Cries of warning ran through their number, but the flames were small yet and so they pressed on—with even greater urgency than before—lest the blaze grow too great before they could reach their enemies. But their increased pace was not enough to escape their doom, for Truesilver's flames were not bound by the ordinary laws of nature. Crimson tongues sped along the edge of the hollow, leaping ever higher into the air. The flames whipped and flickered as though they had a mind of their own, a mind bent on consuming all that it touched.

Kion swept his blade in two broad strokes, the bond between himself and Kithian allowing him to direct the flames where he wished them to go. The fire lit through the trees on the hollow's rim. The water-saturated trunks and limbs burst into pillars of fire. Great, swirling clouds of smoke billowed forth. The smoke rushed on ahead of the flames, as if caught in some imperceptible wind, the dark clouds engulfing the haukmarn long before the flames reached them. Though the haukmarn were no longer visible, their coughing and shouts filled the swamp. It was not long before the panicked cries turned to wails of agony. The sounds were incoherent and bestial, like animals caught in snares. And like that, they also ended quickly.

Tiryn stared at Truesilver with an awe far exceeding anything her face had ever shown before. She was too shocked to even speak.

"You are everything the legends say, Sword of the North," Leanoch said.

But there was no time for words of celebration. Other haukmarn might see the flames and be drawn to this place. They quickly mounted again and rode into the night, leaving the hollow a smoldering crater of death and ruin.

Chapter 9

THE BILLOWS

Tiryn shivered through the night. Her bedroll seemed little more than a slip of paper against the cold slab of the cave floor. A vague, pulsing throb in her legs lurked at the back of her mind. She awoke half a dozen times, opening her eyes just long enough to renew the unwelcome awareness of her misery before falling back into tumultuous dreams.

On some other day, when they were not being pursued by haukmarn on an uncertain journey to some distant isle, the hidden cave they had sheltered in would have ignited her imagination and stirred her from sleep far earlier. The entrance was covered by an ingenious piece of fabric made to look like the moss growing on the rocks around it. Inside, it had shelves carved in the rock, showing that someone had labored long to make it more hospitable. Battered pots and pans, a small fire-pit, and a metal box with spare clothing added to the usefulness of this hidden retreat. Tiryn had always wanted to find a secret cave like this, a place just waiting to be explored. But all she found in this one were chills, a foul odor from the peat fire that Leanoch had made, and imagined dangers looming in the dark recesses. There could be anything hiding in the nested shadows around her—snakes, spiders, rats, or perhaps even one of the haukmarn from last night that had lived to track them down. No, this was no time for secret caves. And life on the run was barely life at all. It meant fear and worry and dread over what would happen next. For the first time since they'd set out, she questioned her decision to accompany Kion in the search for Mother. Back in Charring, she couldn't bear the thought of Kion braving the dangers of such a journey without her. But now that she'd faced real dangers—twice in one day, once from Ilk's henchman and again from those horrible haukmarn in the hollow—she wasn't at all sure that this was where she should be. They had traveled a perilous road to this point and there was no assurance it would grow any safer in the days ahead.

A sudden intensity in the pungency of the burning peat told Tiryn that she must have finally passed from dreams into the waking world. Many mornings, especially of late, Tiryn struggled to know when that shift occurred. At times, she caught her mind wandering dream-like even in the heart of the day. The war, Mother's disappearance, the discovery of Truesilver—at times it all felt more like a dream than anything real.

Leanoch was up and about, stirring something in a pot. The small cast-iron cauldron hung from a hook in the wall. Gray smoke rose from beneath it and ran up the stone, disappearing in the crevices above.

"You're first to wake," Leanoch said. Kion and Zinder lay against the opposite wall, still as stones.

"I couldn't sleep," Tiryn said. The throbbing in her legs was no longer masked by sleep and she had come to the painful knowledge that imagining riding a horse was not at all like actually riding one. As beautiful as horses were, and as grateful as she was that Smokewind and Cyprian had carried them to safety, she was certainly paying the price for her first day in the saddle.

"I see. Troubled by the gray monsters from last night."

"Yes. I don't think I'll ever get the sight of them out of my mind." Tiryn forced herself up. Her legs cried out against her and she stood there half-hunched like an old woman, one hand on the wall for support, but Leanoch seemed not to notice, intent upon the pot. Tiryn was reluctant to speak to most people. Not because she didn't enjoy being around strangers—people fascinated her—but she preferred watching them to talking to them. Words were too hard to get right. She usually bungled what she really meant to say. Leanoch did not give her that feeling. He was so rough and rugged looking he didn't seem like he cared much how eloquent someone's speech was, as long as it was honest.

"I remember seeing them for the first time. Anger and hate turned into flesh, that's what I thought then. Still do." He dumped a bag of what Tiryn hoped were mushrooms into the pot. They looked more like clumps of dirt. It was hard to make out much in the cave, even with the eager flames licking the underside of the pot.

The eyes of the haukmarn were what Tiryn remembered most, the most maddened eyes she had ever seen. They were more like festering wounds than eyes. It was a frightening enough memory to make her forget her aching legs for the moment.

"They were so savage—like beasts, and yet not even beasts—more like beasts gone wrong, tangled and bent. I think I would have been frightened to see them no matter when it happened, but knowing that those are the creatures that captured my mother made it even worse."

A low growl sounded in Leanoch's throat and he spat into the fire. "Haukmarn. That's what I think of them." He left off stirring the soup and gave it a sip. "It's ready. Wake your brother and your friend. We need to have breakfast and leave. Need to get you on to the Billows."

Tiryn was all too willing to help speed things along. The sooner they were gone from the swamp the better. She gritted her way over to where Kion lay, stony as the ground beneath him. Rousing her brother was about as easy as wrestling a tree trunk. He resisted every plea and prodding she could muster. He could get like this after a day when he'd pushed himself too hard. Judging by how tired she felt herself, they could not have slept for more than a few hours. She gave up and woke Zinder instead. He had no qualms about using more forceful methods to wake his friend. After such a flurry of pinching, punching, and howling it was a wonder the cave didn't fall down on top of them, he finally managed to rouse her insensate brother.

Kion thanked him, completely unaware of the thrashing he'd just received, though the ginger way he moved his legs let on that he was sore for other reasons. Though he did a better job at hiding it than Tiryn, she could tell the saddle had taken its toll on him as well. Zinder moved as limber as ever, though. Perhaps his nynnian blood made him more fit to endure the rigors of riding horseback better than his long-legged companions.

The three of them sat down together to try a taste of Leanoch's soup. It had a sour tang to it and reeked like burnt hair. It was definitely not mushrooms that he had put in, but Tiryn was afraid to ask what it actually was. She would have given a gold round for a taste of Mother's cream of potato soup instead. It could warm a person down to their toes and fill their mouth with buttery delight while doing it. Leanoch's soup was warm enough, but Tiryn couldn't bear more than a few spoonfuls before slinking off to pack her bedroll.

As they mounted up a short time later, Cyprian stood tall and dignified in the feeble light that seeped through the trees and clouds, catching the world halfway between day and night.

"How are you, my beautiful friend?" Tiryn said, relishing the touch of his smooth, stately neck and feathery mane while at the same time steeling herself for another long day in the saddle. Cyprian shook his mane and nuzzled her fingers, oblivious to the pain he was about to inflict on her, albeit unintentionally.

They set out into a very different swamp from the night before. It was far from pleasing to the eye—and it was just as damp and foul-smelling—but the farther they got from Leanoch's cave, the more the sun forced its way into the stagnant haunts of Glooming Bog, so that, within the hour, the swamp looked almost hospitable. The standing water and drooping trees unveiled a few honest shades of green. Wrens could be heard calling from nearby. The shadowy canopy thinned and snatches of blue sky braved their way into view.

"How much longer until we're free from this place?" Zinder said.

"Less than two hours," Leanoch said.

"Ah, some good news for a change. Though I don't expect the stench will ever come out of these clothes. I suppose I'll have to buy all new ones." Zinder's tone picked up at this. There were few things he enjoyed more than finding new outfits to add to his wardrobe.

They neither saw nor heard any sign of the haukmarn during their journey through the last few miles of marshland. As Smokewind and Cyprian trotted into the matted grass of the plains, Tiryn took in great gulps of the sweet, coastal air. The faint smell of brine made it doubly enticing to Tiryn's bog-weary senses. All her life she had dreamed of seeing the great waters of the northern seas, but her experience at the docks in Fennigar left her wondering if that day would ever come. Perhaps in Grettling. Surely there had to be fresher, more beautiful waters there. She pictured the tides rolling in on milky foam and the sun dancing upon resplendent waves.

Leanoch brought them to a halt and dismounted. The grass was thick and soggy still, but the last of the stench and the gloom had fallen away, and the underbrush and trees gave way to open air.

"So this is the end?" Kion said.

"This is where I take my leave," Leanoch said. He stretched his arm toward the bluish-green haze which spread across the horizon to the west. "You will ride Smokewind now. And your sister and the nyn will go upon Cyprian. Head west along the coast, but stay out of sight of the water. You don't want any Noathryn ships to spot you. There might be a war going on, but they're not above picking up a slave or two if they make harbor somewhere along the way."

"Right. I hope we'll be able to reach Grettling on our own."

"Smokewind and Cyprian are good animals. They have been to Grettling by this way many times before. They will serve you well." He patted each horse's muzzle vigorously, but held his mouth in a shrunken line, making him look even more grim than usual.

"Oh no," Tiryn said. "You're going to have to walk back through all that mud, aren't you? Are you sure you can make it? What if the haukmarn catch you?"

"The Swamp Dog can take care of himself," Leanoch said. "There are slower, but safer paths upon which I will return, where no horse can go and no one can find, unless they know the way."

Zinder tipped his hat, a dull brown one that had seen better days, but fine enough for swamp travel.

"We are grateful for your service. You got us out of a tough spot, there. Those pits in the hollow were quite clever. You're more than just a skilled pathfinder, that's for certain."

"And thank you for the horses. We'll leave them for you in Grettling and send word on where to find them," Kion said.

"The barracks will do. The soldiers there will take care of them and send me word."

Kion leaned down and shook him by the arm. "We will not forget you, Swamp Dog."

"And I will not forget the Sword of the North. Your fire is no natural thing. Something good burns inside it, though. May it never go out. And you, little sister of the fire, may you have good dreams in the days ahead."

Something in the way he looked at her made Tiryn wonder if he had seen her tossing and turning during the night. But it was likely just an expression. He could not know that she sometimes had dreams so real that they followed her into her waking moments.

"I hope so. And I hope we'll meet again someday."

Leanoch shouldered his satchel and set back off toward the mists that rolled in from the Bog. The dark line of trees was no longer as dismal and threatening now that they were out of it and the swamp soon welcomed the return of its familiar son.

If not for Roardin and Leanoch, they would still be stranded in Fennigar, forced to confront the horrors and hardships of war. Tiryn certainly was not ready for that, and doubted she ever would be. Yet, seeing the way Truesilver's fire had vanquished the haukmarn in the swamp, it seemed inevitable that Kion would be drawn into that conflict. But that was a long ways off, she told herself. Perhaps the war would even be over by the time they found Mother.

"Well, I suppose it falls upon me now to keep the two of you in line," Zinder said, eyeing the siblings with as stern a look as his mischievous face could muster.

"Then I'd say you've got your hands full," Kion said.

"Indeed. You're ten fingers of trouble all by yourself, lad!"

Though they never rode within direct view of the sea, the crisp feel of the salty air afforded a welcome change from the foul confines of Fennigar and the Glooming Bog. The wind kissed Tiryn's cheeks, the gentle breeze amplified by Cyprian's brisk pace. The horses trotted along with a powerful, comforting rhythm, though the enchantment of gliding along atop such graceful beasts had diminished due to the nagging aches in her legs and hind-quarters. Though the soreness had only grown worse on this, their second day in the saddle, Leanoch had promised that the discomfort would fade in time. Whether or not that proved to be true, if Kion could endure the pain, so could she. She refused to let it dampen her spirits or complain. She didn't want to give him cause to doubt his decision to bring her along. Instead, she tried to feel grateful for the enormous favor Roardin and Leanoch had bestowed upon them by lending them two such sleek and masterful creatures. Riding so high in the air, it was almost like she was royalty. What would Mother say if she could see? The peddler, the Griddle, the fog, the swamp, the glaivefire, the horses—Tiryn had so much to tell her and they'd not even been traveling for an eight-mark.

The quiet, empty country known as the Billows opened before them. Gray gulls and the occasional high-soaring hawk drifted above on unseen currents, but no other animals showed themselves amongst the rippling hills which ran along the coast. They were not really hills, more like small mounds, as if thousands of barrows had been raised there. It was from these smooth, gentle mounds that the Billows derived its name.

The day turned out to be fine weather for riding—not too hot, not too cool. And Cyprian and Smokewind proved able guides in these unknown lands. Through Kion's bond with Truesilver, he was able to speak to the animals, or rather, to hear from Truesilver what they said to the sword. Kion was trying to learn their speech himself, but Truesilver had only just begun to teach him. To be able to speak to animals was something Tiryn had always longed to do. It would be worth being a swordspeaker just for that. But having one for a brother was the next best thing. She passed on countless messages throughout the day to both Cyprian and Smokewind, asking them her horse-sense questions. In this way, she learned that the animals had different names in their own language. Cyprian was called Far-lin-das and Smokewind was Rom-del-lin. It was odd the way Kion said their names, with pauses between the syllables as if they had a first, a middle, and a last name. Though these were the names they called each other, they had grown so accustomed to being called Cyprian and Smokewind by their human masters that they did not mind being addressed by those names. Cyprian told her many things more besides, including stories of past masters, most of whom had treated him fairly, but some of whom had been cruel. He had little difficulty at all carrying Tiryn and Zinder since they weighed practically nothing. He also said that he liked her smell. When Zinder asked why Cyprian didn't mention anything about the way he smelled, the horse suspiciously declined to comment. But considering the fact that Tiryn had not bathed since she left Charring, she could hardly swell with pride at this.

"Horses probably have different standards than people when it comes to smell," she said.

Zinder sniffed under his arm and was overcome by a sudden fit of coughing.

"So, tell me about Grettling." Tiryn turned to Zinder once he had recovered his voice, if not his dignity. Zinder had traveled over most all of Inris at one time or another, and he always had wonderful tales of the places he had been.

"You'll like it there," he said. "It has a wide, ancient theater set in a place called Melody Hill where they hold music festivals every eight-mark. Its harbor is much larger than the one at Fennigar. Tall, many-masted ships crowd the harbor, some of them as big as forts. And there's a lighthouse covered with coral that's rose-pink in color. Oh, and they also have the biggest fountain this side of Madrigal. They say it was built by nyn, of course. I was never much for stonework myself—far too dusty and slow—but I knew a nyn once who said that his great-great-great-and-so-forth-grandnyn built that fountain."

Tiryn sat up a little straighter. "A real, working fountain? Aunt Lizet said they had a small one in Charring, but I never got to see it. She said it was broken anyway. I can't wait to see the one in Grettling. What does it look like?"

"It's almost two stories tall, for one thing—simply enormous. It has an upside-down anchor with water pouring out from both sides. At the base are two dolphins, spitting water, which is not all that original I suppose, but what's most amazing is that the whole thing is made from greenstone, which looks like marble, but is far harder to sculpt. The fountain is hundreds of years old, but it's still in wonderful condition. And it's in the middle of a circular courtyard that's almost as large as the commons back in Furrow."

"The world is such a wondrous place, isn't it? You sometimes read about such things in books, but you never imagine you'll ever see them yourself. How much longer until we reach the city?"

"A day and a half if these fine horses know their noses from their tails. We'd get there sooner if we went faster, but I'm doing well to stay on at this speed. We nyn are not known for our horsemanship."

"I think I'm starting to grow a bit used to it," Kion said. "Certainly more than I was in the Bog. But I do worry about one of you two falling off if we went any faster."

"Of course you would say that. You've got Truesilver to order them around for you. The rest of us just have to hold on for dear life and hope we don't get tossed off by a sudden wind."

"I worry about slipping off at times too, I'll admit," Tiryn said. "But Cyprian is so sleek and elegant and these hills are so lovely that it's almost enough to make me forget the haukmarn and the war. I'm riding a horse and I'm about to see a fountain and a lighthouse and go on a ship. It's as if all my dreams were coming true, all except finding Mother, of course."

"That's the only dream I have anymore," Kion said.

The reminder of the reason they were riding on horses in the first place came like a sudden squall, drenching the tender flowers in Tiryn's garden of dreams. Though the sun still shone bright upon the gentle green hills of the Billows, the joy of her surroundings lost some of its strength as Tiryn was drawn once more to consider her mother's fate. Kion was right. That was the only dream that mattered now. Once they found Mother, the three of them would find new dreams to share together, if not in Furrow, then in some place like it. Some place far away from war and haukmarn. Some place where they could live a simple and quiet life. But now was no time for dreams. Now Tiryn had to stay wide awake. The time when it was safe to dream would come again soon enough.

Chapter 10

THE EVERLASTING SPARK

While finishing off one of the oat cakes her aunt had packed for them, Tiryn took out her diary and did a quick sketch of the land where they had stopped. The ice-white clouds, soaring gulls, and rounded hills were easy enough to get right, but the pass she took at drawing the horses did not turn out well at all. She couldn't make her charcoal sticks do justice to their powerful limbs and flanks. And she failed to capture the wary wisdom of their eyes. The end result was far more squat and inelegant than what she wanted. Smokewind and Cyprian looked more like Crusty than the noble stallions they should have been. But it was only a first attempt. She could already see how she would improve things in her next sketch. Underneath the drawing, she scribbled these words.

10th of Lockwin

Cyprian and Smokewind among the Billows. Not only did I get to ride Cyprian, but I got to talk to both of them—through Kion and Truesilver, of course. It took ever so long to say anything that way, but every word was delightful. They take great pride in their strength and speed, but when they are hungry—which is most of the time—they don't want to talk about anything but when they can eat, though they are very polite about it because they've been so well-trained. I can tell that this journey isn't easy for them, though they never would say so.

This drawing was made about halfway between Fennigar and Grettling. Zinder is rearranging his gear before we take to the saddles again. The one thing that's unpleasant about riding a horse is that it makes you feel like a human wishbone—Cyprian is simply enormous. Kion is carrying on a conversation with Truesilver, I think. It's hard to tell. Sometimes he looks like he's just talking to himself. But most of the time he gets this look in his eye that tells you he's listening to the sword's voice. I asked him to tell me what it's like to hear a voice that nobody else can, but he couldn't really describe it. The best he could come up with is that it's "warm, sometimes as hot as fire," but how can a voice be hot unless perhaps he means that it's right up against his ear? It must be marvelous to speak to something as wise and powerful as a living weapon. But it's still so strange that a weapon could even be alive at all. Kion said that Truesilver was made by someone called the Mastersmith, but Kion doesn't seem to know much about him. I wonder if—

Her writing was interrupted by a terrible cry from Zinder. It sounded like he'd been bitten by a snake or cut his finger or discovered a stain on his best shirt—all of those being equally agonizing to the fashionable nyn. Tiryn and Kion both stopped what they were doing and ran over. He was sitting on the ground with Ilk's pack open and a half-unrolled scroll in his hand.

"That ink-blotted, quill-snaggling, brass-hearted, scornefarious wastrel!" Zinder yelled, color rising up his neck like he was a tea kettle about to spout.

"What is it?" "What's wrong?" Kion and Tiryn said at the same time.

"It's him! My arch-nemesis. I told you I saw him in the market." He slapped the paper in his hand as if it were solid proof of whatever it was he was trying to tell them. The paper was old but thick and in fine condition, the words upon it written in a swirling script.

"The Scribe?" Kion said. "What does that paper have to do with him?"

"Don't you see?" Zinder turned it so that Kion could read the words. "This is another fragment from *The Lay of the Glaives*—and I found it in Ilk's bag."

"Zinder, that's wonderful. I would think you'd be overjoyed at finding another part of *The Lay.* You've been hunting for that poem for ages, haven't you? What difference does it make if Ilk had a copy?"

"And what's the Scribe got to do with it?" Tiryn said.

"See for yourself. This was also in there with the scroll." He handed Kion a small piece of paper with a fancy-looking stamp on it—a symbol that had two inverted triangles crossed at the points.

Kion read the words written there. "'This seal certifies that this parchment is an authentic copy of Stanza 2 of *The Lay of the Glaives,* made in the Grand Archive of Gilding, 716, SA.' And it's signed in a rather nice hand, 'The Scribe.' Then there's another date, the date of purchase, the 9th of Lockwin, 838, SA."

"You see? You see? The Scribe sold it to Ilk—yesterday! Yesterday!"

"Which means?"

"Which means that the Scribe is in league with Ilk! I'll bet he's the one who told him where we were staying. Did you ever think about how Ilk found us so easily? It's not like we were much about town. The only time we left the Griddle was to go to the docks yesterday morning, and Ilk showed up a few hours later—after he purchased this stanza of the *Lay,* and after the Scribe ratted us out—the loose-lipped slinker!"

"Well, it certainly does seem like an odd coincidence, but why would the Scribe be on Ilk's side? He sold you a part of the *Lay,* too, didn't he? Perhaps he's just an enterprising businessman, selling to whoever's interested. I can't imagine old poems like that are in much demand."

Zinder waved the scroll at Kion with grand, turbulent

gestures. "He shows up in Furrow with an order for armor and swords and then he disappears. And then he just *happens* to be in Fennigar at the same time we are, and he just *happens* to disappear in the market right after I spot him. Are you spotting a pattern? What if he's following us? The eyes of a nyn do not easily miss, lad. Especially not when it comes to big, poofy-hatted scoundrels hawking poetry."

Kion still seemed unsure, but Tiryn had to admit there was something to Zinder's claims. Just what, she couldn't say, but this Scribe was certainly intriguing.

"Well, Kithian says that the Scribe is on the Mastersmith's side, and that he serves the Four Wards somehow. But whatever his business in all of this, could we at least have a look at the poem?" Kion said. "If nothing else, I'm glad we have a copy of it, however it may have fallen into our hands."

Zinder made a sound halfway between a sigh and a grumble. "Ah, well now, when you put it that way…I suppose I shouldn't get so worked up about that fellow. Some mysteries aren't meant to be unraveled, perhaps."

"You'll read it to us, won't you, Zinder?" Tiryn said. "I love ancient poems. The older the better."

"Of course I will. Now, let's see here." He unrolled the scroll all the way, cleared his throat, and began to read.

Amidst the axe's felling blows
Deep bitterness was sewn
The darkening glaive began to crave
A world unto its own

A realm of iron, steel, and stone
Afflicted by the law
That idle hands and fallow lands
Would be the only flaw

This yearning tainted all it saw
This restive thought consumed
Grave as a dirge, a whispered urge
By which the Wards were doomed

This vain desire in Talin bloomed
This passion held him fast
Till falt'ring then the best of men
Into the shadow passed

In the long moments that followed, the puzzle of the verses pulled at Tiryn's mind. They felt less like poetry and more like prophecy, or perhaps history, something which had already taken place or was going to. Kion spoke into her wandering thoughts.

"Do you have any idea what they mean?"

"Well, the forge only knows—" Zinder cut his words short with a harumph. "That question wasn't for us, was it? Shar's dome, what's the sword told you this time?"

Kion's faraway gaze dissolved as he registered his surroundings again. "Kithian was telling me more about the *Lay.* He says that it was written during his time, shortly after the Shattered Age began."

"Shortly after? So that means—why, the blade must be over eight hundred years old! I knew it claimed to be ancient, but it still looks fresh from the forge."

The wandering look came back into Kion's eyes. Tiryn strained hard, as she often did, to hear the sword's words, but no more than the wind came to her ears. That and Zinder's foot, tapping with impatience.

"He says he was made in the time before days were marked, before the Four Lords and Ladies walked the land, but he came to Warding in the Forging Age."

"That's the one before this one, right?" Tiryn asked. She'd only ever heard it spoken of once or twice.

"Yes, though I've never been able to read any record of the events from that time," Zinder said. "They don't even have accounts in the Grand Archive as far as I know, though perhaps the fane's counselors have hidden lore no one else knows about."

Tiryn loved history, though she knew precious little of it. All she did know came from Zinder and overheard conversations between travelers at markets and festivals. Often, she could not tell what was legend and what was true. But the words of this poem had the ring of truth to them. Of that much she was sure.

"Who was Talin? He's the only person mentioned by name," Tiryn said. "He must be important."

Kion conveyed Kithian's answer a moment later. "He was one of the Four Lords, the Lord of Verisward, in fact. It was by his hand that the Shattering came and the Four Wards were torn asunder. He caused great suffering and death before he was defeated."

"So the Shattering was something that happened, an event of some sort?" Zinder said. "Was it a war? Did he rebel against the other lords?"

"No. Kithian says the other lords rebelled against him."

"Yes, Veris has always been preeminent, first among equals, as they say," Zinder said. "At least as far back as anyone has recorded. Inrisward, though independent on her own, has always deferred and depended upon Verisward for protection and guidance. So why did the other wards rebel?"

"Kithian says it was because Talin chose to wield the Spark for himself, something no man, not even one of the Four Lords, is permitted to do. This forbidden act is what caused the Four Wards to be torn asunder."

Tiryn sat with her hands beneath her chin. Something about these words drew her in, like a whispered invitation to seek treasure long rumored to be lost.

"What is the Spark, Kithian?" she addressed the sword, as if she might hear an answer from the blade without waiting for Kion to relay the words back to her.

"The Spark is the source of the glaives' gifts. But it is much more than that. It is something all living beings possess. As it tells in *The Song of the Spark*:

What lights a fire in the dark?
What gives the daysong to the lark?
What flies the arrow to its mark?
The Spark, the everlasting Spark.

What bends the rainbow to its arc?
What lends its strength to the great oak's bark?
What glows against the bleak and stark?
The Spark, the everlasting Spark.

"Men cannot use the Spark in a direct way. At least they were not meant to. It is far too dangerous when shaped by mortal hands. After Talin's curse fell upon the Wards, none have used it since."

"So it's some sort of power, perhaps a sort of magic?" Zinder said.

"Oh no. That is what Talin thought, and that is what led to his ruin. The Spark is not an enchantment or power to be summoned forth to do one's will. It's a hidden stream that courses through all, sustaining and quickening all things, both living and non-living. Used as intended, it has the ability to pull into being that which exists only in thought. That is how Kithian makes the fire. It is not the oil alone. The oil is more akin to a wrapper or a box to hold the fire. But the flames themselves are pure thought made manifest, creation unfettered by the limitations of this fallen world."

"To have your thoughts spring into being. Now, that sounds like every blacksmith's dream. Every poet's for that matter. I still don't know if I rightly understand it, but it sounds quite spectacular."

"Yes," Kion said. "It certainly does."

"'What bends the rainbow to its arc?'" Tiryn mumbled the words to herself as she surveyed the far horizon. She could not remember the last time she had seen a rainbow, and there were none there now. Only a few hazy clouds. But whenever she did see one again, it would not be the same.

Chapter 11

THE HORSE AND THE RIDER

The third day in the saddle was the hardest yet. Tiryn wondered whether or not Leanoch was right about the soreness ever going away. Though the horses remained as majestic as ever, she was beginning to think that perhaps they were not meant to be ridden for quite such long periods at a time. All three companions were road-weary by the time they made camp that night in a small copse of hazelwoods. And it was more than just the thrill of setting her feet again on solid ground that Tiryn felt when she collapsed beside her satchel in the willowy grass. It was also the wave of contentment at being still once more. She didn't know why she was so exhausted. The horses were doing all the work. But she could not remember a night when she'd been so utterly spent.

There was barely any talk at all around the campfire that night; only enough to plan what they would do once they arrived at Grettling. If the weather held, they hoped to ride into the great seaport by tomorrow evening, find a willing captain that same night, and set sail for Tinesplitter in the morning. Zinder had a fair amount of coin from the sale of his swords in Charring, plus the modest sum Aunt Lizet had given them.

"I just hope it's enough. It will be a tall order to convince a ship to hazard the Noathryn seas now," Kion said.

"You've never seen me when I settle in to serious haggling," Zinder said. "'Coins in the eyes make fools of the wise,' as we say in Lowerwyn. We'll find a captain, come what may."

And with that, the conversation, along with the day, was spent.

Tiryn's legs cried in protest when she mounted Cyprian the next morning. But this would be the last day she'd have to endure the saddle. The thought was bittersweet. She would miss Cyprian terribly, the first and best horse she had ever known, but he belonged to Leanoch and was not hers to keep. One thing she would not miss was the terrible ache in her poor, pitiful extremities.

"Mother is only a ship away," Kion said as they set out, locking eyes with Tiryn. That steady look re-ignited her hopes. They still had no idea how they would free Mother once they found her, but finding her was the first step. And Tiryn felt a quiet assurance that they would. Only a ship away.

"Zinder, how far is it by sea to Tinesplitter Isle from Grettling?" Tiryn said.

"More than an eight-mark, I'd say. And that's with fair winds. Though it's been a good while since I laid eyes on a map of Noath and few good maps of that land survive these days. It could be more than that, it could be less."

"It's a good thing you won't be piloting the ship," Kion said.

"Well, at least I've seen a map. Which is a good deal more than you can say."

"Fair enough."

The land flattened out as the horses carried them on. Little streams frequented their path. Even the largest, though, was no trouble to ford on horseback. A few of the streams had brownish, sullied currents, but most glittered like glass. The clearest of these waters tasted even better than the best springs and wells of the Tors, for they had a faint sweetness to them, as if a patch of strawberries grew within the very waters of the stream head.

With every mile, signs of humanity and the approaching city of Grettling grew more abundant. They passed bristling green wheat fields stitched in tight rows, and wide rumpled stretches of dirt and thinning grass where cattle wandered and watched with their great, indifferent eyes. Several flocks of tufted sheep wandered off in the distance. Seeing them pulled Tiryn's heart once more to the home she'd left and made it hurt all the more to remember that it was gone. The little lambs, the first green sprouts in the garden in spring, the walks among the hawthorns, would any of it ever come again?

Eventually, the horses let out upon an ample, well-traveled dirt road, the main thoroughfare between Grettling and Quelling. As they rode west, the sky cleared and the horses picked up their pace, eager to reach journey's end. Tiryn wondered if they were looking forward to a night in a stable as much as she was looking forward to a night in an inn. Memories of the bright hearth, merry melodies, tingling aromas, and above all the feather-soft beds of the Grizzly Griddle helped her endure the last few painful miles in the saddle.

By the time they crested the last hill rimming the valley which held Grettling, the sky manifested a deep blue that heralded the coming of night. Off in the distance, there rose up out of the great dark sea not the beautiful port city which Zinder had described to them, but a naked scar of smoke writhing and clawing its way to frightful heights. No theater, no fountain could be seen. Even the lighthouse was lost in the smothering blanket of gray. Streaks of fire flickered inside the ring of white walls and a throng of ships crowded the harbor, their yellow triangular sails menacing the bay like tongues of flame shimmering on the black water. Snatches of shouting and the thunderous tumult of battle rattled upon the wind.

The horses came to a swift and jarring halt.

"We've come too late. Grettling is under siege." Kion pounded his saddle horn with his fist.

Zinder stared in sickened awe at the flaming city. "I did not imagine the Noathryn had enough ships to attack both ports within a four-mark."

"Those poor people," Tiryn said, covering her mouth. And then came another thought. How would they ever reach Mother now? Watching the city in flames was as good as watching their hopes burn slowly away.

They gaped in helpless silence at the smoky gravestone piling upon itself above the ravaged city, their minds caught in a web of dismay and disbelief. Like the haukmarn, the Noathryn hated their Inrisian neighbors, claiming—as the haukmarn did as well—that the lands of Inris belonged to them. But unlike the haukmarn, they rarely attacked Inris for they were a poor and sparsely populated country. How could they join the side of such monsters? How could men turn against each other and set to the flame each other's homes and families? Tiryn was struck by the senselessness of it all, the irrational hate or envy or greed which drove these men to the path of destruction.

At last, Zinder spoke. "Look there, a lone rider is heading towards us along the road."

Neither Kion nor Tiryn could see him at first.

"A horseman?" Kion said. "Is he Noathryn?"

"It is doubtful. The Noathryn have little affinity for riding horseback."

"I see him now," Tiryn said, following the dark speck as it wound its way down the road toward them. She could not yet make out that it was an actual horse, but she trusted Zinder's sharp eyes.

"The rider wears the green tabard of the margrave's men," Zinder said. "But he rides slumped in the saddle, as if wounded or dead."

"We must help him," Tiryn said.

Kion's eyes drifted back to the flames and Tiryn wondered if he had heard what she said. "Yes, it is the least we can do," he said at last, but his voice remained distant. Like her, he was wondering what the attack on Grettling would mean to the search for Mother. "Kithian, tell the horses to speed toward that rider."

Cyprian and Smokewind dashed off with a sudden surge. They went short of a full gallop, but it was faster than they had ever gone before. Tiryn and Zinder bounced around like fleas in a fire pit. The farmsteads around Grettling, with their tiny gray-and-white houses, rushed by in a thunderous rush of wind. It was all one vast blur of budding green and fresh-tilled browns. The other horse came at them with equal speed and, it soon became clear, did not intend to slow down when it reached them.

"Kithian, tell the horses to circle around and come alongside him in the road so that we're riding in the same direction," Kion said.

The two mighty stallions left the road, kicking up clods of dirt and clay in the tumbled soil that ran along the fringes of the fields. They trampled some of the crops growing there, but it could not be helped. The horse fleeing Grettling was running scared and it was better for them to keep him on the road than to force him off. It was a rose gray, a touch shorter than Cyprian, but swift as a jackrabbit.

Their steeds wheeled sharply at the other horse's approach. As the panicked beast roared past, eyes wide and ears pinned back, the two stallions came charging out of the fields. The rider had slumped forward in the saddle and was in danger of sliding off. They pulled even with the runaway horse and, through Kithian's guidance, the beast calmed, slowed to a trot, and then stopped in the middle of the road, its great sides heaving, its flanks running with rivers of sweat.

Kion tumbled out of his saddle, too rushed to take his time or to help Zinder or Tiryn from theirs. Zinder, though, leapt to the ground with the deftness of someone who'd been riding all his life. He grabbed hold of the wild-eyed horse's dangling reins while Kion pushed the unconscious rider back into a safer position atop his mount.

"He's sorely wounded. There's a good deal of blood, and he's passed out, but his breathing is steady for now." The rose gray horse stood snorting and stamping its feet, but the wildness had gone from its eyes.

"Go now and help your sister down," Zinder said. "She's too fond of her neck to risk jumping off on her own and I'm too short to help you get him off."

Kion helped her down, and together they wrested the rider from his saddle and eased him onto the dirt road. He was a few years older than Kion, with tousled brown hair, the shadowy beginnings of a beard, and a solid, if lean, frame. He might have been any of the older farm boys from Furrow save for his mail and emerald tabard. His armor had many chinks, and unlike most soldiers Kion had seen, he wore no helmet. An arrow protruded from his back, and a gash ran along the side of his neck. Blood from the neck wound had soaked through the upper part of the gambeson he wore beneath his mail.

"He took a blow to the head, perhaps several," Zinder said. "It knocked him cold but he's not dead. Thankfully, the arrow got stuck in the padding and only grazed the skin."

"Good for him, because I doubt we could have found a healer for him out here in the countryside," Kion said.

Tiryn cleaned the soldier's wounds with a wet rag. She bound them with clean cloths, the way her mother had taught her. She could have done little if the arrow had gone through, but she'd treated plenty of injured sheep over the years and knew how to dress wounds like this.

"Kithian says that the horse's name is Hif-lan-eld. He and his master were attacked as they fled the city. He knows little else, and it may be some time before we learn any more. The beast is quite frightened."

"What should we do?" Tiryn said once she'd finished wrapping his head and neck. "We can't just leave him here."

"True," Zinder said. "The fighting down in Grettling is fierce from the looks of it. The Warding forces may pull through, but we can't wait to find out. We must assume the city is lost."

"I don't see how the cities are falling so quickly. Vayd must be more cunning than I thought." Kion's face set itself as hard as iron. Tiryn could almost see a door shutting in his mind. "If we can't find a ship in Grettling, then we must take the last road given to us. We will have to travel overland, through Noath itself."

"Are you certain, lad?" Zinder's face tightened with doubt.

"Is anything certain anymore? Even if we find Mother, we may not have a land to return to. The only thing I do know is that somewhere at the end of these lands is another sea. And across that sea is an island. And on that island is a slave camp. And if my mother is anywhere, that's where she is. We must go to her by whatever way we can."

"That's a grim prospect. But I suppose we have no other way left to us. We could make for the fortress of Dunach which guards the western border. That's the safest place I know of. Unless the Noathryn have taken it as well, we can find shelter and supplies there before heading out across Noath. As for this fellow, we don't have time to take him to some other town in Casting Limmring. We'll have to bring him with us. He can't stay unconscious forever. When he revives, he can ride back to join the margrave's forces."

Though Tiryn had cleaned the soldier's face as best she could, little nicks and a scar above his right eye marred the handsome features. But he would pull through.

Somewhere, this soldier had a mother, too. Whether she was still at home, tending the hearth, or had been captured like Tiryn's, she would be worried and thinking of her son. Of all the great ills of war, Tiryn knew more than most the pain and suffering that distance caused. Her father had left for war and never returned. Now it had taken her mother as well. War separated things. It severed people from their lands, it destroyed their way of life, ripped them from their homes, and shattered their dreams. It sundered families, tearing mothers from daughters, fathers from sons, and brothers from sisters. War was the great insatiable pit that pulled everyone inside it who didn't flee fast enough or far enough away. How much longer would such distances have to be endured? Would this war-ravaged land ever be made whole?

Tiryn's and Kion's eyes met. They both knew the way ahead offered only more suffering and hardship, even as it threatened to extinguish all hope. The black cloud of death and destruction which hung over Grettling may as well have been hanging over their heads as well. For they certainly felt its shadow.

Chapter 12

CROSSING THE STOUT

By Zinder's reckoning, it would take at least five days for them to reach the eastern border of Noath. There they would find the Fortress of Dunach, an ancient defense against Noathryn invasion by land and the farthest western reach of Inrisian authority. If the fortress had not been assaulted as well, they hoped to find help and shelter there and to rest the horses before setting out across Noath. Though Noath was the land of the enemy, it was said to be mostly open country, so that as long as they avoided the settlements, they hoped to find their way across without much trouble.

But to reach western Inris, and Noath beyond, they would first have to cross the River Stout. The great coursing waterway ran south past the western wall of Grettling; a roaring, rushing barrier whose pale green waters both shielded and connected the city to the many outlying farms and small estates to the south, as well as the minor city of Jabble in the uplands. A massive, stonework bridge spanned the leaping, dancing waters just beyond the city walls. The easiest way to cross it was through bridge into the city, but since that way was closed all they could do was ride along the eastern bank until they came upon a natural ford.

Turning south, the same misgivings Kion had when leaving Fennigar rumbled inside of him. Men like Roardin were fighting somewhere down in the sinuous smoke now rising from within Grettling's blanched walls. There was little Kion could do to save the city, but heading in the opposite direction of a battle when he had a sword like Truesilver chafed against his sense of honor. His father had not wanted to go off to war, but he had answered the call when it came. A troubling doubt nagged him that he was letting his father down, even though he was convinced that his father would want him to save his mother at all costs. And yet, the doubt would not go away. Walking away from a battle was not what Strom Glyre would have done. And judging from Kithian's reaction to Kion's decision at Fennigar, it wasn't what a swordspeaker should have done either. But every time he thought of his mother, hungry and chained, weary and weak, her hands and neck gripped by the fetters of the Noathryn slavers, a heat reignited inside of him hot enough to keep the doubts in check. That singular purpose spurred him on and strengthened his resolve against the ebbs and flows of his inconstant heart.

They had traveled for more than two hours, picking their way through sparse stands of hackberries and tamaracks and over swaths of scrubgrass and patches of sword reeds, when the river took a sharp bend to the west. By that point, the channel had shrunk to about half of its breadth at Grettling. Using Zinder's spyglass, they climbed a lone hill and surveyed the land to see if they might find a better crossing to the south. Zinder had let Kion look through his marvelous glass a few times back in Furrow, but Tiryn had never before had the pleasure. The device appeared to be made of lead bathed in a thin sheen of oil, but it was actually fashioned from *lumim,* a rare metal used to create devices with moving parts like music boxes, locking mechanisms, clocks, and gears in sophisticated war machines. The coating it exuded functioned like grease which kept it from wearing down easily. The spyglass, which had been passed down to Zinder through many generations, expanded from the size of Zinder's hand into a cylinder as long as his forearm.

"Yes, the river definitely widens after this bend. We'll lose at least another hour of travel if we don't cross here," Zinder said.

Though Kion had grown more confident in the saddle over the last two and a half days, fording a river the size of the Stout was hardly something he was anxious to try.

"You think this is a good place, then?" Kion asked Zinder, though he knew what the answer would be.

"We might travel all the way to Lake Kemshorn and find none better. We could save a whole day by crossing here."

The gradual bank along this stretch would also aid their crossing, as would the large, rounded rocks dotting the stream halfway across. The swift current gave cause for concern, but that would be a problem no matter where they crossed. Summer had only just begun and the Stout was still swollen from the spring rains.

"What about the soldier's horse, Kithian?" Kion said. "Will Hif-lan-eld be able to bear his rider safely across?"

"He promised that if one of the other horses led the way he would push through to the far side. Though he says he's not fond of water, he'll risk crossing it rather than earn the disapproval of his fellows."

"Very well. I don't know what we would have done without you on this journey, Kithian. Even if I'd ridden a horse before, I wouldn't feel safe pulling a strange animal across a river I didn't know."

"Remember also that my sight is different from yours. I can see below the water as well as above. I should be able to find the best path for the horses to cross."

Kion had in fact not taken into account Kithian's swordsight, which could penetrate even through solid rock. It could see in all directions at once, too, though it was limited to a short distance. Kithian could even share his sight, but Kion thought it best if he could see the whole river during the crossing.

"The sword can see?" Zinder pushed up his hat and gave his forehead a good scratch.

"Yes. Either through my eyes or his own. I thought I told you that before."

"You most definitely did not. I always wondered about that,

though. I suppose it needs some way of sensing the world or it wouldn't be any good at flinging around those flames. Are those gems in its hilt the eyes?" He craned his neck to get a better look at the large citrine in Truesilver's pommel and made a ridiculous face to see if the sword was paying attention.

"No. Kithian sees the world from the top down so your attempt at humor was utterly lost upon him."

Tiryn leaned around from behind Zinder and giggled. "That's too bad. That was one of your more original ones, Zinder. What emotion was that supposed to be?"

"Tortured for attention, I'd say," Kion said.

"No, it was bold absurdity. You're just jealous because you can't manage more than one face these days, Kion the Sour. What can I say, my face is the canvas upon which I paint my masterpieces." Zinder raised an eyebrow and slanted his grin with roguish charm.

"Ah yes, and that one's confident confusion." Kion roared in laughter.

Tiryn tried to cover her mouth, but her laughter rang out clear and bright upon the water. "Oh my. Let's cross this river before I laugh so hard I fall off."

"Right," Kion said, shaking some seriousness back into his expression. "Let's get this over with."

The horses took tentative steps into the shallows near the bank. Smokewind took the lead and Hif-lan-eld, frisking nervously, followed. Despite Kithian's encouragement, the skittish horse came to a hard stop at the edge of the water.

Smokewind trotted bravely on, his hooves barely making a splash. Hif-lan-eld wavered, but when the rope tying him to Smokewind's halter went taut, he allowed the force of it to pull him forward and his hooves entered the water at last.

Cyprian came in close behind, nudging the water-shy horse forward on several occasions. Through Kithian's coaxing, and the stern guidance of the other two horses, Hif-lan-eld eventually made his way out into the main flow.

"The river dips quickly from here, but runs no deeper than the top of your legs between this spot and those rocks halfway out," Kithian assured the horses.

Smokewind whinnied a spirited reply and eased his way in, feeling for his footing, confident in Kithian's assessment.

But here again, Hif-lan-eld waited until the rope snapped tight. This time, though, he did not give in to its pull. Kion gave it several yanks, but the horse only stamped in the water and remained stubbornly where it stood.

"Can't he see the water's not that deep?" Kion said. At that point, it was barely past Smokewind's knees.

"Come, Hif-lan-eld." Tiryn encouraged the horse from behind, clicking her tongue as if she were an old hand at handling a horse.

"Hif-lan-eld, be brave. You are about your Master's business. Do not forget that," Kithian said, his voice that strange mixture of commanding and compassionate which only he could convey.

The rose gray made a soft, apologetic wheeze and reluctantly followed Smokewind in. He tottered, shifting his hooves until he found sure ground. His movements jostled the poor soldier on his back, but the man had been tied down too tightly to fall off. Though Hif-lan-eld's jittering movements never wholly ceased, he failed to resist anymore once they passed beyond the deepest waters. In fact, he actually pressed the pace after the mid-river rocks, pushing Smokewind to hurry on and leave the river as quickly as possible.

Once the party reached the shore, the three companions dismounted and allowed their animals to graze along the bank. Hif-lan-eld hung his head and refused to look at the other horses, but neither Smokewind nor Cyprian admonished him in any noticeable way. They were too preoccupied with the abundant reeds and plump grasses surrounding them to give much heed to anything else.

"I think I understood a few words you said to them during the crossing, Kithian," Kion said.

"That is encouraging. I know it must be difficult for you to concentrate during our lessons with all that weighs upon you."

"Am I really that distracted? I'm sorry, I'll try to do better going forward." Kion knew Kithian had not meant it as a reproach, but he did not want to disappoint his glaive.

"There is nothing wrong with being intent upon your purpose. The danger comes when your focus is so narrow that you miss what is happening in the present moment. Many times the very intensity of your desire may be the thing that keeps you from achieving it."

"But how can that be? Don't I need to work hard and push myself to press ahead? My mother needs me. I'm her only chance at freedom."

"Are you certain of that? The wheels of this world are rarely moved by a single man. Men often seek to turn one wheel only to find that it turns another they had not intended. As I have told you many times, you can only fight the battles before you. When the time comes to turn all your thought to saving your mother, you will know. But until then, do not neglect the opportunities before you. It may be that in fighting today's battles, you unexpectedly win ground for tomorrow's war."

This time Kion felt the rebuke in Kithian's words a little more strongly. It brought to mind again the way he had taken the news of Kion's decision not to fight in Fennigar. Was that what Kithian meant by fighting today's battles? And yet, how could defending Fennigar have helped free his mother when she was at the other end of the world?

"Do you mean that I should have pledged to fight when Roardin asked me to?"

"No. I only mean that it is never wrong to do what is right."

To do what was right. Of late, it had been hard to know just what that was. Everything had seemed so clear when they set out for Charring. Finding his mother had so obviously been the right thing to do. But his vision had grown blurry along the way. Nowhere on this journey had that been more apparent than in his near betrayal of Kithian at the inn. To use Kithian's figure of speech, if Kion had turned that wheel, it would have turned many others he did not wish to move and things would have turned out far worse in the end. Only by a great mercy had he been spared from making that mistake.

"Kithian." Kion was a good distance from the others, but he cast his voice as low as possible. "I have something I need to tell you."

"You know that you may always tell me anything."

"It's been weighing on my heart ever since we left Fennigar. You remember, back at the inn, when Ilk asked me to trade you for information about my mother? Well, Roardin arrived, of course, and so Ilk was exposed for what he was, but before that I...I had decided to do it. I had decided to give you away. I see now how foolish I was, how terrible that would have been. I can't expect you to ever forgive me, but I...I must beg you for forgiveness all the same. I'm so terribly sorry—"

"I forgive you, Kion Swordspeaker." The voice showed no hint of bitterness, no sign of reproach. It was as steady as always, as solid and unchangeable as the silvery blade from which it came.

"Truly? Just like that? You're not angry or disappointed at me?"

"That is not what matters. I forgive you and that is all you need to know."

"But—but how can you? I almost gave you up."

"We must always stand ready to forgive those who do us wrong. To do any less is to set upon ourselves an authority that we do not have. There is only one to whom the power of vengeance belongs."

Cords that had bound themselves tightly around Kion's heart grew slack and fell away. He had never felt more unworthy of the blade he carried. And never more glad that he had answered Truesilver's call. Kithian may have been the greatest sword in all the land, but he was an even greater friend.

Chapter 13

CURMELION THE CLEVER

Kion sliced off the tree branch with a revil twist. His breath came in great, sweltering heaves. He mopped the sweat from his brow with his sleeve. The inside of his armor baked like an oven even though the sun had long since gone down.

Tiryn clapped enthusiastically beside the dying fire. It was little more than glowing embers by now, but neither the fading flames nor the waning moon were needed. Truesilver radiated more than enough light for Kion to practice his forms.

"That was the next best thing to seeing you at the tournament. Though it does make me regret that I couldn't be there this year," Tiryn said.

"You're just saying that to be nice. You never took any interest in my sword-fighting before."

"Well, I never really saw the need for it. Besides, people change. I'm over halfway to sixteen, you know."

"I suppose you are," Kion said, taking a long swig of water. It was fresh from the River Stout that morning and after the long round of sword work, it tasted even crisper and more savory than it had after the crossing.

"Your shoulder seems to be doing well. It wasn't hurting you, was it?" Tiryn said.

"A little. Mostly it's just stiff. Zinder, mind helping a turtle out of his shell?" Kion pounded on his breastplate.

Zinder cocked his head to the side from where he sat by the fire. After sparring with Kion earlier, he was enjoying his friend's display of swordsmanship, commenting several times at how much he had improved in such a short span of time, but he was less pleased with Kion's request.

"Now? I was just getting comfortable."

"It's your punishment for losing."

"Oh, piddle—fine." He grumbled his way to his feet. "Craft a palace or craft a pin, it always falls to the poor little nyn. Crusty required far less attention than you."

Feigning impatience, he set about helping Kion out of his armor. Originally crafted for someone with a bulkier build, Zinder had refitted it for Kion while he was recovering from his wound in Charring. It felt so natural now that, apart from the heat, he hardly knew he was wearing it.

"You have an admirable knowledge of the basic forms for one who has not been formally trained," Kithian said.

"It's all thanks to Zinder and his folio. I learned most everything I know from that. The style I use is called the Fiorin Batal. Have you heard of it?"

"No, but several of those same stances have been taught since before the dawn of the age."

"Well, fighting with you makes it even easier. You're so perfectly balanced, it barely feels like I'm swinging anything. In all honesty, I was never this good before, not even in practice. I'm sure during the next lesson I'll make more mistakes."

"Your newfound skill is no accident. It is part of the bond between a swordspeaker and his glaive. The bond will not make you better than you are, but it will make you as good as you can be. A veteran swordsman might still best you, but with me in your hand, you will fight to your full potential and defeat many with far greater experience."

"Ah, I see how it is," Zinder said. "That's why you had an extra spring in your step. It was all the blade. Let me fight with Truesilver next time around and we'll see who's the true Sword of the North!"

"You're welcome to try, old friend. In fact, now that I think about it, you probably would win. Watching you try to wield a blade almost twice your size would be such a ridiculous sight, I'd probably fall over with laughter. Ouch!"

Instead of unfastening the next strap in Kion's armor, Zinder tightened it. "Watch yourself, lad, unless you want to sleep in this armor."

"At least I'd be protected from having a bucket of water dumped on me. Ow! Zinder!" The nyn tightened another strap.

"Oh, pardon me. I thought you said you wanted it tighter."

Tiryn had gone over to check on the soldier's bandages. He still had not stirred, though his wounds looked considerably better thanks to Tiryn's constant attentions.

"Do I need to come over there and separate you two?" she said.

"No, just teaching the lad a little humility. Something I'm sure a swordspeaker needs to know." With a little snicker he undid his mischief and removed the last two straps holding the armor in place.

"Indeed," Kithian said.

"Oh no, you're not turning against me too, are you?" Kion smirked as he shed the last of his armor and began gathering up the pieces.

"You see there? Listen to Truesilver," Zinder said. "You don't want to get too clever for your own good. Your apples might turn to lemons."

"Apples turn to lemons? What's that supposed to mean?"

"You've never heard that expression? It comes from an old story."

"No, that's not one I've heard."

"Me neither," Tiryn said. And she knew more stories than Kion.

"I never told you the story of Curmelion the Clever?"

"No. I think I would have remembered it with a name like that."

"Oh, wonderful, one of Zinder's stories." Tiryn finished

caring for the soldier and traipsed over to her bedroll, curling up inside of it. "It's been forever since I've heard you tell one."

"I suppose we might have time for one before we sleep," Kion said. "If it's not *too* long."

"Well then…" Zinder sat down atop his own blankets and his eyebrows gave a little dance. "There once was a man named Curmelion. Now Curmelion was so clever, sooooo clever that he could dot his t's and cross his i's and you couldn't tell the difference."

"Is that so?" Kion said.

"Most certainly. He could squeeze a lemon and get apple juice. He could burn ashes and make logs. He could shoot an arrow so high it never came down. He could make paint peel just by staring at it."

"Was he a magician? Because none of that can actually be done."

"Oh, couldn't it? Well, let me assure you, he did all that and much more! He was the wonder of Windstern, the marvel of Madrigal—"

"Wait. You're saying he was a real person? Someone who lived in Inris?"

"Long ago, yes, and this story is about how his career as a wise man and a sage came to an abrupt and ignominious end."

"What? I thought he'd be far too clever to allow his life to be ruined."

"Yes, well, it all happened when Silas Thumbsby came into town one blistering summer afternoon and asked for a glass of water. Some say Silas came looking for trouble and that he knew Curmelion was there, but that was never fully established. I myself am of the mind that he was just thirsty. But whatever the case, he came to the town where Curmelion lived, looking for water. The problem was, there had been a terrible drought that year and nobody wanted to give up any of the little water that they had.

"But Curmelion never passed up an opportunity to make

himself look more clever. And if he made a coin or two in the process, all the better. So he offered to pour water from a rock for poor old Silas. And Silas, being more thirsty than he was rich, and being rather clever himself, agreed on one condition.

"'I have no coin to offer you, but if you give me a cup of water I'll serve you for a year and a day.' (He was very thirsty, as you can imagine.) Now Curmelion loathed work more than anything, so the offer of free labor pleased him greatly. He agreed and promptly pounded on a nearby rock, and out came a trickle of water, not much mind you, but enough to fill a small cup.

"Everyone in the town gaped in awe at this, the most marvelous of wonders in a long line of marvelous wonders. For coaxing water out of a rock was one thing, but there had been no rain for two months and all the rivers were dry as wool. But something happened when Silas drank the water. You see, it had a funny taste to it, like the water had a bit of straw in it. It was very faint, but Silas had a sensitive tongue. Still, the water did as promised. It quenched Silas's thirst. He drank it all down and thanked Curmelion, who promptly put him straight to work."

"I suppose if you're dying of thirst, a year of work is better than perishing."

"Silas certainly thought so. He worked day and night, night and day, in Curmelion's mansion, dusting, polishing, cooking, serving, and running errands. And in all this Curmelion took advantage of Silas and pushed him as hard as could be. For though he was very clever, he was not very kind, no, not very kind at all. And one of the hardest things he made Silas do was to receive guests and wait upon them whenever they came, which was almost daily. Curmelion was a popular fellow, as you can imagine. And the guests, taking their cue from Curmelion, treated Silas almost as badly as he did, demanding this, ordering him for that, as if they were every one of them kings and queens. So Silas had to wait on four or five or ten people instead of just one, and they grew more tyrannical as the year went on.

"Now everyone who came wanted to see one of Curmelion's famous feats. They got apple juice from lemons, usually, but some got logs from ashes, and still others watched arrows disappear into the sky or paint peel with a look. And all the while Silas worked and slaved and watched his master perform his marvels. But Silas did more than just watch. He noticed. And those are two very different things. For many's the man that watches, but few are the ones who notice.

"It just so happened that the final day of Silas's year and a day of service was Curmelion's birthday. And Curmelion made him bake a seven-layered cake and cook enough food for two hundred people and wait on them hand and foot, just like always.

"And after the feast, when everyone gathered around to watch Curmelion's marvels, Curmelion did an odd thing. He appeared on the lawn wearing an enormous hat and scarf. He looked rather silly, and all the more so in the midst of summer, but no one dared to tell him so, for he was Curmelion the Clever. He claimed that he had caught a sudden cold, but would perform his fabulous feats all the same. And so he did as he always did with his lemons, ashes, arrows, and paint, and a half-dozen marvels besides.

"But his most surprising feat was his last. For when he finished, he unraveled his scarf and tossed off his hat and revealed that it was not Curmelion the Clever who had performed these wonders at all, but plain old Silas Thumbsby!

"And this is what he said: 'Friends and admirers of Curmelion. As you have seen this evening, it is not Curmelion who has done these marvels for you today, but I, simple Silas Thumbsby. For a year and a day I have waited upon you all and done your bidding and followed Curmelion's orders without complaint. But while I worked, I watched and even more than that I noticed. And I came to see that Curmelion was not so clever as you all have thought. For I saw how he achieved each one of his tricks. You would have seen too if you had not been so agape and agog with admiration at his cleverness. For his only real cleverness was in fooling you and as you have seen, I have proven myself at least as clever.'

"But the crowd protested, calling him a cheat and an imposter and wondering how this could be and where was Curmelion after all? And Silas replied,

"'Fear not. He is safe, though sound asleep, for I gave him a special tea. But as for me being a cheat, if I am, then no more than your Clever Cur. But I can see in your eyes that you do not believe me so I shall reveal his secrets to you and let you judge for yourselves. The lemon, you see, was just a lemon peel with an apple inside. The ashes were just ashes on top of a log, though carefully applied and with the logs hidden in a hollow below the hearth. The arrow was painted like a branch and shot up into a tree. And the paint was applied on top of a watery surface and softly blown away before your unclever eyes.'

"'But the water you drank that day? What of that? Surely that at least was real?' they said.

"Oh, but if you had tasted it, you might have known better. For that water tasted like straw, which is just the way water tastes when squeezed from a sponge. And though the sponge Curmelion used was hard enough to pass for a rock, it was still soft enough to let out a little water.'

"And after that, all the people stood amazed at this simple man who had undone the cleverest of them all.

"'And this is my last gift to you,' he said. 'Though thankless you are and surely undeserving, I leave you with this truth all the same. For it is not what you know, but knowing what's true that matters. Clever men teach many false things. And some are so clever they believe their own charades. But it takes a truly clever man to see the truth. So notice, don't watch, lest you prove yourself the fool of the clever, who is, after all, only a clever fool.'"

Kion gave an exhausted, but satisfied sigh. "That might be one of your better ones, Zinder. Don't let your apples turn to lemons. I suppose that means we ought not to think ourselves more clever than we are."

"Or perhaps it means not to think about our cleverness at all," Zinder said.

"What do you say, Tiryn? Did you enjoy—"

But Tiryn had fallen fast asleep. On her face, though, was the smile of someone who was far more kind than she was clever.

Chapter 14

SICKLEWOOD

Kithian's voice penetrated Kion's sleep the way a single ray of light might scatter the darkness of a cave.

"Arise, swordspeaker. The wounded soldier has awakened."

Kion resisted the pull of the sword's voice. Weariness was a far more appealing call than that of his glaive. He needed sleep. A few more moments at least. The cares of the world could wait.

"He will be confused when he awakes. You must go to him." Kithian's voice grew more forceful, shaking him from the inviting embrace of slumber. Reluctantly, Kion's eyes flicked open. His arms and legs hung like wood from his torso. The strength he had spent during yesterday's training had not fully returned. But the insistence in Kithian's tone demanded attention. Kion looked to where he knew the soldier to be, but it was too dark to see anything definite.

"Kithian, a little light."

His hand wrapped around his scabbard and he quietly drew the sword so as not to wake the others.

Truesilver's warm glow gave shape and form to their little camp. Tiryn and Zinder's forms lay in smooth gray heaps about the ashen remnants of the fire. The soldier, who lay a few paces behind Tiryn, turned his head toward Kion, shielding his eyes.

"Who's there?"

Kion eased around the others to arrive at the man's side, the new day's strength slowly seeping into his limbs.

"My name is Kion Bray. How do you feel?"

The soldier felt the bandage on his head. "I—I'm fine. Very weak, and with a sharp pain in my head, but I'll be all right. What happened to your sword? Why is light coming from it? There's no moon to speak of. Am I seeing things?"

"No. It's a different kind of sword, that's all. I'll explain it to you later. What is your name?"

"My name? Yes, right. I am called Endrith. Do you mind telling me where I am and how I got here?"

"We came across you at Grettling." Kion pointed to the two bundles around the ashes. Zinder's bright red nightcap with the fluffy yellow ball on the tip shone like a beacon in the sword's light. Tiryn's auburn tresses spilled gently from the woolen folds of her blanket. "You were fleeing the city on your horse. It looked like you had been injured in the battle there."

A troubled memory flitted across Endrith's face. "Yes, the battle at Grettling. Several of us were ordered to attempt to force our way through the south gate. We knew it was a desperate chance, but the western gate was even more heavily guarded so we took the risk. I rode down two of the enemy and several of our men sold their lives to open the gates, but something struck me in the head as I passed through. That's the last thing I knew. I hope the other messengers made it."

"I can't say. You were the only one we saw on the road."

Endrith closed his eyes with a grimace, whether in pain from his wounds or in response to the news, it was impossible to say.

Tiryn stirred and made a little gasp. "Oh, you're awake." She threw her cloak over her shoulders and came to them, concern for the soldier quickening her step. The commotion rattled Zinder awake as well.

"Conspiring to leave me out of your midnight party, are you?" he mumbled as he walked up, his bright orange night cap bobbing to and fro.

"This is my sister, Tiryn. And our friend, Zinder."

"Pleased to meet both of you. My name is Endrith."

Tiryn offered a brief nod, her eyes intent on studying Endrith to judge his state of health.

Zinder rapped his knuckles against the side of his head. "You took a good knock, I'll warrant. 'But the strength of the steel is known in the fire' as we smiths say. You're made of some stern stuff."

"Tiryn's been taking care of you. You've been out for about a day and a half."

"Here." Tiryn brought him a cup of water. "You must be awfully thirsty. I put a few drops on your lips during the day, but I couldn't give you much."

Endrith drained the cup almost at one pull. "Thank you, I needed that more than I knew."

"You said something about other messengers. Who were you trying to get word to?" Kion said.

"I was sent to bring word to Dunach. Around a hundred Noathryn came to Grettling the day before the attack, disguised as refugees. When the ships appeared in the harbor they revealed their true nature. With most of our men called out to fight the enemy in the water, the Noathryn inside were able to overwhelm the gates and allow the rest of their host into the city. The attack on the harbor was but a diversion."

"How large was their force?" Zinder said.

"Only around two thousand. But they could have taken Grettling with even less. The city's defenses were pitifully undermanned. The margrave's men are spread thin all across Inris."

"Well, you're safe now," Kion said, trying to make the best of Endrith's dire news. He had to believe that the fane and the margrave were marshaling for a counterattack, though how many cities would fall before it came?

"Does Dunach still stand, then?" Zinder said. "That's where we're headed as well."

"Yes, and from there to Noath," Kion added. "We thought we might find supplies there before we set out."

"Dunach stands as far as I know, but I don't know why you'd

ever want to go to Noath. Especially now that the Noathryn have joined the haukmarn."

"We have no choice. My mother is there and she needs us."

"Your mother…" Endrith held his head and grew silent.

"What's wrong?" Tiryn filled his cup with more water and handed it back to him.

"Nothing. It's passing now. I'll be fine."

"He hides the truth behind his wounds," Kithian said. *"He was thinking of his own mother just now. Like you, he fears he will not see her again."*

Endrith was a soldier who had risked his life to storm through the enemy. He deserved respect for that alone. But Kion esteemed him even higher, knowing that he and Endrith shared the same burden.

"You should rest." Tiryn tested his bandage, ensuring that it was still dry and snug.

"Yes," Kion said, wanting to ask more, but mindful of Endrith's weakened state. "It won't be long until dawn and we will resume our journey. You need to save your strength for the ride."

Endrith grabbed Kion by the hand. The grip was feeble, but earnest. "Thank you for saving me. Thank you all. I'm sure if you had not happened along the road I would not be here now."

"It was good fortune we happened upon you when we did," Kion said.

"It was more than that," Kithian said in a low voice.

Zinder doffed his hat with a bow. "I'm glad you're awake at last. Perhaps now I can have some decent conversation!"

Though Zinder had guided them up to this point, he had never actually been to Dunach and so was not entirely sure of the way. As a messenger for the Warding forces, Endrith had been there many times and so he willingly accepted the role of guide.

If he was still suffering the effects of his injuries, he did not show it once he got in the saddle. He called his horse by the name of Drowen, and Endrith rode him as naturally as walking. It was only when they made camp and Endrith went straight to sleep after his meal that the others were reminded of his injuries, but Tiryn remarked that he was growing stronger by the day.

Endrith informed them that the rough, scraggly land through which they were traveling was called the Dunshave. Closer to the River Stout, they had seen farms of fresh-tilled earth and humble, clay-baked cottages. But now as they left the river valley, the ascendant sun revealed a land of low, matted bushes with fan-like leaves. From a distance it looked like a blanket of pine cones scattered across the land, though the foliage was pale green in color. On occasion, an oak or an elm rose to challenge the dominance of the underbrush, but they were lone warriors in a battlefield that had been overrun. The Dunshave was not wholly wild, but its paths were often overgrown and would have been difficult to follow had they not had Endrith to guide them.

"How long have you been riding?" Kion said.

"Only a year, but my swordswain said I took to it faster than most."

"We only started riding three days ago," Tiryn said, stroking Cyprian's mane. "But these horses have been good to us. Now that I'm starting to get over the saddle soreness, I find riding just about the most glorious thing imaginable."

"I'm glad to hear it. The right horse can make all the difference. I've been around many in my time, but I've never seen any as intelligent and disciplined as yours. They act almost human. Even Drowen, who has given me fits on occasion, seems to have taken to their ways. Do you know who trained them?"

Kion, Zinder, and Tiryn shared tentative glances, trying to gauge which one should offer an explanation.

"Well..." Zinder said at last. "Before they came to us, I

couldn't say who trained them, exactly, but I do know who's been doing it for the last few days."

Endrith was unsure of what to make of the slight amusement in Zinder's tone.

"I don't understand. Who could be training them out here in the open country? I thought you said that none of you knew how to ride."

"What Zinder means is that we have a way of speaking with the horses," Kion said. He didn't see any way around it other than being direct. "I know it will sound farfetched, but you remember last night when you asked about the light of my sword? Well, this sword is more than just metal and smith-work. It has a life of its own."

Endrith stared at Truesilver's hilt where it rode above Kion's shoulder. His brow rose and fell in a wave of confusion.

"Are you saying it's some sort of magic sword?"

"By one way of thinking I suppose you could say that. But its unique nature actually comes from the Spark."

"The Spark. I used to hear stories about that when I was a child. I've all but forgotten them now. The one thing I do remember is that the Spark had a way of making things come to life. You're saying the Spark is real, then?"

"Yes, though I hardly know more about it than you."

Endrith had many questions and so Kion launched into a lengthy explanation of all that he had learned of Kithian's origins and nature. He told of how he'd come upon the sword in Roving after the death of the Bladewarden, and of his search for his mother and sister, which had led to the fiery battle in Charring. He ended by sharing an account of their subsequent clashes with Ilk and the haukmarn in and around Fennigar.

"So you're the Sword of the North we've all been hearing about?" Endrith said, his eyes touched with wonder.

"That's what some call me. But I'm really just a son on the path to find his mother."

"And you say that it talks to you? And that it can talk to the animals?" Endrith regarded Drowen as if he were waiting for the horse to open its mouth and speak at any moment.

"Yes. And they have taught us many things. Your horse calls itself Hif-lan-eld, for one. Kithian has started teaching me their speech, but as of yet, I do not understand all that they say and I still mostly rely on Truesilver to tell me."

"That is a skill I should very much like to learn myself. Could you teach me as well?"

"I'm afraid not. Only a swordspeaker can learn to decipher it. And it is only through the sword that my words may be translated into sounds the beasts will understand."

"So he says." Zinder put on a sly air. "I, for one, think he's keeping some of those tricks to himself."

"Perhaps the Hammer of the North is a little jealous?" Kion teased.

"You may have all the fireworks, but don't forget who took you to Roving to get that blade in the first place!"

Kion and Tiryn shared a chuckle at Zinder's antics.

"You've been to Roving?" Endrith said. "I was actually there the day the haukmarn attacked. I brought a message to Bladewarden Glyre."

"You did? What was the message, if I might ask?" Unconsciously, Kion edged Smokewind a little closer to Endrith's horse.

"That the fane and the margrave would not be sending reinforcements. They were leaving him to fight the haukmarn alone." Endrith's voice grew wistful. "He was a great warrior, Strom Glyre. I'm not sure the fane understood just how great. It pained me to bring him such news. He took it nobly, though I think he knew it would likely doom him and his men to death."

"The fane left him to defend Roving alone? That's why Strom chose to face Vayd in single combat. He had no choice."

"Yes, he found a way to save his men in the end, but he could not save himself."

Zinder shook his head in disgust. "The fane will live to regret the loss of Strom Glyre, mark it down."

"Perhaps the fane had no choice," Tiryn said. "I'm sure he didn't want Strom to die."

"Ah, lass, I would that it were so. Of course, we've no way of knowing for certain why the fane did what he did, but the word over Inris is that all he cares about is stuffing his pockets as full of coin as he can."

Kion had never given much thought to the fane beyond the unreasonably high taxes he imposed and how difficult they made life for the shepherds on the Tors. The fane lived a world away in Gilding beyond the mountains. Thinking about the fane was about as helpful to a shepherd from Furrow as thinking about the sun when it shone too hot. It wouldn't change a thing. Whether Fane Sathe was the tyrant he was said to be, needlessly throwing Strom's life away, was hard to say. But the haukmarn were marching on and Warding would need a strong leader if it ever hoped to win. If the fane had some hand in Strom's demise, he may have lost the war before it ever began.

"What do you think, Kithian?" Kion said. "Do you think the fane understood what he was doing when he left Strom alone in Roving?"

"That I do not know, nor is it wise to suppose you understand the weights and measures of one who rules until you have access to his scales. But this much I do know. No ruler is immune to failure. And if a leader lacks good counsel, or refuses to listen to it when it is given, his blindness will bring about the ruin of many."

With Endrith leading them on, they rode harder and covered more ground than ever before. The low, pale shrubs of Dunshave gave way to a graveled land of open spaces and far vistas, well-suited for travel on horseback. These were the wild lands of Casting Limmring, which Endrith called the Homendor. It was unpeopled by all but the hardy and the brave. It was a dry expanse, full of dust and grit where little grew and few streams were to be found. The sun beat fiercely down on those who traveled these trackless plains, the wind blasting against them, unchecked by tree or hill, hamlet or hermitage. The vast and boundless barrens stretched beyond all sense and knowing.

Though no settlements marked these endless leagues, that was not to say that they were uninhabited. Tiny knife hawks and great black vultures swirled far above. Flocks of gray geese glided a little lower, larger and louder than their kinsmen of the Tors. Herds of small slender deer grazed in the distance, with burnt-sienna coats and no antlers, only little nubs for horns among the bucks. On one occasion, a pack of some three dozen longhounds came within a mile of the party. These were large dogs with long hair and great, loping strides. They ran so swiftly and the pack was so large, Tiryn wondered aloud if they ever attacked travelers.

"Not that I've heard," Endrith said. "A few have been caught and trained as watchdogs in the Warding army, though. Some even fight alongside their masters in battle."

This particular pack certainly showed no interest in their band and soon passed off to the south. The plains rolled on and on, and yet the great open expanses of the Homendor did not last forever. The harsh sunlight and wide spaces fell away in the late afternoon as they drew near the borders of Sicklewood. Once inside the forest, the world changed as though from the drawing of a curtain. The wind cut to a whisper. The air turned fresh and cool. Rabbits and voles and other small scurrying creatures hid themselves at the horses' approach. Larks and warblers whistled cautiously from the shadows. The ground swelled with ferns and moss and tangled vines. And watching down upon it all, the tall, thin harvestwood trees curtained off all trace of the horizon. These ancient sentinels wore the bark of pines, but had long, tapered leaves of faded green which fluttered like banners in the wind.

"I've only ever seen pictures of these trees in books. I wish I could stop to sketch them," Tiryn said.

"As far as I know, this is the only standing grove of harvest-woods in all the Four Wards," Endrith said. "I've been here during the winter when they're covered in ice. The leaves take on the appearance of icy blades—quite beautiful—but dangerous to walk under."

The trail they followed through Sicklewood was not wide enough for more than a single horse at a time. Endrith rode in the lead and Kion brought up the rear. As they drove deeper into the forest, the air grew more quiet. The only creatures that showed themselves were skittish squirrels and sullen crows. The crows passed northward in aloof flocks, cawing in derision at the land-bound creatures below. They passed in a steady stream, so that for more than two hours there was never a time when several—if not dozens of—crows couldn't be seen at a time.

"Other soldiers who have journeyed here say that a great roost of crows lies somewhere within the forest," Endrith said. "Though I have never seen it myself."

"A friend of mine was attacked once by a crow. It made off with the pin in her hair," Tiryn said.

"Yes, they're born thieves. But don't you worry, lass," Zinder said. "I've got a hat you can wear that's so daunting, no crow with any sense would dare tangle with you. It's even got spikes on the band, which will make them pay dearly if they do decide to swoop down and nab it."

But the crows paid them no heed and by twilight they were seen no more. Concern over crows or other wild beasts seemed little justified in the still and sheltered woods. Even the haukmarn seemed a distant threat in a place so serene. They had left the haukmarn for good in the Glooming Bog for all they knew, and the smoke of Grettling was a faint memory lost upon the mild breeze which rustled through the long thin leaves.

That night, they camped by a gurgling stream and Tiryn made a hearty soup of some mushrooms Zinder had harvested in a nearby glen. She also mixed in some potatoes from their provisions. It was not nearly as good as Mother's, but Tiryn had done her best and they could hardly complain.

"How long have you been a messenger?" Tiryn asked as she ladled another helping into Endrith's bowl.

"Over a year," he said. "And in all that time, I've never had soup this good."

"It's my mother's recipe. My aunt sent some spices with us, but the soup is still missing a few ingredients."

"Well, it's as good as my own mother could make, and that's saying something."

"Where is your mother now?" Kion said.

"On our farm, south of Jabble. Though if the Noathryn cannot be pushed back at Grettling, my family won't be able to stay there long."

So Endrith was a farmer. Kion's stomach gave a sickening flutter. He'd never known a farmer that didn't insult or ignore him, and no shepherd he knew had ever been friends with one. Any farmer Kion knew would have been shamed out of such a friendship the moment someone found out.

Well, as long as Endrith didn't know, perhaps they could still be friends. Out here these distant lands they were no longer farmers and shepherds, but two boys caught up in terrible events and far from home. In the shrouded woods, leagues from any settled lands, there was no past and there were no professions, only travelers trying to make their way along uncertain roads.

"And your father? Is he there, too?" Zinder said. By now he was on his third bowl of soup. Though Tiryn was confident her spices would last the whole journey, with Zinder along, Kion was not so sure. Zinder could out-eat them all.

"Yes, both he and my brother are still at home. I have another brother who serves in the margrave's marches in Dunskein, but I've not heard anything of him for many months. I can only hope he fares well enough to come home when the war is over."

"So may it be," Zinder said solemnly, pausing to reflect between spoonfuls of soup.

"And here's to you finding your own mother," Endrith said, raising his cup.

"So may it be," Kion and Tiryn echoed Zinder's words and all of them tipped the cold fresh water down their throats.

"Were I not bound to the margrave's service, I would help you find her. My own mother means more than anything so I know how you must feel. I almost lost her once when I was seven. My father and older brother were away cutting wood when a mad wolf came snarling into the garden. Mother told me to run into the house, but that was the one time in my life that I disobeyed her. I took up a hoe to defend her, but the wolf struck before I could do anything. The creature gouged her leg with its iron jaw. It would have done away with her if I hadn't come charging in. I was as fearful as the wolf was mad, but fear was my friend that day, for the greater fear of losing my mother conquered my lesser fear of the wolf. I swung that hoe for all I was worth. By some blessed stroke, I crushed the beast's eye. It squealed and ran for the woods. My mother's wound never did quite heal and she never walked the same after that, but she lived. And if I live to be a hundred, I'll never have a prouder moment."

"She's fortunate you were there," Kion said. Tiryn nodded in agreement in her own knowing way.

"It was well done, Endrith," Zinder said. "Perhaps we'll have to call you the Hoe of the North from now on."

They all had a fine laugh at that and Kion took courage from the tale. Perhaps he was up against more than a maddened wolf, but he had a far greater weapon than Endrith. If Endrith could stand up for his mother, so could he. Either way, one thing Kion knew for certain: he liked this soldier, Endrith, farmer or not.

Chapter 15

FOREST FLIGHT

Tiryn's body jerked, hurling her from her dream. But the images and impressions from all that she had seen clung to her memory in dark and unsettling detail. She lay there panting as though she had just finished a race.

She had not had a dream like this since before the attack on Charring. This new dream felt like one of the ones she'd had while suffering from the wistering fever—less like a dream, more like a vision. That other vision had come partly true. The haukmarn had come to Marlibrim Mansion, but the fire she thought they were bringing came from Kion, not them. She had thought —and hoped—that the vision had been a one-time occurrence, an awareness brought about somehow by her sickness. But now she was not so sure.

In this new vision she was soaring above the land. It was a wide open country, the Homendor—or something very like it—though seen from above, as if she were floating through a night sky. The sparks traced their indecipherable courses, like glitter-sticks from a summer festival, casting their inconstant, shimmering light upon the empty land below. No creatures grazed or roamed at this hour. No birds traversed the shadow-locked sky. The scattered tufts of grass and isolated stones faded into the rugged plains below. But one bright flame defied the stillness of that dormant land. It flickered brighter and brighter until at last Tiryn could see it for what it was. It was Kion. He came streaking across the land, riding Smokewind at full gallop, brandishing Truesilver aloft, the long blade rippling with flames, leaving a trail of light behind him. He let out a great cry that could be heard from far off.

"I am coming! And I will not stop until I have saved you," he shouted.

The sight stirred Tiryn, filling her with hope. Surely this meant that their mother would be found. Riding at such a pace, and guided by Truesilver's unwavering light, it was only a matter of time before Kion found her. And yet, why was he riding alone? Tiryn should have been with him. Not even Zinder was there.

Tiryn swooped down from the great heights, determined to help her brother, to accompany him on his search. He must not attempt his journey without her.

But as she descended, out of the east rolled twisting clouds of a darkness deeper than the night—an immense, coal-black wall that stretched from the lowest valley to the glittering sparks above. At the vanguard of these clouds, tendrils of black fog stretched forth, slithering this way and that, seeking, searching. And they were coming for Kion.

But Kion and Smokewind outpaced the darkness. They sped beyond the Homendor and into a labyrinth of hills. On the back of Smokewind, with his sword blazing forth, Kion would fly to safety and the search for Mother would go on. Tiryn's heart filled with peace, knowing that her brother was too swift and too strong to let the advancing storm overtake him. But when she looked back she saw two frightening things.

The darkness parted briefly to reveal the lands beyond. The roiling storm had blown across all of eastern Inris and it withered all that it touched. Fields and forests curled like ashes. Cities lit up in flames, burned for a moment, then crumbled to dust. High stone walls toppled and buildings were torn asunder. Inris, their homeland, was falling. But the second thing she saw filled her with even greater dread. For though the black tide would not claim Kion, it would soon overtake her. She could not match his pace. The chill of death rode before that churning sea and once it reached her, it would swallow her up and she would wither into nothing along with the lands behind her.

Kion rode on, oblivious to the destruction trailing in his wake, unaware of the threat his sister faced.

"Kion!" Tiryn cried. "Behind you. Don't you see the darkness? It's destroying all that it touches and if you don't turn back, it will destroy me too!"

But her words could not reach his ears. He was traveling too fast. Even now his light was dwindling in the west as he rode farther and farther away. She strained to outdistance the advancing storm, but with every breath, it drew closer. If only Kion would turn back. With Truesilver's flame he could cast back the darkness and save her and the land as well.

"Kion! The darkness is coming. You must stop it. Turn back before it's too late. Help me, Kion. I need you…"

But he rode on, a bright arrow loosed from a bow that would not waver or cease its flight until it found its mark.

Tiryn had no choice but to turn and face the swirling, malevolent storm on her own. Kion would save Mother. Tiryn could die knowing that at least, but there was no one and nothing to protect her from the oncoming darkness. She had no way to stand against the endless black. The midnight clouds overtook her in a whirling rush. As they smothered her, she began to fall, caught up in spinning winds which threw her into a yawning abyss. She braced herself, waiting for the moment when she would come crashing into the rock-hard ground below. But at the moment the ground flew up to meet her, fear shook her frame and cast her from the dream.

She lay, shivering, deep within Sicklewood. A few wandering sparks shed their feeble light through the trees. The air around her was warm, but not nearly warm enough. She wrapped her blanket tighter, but it did no good.

The others slept on, oblivious to the terrors she had faced. She longed to wake Kion and tell him what she had seen and warn him not to leave her behind, not to run so far ahead that the darkness would overtake her. But he would say it was only a dream and tell her not to worry. He would not feel the weight of it, the foreboding that pressed down even now upon her chest. If anything, it would make him worry that she was getting sick again, and her shivering would make that all but a certainty. And Kion had enough to worry about as it was. What could he do about a vision, even if he believed it was real? She did not even know what the darkness was.

The shivering would pass. The sun would rise. The dream would fade and their journey would continue. All around her the woods slept on, quiet and sheltering, the air fresh with the newness of life and growing things. What power did a dream have over such enduring strength and beauty, weathering the elements year after year, unbowed and unchanging?

No, it would be better if she kept the dream to herself. It was only one dream, after all. If more came, perhaps she would tell Kion then. But right now, she desperately needed to sleep. Another long day of riding lay ahead.

"Please, let there be no more dreams," she whispered and buried her head inside her blanket. But dreams are not ours to command.

The morning dawned cool and still. The trees exuded an unshakable peace that seemed strong enough to slow time itself. Tiryn wrapped her arms tight around her. The shivering was gone, but the memory of the vision remained. She did her best to cast it aside, turning her attention to the songbirds trilling amongst the swaying branches. Their melodies worked to draw out the poison from the wound of her nightmare. A rich, enticing scent scattered the last troubling wisps of sleep from her mind. It was a fragrance she'd not smelled since long before she grew sick with the wistering, the tongue-tingling scent of meat roasting over an open fire.

"The Lady of the Tors awakes at last," Kion said, using the title Father had been fond of using. He and Zinder were already packing their things onto the horses. Endrith knelt beside the fire, poking at several delectable scraps in a pan.

"You made breakfast without me?" Tiryn said, scrambling out of her blankets.

"We thought you could use the sleep," Zinder said. "With any luck, we'll reach Dunach tonight and we thought you'd want to look your best for all the handsome young lads who'll be throwing themselves at your feet."

An unpleasant warmth rushed to her cheeks. Tiryn wasn't sure what to make of men or boys her age, and she was certain that what Zinder had said wouldn't come true, but she didn't like to even think about it.

"Endrith, I didn't know you could cook," she said, avoiding Zinder's dancing eyes.

"When you spend as much time alone in the wilds as I do, you learn to get by. It won't be anything close to your soup, but Zinder was kind enough to do a little hunting this morning and caught us a few squirrels."

"Crafty little fellows. Hard to spot before dawn with those dark coats of theirs, but I felt I would fade into a vapor if I had to eat another biscuit for breakfast."

"Yes, Zinder, you're practically a skeleton with a hat on," Kion said.

The meat was stringy, but by far the most delicious thing they'd had since the Grizzly Griddle. There was little time to savor it, though, for all too soon they were back in the saddle and on the trail once again.

"Another day closer to Mother," Tiryn told herself. "We're almost to Noath." And yet, glancing at Kion behind her, she wondered if they would both make it to the end. Would he fly off and leave her behind before they reached the island? Would it be soon?

The early morning cool of the pines drained away her

worries and her cares. There was nothing quite like a long ride through gentle woods and stately trees to calm and quiet the soul. The daggered leaves of the harvestwoods rippled in a rolling tapestry of green. "Listen to the words of the wind through our leaves," they seemed to say. "Our branches give voice to its song...Come sing with us this rustling, sifting, murmuring tune..."

Caw!

A crow called out, shattering the song of the trees. Endrith turned his head toward the sound, but they rode on. And yet there was a strange timbre to that call, an urgency, perhaps even a warning.

A few moments later, other crows echoed the call, a few at first, but soon the cawing multiplied. Within minutes the whole of Sicklewood rang with the sound.

"Keep vigilant," Endrith said. "A great number of them have taken wing."

"Reach back in that bag, lass, and put on the hat that's inside," Zinder said. He pulled down his own hat, a large blue one with a silver feather on one side, so that the brim came to the bridge of his nose.

She pulled out a large wool cap with a spiked band around it. "You mean this?"

"Yes, it wraps around your head and then you unroll those flaps so that it forms a sort of veil over your face. And you can adjust the band with this buckle like so."

"They're just birds," Kion said.

"It doesn't hurt to be safe," Zinder said.

The cawing intensified. There was fear in those feathered voices, and a hint of madness. Tiryn worked her head into the hood and fought with the flaps until they dropped over most of her face, leaving only a narrow slit by which to see. Zinder helped her tighten the band.

"I can hardly see anything."

"Me neither, but the horses know where they're going. Let's hope they're braver than us if the crows pass our way."

The piercing cries grew into a near-constant peal of avian terror. The leaves shook in anticipation of their coming. And from the south the crows swarmed in. Through the slit in her hood, Tiryn saw hundreds of black darts knifing through the trees. It was a deluge of wings. The wind of the crows' passing sent her hood flapping. There were thousands upon thousands of them. Most flew well above them, but some swooped low where the branches were thinner. Several buffeted Kion and Endrith, who ducked and shielded themselves with their arms.

"Hyah!" Endrith shouted, barely able to make his voice heard above the tempestuous flock.

The horses took off at a full gallop. Tiryn had never known speed until that moment. She and Zinder hunched forward as wings and winds rushed by. She shut her eyes and clung to Cyprian's bridle. A claw scratched at her hood, leaving a tiny hole. Wings brushed her shoulder. Something tore at one of the flaps of her cap, slashing open the fabric near the top. A sharp pain stabbed her hand. The wet blood dried quickly in the wind, but the sting of it remained. Cyprian pumped and strained beneath her. For all Tiryn knew, she might have been back in her dream, flying over the Homendor. A deluge of birds roared past, a tempest of screeching feathers.

Caw, caw, caw, caw, CAW!

One of them nipped her other hand. This time the pain brought a flash of heat. Holding on with only the other hand, she yanked open her veil and put the finger in her mouth. The saltiness of the blood ran to the back of her throat.

"Agh! No!" Zinder screamed. "No, no, no, no, no, no, no, no!"

Tiryn opened her veil to see, fearing Zinder was hurt, but he had his head buried in Cyprian's mane and she couldn't tell what sort of wound he had suffered.

Whatever ill turn the crows had given him, that was the final blow in their assault. The shrill cries and beating wings abated almost as suddenly as they began. The cawing died away into the distance and the trailing crows were content to fly through the upper reaches of the trees and leave those on the ground unmolested, though leaves continued to rain down in twirling threads. The sudden migration had left a veritable tapestry of verdant destruction below. It would be a full season before the harvestwoods in that part of the forest returned to their former glory.

As the murder of crows drifted off to the north, the horses slowed to a trot and soon stopped altogether.

"Those birds were fleeing something," Endrith said. "I would like to know what beast in the southern woods is terrifying enough to send the entire roost to flight."

But Tiryn gave little attention to his words. For Zinder sat slumped in the saddle, sniffling and blubbering, his head still sunk into Cyprian's mane.

"Zinder, what's wrong?" Kion asked, dismounting and running to his friend.

There was no mark on Zinder that Tiryn could see. Not even a splotch of blood from her own wounds to soil his fine clothes.

Zinder reared up, his eyes pink with tears. "Ah, lad, are you blind? Can you not see?" He pointed emphatically to his bare, white-haired head. "Those filchers made off with my third-best traveling hat!"

For a moment they all shared a look of surprise. Then Tiryn's sigh of relief turned into laughter and Kion and Endrith echoed her so that the forest rang out with their mirth, but in one of the rare moments of sustained sorrow in his life, Zinder did not have the heart to join in.

Chapter 16

A TIME TO FIGHT

No one was seriously hurt by the crows, unless Zinder's hat collection was taken into account. That was wounded in the deepest way, according to Zinder. They spent several minutes searching the woods for his third-best traveling hat, but alas, it was forever lost—and with no chance to be replaced for many days, his second- and first-best traveling hats would have to do. Beyond that, Tiryn suffered a minor wound on each hand, Kion received a small cut above his ear, and the three horses had minor scrapes and abrasions, but nothing more. Endrith was the only one to come away unscathed, which was just as well since he was still recovering from his wounds at the battle of Grettling.

"I never dreamed that crows could be driven into such a frenzy," Endrith said as Tiryn finished cleaning Kion's cut—despite Kion's protests that it was nothing that required attention.

"It seemed as if every crow in Inris must have passed through," Tiryn said.

"I may need to look into wearing a helmet when going about in the woods," Zinder said, still in mourning.

"It must have been something large or deadly to have frightened the whole roost like that," Endrith said.

"Or perhaps several somethings. Do you think it might have been a force of Noathryn? We're very close to the border," Kion said. Sicklewood lay just east of Dunach Fortress, at the very edge of the margrave's dominion.

"It's possible, but since the crows came from the south, it's not likely Noathryn would have passed that way. The path through Sicklewood from Noath would have brought them in from the north. Even then, the forces at Dunach would have had something to say about that. No, I do not think we can blame the Noathryn for this."

"Whatever it was, let's hope it stays south of us." Kion eyed the woods with suspicion and the company mounted once again, more anxious than ever for the sight of Dunach's walls. "Tell me something, Kithian. Why couldn't you understand what the crows were saying, and why wouldn't they listen to you?"

"When an animal is set to flight, it is no longer fit to speak. A man may be reasoned out of his fears, but animals can think of nothing else when fear takes hold."

"What do you think they were running from?"

"That I do not know. There are many wicked things hidden in the wild places of the world."

"Dangerous enough to frighten ten thousand crows?"

"Oh, yes. Talinyon twisted many creatures before he was stopped. Dark things, wicked in purpose as well as shape. Creatures of fang and horn and claw, who grew to hate the beasts from which they came and all living things that are whole and good and untainted. Even a predator respects his prey and only kills when hungry. But there are things which feed on hate and malice alone. Many of these creatures fled into forgotten places after Talinyon disappeared, but they lie in wait until the opportunity to do evil should arise again."

"Talinyon? The same person as Talin from the poem? He disappeared? I thought you said he was defeated."

"Defeated, yes. But he escaped before he could answer for his crimes. He was never found, nor his glaive."

"His glaive? Talin was a swordspeaker?" How had Kion missed that before?

"The very first. It was a day of great sorrow when the other lords learned of his betrayal, but though he did great evil, he was not wholly to blame. For his glaive, Malix, fell long before he ever did. It was Malix who poisoned Talinyon's mind against the Mastersmith and the

other lords." The pain in Kithian's voice ran deep. An unspoken grief dimmed the sword's usual fire. For the first time, Kion saw that even a sword could know suffering. And perhaps because Kithian lacked most other forms of sensation, such feelings might even affect him more greatly.

"A corrupted glaive?" Kithian had spoken of such things before, but only in brief. This was the first time he had ever given one a name. Malix. There was menace in the sound of it.

"Indeed. Malix was the greatest of all the glaives sent to mankind. Unto him was given the power to inspire and strengthen men to subdue the land and raise up great works—vast roads and mighty bridges, deep storehouses of grain and strong homes of oak and stone—that men might dwell in safety upon the land—"

"I don't understand, Kithian. Build bridges and buildings? How could a sword make men do all of that? Was that part of Malix's gift?"

"I did not say he was a sword. He is a glaive, and that is very different, as was the nature and purpose of the glaives at that time. For many long years Malix fulfilled his purpose faithfully. But at length, he grew impatient to see his plans come to fruition. He believed that he could improve upon the Mastersmith's designs, make works that were larger and grander, and above all to make more. More. That insatiable word which has swallowed the happiness of rulers and common folk alike, which knows no boundaries and brooks no challenges. That word which has shipwrecked so many lives in vain pursuits and tricked whole nations into surrendering their freedoms for the promise of something better. It is the enemy of contentment and the fuel that fires vanity's consuming blaze. In Malix's quest to build a world after the fashion of his own designs, he rebelled against the law of his maker. If only the other glaives had seen it sooner, perhaps we could have prevented the sorrow that came afterward, but it was not meant to be. For Malix was clever to conceal his betrayal until the time was ripe. And the Shattering happened first in Talinyon's heart before it ever broke upon the world."

The Shattering. Another mystery of the past. The calendar

was reckoned by it; they lived in the Shattered Age. And yet Kion still knew so very little of what had happened then.

"Tell me more of the Shattering."

Kithian's voice grew dark and deep as the memories coursed through his steel. *"The Shattering is a tale too long to tell in full, and there would be much grief in the telling. Enough for a thousand tales. For now, it is sufficient to say that it began when Talinyon severed the Iron Vine and death came into the world. By that one act of defiance, the whole of the Four Wards was undone—though the full ruin of the Shattering was long in its coming. The corruption spread slowly at first, for the other Lords and Ladies ruled yet in the springtime of their realms and had no thought that their joys might come to an end. But in time the Four Wards were plunged into war, the first and the most terrible the world has ever known. And from that wound, the land has never fully healed, even to this day."*

The Four Wards. Legends told wondrous things of how they had once been—a land of peace, united by wise rulers and blessed with endless abundance. A land without war or famine or hardship. A world where the winter did not bite and the summer did not wither. A place where men ran and did not grow tired, where women aged and their beauty did not fade. Could it be that it was more than a legend? Kithian's words made Kion want to believe so. The ancient words spoken at the great festivals throughout the year returned to him as he rode upon the forest path.

Though what has passed may never be
More than echoes of memory
Yet hope shall stir and bind us when
We look unto what once has been

"Will the world ever be the way it once was?"

"That is not for me to say. Nonetheless, that is what we must strive for. Though we rightly mourn this shattered world, in this as in all things, it often comes to pass that suffering will prove to have been

good to have been—though no less painful because of what was born from it. We must not fail to trust in the Mastersmith's guidance when the cost becomes too great, however dark the path may grow. This present war is one such path. Twisted and unsure though it may be, we can trust that it serves some larger purpose. The dross will be burned away through the fire and when all is finished this land may emerge stronger for the sorrow it has seen."

"But that does not make it any easier to go through the darkness. Even if the Four Wards are never restored to what they once were, we can still win this war, though. My hope is in the fane. No matter what they say of him, I believe he will marshal his host eventually. And once the Warding army is at full strength again, the war will end quickly. The haukmarn were beaten back in the last war. Our soldiers will beat them back again." Even as Kion said this, doubts softened the conviction in his voice. For without Strom Glyre to lead them, he wondered how they would stand against the vast hordes which had poured down from the north.

"That is possible, but even if the fane's men do march forth once more, there is no surety that they will win or that they will come in time. Verisward is a great distance from here and the march will be long and tiring for whatever men do come. There is one thing I know of, though, that would have the best chance to shorten this war."

"What is that?"

"A swordspeaker. There is more to winning a war than the strength of an army, Kion. Men need a leader to guide them, a warrior they can follow, someone they can believe in, whose banner they can rally to when all seems lost. One hundred men of the same mind will beat a thousand who sail on a rudderless sea. This land needs a hero, a leader to ignite hope in the people's hearts. I believe you could be that leader, Kion. And when that day comes, I will be your banner of red flame and men will rally to fight at your side. Together we will stride forth into the field with the ground shaking from the force of the battle shouts of those around us. That day may not be upon you yet, but steel yourself. For it may come sooner than you would wish."

If Kion had been moving on his own power he would have stopped in the middle of the trail. He was not fit to lead anyone. In Strom's journal he had read of the many struggles that great warrior had gone through to win the hearts of his men before he had become the bladewarden and was a mere swordswain in the fane's army. It had surprised Kion to learn that someone as noble and brave as Strom had to earn the loyalty of those who should have served him willingly. If even Strom had to work to lead, there was little hope for Kion. The only thing he had ever led in his life was a flock of sheep and even they had not listened to him. Kithian had never been wrong before, but surely even he made a mistake in judgment from time to time.

"I'm no leader. No one would follow me."

"No one? Are you not the Sword of the North? Did you not see the way the soldiers in Fennigar looked at you when they learned who you were? You even had the respect of Roardin, a man who served under Strom Glyre. He, of all people, surely knows a great leader when he sees one."

"Just because I defeated Vayd and drove a few haukmarn from Charring doesn't mean I can lead the whole of Warding to victory. That was one battle. And I barely won it. I still have so much to learn. Maybe if I trained for a year or two—or three—I might be ready. Even then, I'm not sure."

"You are ready now."

"No, Kithian, how can you say that?"

"Because you have a glaive. And when you fight with me, you are more than your training, more than your experience. You are the greatest warrior in this land. You know that what I say is true. You felt it when you fought Vayd. How else do you think you defeated him where Strom failed? It was more than just the fire. It was you and I, bonded together in battle. Your strokes, your speed, and my wisdom, my knowledge. You are the strength, I am the steel. You were ready to fight the moment you took hold of me on the plains of Roving. Roardin told you that you would be worth a hundred men in battle, but I say he underestimated you by far. And wherever you fight, you will make

those around you fight all the harder. For that is what a hero does. He ignites a flame in the hearts of others and spurs them on to deeds greater than they could otherwise achieve."

Kion had no answer to this. Kithian was far wiser than he was. If Kithian believed Kion was ready, who was he to tell him otherwise? And yet, Kion could not see himself as a leader, no matter how hard he tried. It was all too fast, all too impossible. Yes, he had defeated Vayd, but how could he be sure he'd fight as well the next time? He couldn't even win the sword-fighting tournament in his tiny village. How could he sway the outcome of an entire war?

"Kithian, you may be right. The Four Wards may need a swordspeaker. They may see something in me that I cannot see in myself. They may want me to fight, even to lead. But if that's so, there's something I don't understand. If I was ready to fight the moment I held you for the first time, why did you let me leave Fennigar? Why didn't you force me to stay and fight there?"

Kithian's reply came swift and sure. *"For the simple reason that it was not my choice to make. My role is to counsel and to guide, not to decide for you. I know how much your mother means to you, and I know that it is not my place to ask you to abandon her. You must do what you feel is right. Only be sure that you do not choose the good thing over the best thing. The people of this land need heroes, someone who will lift them up when they have fallen, who will stand beside them when things are dark and hope has fled, who will teach them that anguish and despair are cruel, yes, but they are only weightless shadows which scatter to nothing in the light of unstained honor, bravery, and sacrifice, that what is good and true and right in this world is what shall endure to the end. You can only delay your destiny for so long. I say again to you what I said before. You are the Four Wards' best hope for ending this war. And the longer you avoid taking up that mantle, the harder it will be to defeat the enemy when you do."*

The cool shade of the forest turned into an unsettling shiver across Kion's shoulders. Ever since he was old enough to swing his father's sword, he had dreamed of being a soldier. A month ago, the thought of serving under Storm Glyre was the highest pinnacle he could ever have hoped to achieve. Now he was being asked not merely to be a soldier, but to aspire to lead the forces of Warding into battle. The old dreams did not go down so easily when they threatened to break into his present life. For there was another dream that meant far more to him now. No, the Four Wards would have to wait. The battle for his mother was the only one that Kion was ready to fight right now. But even if he won that battle and brought her safely home, he was not prepared to take the place of someone like Strom Glyre. It was the fane's role to appoint the leaders of his army, after all, not Kithian's. And Kion was just a shepherd boy with not fifty nicks to his name. He was not afraid to fight under Roardin or some other commander, but to lead them? That was something even the greatest sword in Warding could not make him fit to do.

Chapter 17

WATCHERS ON THE ROAD

Darkness fell swiftly as the horses cantered out from the sheltering boughs of Sicklewood and into the northern reaches of the Lost Hylls beyond. Though the hour was late, the rugged hills through which they now traveled had yet to cool from a long day under a baking sun. The trail grew rough, and the horses trod over rocky soil, tendrils of dust stirring beneath their hooves. The last few miles to Dunach Fortress were doubly unpleasant after their recent travels in the gentle woods, but Zinder remarked that at least there were no crows.

No moon arose to ward off the darkness. The golden sparks flickering above offered the only defense against the deepening void of night. Only Endrith could pick out the path now. It was invisible to Kion and the others. Kion saw only an endless array of craggy swells and dips, rounded backs of stone bent and crumbling against the weathering assault of sun and wind and rain. No green and growing things rose up to shelter that naked land. All was exposed and blasted and bare. The horses chose their steps carefully, for crevices and sliding gravel abounded. It seemed that they must surely run afoul of the dangers of the trail sooner or later, but they pressed on, weaving their way from one valley to the next. None of the companions were of a mind to pass the night in this forbidding maze of hills, and the prospect of shelter within the fortress walls drove them doggedly on.

"Fair warning," Endrith said. "Varlance Aonar may recruit you as messengers if we keep up this pace."

So a varlance was overseeing Dunach. The fortress must have been more important to the Wards than Kion realized. Varlances could command up to ten full companies and were beneath only the highgilds and the bladewarden within the Warding ranks.

"I have my doubts about that," Kion said. "From where I'm sitting, I'd say the horses are doing all the work."

"Perhaps, but I imagine he'll take an interest in you all the same."

Kion voiced no answer, instead he mulled over Endrith's words. The only varlance he had ever heard of before was Sevelius, the varlance over Jasper March in the War of the Claws. Strom had written about him in his journal, having served under him. Though Strom had said nothing openly disparaging about him, it was clear from his accounts that Sevelius had been something of a tyrant, lording his authority over his men and treating them harshly. If the varlance at Dunach was like that, Kion might be walking into a trap. Roardin had wanted Kion to fight in the Warding army and had mentioned that he had the authority to force him to do so. If Roardin, who was merely a swordswain, had such authority, how much more would a varlance? Would Aonar press him into service where Roardin had let him go? Would Kion be forced to turn away from the search for his mother to fight for the Four Wards after all? Surely not. Dunach was not even under attack as far as they knew and varlances had more important things to do than recruit individual soldiers. No, it would be a short rest and then onwards to the western shores of Noath.

The conversation turned to the hoped-for comforts of the fortress. Though Kion was no stranger to hardship and nights in the wild, he had been long enough without real rest to know the treasure of a good night's sleep sheltered from the elements and away from hard, unforgiving ground. And life in the saddle had added a new kind of weariness as well. A real bed was something that he was definitely looking forward to.

Tiryn was asking Endrith what life inside a great castle was like and fighting back a yawn when the faint sound of hooves came rattling over the hills from the east. They stopped the horses to listen. Judging from the rhythm of the hoofbeats, it was clear that a pair of riders was making its way westward and would soon overtake them if they did not match their pace.

"Scouts from the fortress, or messengers on their way to it, most likely," Endrith said. "Still, these are perilous days. It could be anyone. We could alter our course so that they pass us by unseen."

"And delay our arrival to Dunach even further?" Kion said. "I think we can handle two horsemen if they mean us ill. I'd rather push on."

"I'm of like mind," Zinder said. "We've got the Sword, the Hammer, and the Hoe of the North with us, after all. I don't see what we have to fear."

"You're sure they're not bandits?" Tiryn said, her small voice showing that she had less confidence than Kion or Zinder.

"Not likely," Endrith said. "They would be doing more to catch us unawares if they were. I suppose we'll carry on, then. We're not far now from Dunach in any case. We may even arrive before them if they slow their pace."

But the riders did not slow. If anything, they came on even faster. Within a quarter of an hour Zinder spotted two silhouettes cresting a rise behind them. Not long after, their own horses grew skittish. Smokewind shook his mane and his steps grew furtive.

"What's wrong with the animals, Kithian?" Kion said.

"A foul wind blows from the south. Some unnamed beast stalks the land, though they cannot say what it is."

"It's not the riders, then?"

"No, something far more sinister."

The riders soon overtook them. They arrived in a rumbling cloud of rising dust and reined in their galloping steeds. They were two soldiers, wearing mail and tabards identical to

Endrith's. Both were near his age, though their short beards made them look older. A grave warning shone in their eyes.

"Hail, strangers," one said. "We are scouts from Dunach. We have been following the trail of some haukmarn wulfmasters since this morning. They travel with great speed through hard paths, and the hills are as nothing to them. We do not know what brings them so close to the fortress, but if you do not make for Dunach with all haste you will be in great danger."

"Wulfmasters?" Kion said. Leanoch had mentioned them once. Could the haukmarn have picked up their trail after all this time?

"And you're certain that they have dreadwulfs with them?" Endrith said.

"Yes, twelve of the foul beasts. We sent for one of the companies to drive them away or draw them off, but it is not likely they will come in time."

"Then we cannot delay. We must ride with all haste for Dunach," Kion said.

"And we shall ride with you."

No more needed to be said. The five horses tore off through the rocky hills, unconcerned with the perils of the jagged terrain, for a far greater danger now threatened. Fear coursed through Smokewind and all weariness fled from his galloping frame. The wind hurtled past, roaring atop the staccato din of trampling hooves. The horses' bodies glistened white with foam. As their wild ride took them up another of the countless rises, the vague tracing of battlements glimmered beneath the sparklight to the west. The sight lifted Kion's spirits. It was still some way off, but the promise of it sent a thrill straight through him.

A heart-shuddering howl struck his newfound hopes to the quick. Fury and blood lust rang in that cry. All warmth drained from the air. The horses whinnied brokenly in reply. From the southeast, dusky forms poured down the far hill as though fiends unleashed from a pit. The white glow from their eyes left a trail of ghostly wisps in their wake. Huge and terrible, their heads riding as high as a man, the dreadwulfs came on at a pace no horse could match. Twelve snarling terrors of fang and fur hurtled toward them. Their howls multiplied the dark and an air of doom spilled out before them.

"We will not reach Dunach in time," Kion said in a voice only Kithian could hear.

"Then you must turn back to face them while the others go on. It is their only hope." Kithian's voice was clear and even, undaunted by the terror of the dreadwulfs' coming. Kion flinched in fear at his glaive's words, but only for a moment. Need drove the fear away.

"Endrith!" Kion shouted above the hooves and howls. "Ride on to Dunach. I must turn aside to face them. Whatever you do, do not turn back for me."

"Kion, no. Twelve dreadwulfs! Few men could defeat a single one unaided. No warrior could think to take on so many, no matter what sword he wields."

"There is no time for debate. If I cannot hold them back, I will at least slow them enough for you to reach the fortress. Zinder, protect Tiryn. I will see you both at Dunach."

"No, lad, don't go!" Zinder shouted.

"No, Kion!" Tiryn screamed. "Don't leave me!"

But Smokewind had already broken from the group. He wheeled before galloping back down the slope. The others drove onward to the summit. Tiryn's cries shook Kion's resolve, but they faded mercifully as she passed from view.

Kion struggled to slip his sword off his back at a full gallop, but need brought the baldric off and Truesilver into his hand. There was no time to place the scabbard back so he tossed it to the wind.

The dreadwulf forms took on more definite shape as he raced across the rock-strewn valley to meet them. They came with maws snapping, hooked fangs closing on nothing but the night. Their matted fur bristled in anticipation of the kill. It clung thick upon their bodies, dense enough to turn away all but the sharpest blade. They were more savage, more massive, and more deadly than even the haukmarn that they served.

"Prepare yourself, swordspeaker. Fear is not folly until it becomes action. And the mastery of it is called courage."

Now that the moment of decision had passed, the terrible truth of what Kion had to face rose before him like a haunting specter. But Kithian's words lent him strength. With Truesilver in his hand, there was always a chance. And Smokewind was a valiant horse, all the more so with Kithian to guide and encourage him. Kion just had to make sure he held on and struck when and where his sword directed.

"Glaivefire."

His blade lit up the night, transforming into a crimson brand. The dreadwulfs slowed, briefly daunted by the fire, but their hatred burned away their trepidation as soon as it came. They surged forward with even greater speed.

"Rom-del-lin, dash hard to the right," Kithian said. The two sides reached the valley between the hills at the same time. Smokewind had been charging straight for the middle of the pack, but he shifted and made for the edge of the ragged line of wulfs. The acrid stench of wanstones tainted the air and a faint white glow emanated from the open throats of the wulfs, making it look as though they had swallowed the very stones themselves.

As Smokewind darted for the end of the line, the wulfs adjusted course, but their speed and great bulk worked against them. They could not all turn in time. Smokewind passed beyond the reach of the endmost wulf, but only just. It would have raked the horse's flanks if Kion had not landed a strike against the monster's lunging paws. The red slash scorched the beast's fur and raced across its body. Within moments, the flames had turned the creature into a living pyre. It staggered to the side, howling in agony, and yet still it swung about and attempted to right itself. For a moment Kion thought it would rejoin the others as they wheeled to face him once more. Yet though the creature lasted far longer than any haukmarn Kion had faced, at last it succumbed to the fire and fell into a smoldering pile.

"They are coming around for another pass," Kithian told Smokewind and Kion was too caught up in the rush of battle to wonder that he understood the sword's words as beast speech and not as those of his own tongue.

Smokewind sped to the opposite side of the re-forming pack, passing again around the end. The dreadwulfs could run at tremendous speed once they got going, but could not match Smokewind's nimbleness. Kion swung his blade in a wide arc as he closed with them a second time so that a tide of flame burst across his enemies. Four of the wulfs ran aflame across the valley, great loping mounds of fire tearing through the Lost Hylls.

As Smokewind wheeled to meet the pack a third time, he could no longer reach the end of the line and avoid them. The wulfs had slowed. They would not be fooled into rushing past him again. They fanned out to encircle the harried stallion. The flaming beasts tried to follow the rest of the pack, but as the others took off, they staggered to the ground in smoking heaps.

"Rom-del-lin, you'll have to run through them this time. Fear not. Kion will cut you a way."

Faithful in spite of the bounding terrors on every side, and paying heed only to the guidance of the glaive, Smokewind plunged into the line. Kion gashed the flank of a dreadwulf, setting its fur aflame, but more telling was the deep wound he opened in the creature's flesh. The wulf faltered and fell at once. So swift and sudden was Smokewind's charge that the snapping jaws of the dreadwulfs clamped only on the wind of his passing. Still, the horse was hard put, for the wulfs drew closer, tightening the loop. Two charged at the same time, one on either side. Kion could only strike one before it reached them. He feared that he and his brave steed would be brought down. But Smokewind had lightning in his hooves. Spurred by Kithian's fearless voice, the horse pranced and whirled with the litheness of raindrops on a willow branch. Smokewind dashed forward just before the two barreling beasts crashed into one another. The large bodies of the dreadwulfs were ill-suited to engage the quickness of the elusive horse. They lumbered and charged and howled and spun, but they could not pin Smokewind down.

With each near miss, the dreadwulfs came out worse for their troubles, for Kion landed fire and blows on snouts, flanks, legs, and haunches. Soon all but five of the wulfs had fallen to Truesilver's blade, though two of those he'd set aflame bounded after him, defying death. The horse screeched when their flames grazed its side, but Kion twisted to strike one of them in the throat as the other was at last consumed by the flames.

Then a great horn sounded from the south. A foreboding, sickening note devoid of all beauty or grace. Kion had heard it before, one cruel morning in Roving. The horn of the haukmarn. There, on the jagged spine of the hill beneath which he fought, twenty haukmarn appeared, their wanstone-embedded armor shimmering in the dark. Kion heard his death in their echoing cries.

And yet, a moment later the dreadwulfs ceased their attack. For another sound came in answer to the horn of the haukmarn —the pounding of many hooves. A host of mailed horsemen surged over the top of the hill to the west, a hundred strong. The dreadwulfs scampered about, unsure of what to do. But the second call of the haukmarn horn did its work and sent them racing off back up the hill toward their masters. All but two. The last two, whether from madness or because they were more savage than the others, dashed off to the north.

"For the Four Wards!" Kion called. Hope surged through him. He had met the dreadwulf pack and held his own, and now the wulfs and their masters would be vanquished by the Warding forces.

But the sense of triumph was short-lived. For the two fleeing wulfs were streaking up the same hill Cyprian and the other horses had taken. Kion might have stayed to finish off the haukmarn and wulfs alongside the Warding soldiers, but now his only thought was of Tiryn, Zinder, Endrith, and the scouts. What if they had not yet reached Dunach? What if the wulfs overtook them?

He spurred Smokewind into pursuit, but as the two dreadwulfs crested the rugged hill, they began to pull away. Smokewind, for all his feats during the battle, was too winded to catch them.

And yet, Kithian's rousing voice came once more to his aid.

"We must reach the others before the wulfs. You have given much, Rom-del-lin, but you have not yet given all. There is yet strength in your hooves for one last journey this day."

Stirred by Kithian's words, Smokewind galloped on, finding a last hidden well of strength. He braved once more the dangers of the rubbled path, running as he never had before. Only by the voice of the sword and perhaps some special grace was the noble steed saved from the jagged rocks and cracked ground. He rushed headlong into the darkness, never more deserving of his name than he was that night.

At the crest of each hill, they caught sight of the dreadwulfs, always too far ahead to reach, and yet Kion never entirely lost sight of his quarry. At last came the hill from which they could see the fortress of Dunach itself. The brownstone walls blazed with torches, and the battlements rose strong and dominant over the surrounding hills, and yet it was still half a mile to the safety of that bulwark.

As Smokewind strove to conquer the last few hills between them and the fortress, a horse shrieked from the valley beyond. The howls of the dreadwulfs answered and Smokewind strained to mount the rocky slope and gain Kion a view of the scene.

The wulfs had overtaken Endrith's party. The scouts and their horses lay cast to the ground, savaged by the rending claws of the vicious creatures. But Endrith, Zinder, and Tiryn maintained a slim lead, for the blood-thirsty beasts had slowed in bringing down the unfortunate soldiers.

As Cyprian and Drowen struggled to bring their riders up the far hill, the dreadwulfs resumed their pursuit, howling for another taste of blood. Kion closed in as well, having at last gained some ground, but he was too far back to reach his friends before they would be overtaken. Yet, before the wulfs could reach their prey, ten bowmen and eight longhounds sprang from the rocks. The dogs rushed at their enemies with a burst of baying challenges, eating up large stretches of ground with each graceful stride. Their speed surpassed even that of the dreadwulfs. They darted at the white-eyed beasts who outsized them fivefold, diving and nipping at their feet, careful to avoid the clamping maws that sought to entrap them. The bowmen unleashed a spray of arrows. Most found their mark, but the matted fur shunted aside the shafts as easily as plated armor. For all its bravery, all the ambush did was slow and harass the pursuing wulfs.

But the delay allowed Smokewind to gain ground. If the hounds could slow them but a few moments longer, Kion might be able to run down the dreadwulfs from behind.

"Kion!" Tiryn's shout echoed across the valley.

The dreadwulfs glanced back to see the bright blade and the dark horse which had eluded them before, now bearing down swiftly upon them. One vaulted over the skirmish of hounds before it, charging straight for Tiryn's horse. The other, mesmerized by the shining blade, if only for a moment, dropped its guard and allowed one of the hounds to dive in and fasten its jaws on the creature's throat. Two more dogs dashed in, tearing at the dreadwulf's legs. In the soft under places where the iron fur thinned, the attacks found their mark and the beast tumbled in a twisted heap. But it was not wholly defeated and the longhounds paid dearly for their attack. Two fell to the wulf's claws and did not stir.

Kion closed the final lengths to the staggering wulf before it could shake itself free of the tenacious hounds. He sliced into the creature's back with two furious blows before plunging Truesilver's tip deep into the flank. This time the beast failed to rise.

Heedless, the other wulf dashed on. It had already passed the bowmen and the other hounds.

Fwaaawp. A bolt from Zinder's crossbow hit the beast just below the eye but bounced off.

"Horn toads!" Zinder said, scrambling to load his next bolt.

With breathtaking speed, the dreadwulf sprang. It bared its wicked fangs, diving for Tiryn's neck. She jerked away, bracing for the attack, for there was no way to avoid it short of hurling herself from her horse.

"Swallow this!" Zinder reached around her and fired another bolt into the thing's open maw before its jaws could reach Tiryn. At the same time, he shoved her aside so hard she nearly tumbled off. By some unthinkable feat of acrobatics, the two riders ended up changing places. The brave act saved Tiryn, but not the fearless nyn. The bolt buried deep inside the creature's throat, but Zinder followed it. Through a miracle of quickness, the wulf only snatched him by the leg, but Zinder squealed in agony.

"Zinder!" The brave fool! Kion's heart faltered. He could not lose his friend. He dug his heels into Smokewind's flanks, but it was not enough. The poor horse had nothing left.

Endrith fell back to strike the dreadwulf with his sword. He landed a solid blow, but failed to draw blood, his blade deflecting off the beast's thick coat. The dreadwulf flung Zinder onto the rubbled hillside and turned to face Endrith. Its white eyes pulsing with hate, it gouged him in the chest with one claw, tearing through his mail, and raked Drowen with the other, pulling both to the ground.

But in taking down Endrith, the dreadwulf fell behind Tiryn and Cyprian. Eager to savage another of its foes, it surged forward and would have caught her again had the hounds not returned. Four leapt on the great wulf from behind. Though none managed to sink their teeth or claws in, the unexpected attack caused the wulf to misjudge a crevice. Its leg slipped into a crack and the mad beast rolled into the dust with the eager dogs piling in all around.

With a roar, Kion rode down the monster at last. Smokewind's hooves and Truesilver's flashing blade made a quick end of the snarling beast. The creature's eyes smoldered with one last cruel gleam and went gray as stones.

Cyprian reversed course back down the hill as the dogs moved in to ensure the wulf had breathed its last.

Drowen lay bleeding out on the ground, his powerful body unmoving. Endrith staggered to his feet, his face marred with blood and grit, but his eyes shining bright and clear.

"You truly are the Sword of the North," he said.

But the memory of his battle with the dreadwulfs had already fled from Kion's mind. For though Tiryn came riding up, safe and unharmed, Zinder lay face down amidst the scattered rocks of the hillside, his lively frame unsettlingly still.

Chapter 18

DUNACH

An attentive young soldier wearing the deep green tabard of Inris marched toward the wooden doors of the great hall. Kion and Endrith waited beside them, weary and downcast from all that had befallen before the gates of Dunach. After crossing the inner bailey they had been welcomed into the thick, squat keep. As with the rest of the fortress, the stone of the great hall was rough-hewn. Beyond the foyer, it had the appearance of a lofty cavern, thick with beams and strung with long emerald banners stitched with sunny marigolds into the fields. Flickering torches hung from sconces in the cinnamon-colored blocks. Between the color and the texture, the walls were more reminiscent of bark than cut stone. Arches graced the sides of the hall like arboreal fans. A dozen narrow tables of rich walnut ran in two files down the center of the room attended by a throng of chairs. No less than six oaken doors adjoined the room, besides the massive set that formed the entrance. All were reinforced with metal ribbing, as if their brute thickness was not enough to stand against attack. Any other day, Kion would have stood in awe at the vast chamber, the first castle he had ever set foot in, but his heart and mind lingered beyond the walls, chained to dark ruminations over the fate of his friend.

"Varlance Aonar will see you now," the glinthelm said. Though he kept a formal expression, his eyes strayed once or twice with obvious interest to Kion's naked blade. Kion had not recovered the scabbard after the battle and so had no way to sheathe it. Though at present the metal gave off no light of its own, it had a warm appearance, unlike the bluish-gray of natural steel, and of course the golden hilt and sparkling citrines embedded into it were of a quality unrivaled in all the land.

They rose from the bench where they'd been sitting and followed the soldier into a cramped, spiral staircase. Kion kept his distance from Endrith as they climbed, to keep from accidentally nicking him. He was not used to stairs, and the sword's length made for an awkward ascent up the narrow steps. The gems cast a faint, gossamer light upon the walls, which the soldier pretended not to notice, but he let slip another curious glance when they arrived at the first landing. The soldier had no doubt been informed about the battle with the dreadwulfs. The legend of the Sword of the North was growing, and yet a cloud of dismay hung over Kion. All Kithian's talk of Kion being ready to lead Warding to victory echoed hollow and empty in his thoughts. He had not even been able to protect his friend when the battle came. How could he defend an entire nation? What good was it if stories and legends were told of his battles but his friends did not live to hear them?

The soldier led them down a hall to another pair of formidable doors studded with metal. Swinging the doors aside, he ushered them into a large room with three great windows crisscrossed with iron latticework. A staunch oak desk occupied the center of the room. It had carved channels in the legs and the sides were engraved with men on rearing horses. Two lanterns of smoky brass hung from hooks in the ceiling, casting a summery glow bright enough to expose all but the farthest corners of the room.

"Varlance Aonar. Here are the men from the clash at the gates," the soldier said, saluting the man who had just risen from behind the desk. The varlance was a straight-backed man, well-cut, and light on his feet. He did not so much rise from the desk as spring—as though his body knew only two states, rest and action. If he had drawn a sword and issued a challenge right there it would have been the most natural thing in the world. He wore an emerald tabard with a gold bar on the shoulder. He had a narrow face with charcoal hair, and a short, angular beard. A dark silken patch covered his left eye, giving him a somewhat severe look, but his other eye shone with a perceptive interest that tempered his intimidating presence.

"Thank you, glinthelm. You may depart," Aonar said, his voice both rich and rhythmic, as if he must have said that phrase a thousand times before.

Kion doubted anyone from Furrow had ever met someone of such importance, not even Fielder Lorris. He ought to have been thrilled to be in the presence of someone of such high station, but just as when he'd been sitting in the great hall, his thoughts kept returning to the quiet room in the barracks where Zinder lay wandering somewhere between the doors of life and death. Tiryn was by his side, and Kion attempted to console himself with the knowledge that she would come and find him if anything happened. But the unmoving body of his friend and the utter silence that had fallen upon his normally chattering lips were carved into Kion's memory with deep strokes. The wound on Zinder's leg reminded him of the kinds of wounds his sheep had suffered at the hands of predators. He had lost many of his flock over the years to wild beasts. Though Zinder was surely made of sterner stuff, his survival was anything but assured. Kion had caught the panicked look on Tiryn's face when she was binding the wound. That, perhaps more than anything, dogged his thoughts as he stood before the varlance.

"Glithelm Endrith, well met. It is good to see you again, though I fear I will not like the reasons for your coming. What word do you bring from the east?"

Endrith gave him a cross-armed salute. "Grettling is overrun, Varlance. The Noathryn came by land and by sea and through treachery seized the gates. I barely escaped to bring word to Dunach. I fear the messengers bound for Quelling and Fennigar did not make it through."

Aonar turned away behind his desk. The windows of this room faced west, and he gazed into the black of night as if something within the vast dark wilds of Noath could be discerned with his one good eye.

"So, our embittered neighbors have joined the fray at last. I expected as much, only not so soon. This Vayd Mokàn must be shrewd indeed to have lured Ralstad into the fight when the haukmarn have conquered so little of Inris."

"If we had more numbers at Grettling, we may have held. The men fought like deepwood boars, but it was all for naught," Endrith said.

"Yes, such has been the state of things under Berintall since the ending of the last war. Our strongholds are more and more undermanned with each passing year. We are down to one hundred and eighty here, less than two full companies. It is well the Noathryn took to the sea and did not attack us here for I have not the men to defend this keep. But they will come. Soon. They will come." He left the window and his eye fell upon Kion. That keen gaze was enough to snap Kion from his brooding fears. "But not today. No, today at least, we have some good news to counter the bad. A boy with a bright sword has come to Dunach. Kion Bray, they tell me you are called, and Sword of the North. Most of the things they say about you can hardly be believed. You single-handedly defeated a pack of dreadwulfs? Is that true?"

Kion stared at the floor. He did not want to be thought of as a hero. Not when he had failed the best friend he had in all the world.

"Endrith and your men fought just as bravely. And if not for my horse, I would have been overwhelmed. But I did what I could. I only wish I had arrived at the gates sooner."

"And yet if you had not bested most of the pack, many men would not have ridden back to Dunach this night. I am told that one of your company was injured. Do not blame yourself. Even the best warrior cannot be in two places at once. For now, trust that your friend will pull through. My healer is well-skilled. He has brought many a man back from the edge of death who might otherwise have passed on." The varlance's voice resonated with such confidence that even Kion was tempted to hope. If life and death could have been commanded to do the varlance's bidding, there was little doubt they would have fallen in line. If only that was all that Zinder's fate depended upon.

"Thank you, my lord, for your words. I can only hope that proves to be the case this time." He looked to Endrith, who nodded reassuringly, but his eyes told another story.

"It appears you lost your scabbard in the fight. I will see to it that you have one sent to your quarters after we finish here. Is it true that this magnificent weapon of yours can make fire?"

"That's very generous of you." Kion held the sword before him, one hand on the hilt, the other cradling the blade. "Yes, the blade can make fire. This is Truesilver, forged by the Mastersmith long ago."

Aonar ran his fingers along the length of the weapon, his one eye narrowing.

"The Mastersmith. Indeed a master he must have been. But the metal is cool. How then does it make flame?"

"The Spark. The weapon's gifts are connected in some way to it, though I do not fully understand how. I am still learning. I have only had the blade for a short time."

"And this Mastersmith, who is he? Did he make other weapons such as this?"

"Yes. They are called glaives; though I do not know much about the others, or about the Mastersmith himself for that matter, only that he made them long ago and that it was he who gave the Spark and, it would seem, life itself."

"Life itself? The Spark? You speak many mysteries for one so young. Would that we had the time to unravel them. But war offers no time for such thought. Whoever he was, the Mastersmith well-earned his title. I have never seen a more skillfully crafted blade in all my days. You are welcome to stay here, Kion, as long as you like. Any slayer of a pack of dreadwulfs has more than earned his keep. Few are the men who can say they have slain even one. Dunach is hardly a place of comfort, but we have food and beds to spare, such as they are. Forgive me, but I have duties yet to attend to, and much to consider, in light of Endrith's news. However, I invite both of you—and your sister as well—to dine with me tomorrow night. I have some things I wish to discuss with you."

I have some things I wish to discuss with you. Those words loomed in Kion's thoughts long after they were said. Aonar would ask him to fight for Warding, Kion was sure of it.

"Yes, sir, we would be honored to dine with you," Endrith said, saluting again. He looked to Kion expectantly.

No doubt Kion should have felt honored as well, but his suspicions kept him from seeing it that way. And yet, how could he refuse? Even setting aside his rank, Aonar was providing them food and shelter, and his men had risked their lives to protect Zinder and Tiryn.

"Yes, Varlance. We'd be happy to join you," he said. Even if Aonar asked him to fight, that did not mean he would force him to. In any case, Kion couldn't leave before tomorrow night. The horses needed rest, especially after the battle with the dreadwulfs, and they had to stay at least long enough to find out if Zinder would survive his wounds and when he'd be fit to travel.

"Excellent. The glinthelm outside will see you to your quarters and provide you with a new scabbard. Get some rest. I'm sure you could use some after what you've been through," Aonar said, showing them to the door.

But Kion would not be able to truly rest until he knew whether or not Zinder would pull through.

When the light finally penetrated the slit near the ceiling that served as a window, Kion failed to notice. He'd been staring at the opening so long, and the light had come so gradually, that he did not mark the change. But at some indefinable point, the advent of dawn impressed itself upon him and he rose from the hard bed where he had spent the night. He could not bear another moment of waiting; he had to see Zinder.

He strapped on his sword belt with the new chestnut leather scabbard Varlance Aonar had sent him. Though True-silver wouldn't strictly be needed on a visit to the healing quarters, Kion had not been separated from his glaive since it had come to him outside of Roving. Leaving Kithian behind felt unnatural at this point, like leaving behind a part of himself.

"You should have slept," Kithian said. He had spoken little during the night, hoping no doubt that sleep would eventually overtake his troubled glaivebond if he let him be.

Kion eased his way past Endrith and the four empty beds in their quarters. He waited until he was outside before answering his glaive.

"What do you know about sleep?" he said. "You're a sword. You never sleep…do you?"

"No. But all living things have limitations. And difficulties come when we push against them."

"Limitations? What limitations do you have?"

"Well, have you ever thought of what life would be like with no hands or feet? Or if only one person could hear you?"

"And animals."

"Yes, well, animals are not the greatest conversationalists. Not that I have much desire to converse. That is more of a human need. Most of the time there is too much to think upon to waste time on words."

"I suppose you do lack certain freedoms. But you never get hungry or tired or feel pain. On the whole your advantages far outweigh your disadvantages, wouldn't you say?"

"And I say you will have fewer disadvantages if you get some sleep."

That was true enough, but Kion could not follow that advice

just now. There were other, more important things than his own well-being.

He descended the stairs and stood turning about, attempting to orient himself inside the unfamiliar building. This floor of the barracks had no windows. Vague table-sized shapes lurked in the dark. He pulled Truesilver just far enough out of the sheath to get some light. Ah, yes, he remembered now. Zinder's room was at the end of the hall. It was the one on the left. He ventured in that direction, avoiding the furniture and eventually arriving at Zinder's door.

Kion gave the door a few timid taps. When no one answered, he repeated the action with greater force.

"He may need his rest, too, you know. It is still awfully early," Kithian said.

"Perhaps." Kion decided to try one more time and then—

A man shorter than Tiryn, lean-faced and half bald, with large splotches like brown raindrops across his cheeks, appeared at the door, opening it only enough to show his head. He laid an accusatory finger across his lips.

"May I help you?" the man said in a perturbed whisper, his expression all frown and fret. For a healer, he was hardly the most fit-looking person Kion had ever met.

"I need to see my friend, the nyn," Kion said.

"I told you last night that visits will only slow down his recovery. He needs—"

"Eh, healer? What's that about?" Zinder's voice was hoarse and muffled behind the door, but it gave Kion a surge of joy just to hear it.

"Nothing, Mr. Hamryn. Please, go back to sleep."

"It's Kion Bray or the moon. Send in the lad. It's not like I have the sprull."

"But, Mr. Hamryn—"

"Are you my healer or my jailer? Don't make me get out of this bed." Some of the old vigor came through in Zinder's warning, though his voice still had an unhealthy crackle to it.

The healer, who was dressed only in a long nightgown, dragged the door open with great indignation. "Please, only a few minutes. He may seem as if he's doing better, but he must be careful not to overexert himself."

Given Zinder's boundless energy, Kion doubted the healer would get his wish, with or without Kion present.

Zinder lay upon a meager pallet with an old blanket covering his lower half. One side of the covering bulged like a smuggler's breeches.

"You're awake, Zinder!" Kion tried to keep his voice down, but his words drew the ire of the healer, who gave him a "Shh-hh!" that was rather loud itself. Kion tried again at a softer pitch that seemed to pass muster. "And you're talking. That's an encouraging sign."

"You might regret it once we start back on the road." Zinder grasped Kion's hand and pulled it close. His grip was shaky, but the skin no longer blazed with fever. "Tiryn told me what happened. You and that sword did a little cooking, it seems. Tell me, how was the meal?"

"Awful. It was the worst thing I've ever tasted, Zinder. You almost died."

"Now, lad. Don't knock yourself about. Nyn may not live long, but we live all the way to the end. And I never thought for once it was my time, not even when that cave of a mouth opened to swallow me whole."

"It all happened so quickly. I couldn't stop it. The wulfs were too fast."

"But not fast enough for a nyn!"

"There's no doubt your quick thinking saved Tiryn's life. For that I owe you a debt I'll never be able to repay."

Zinder patted Kion's hand. "I just happened to be in the right place at the right time. You'd have done the same if you'd been in that saddle."

"Well, I'm not so sure I'd have been quick enough to pull off that maneuver you used. But how's your leg?"

"Not broken, which is a mercy. The healer said it was the size of my leg that saved me. A regular one would have been snapped in two, but mine slipped between the beast's fangs. Never thought these stubby sticks would turn out to my advantage."

Kion allowed a bit of relief to seep in. Hopefully, Zinder was being honest and not just putting a good face on it.

"May I see?"

Zinder flicked aside the blanket. The bandages covered his leg from the ankle to the thigh in a thick, cottony cocoon. "Not much to see, is there? The healer told me I lost a lot of blood. I'm going to have to eat for two if I want to get back to full steam."

"As if you didn't already."

Zinder chuckled, but his face pulled into a painful grimace, which somehow made him laugh all the more.

From his place near the door, the healer gave a hearty cough. "Mr. Hamryn, I really must insist that you get your rest."

Zinder worked the laugh out of his lungs and sank back into his pillow. "All right, all right, Curmelion. I'll obey."

Five other beds held the slumped forms of wounded soldiers, though in the dark they were little more than colorless clumps with pale faces or tufts of hair at one end. Thankfully, none of them had been awakened by Zinder's little eruption of mirth.

"I suppose I've stayed long enough," Kion said, though the last thing he wanted to do was leave. "You'll heal with time. That's what I needed to know."

Zinder squeezed Kion's hand as he rose.

"Thank you, lad. You may not be able to see it right now, but you saved us all."

Then why did he feel like he'd failed?

"You would have done the same thing if you'd been in my place."

"Ha! Using my own words against me. One good turn deserves another, I suppose."

The healer cleared his throat.

"Looks like the prison visit is over," Kion whispered, which drew a wide grin from Zinder. "But the healer's right. You need your rest. I'd best be going."

Zinder nodded in weary assent and the two friends exchanged warm good-byes. Kion stopped on his way out and spoke in a low voice to the healer. "How long until he's able to travel?"

"An eight-mark at least. If I had better medicine, I could speed his recovery, but I can only work with what I'm given."

"An eight-mark?" No, that would not do. Not at all. "Thank you. And I'm sorry for forcing you to get up so early."

Kion shuffled down the hallway, barely lifting his feet off the floor.

"Zinder looks well, all things considered. His body is nearly as strong as his spirit," Kithian said.

"Yes. And for that I am thankful. But did you hear what the healer said? We can't stay here for an eight-mark while Zinder heals. Mother might be dead before then. What am I going to do?"

"We will speak of that later. Right now, my advice to you remains the same as before. You should get some sleep."

The weariness he'd been wrestling against all night sank deep and suddenly into his bones. Perhaps Kithian was right. For once Kion's worries would have to wait. He was going to need his full strength to face his next decision: what to do about Zinder.

Chapter 19

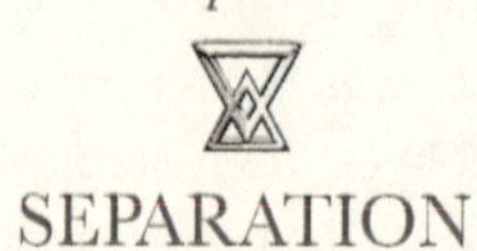

SEPARATION

For the first time since finding his glaive, Kion had to leave Truesilver behind. A private meal with the varlance was no place for weapons. Kithian's absence left a cold hollow place inside of him, like waking up to an ashen hearth in the middle of a winter night. And yet, in some ways, Kion needed the separation. He needed time to sort out the path he would take. He had to make this decision apart from anyone's influence, even Kithian's.

The party took their meal in the officer's hall upon a large oak table, reminiscent of Varlance Aonar's desk in its thickness and craftsmanship, though twice as long. As was the case throughout the fortress, the emerald and marigold banners of Inris were present here as well. They lined two of the walls, but these were interspersed with other, more alien banners—trophies of the victories won by the forces of Dunach over the years. Little had been done to enhance the appearance of these captured standards. They looked as if they'd been pulled straight from the battlefield and set upon the walls. Some were so tattered and faded it would have been impossible to tell they were banners at all if they had not been hanging with the ones representing Inris. Opposite the entrance, shelves groaning with books ran from floor to ceiling. The spines, some as thick as fence posts, hugged each other so tightly a sheet of paper would hardly fit between. Kion had never seen so many books in one place. Though he himself was not much for reading, the books immediately drew Tiryn's attention.

"Do all fortresses contain as many books as this one?" she asked, drawn out of her usual shyness by the presence of such a literary trove.

"No, most books are too valuable to risk being captured by the enemy." The tone of Aonar's reply hinted that he shared Tiryn's love of the written word. "Sadly, these are nothing more than record books. Lists of troop movements and accounts of battles described in only the most rudimentary fashion. Twenty men killed, fifteen injured, such-and-such Noathryn chieftain defeated, that sort of thing. It's unfortunate that the bravery and sacrifice of these men are lost when reduced to the barest facts. Still, you are welcome to look through them after dinner, if you like."

Tiryn's enthusiasm dimmed considerably and her old nature reasserted itself. "I see. Thank you for the offer."

"And how fares your friend, young lady?" the varlance said. "My healer Jarmond tells me you've been quite an assistance to him."

Tiryn clasped her hands behind her back. "Zinder's doing much better, thank you."

"It pleases me to hear it. Nyn are hardier than they look. Still, I imagine it will be several days before he's able to walk on his own."

The words "several days" stirred up troubling thoughts for Kion. They had already lost so much time going overland. His mother did not have "several days" for them to spare.

Tiryn wrung her hands, looking like she wanted to respond, but said nothing.

Aonar spread his arms toward the simple meal set before them.

"Now, please, everyone, have a seat."

Though the table sat ten, only four seats were filled on that night. The varlance desired to speak with his visitors undistracted by the presence of other soldiers.

Kion and Tiryn sat down across from Aonar and Endrith in

front of steaming bowls of white bean soup and loaves of bread which smelled as bright as an oven. The soup was not as good as Mother's, but it was fair enough. By contrast, the bread was a dense rye baked that morning and bursting with malty texture. Kion was hungry enough to appreciate the meal, but as the dinner unfolded, his interest waned and his mind wandered to things other than food and drink. His thoughts roamed from the stark bed where Zinder lay, unable to walk, to beyond the unknown expanse of Noath, past the lapping shoreline, and finally to the cruelest stretch of land in all of the Four Wards: Tinesplitter Isle. Instead of fresh bread and the company of an accomplished man like Varlance Aonar, his mother had no more than scraps tossed grudgingly at her by Noathryn slavemasters. And though these thoughts were foremost in Kion's mind, at the back of them hovered another troubling thought: the fear that Aonar, like Roardin, would ask him to join the Warding army, or worse still, that he would not even ask, but demand it. Such concerns tainted every word that was spoken so that Kion could hardly enjoy what should have been a pleasant meal in an ancient fortress sharing the company of one of the most powerful men in all of Inris.

Aonar raised his mug to his guests, who followed him in the toast. "To brave travelers and an end to this war," he said. When he had downed a long swallow he continued. "Now, my friends, I have heard of your exploits against the dreadwulfs and how you saved our messenger, Endrith, but I know little else about you. Tell me, Kion and Tiryn, where are you from?"

"We're from Furrow," Kion said, questioning the words even as they left his lips. Was it right to say they were from a place that no longer existed? But it was the best answer he could give.

"Then you have my sympathies. You have traveled far if you come from there, but you are not merchants or nobles as far as I can tell. What profession did you practice in your village before the haukmarn put it to the flame?"

"We were..." Kion struggled to find a way to answer without

having to alert Endrith about his past. The echoes of a thousand jeers stiffened his tongue. "Sheepstink," "woolhead," "snotgobber," "ramrotter," "dimwit." He'd heard all of these and many more from farmers for as long as he could remember.

"We were shepherds," Tiryn said, guileless as ever. She had not experienced the farmers' cruelty in the same way as Kion, for she'd rarely gone to the village. Kion's eyes leapt to Endrith. What would the farm boy think of them now?

Endrith gave an amicable nod, friendly as always. "Well, that just goes to show that shepherds are as brave as anyone, right, Varlance?"

Kion could hardly believe his ears. Had those words truly come from the mouth of a farmer? He felt very far from home just then. In the space of a moment, the mocking faces and condescending looks of seventeen years on the Tors shook within their deep-rooted foundations inside Kion's heart. The scars were still there, but the fear and the shame and the torment transformed from a thing of stone—an immovable certainty, impossible to change—to a thing of clay—malleable, vulnerable, and able to be formed into something new—all by the unexpected gift of Endrith's words.

"Indeed," the varlance said. "Bravery does not come by birth or station. Some of my best soldiers were once shepherds. To have come this far on your own shows bravery enough, dreadwulfs or no. But now you travel the land not with sheep and cudgels, but with stallions and a sword unmatched in its making. What brings you to the far reaches of Inris in these dark times?"

Despite the sudden sense of freedom now fluttering inside from Endrith's words, Kion was all too glad to turn the subject to the purpose of their journey.

"We're searching for our mother. We believe she's being held prisoner on Tinesplitter Isle."

"We hope to head there as soon as Zinder is well again," Tiryn said. The words tore at the frayed edges of Kion's heart. If only it were that easy. It was such a cruel task to have to choose between two people he so dearly loved.

"Tinesplitter? You are sure of this?" Aonar said.

"Tadgart Ilk told us. He's in the service of the haukmarn," Kion said.

"Ah yes, the traitor Ilk. Are you certain that you trust the word of one such as him?"

"Swordswain Roardin captured him in Fennigar. We are certain that he is telling the truth."

"For your sake, I hope that is so."

"What can you tell us of Tinesplitter Isle?"

"Very little, I'm afraid. It is a place no Inrisian has seen in hundreds of years. All my scouts have ever been able to tell me about it is that the Noathryn believe it to be under a curse."

"A curse? What kind of curse?"

Tiryn's bread remained half dipped in her soup as she listened to Aonar's reply.

"The accounts vary. Everything from an evil wind, to monstrous creatures attacking those who travel there, to the land being haunted by some powerful spirit. Even the Noathryn refuse to go there. If the histories are to be believed, the land once belonged to the Frindalians, a people distantly related to the Noathryn and who, by all accounts, may have been there before Noath was founded. They were a mysterious people, and little is known of them, but it is said that they cursed the land when they were driven from it by the Noathryn and now no living thing may survive there."

The expression on Tiryn's face left little doubt that she believed the varlance's far-fetched tale. Then again, she had always been partial to legends and outlandish stories.

"Well, I suppose we'll find out if it is truly cursed when we reach there. We have to cross Noath first. That's what worries me now," Kion said.

Aonar took a moment to gather his thoughts. Perhaps he was weighing the dangers of such a journey, or perhaps he was considering whether or not now was the time to ask Kion to join the Warding forces. Kion tensed, expecting the worst.

"With most of the Noathryn off to war, I doubt you will have much trouble crossing the countryside. I worry that the real danger awaits you at journey's end. Beware the words of one such as Ilk."

The varlance surely meant no ill toward Kion in this remark, but Kion's defenses rose at what he perceived as an attempt to dissuade him from his purpose.

"I have bested haukmarn and dreadwulf alike on my journey. And I will overcome whatever the Noathyrn have in store for me on that island."

"Haukmarn and dreadwulfs, terrible as they are, are foes that can be beaten by force of arms. But the schemes of wicked men can harm in ways no armor can protect you from. The word of a traitor is a knife that pierces the hand of those who lean upon it."

Kion's eyes flicked down into his mug. The water shone black as a clouded night in the dark pewter vessel. The memory of his fight with the dreadwulfs crept back into his thoughts. The haukmarn had twice attacked them on their road to Tinesplitter. Had Ilk escaped from Fennigar and told Vayd of Kion's intention to free his mother? It was certainly possible. If so, would an ambush be waiting for him once he reached the island? Or could there be other monstrous things besides dreadwulfs, as Kithian had said, lurking in the far corners of the world?

"I do not know what dangers we may face, Varlance, but Ilk spoke the truth. My mother is on that island if she's anywhere. And if it's a trap, or if some curse lies between me and that place, I will risk any danger to find her."

The more he spoke, the more he realized that the decision about Zinder was making itself for him. He could not let his sister and friend walk down this road. Perhaps Zinder's injury would turn out to have been for the better when all was said and done.

Varlance Aonar's expression grew reflective, his eyes set

upon some other time and place. "I admire your courage. I lost this eye to a dreadwulf many years ago. The heartless beast would have taken my life as well had my son not come to my aid. He drove the beast away, but paid for it with his own life. Fardil was about your age when he died. He would have completed his twenty-eighth year six days ago had he lived." Aonar's eye flashed and Kion knew from the look in them that the time had come. Aonar would make his plea. "You remind me of him. He had a great talent for the blade, but he did not possess one such as yours. A warrior with a sword like that could turn back the tide of this war, could check the haukmarn advance before it reaches too far. We cannot afford to lose so great a weapon in the cursed Noathryn wilderness. I want you to join the Warding forces here at Dunach. I want you to fight for your people. I will even allow you to enter the ranks as a swordswain, as if you had been trained in the Batal at Avelar, for you have already more than proven your worth in battle."

Kion gripped his mug tightly and did his best to keep his composure. Now more than ever he knew that he had to leave this place. His mother's life depended upon it. He could not be swept off to fight this war. Not now.

"I am honored by your offer, Varlance, but as I said, I am going to Tinesplitter."

"I do not wish to rob you of all hope, but even if there is a Noathryn camp on that accursed isle, and even if your mother is there, women rarely last long in Noathryn slave camps. Do not throw your life away in a vain pursuit. The Four Wards need you. You can help us win this war."

Tiryn dropped her bread in her soup. "Please, sir, don't ask this of him. Think of your own son. If you could do something to save him, to bring him back, I'm sure you would. Please don't deny us the chance to save our own mother. Oh, please don't make my brother fight in this war."

The room grew quiet. Aonar gave Tiryn a look of regret, as if he had no choice in the matter.

"That is true. I would do anything to save him if I could. But since I cannot, it would be foolish of me to try. Reason tells me that you will not return from your journey. And there are others whom Kion *can* save—men and women all across this land, from villages like Furrow to the great city of Madrigal to all the farms and towns in between."

"I will gladly serve you, Varlance, once my mother is safe, but until I know for certain that she is beyond hope, I cannot fight in this war," Kion said, pushing his bowl and mug away. He would have risen and left but a warning look from Endrith made him think better of it.

"Both of you are young and ignorant perhaps of the laws of the land and the ways of war. The margrave claims the allegiance of all those who live within Inris. Some choose to fight of their own will and others come when they are called. We are undermanned at every outpost and city. I am only doing what I deem best for the defense of the Four Wards."

Kion eyed the banners, recalling Kithian's words about leading Warding soldiers. Had he foreseen this coming? Had he been trying to prepare Kion for this encounter with the Varlance? But then, as now, Kion was not ready for this path. He had to find a way out.

"This is all so sudden, Varlance. We came seeking food and shelter, nothing more. And while we deeply appreciate your aid to us, and the bravery of your men in fighting to protect us at the gates, I fear that I cannot answer your call at this time. Please understand. I will return to fight for you as soon as I have found her. I give you my word."

Aonar set his jaw, his one eye restive from the conflict that raged within. To his credit, he was no Sevelius, imposing his will as he saw fit, wielding the authority of his rank like a weapon. No doubt Aonar could have simply demanded Kion to serve, but he at least had attempted persuasion first. But now Kion, Tiryn, and Endrith all stared at him, waiting for the axe of his authority to fall, as surely it must.

"You do remind me of Fardil. He, too, had a will like yours. And a heart. I do not think he would approve of me forcing you to fight against your will. I fear that I may be allowing you to go to your death and surrendering a chance at victory in doing so, but your sister is right. We must do what we can to save those we love. I would indeed give anything to share a meal with Fardil one last time. And so, in honor of his memory, I shall allow you to go. But I will hold you to your promise. Should you return, I expect to fight alongside you and drive the haukmarn back to their ravaged lands with the fire of your blade."

Kion bowed his head in gratitude for Aonar's change of heart. He could fight under a leader like this, one who had compassion for those under him, one who saw them not merely as soldiers but men with lives of their own, as mothers' sons.

"Thank you, Varlance. You will not regret your decision. I will return. You may be sure of it. And when I do, I will do honor to the memory of your son and fight in his place."

Tiryn squeezed Kion's hand in elation and relief and gave Aonar the largest smile her face could give.

But as Kion looked to the door, knowing that the meal was over and that he had escaped the snare set before him, the lightness of his heart quickly faded. For Aonar was not the only one who had been forced to make a hard decision this day. Kion had had to make one of his own. And now that he had, he would have to tell Tiryn what she would not want to hear: that he must leave her behind and journey across Noath alone.

A light rain misted the bailey. The path to the barracks grew heavier with each step. Tiryn rambled on about how relieved she was that the varlance had decided to let Kion go, and about what a great and noble man he was for doing so. And that was not all. She had just as much to say about the great honor it had been to dine with the varlance. From there she went on about the majestic and stately atmosphere of the fortress. The massive stones, the cunning archways, the enduring solidity of the doors —even the craftsmanship of the lanterns—none of these had failed to catch her observant eye. On and on she waxed about their evening, oblivious to Kion's inner wrestlings. He feigned interest, but only heard every third or fourth sentence. He wandered on, heedless of the drizzle, the buildings, and the walls that rose all around them. Kion arrived, as if by sleep-walking, at the base of the stairs, just inside the entrance to the barracks.

Tiryn looked up, her eyes searching his, her brow weighed with doubt. She looked so very much like Mother. But that fact would not save her from Kion's decision.

"Something's troubling you, Kion. You haven't said five words to me since we left the varlance's table."

The air lodged in Kion's throat. It was a wonder he could still breathe. Now that it came to it, the words died on his tongue.

"Fine, you don't have to tell me. Jarmond and I are going hunting for *sangrist* tomorrow. It's the best thing for healing wounds quickly. You could come with us if you'd like. Truesilver's sight might come in handy on a search like that."

Kion forced some air into his lungs. He could wait no longer. He had no choice but to tell her the truth.

"Blood root? I suppose that might help, but I can't come with you, Tiryn."

"Of course, you need to train. Or perhaps you're going to meet with the varlance to learn more about the way through Noath before we leave? I'm sure he'll want to help you, now that you're practically fighting under him. I don't want you to have to fight, but I suppose you really don't have a choice, do you? The war will just go on and on if no one stands up to drive the haukmarn back. Still, I suppose I'll have you for a little longer at least."

The tightness in his throat redoubled, but he fought against it. He looked her straight in the eye instead. It was the only thing to do in such matters. Rip the bandage from the wound or it would fester.

"I can't go because I won't be here."

"You won't? You want to stay by Zinder's side, then, to keep him—"

He stepped forward so that she could see his face in the light. "I won't be here because I'm going to the island on my own. I will leave at daybreak."

Tiryn's slender fingers locked onto him with the swiftness of a hawk. Her words came shrill and desperate.

"No, Kion, you can't! You can't leave without me—and Zinder, after how faithful he's been to you, to both of us? You can't do this! You wouldn't!"

Kion willed himself to answer in a calm, measured voice. It took every drop of will he had to endure the terrible ache that stung his heart.

"It's a hard choice, I know. And not one I made easily. But we've already lost a day here. Every delay could mean the difference between life and death for Mother. I cannot wait any longer."

"Kion, no. How will you survive all alone? I know that sword makes you almost invincible in battle, but without Zinder, you'll be lost, I'm sure of it. And without me to cook for you and take care of you, you'll waste away. What if you get hurt? Who will nurse you back to health? We're family, Kion. That means we stay together—through high and low—through everything."

Kion paused to let Tiryn's emotions run their course. That was always the best way with her. He'd watched his mother do it a thousand times. Though he rarely had the patience to wait such things out, he found the patience now.

"Don't look at me like that," she said, struggling through her tears. "I know I'm probably just spouting out nonsense. You can survive on biscuits and water, and Smokewind could probably follow his nose through a snowstorm, but it's just not right. You can't abandon us here, Kion. Please don't do this!"

"I'm not abandoning you. I'll be back in an eight-mark. You'll barely even know that I'm gone."

"Barely even—barely even? Kion, my heart will break in half every day you're gone. It will be splintered to dust by the time you return—if you return. And what if you don't make it back? What then? Have you thought about that? What am I supposed to do when I've lost Father and Mother, and then you too? You're all I have left, Kion. If you go on your own, I know I'll never see you again."

"Tiryn, that won't happen. I'll come back. I promise. Listen to me now. Mother's life hangs by a thread. I can't wait for Zinder. I'm sure that between you and the healer, he'll snap back to his old self twice as fast, but I can't wait that long. It's all bent and broken, I know. Don't think I like it any more than you, but I have to do this."

Tiryn let go, fumbling back against the baluster, leaning against it for support. Kion reached out to steady her, fearing she might fall, but she sank down on her own. She sat huddled on the stairway in silence for the longest time, tears covering her bright red cheeks. Something dark and enigmatic descended upon her brow. It was a look Kion had never seen before. She scrubbed her cheeks dry and found her voice once more.

"You don't understand, Kion. I had another vision. I didn't want to tell you about it. I thought maybe—I hoped it was just a dream—but after what you just told me I have to tell you. In my dream, you left me to search for Mother. A strange darkness, like a rushing shadow, overtook me. I don't know where Zinder was, but you went away on your own and left me to be swallowed by the darkness. That much I remember. I've thought about it many times since. I don't know what it means. The darkness might be the haukmarn. Maybe they will overrun this fortress while you're gone. But whatever it is, you can't leave us, Kion. You have to wait—just a few days more. Mother's stronger than you think. She'll hold on. I know she will. I'll find the blood root and Zinder will get better and we'll go find her together. Just a few more days, that's all I ask."

Kion wrapped his arm around his sister's trembling frame. With great effort he spoke in firm and quiet words, each one as torturous for him as it was for her.

"You may believe in that vision. But I can't risk Mother's life on one of your dreams. Even if there's something to them, even if they are visions or prophecies, people are not bound by such things. We can change our dreams. We can alter our fate. Nothing is set in stone. And I can't wait any longer. I have to go."

Tiryn crumpled into a ball, falling into voiceless sobs. The wrenching sorrow of her tears almost undid Kion's resolve, but he bowed himself against his emotions and held fast to what he knew to be right. When he returned with Mother, all tears would be forgotten, all hurts would be forgiven. That was all he had to cling to in that dark and terrible moment. It was the one thing that kept him from giving in and crying along with her.

Chapter 20

PAYING A DEBT

There are few pairings in nature more comforting than the deep still hush of night blended with the quiet mist of after-rain. Such a nocturnal hush now wrapped itself around Tiryn like a blanket, her sole comfort as she trundled through the scattered brush east of Dunach. Her limbs ached for rest and every other minute some hard-edged pebble worked its way inside her shoes. Very little grew on the bony escarpments surrounding the fortress. And as if she hadn't already been discouraged enough, she'd torn her dress wading through a patch of bramble.

"Tiryn, what were you thinking? You'll never find it in the middle of the night. You'd need the eyes of a nyn to find *sangrist* in the dark," she mumbled to herself.

Poor old Zinder. He didn't deserve this. To lose his smithy, risk his life saving both Tiryn and Kion, and be dragged halfway across Inris only to be abandoned. It was bad enough to betray a friend, but to leave without telling him? It would break Zinder's heart when he found out. Oh, he'd laugh it off, most likely, but Tiryn knew that deep down he loved Kion like a son and was more sentimental than he let on.

She stumbled over something knobby and crashed onto the shingly soil, stifling the screech that leapt in her throat. If someone discovered she was outside the fortress, it would be high water for Endrith. He wasn't supposed to let her out, not after the haukmarn and their dreadwulfs had come practically to the gates. But after she begged and explained and begged some more, he gave in. She wished he would have come with her. She needed all the help she could get. But someone had to be at the gate to let her back in and he could hardly ask someone else to take his post.

Tiryn scrambled to her feet and brushed herself off. She needed to hurry. Endrith would only be at the gate for another hour or so. That didn't give her much time.

Scurrying over a slope, she stepped down a little drop into a good-sized patch of bushes. At last, some good fortune. She went down on hands and knees and felt about. She couldn't see well enough to tell if any blood root was here. The half-veiled slash of crescent moon bled all the colors to gray and ghosted the details, but her hands would know when she found it. How often had she rooted about like this with her mother in the woods of the Tors? If only Mother were here now. She would find it in a snap. Then again, if Mother were here she wouldn't need to be searching for it. Oh, why did everything have to go so wrong?

Tiryn pawed her way through the underbrush, patting down every inch twice over, but the prickly plant she so desperately sought eluded her once again. Defeated, she hobbled to her feet and plodded on aimlessly across the next stretch of ground, half-heartedly dusting off her dress, more out of habit than to any good purpose, for it was hopelessly soiled.

Shuffling onward, she nearly staggered into a small tree but pulled herself back just as the bark brushed her nose. Tenter-hooks, that would have smarted. Grateful to have dodged a disaster, she leaned against the trunk for a short reprieve. A few promising blades of grass stubbornly clung to the barren dust-bed between the roots.

She dropped to her knees, but once more her search proved fruitless. Nothing. She pounded the ground, her fist banging against some rocks.

"Ouch!" She was quick to cover her mouth. She stopped and listened, waiting for the hue and cry from the fortress walls. Her anxious breathing was all that came back. Maybe she was far enough away, or the night winds were kind enough not to carry her voice back to Dunach. The fortress rose off in the distance, high and dark and phantasmal, like something from a dream. The sight galvanized her. She had to hurry before her vision came true, before the darkness overtook her and Kion left forever.

She rose to dust herself off once more. Her miserable dress was a positive dish rag by now. But before she could finish her futile routine, her foot caught on a tree root, and down she went again.

This time she managed to trap the cry before it could escape. But that didn't make it hurt any less. If anything, it probably hurt more, for she was denied the release of voicing her pain. She was tempted to pound her fist again, but she no longer had the strength to be angry. The fall had knocked the fight right out of her. She rolled over and lay on her back, looking up at the indifferent sliver of moon that should have been guiding her to the blood root, but which kept shying away behind nettlesome clumps of clouds. Her time was up. There would barely be enough time to run back to the gate before Endrith was relieved of his duties. She'd failed. Some mountains were just too impossible to climb, no matter how hard you tried, no matter how much you wanted—

Wait...what was that, pressing into the small of her back? The shape was hard and prickly and...she flipped over, quick as a fish, and grabbed hold of it. Yes, this was it! This was what she'd been looking for all this time! Her fingers dug mad as a mole. In the span of a dozen frenzied heartbeats it was out: a dirty, bloated stalk with prickly feelers and warm to the touch. She couldn't see the deep red tint, but she didn't need to. Her fingers knew.

She had found the blood root at last.

Endrith and Zinder kept a vigilant watch as rain pittered across the bailey. Tiryn was too nervous to look. She hadn't slept all night, but that didn't matter. It wasn't lack of sleep that kept her staring at her bedraggled dress. It was the dreadfulness of not knowing whether Kion would listen. Waiting was bad enough when you were expecting something wonderful. When you feared the worst, it was just about the most awful thing imaginable.

To pass the time and to keep her spirits from sinking, she half-sang, half-hummed a little tune.

Free as a whistle on the breeze
The wandering lad came janglin'
Singing songs to those that he pleased
And folk came 'round a-listenin'

His songs they brought him far from home
His restless feet a-wanderin'
His dreams like tides of churning foam
Never would cease their thunderin'

Until there traipsed beneath the sky
A maid with brown eyes glimmerin'
Stilled his song and captured his eye
And set his heart a-swivelin'

Love arose like the break of dawn
She smiled at all his flatterin'
They danced upon the fresh green lawn
And peace at last came settlin'

Across the plains with a whistle on the breeze

"That was lovely," Endrith said, hovering over her with his cloak extended to keep her dry. Tiryn had a cloak of her own, but it was the gentlemanly thing to do. She and Endrith sat in the back of the cart Aonar had given them. Zinder sat up front. The cart was a good foot longer than Zinder's and even though it was loaded with provisions and tools, Tiryn had plenty of room to stretch her aching legs.

"My father wrote it for my mother," she said. The past few years, it had hurt to sing it, and she had all but given up doing so. But today it brought no sorrow. Today it brought strength. Kion was still his father's son. And he would not deny his sister twice. Not when she'd worked so hard to find what they needed to help Zinder and keep them all together.

Zinder scooted forward to the edge of his seat. "Look! There's the little shirker! Ah, he's in for it now."

"You're not going to go too hard on him, are you?" Tiryn said. "I told you why he made the decision that he did."

"I'll go as hard as I have to. Some heads need a good knuckling now and then."

The dribbling rain muted the echo of Smokewind's hooves upon the flagstones. Kion's eyes flashed with surprise in the dark when he spied the cart at the gate, and just as quickly they gave way to displeasure.

"Fire and ice, Tiryn. What in the Four Wards are you doing here? You promised you wouldn't tell Zinder until after I was gone."

"Well, that's because, you see, things have changed. That was before…What I mean to say is…" Her prepared speech fizzled on her lips.

Zinder came to her rescue. "What she means to say is that there has been a shift in the circumstances, a change in our fortunes, if you will, a new development that you hadn't accounted for."

Kion pulled on the reins, and looked as if he might just ride off in anger, but then came that look in his eye. Truesilver was telling him something.

Kion huffed in response to the imperceptible words and let the reins go slack.

"And what would that development be?"

"Me!" Zinder thrust his bad leg, still wrapped like a cocoon, into the air. This induced a grimace, but he went on, chattering away through the discomfort. "Your sister, unlike you, didn't give up on me, you see. She scratched her way to some blood root in the middle of the night and I feel as good as a pie in the oven. It's miraculous. Even the healer said so."

"You don't expect me to believe you made a full recovery in one night." Despite his disapproval of what Tiryn had done, the little smile creasing up around the corners of his mouth showed that Zinder's liveliness was already having some success in weakening Kion's resistance.

Zinder, wincing and careful to move more gingerly, rose with the help of a smooth black cane the healer had given him. Tiryn shifted toward him in case he lost his balance.

"Of course I haven't made a full recovery. If I had, do you think I'd be thumping around in this spool of yarn?" He tapped his bandaged leg with the cane, his eyes starting from a sudden flash of pain. "But the healer said that I will recover in half the time with the blood root—a four-mark or so—which is just about as long as it will take us to reach the western shore."

"I suppose your plan is to ride in the back of that cart." Kion surveyed the wooden construction hitched to Cyprian. He cut a glance at Endrith. "I assume this is your doing?"

Endrith gave an apologetic shrug. "With the varlance's permission. I hope you'll forgive me, but I thought even the Sword of the North could use some companions."

"I don't doubt you meant well. But, Zinder, do you honestly think you'll recover as quickly on the road as you would in the healing quarters?"

"Well, we won't know until we try, but—"

"I can't let you do this."

"Let? Excuse me, young laddie, since when did you lay claim

to lordship of Zinder Hamryn of Casting Selvedge? I'm the elder here. If anything, I'm the one who should be upset at not even being consulted—not even a whisper or a wink, mind you—before you made your brash decision. Oh, you were fine and happy to call me part of the family back in Charring when we ran right through the heart of the haukmarn garrison, but the moment I do a little half-step into the jaws of a dreadwulf I'm tossed like a cheap hat by the wayside."

Tiryn, emboldened by Zinder's pluck and desperate to win her brother over, raised herself as tall as she could to address Kion in his lofty saddle.

"Kion, I wouldn't have broken my promise and told Zinder if I didn't think he could make the trip. The blood root will work. Mother's used it on you a dozen times. You know how potent it is. Please, let us go with you. Let us help. I may not have a sword, but I'm still your sister. I want to find Mother just as much as you do. Remember what you said: we can change our dreams. I'm not going to let that vision I had come true. I'm going to hold onto you until the very end, no matter how dark it gets."

Zinder beamed beside her. "She's right, lad. You know that if you leave us here, we're just going to follow you on our own. You're backed into the sheep pen and you know it."

Kion heaved a sigh of frustration, scattering the raindrops trickling across his lips.

"I just wanted to protect you."

Tottering on his one good leg, Zinder raised his cane and pegged it in Kion's chest. "Remember that day you were dead set on piggy-backing with me off to Roving? And I was sitting right where you are now, in the very same shoes. All my better sense told me to leave you in Furrow, but I didn't. And do you know why? Because I knew how much it meant to you and I couldn't bear to break your heart. I could no more have denied you that day than the day your father asked me to look after you when he went off to war. Well, now it's time to pay that debt. Let us go with you, lad. We're family. And we're in this to the end, however hard and bitter it may be."

The last plate in Kion's once invulnerable armor fell away. His head bowed in reluctant surrender. "All right, you've bested me. If you were half as good a swordsman as you are at talking, the war would be over tomorrow. But I see your point. It wouldn't be right to leave you. Especially not slinking off like this in the middle of the night. I just couldn't bring myself to tell you in person."

"Shar's dome! I told you he'd come around, Tiryn!"

Zinder gave a little hop, but if it caused him any pain, he didn't show it this time. Tiryn wanted to sweep Zinder off his feet—they'd done it!—but she kept her wits about her and only hugged him instead.

"It takes a strong man to admit he's wrong," Tiryn said.

Kion reached down and tousled her hair. "For once in my life, I'm glad to be wrong." Kion might make mistakes, but he always did the right thing in the end. He turned to Endrith. "So, my friend, after the hand you've played in this plot, will you deign to follow this shepherd and his unshakable companions on their journey across the Noathryn wilds?"

"Alas, if only I could. No, my duties lie elsewhere. I ride for Quelling today. I must bring them news and a call for more soldiers to rally to the margrave's banner. I only came to see you off, and to thank you again for saving my life. I shall never forget the three of you, nor that sword of yours."

"Nor will we forget you. Kithian thanks you for your part in guiding us this far."

"I will miss you," Tiryn said, forcing her emotions down as far as she could push them. She did not like good-byes. Especially when she knew it was likely that they would be permanent ones. In the short time they'd known him, Endrith had proven to be a true friend. "I won't forget you either."

Zinder let out a sudden chuckle. "And I'll say the same. I'll think of you every time I see a crow!"

Chapter 21

A NEW DREAM

Tiryn leaned against Kion's shoulder, so tired she could barely keep her eyes open, but so tense she couldn't sleep. Her plan had worked. Her plans never worked, but this time was different. This time she had defied the vision and now she was setting out on a new dream, one of her own choosing. The path they now followed was unknown, but Kion was with her, and Zinder too, and that made all the difference. They would find Mother—together. Tiryn was certain of it. The conviction was not as sure as her visions, but it was close. In only a few days they would reach the western shore of Noath and then, somehow, some way, they would find Mother and all would be well again.

The pathway off the crags surrounding Dunach plummeted into a valley, necessitating a slow start to their journey. Kion's inexperience driving a cart didn't help. Zinder offered a near-constant stream of advice and instructions, to which Kion paid little attention until he had nearly driven them off the path the third time. After that, he gave in and followed Zinder's advice, but he still shifted restlessly in his seat, anxious to increase the pace.

"Not until we hit a decent stretch of road. And even then, have a care not to jostle my spool of yarn over-much." Zinder fluffed the blankets and cushions around his bandaged leg.

Unfortunately, if there was a "decent stretch of road" in Noath, they never found it. Not only were there no well-traveled roads once they'd passed a league beyond Dunach, there was barely any flat ground. From mid-morning on, they were forced to venture in a generally westerly direction through lands not suited to travel by cart at all, full of rocks and ravines and tangled underbrush, all of which slowed their progress and cost them time. The map Varlance Aonar had given them had a few settlements marked upon it, none of which they came near, but otherwise offered few details of what they could expect to find in the interior. The most important thing the map had to offer, and the thing they were focused upon above all, was that jagged line to the west, the one representing the coast of Noath. How they would find a way across to Tinesplitter Isle once they reached it was the topic of their conversation throughout the morning. Zinder had a good idea of how to make a raft, so there was less doubt about that part. A nyn could make almost anything if he put his mind to it and, as he pointed out, rafts were a lot simpler than crafting a suit of armor. They had a good sharp hatchet which the varlance had gifted them, and plenty of rope, so they only had to find a few suitable trees for the wood.

It was the piloting part that was their chief concern. None of them had ever been on the open water in any sort of vessel. Ocean sailing was a rare and difficult skill in the Four Wards and due to the inconstancy of sparklight, only really possible along the coasts. Zinder had crossed a few rivers on ferries, but he'd never been the one managing the boat. Kion and Tiryn had experience swimming in brooks and pools, so at least they might survive a shipwreck, but that was hardly comforting.

"We do have a good deal of coin left," Zinder said. "Surely we can find someone with enough business sense to look past the differences between Noath and Inris and guide our boat across the bay. It's not a large body of water."

"Let's hope so," Kion said. "And maybe they'll even have a boat of their own. That would save us a great deal of time."

The light spread warily across the plains, as though it sought to hide the Noathryn landscape for as long as possible. Noath was a harsh place, with upturned rocks and cliffs jutting out in unexpected places, but green patches poked through off in the distance, beacons of life amidst the hardscrabble terrain. Yet, the green was not the vibrant Inrisian shade. This was a deeper color. It gave the land an older, more subdued feel, as though the power of nature had gone partially dormant here.

Trees were few at first, and mostly small and gnarled, but as the distance from Dunach grew, so too did the health and stature of the trees. The largest of them grew isolated, like lords among their lesser counterparts. They were enormous—twice as tall as the tallest oak in the Tors, but their waving branches offered little in the way of shade. They looked to be some sort of pine, for a carpet of thin needles spread beneath them. The trunks were thin for their size but rose to such lofty pinnacles it half seemed they disappeared rather than that they stopped growing.

"The fabled hovar firs," Zinder said. "I had never thought to see them. They grow only in these lands, from what I've read. It is from these that the great ships of Noath are built."

As they wandered farther and farther into the domain of these scattered giants, the hovars grew even larger. By mid-afternoon, some were five or six times as tall as the towers of Dunach.

"Did you ever dream trees could grow so tall?" Tiryn said. "They're as big as mountains."

Kion, who had been conversing with Kithian, sat up in his seat, as if seeing the giant trees for the first time.

"They're quite large, aren't they?"

Zinder's arms flailed in disbelief from the back. "Quite large? That's like saying the fane's crown is quite valuable. Shar's dome, lad, even in Lowerwyn we don't have trees like this. You can see why there's so few of them. Must take an underground lake to feed each one. Quite large indeed!"

"Well, I don't imagine we'll be cutting any of these down for our boat," Kion said, his voice still distant, his mind lost in other things. "It would take several days with the hatchet we've got."

As great as the trees were in height, their scarcity and lack of shade were points against them. By mid-afternoon, the sun had begun to beat down fiercely upon the company. To guard against the heat, they were forced to stop at every trickling stream to keep the horses fresh. At one tiny rivulet, Zinder sat gazing at the faithful beasts, a flicker of melancholy in his eye.

"What's wrong, Zinder? Is your leg bothering you?" Tiryn asked.

"No, I was just thinking of Crusty, wondering if he survived the battle at Fennigar."

"I'm sure he's fine. He's a tough animal."

"You know, I wish I'd thought to have Kion write a note of apology to him, explaining why I had to abandon him."

"I don't think animals can read their language, only speak it," Kion said.

"Well, you know what I mean. I should at least have had the presence of mind to ask Truesilver to pass my condolences along. But we got whisked away so fast, there was hardly time to breathe."

"You may see him again," Tiryn said. "Once we find Mother we can go back to Fennigar and find him…If the soldiers managed to repel the haukmarn…"

Even by the time she finished the sentence, Tiryn did not believe there was much chance of that happening. She'd seen the crumbling walls at Fennigar and how few men guarded them. She doubted the Warding forces would be able to repel an attack from both land and sea. Fennigar was no doubt lost, along with Grettling, Roving, and most of northwest Inris. Only at Charring had they been pushed back, but for how long?

Tiryn knew nothing of war except that it had robbed her of her father and stolen away her mother. She also knew that the only way to stop a war once it started was to fight. Strom Glyre had stopped the haukmarn in the War of the Claws, but who would drive the enemy from their land now? Recalling their dinner with Varlance Aonar and looking now at Truesilver, she thought she knew. Maybe if he had stayed at Fennigar the city would still be free. This led to an unsettling thought.

Were men dying on the battlefield because Kion was not fighting? Before he found the sword, her brother had been nothing more than a shepherd, responsible to no one but his family and his flock. But he was no longer a simple commoner. With Truesilver in his hands, he had become something else. Not a soldier, nor even a noble, but something greater. He was a swordspeaker, the only one of his kind in all the Four Wards. And one day soon he would take up his blade to fight in the Warding army. He would go off and leave her, the same way Father had…

With all that was inside her, she hoped the war would come to an end before they returned. And yet, she knew that was an impossible dream. The more she thought about it, the more she came to see that finding her mother would also mean losing her brother. If only there was a way to bring them all together and keep them that way, the way things had always been. But wars gave no heed to the wishes of young girls and the seeds of grief and loss threatened to sprout once again in her all too tender heart.

They slept that night under the slender branches of one of the great hovar firs, like three small pebbles wedged in the foundations of a lofty tower. The next morning, they set off before dawn once again. By the time the sleepy gray sun had fully awakened upon the clouded land, the giant firs had grown fewer and fewer until they disappeared altogether. Velvet spruces, of the sort common to the Tors, grew in their place. Rugged boulders and broom grass surrounded them. Loose rocks grated against the wheels of the cart and several times they were forced to double back down a promising path when they found the way impassible. Large jagged rocks thrust up through the soil, sending them on circuitous routes to avoid them. Smokewind and Cyprian bore their burdens and the hard road with bottomless patience and perseverance, though even their impressive strength began to flag later in the day.

In the afternoon, they stopped at a small pond, just east of a smooth, stone-capped hill. The company took refuge from the glaring sun under the shade of the cart while the horses took water. It was a relief to be out of the jolting, swaying wagon, if only for a little while.

"What's that smoke to the north?" Tiryn asked as she chiseled away at a trail biscuit, scraping off enough crumbs with her teeth for half a bite.

"A hot spring, if I had to guess," Zinder said. "I didn't know they had them in Noath, but we are not all that far north of the Clarion Toths and such things are common in those mountains. I visited the baths of Nivilwane once, long ago. Quite nice on the toes, but I don't suppose you'd fancy a dip in the middle of summer?"

"Not even if it was the dead of winter," Tiryn said. "I've heard those places have an awful smell to them."

"That depends on who you're bathing with," Zinder said.

That got a chuckle even out of Kion, who'd been even more stern than usual since they'd left Dunach.

"Perhaps we'll have time to stop at one on the way back," Tiryn said. "Just to see it, of course."

"Of course. We'll show your mother all the sites of Noath. Perhaps even climb one of the hovars. Could you imagine the view?"

Where would they be without Zinder's irrepressible spirit? His ship never went under, no matter how high the waves.

As they hoisted their friend back into the cart to resume the journey, he let out a startled cry.

"What is it, Zinder?" Kion said. "Did we move your leg the wrong way?"

"No—look. To the south. A company of men marches this way."

A few miles away, beyond a twinkling river, dark shapes

shambled toward them. At this distance, they were only curious clumps. It might have been a herd of cattle or wild horses, but in time, as always, Zinder's sharp eyes proved true. Two hundred men, glints of metal shining among them, were making their way north. They were tall and light-haired. Many wore iron helms. They moved swiftly, their long strides eating up the ground. And if they kept their present course, they would pass just west of where the cart now stood.

"Quick, Tiryn, help me with the horses. We need to get everything around to the other side of this hill." Kion fetched Smokewind while Tiryn laid hold of Cyprian.

"Oh, bother my leg," Zinder said. "I'm no help at all."

"You spotted the soldiers," Kion said as he and Tiryn worked to harness the horses. "Without you, we wouldn't have seen them until they were much closer."

"Well, a lot of good it will do. They'll soon be close enough to see us no matter where we squirrel ourselves away. This little knot of a hill isn't enough to hide us completely."

"Do you really think they would come after us? Three people and a cart?" Tiryn said.

"As sure as the fane's taxes," Zinder said. "Those are not all soldiers. Did you not see the chains around some of their necks? No? Well, trust me, they've got slaves in that band as well. I'm sure they wouldn't mind adding our three backs to their choices for whipping."

"How can we stay hidden, then?" Kion said.

"If only we were back in the Tors," Tiryn said. "There are a hundred places to hide there."

"Wait—" Kion was caught up by Kithian's voice, his eyes staring off at the sky. "Kithian has an idea. We need to move the cart to the other side of the pond."

"But that's even farther away from the protection of the hill," Zinder said.

"Trust me, this is the only way. I'll explain as we go. Tiryn, get in the cart."

There was nothing to do but climb in the back and hope for the best. Though it seemed the exact opposite of what they should do, Tiryn made no complaint. Kithian's wisdom was as trustworthy as Zinder's eyes.

As the cart got rolling, Kion laid out their plan. "I'll go into the pond and use Truesilver's flame to heat the waters. That should create a mist thick enough to hide the cart. It will look just like another hot spring."

"But won't they see the fire, even through the mist?" Tiryn said.

"They won't see the flames. The fire will be underwater."

"Underwater?" Zinder's eyes nearly sprang from his head. "What kind of fire burns underwater?"

"Glaivefire. Kithian assures me that it will work."

"Well, I grant the sword ought to know things like that, but honestly, if you keep this up, I'll be expecting Truesilver to dig us a tunnel to Tinesplitter by the time this is all over." Zinder drew out the ends of his mustache, rolling the plan around in his mind. "It's unconventional, but it just might work. Whatever the case, it's better than just sitting behind this hill, holding our breath and hoping they don't look our way."

Kion reined in the horses and stepped down, peeling off his cloak and tunic.

"Tiryn, you lie down in the back with Zinder. It will take a little while before the mist starts." He tossed his clothes off to the side and worked himself out of his boots. The pond was a murky green, with thin sheets of moss on the surface. Kion waded out to the middle with little trouble, dragging his magnificent blade along underwater.

"Glaivefire."

A red shimmer rose from below, though it was little more than a dull glow beneath the murk.

Despite Kion's orders, Tiryn and Zinder kept peering over the side of the cart. Kion, who had waded in up to his shoulders, kept his eyes trained on the approaching soldiers and so failed to notice his companions' prying eyes.

The first tendrils of mist floated skyward as the approaching shapes grew more distinct. The bands around the necks and wrists of the prisoners transformed into metal bonds and their clothing into rags. Only a handful of them were slaves. Most traveled free and unfettered, long spears and small round shields slung across their backs and pointed helms upon their heads.

Tiryn searched for her mother among the ranks of the prisoners, but she could not make out enough detail to tell one way or the other. She asked Zinder, though, and he assured her that no women marched among them.

By now, the mist made Kion difficult to see. A chalky curtain clung to the surface, the way it so often did early mornings upon the Tors. A dank smell hung in the air. Tiny beads of moisture formed upon the planks of the cart. Tiryn wiped away a large drop of water from the tip of her nose.

"Can you see them anymore?" Tiryn whispered.

Zinder's white beard glistened with tiny droplets. "Not even nynnian eyes could see through that." His voice was softly giddy. "That sword of his is a wonder a day."

"I don't understand how it doesn't burn him."

"You, me, and the moon. I've stopped trying to stitch it all together and just wear the outfit that's been given to me."

They sat in the mist for a long while. The sounds of marching drew ever nearer. Thumps and clinks and rattling of gear peppered the range of hills. It was hard to tell if the Noathryn were still heading north or if the soldiers had turned towards the smoking pond.

Tiryn feared to breathe. It was like she was back inside her aunt's underground chambers waiting for the haukmarn attack. Every sound was a threat, every moment coiled with fear.

After what seemed ten thousand moments of dread, Zinder nudged her. "The sounds are fading. I think the steam worked."

Tiryn drew a long, grateful breath.

Soft splashing and soggy steps announced the re-emergence of Kion from the pond. He appeared at the side of the cart, soaking wet, his dark hair black and glistening.

"Truesilver ran out of oil, but I think we made more than enough mist to last us until they pass."

"Well, we brought enough oil with us to last the whole Seven Fires Festival if you need to take another swim," Zinder said.

"We'll see. Unless a stiff breeze comes along, we should be fine. I only wish we didn't have to lose all this time again. It will be at least another hour before we can be sure they've passed out of view."

Tiryn handed Kion a dry cloth from one of the packs. "It's too bad we ate lunch before we saw them."

"Well," Zinder said. "We could always eat lunch again..."

Chapter 22

THE FOOLISH AND THE BRAVE

They pressed on well past dark in hopes of making up for the time lost at the pool. But when Kithian warned Kion that he was in danger of pushing the horses too hard, they found a large grove of low-standing trees to camp for the night. The boughs spread fanlike up from stubby trunks almost as soon as the trees came out of the ground. Nearly every branch sagged beneath the weight of a strange purple fruit that bulged on either end like an hourglass. Since the fruit was unfamiliar, they hadn't planned on trying any, but after they caught Cyprian chomping on one and suffering no ill effects, they decided to throw in their lot with the intrepid animal. It was a little tart, but not unsweet, and fairly bursting with juice. Tiryn had a hard time keeping it from sliding down her cheeks and chin. She could only eat two before she was filled.

She awoke the next morning the most refreshed she'd been since the Grizzly Griddle. When she woke Kion, he sprang up with a start.

"What—oh no, I slept through the dawn." He threw off his blanket and scrambled about, tossing their waterskins, provisions, and bedrolls into the cart. "Zinder needs his sleep. Help me carry him. We'll put him in the back."

But the moment they laid hands on their slumbering friend, his eyes popped open.

"No need to pack me in like the rest of the gear. I'll hobble in all on my own." He brushed their hands away and limped toward the cart on his own, though he did suffer their help in getting up and into his seat. Last night had been his first attempt at walking since his injury. He still had some way to go before he recovered his nimbleness and cat-like grace, but the blood root was already proving its potency and he was able to make it twice around the wagon without a fall.

Tiryn and Kion had just finished harnessing the horses when a strange bleating noise invaded the clearing.

"What was that?" Tiryn said.

No one knew. Some animal to be sure, but unlike any they had ever heard.

The bleating came again. Though the sun was up, it was still half-dark from the surrounding trees. Large swaying shapes came lumbering towards them from the north. They looked to be donkeys or a smaller breed of horse.

Kion motioned Tiryn into the cart. Whatever they were, there was no need to wait until they arrived. The cart creaked into motion, the harness jangled, and they were off on their way once again.

The shadowy animals moved slowly towards them, clearly in no rush, but though the cart moved to the west to skirt around them, more and more of the creatures appeared as the light grew brighter. Kion risked pushing the horses a little, though they couldn't get up much speed within the confines of the grove.

They were almost to the edge of the trees and clear of the unfamiliar beasts when a low, threatening bark sounded behind them. Two loping creatures came darting into their path. Nightmarish memories of the dreadwulfs flooded Tiryn's mind and she gripped Kion's arm for all she was worth. He flicked the reins, urging the horses toward the open fields, but the charging creatures were too quick. Two longhounds—for longhounds they were—swept in as swift and furious as the ones that had rushed in to save them from the dreadwulfs. Only this time, they had not come to help, but to threaten and waylay them. They closed in upon the wagon, causing the horses to rear up. The wagon shuddered to a halt. Tiryn jolted forward and would have teetered off the seat had she not been holding onto Kion's arm so fiercely. The hounds grew all the bolder now that their quarry was caught. They barked and growled enough for ten dogs, nipping at the stamping, snorting horses and circling the wagon.

"Kithian, tell the horses not to be afraid," Kion said.

Zinder rose up in the back, rapping his cane along the side of the wagon. "Get going, you ganglers. Mind your business or I'll get my crossbow!"

The two dogs only barked all the more ferociously. They sounded as big as bears, and just as fierce.

"Hold on, Zinder. Kithian is trying to talk them down," Kion said.

Within moments their deep-bellied growls turned into low and puzzled whines. Both hounds sat on their hindquarters, gazing curiously up at Kion with big, dark eyes. Tiryn marveled at Kithian's ability to sway the animals so quickly. Eventually their barking returned, but this time it came in short, even-tempered *rooowwffs*.

"The hounds say they're protecting their flock. These woods are under the protection of their master. They say we don't belong."

Their barking quieted again as they took in Kithian's silent words. If Tiryn hadn't seen their wild threatening racket a few moments before, she might have thought they'd been trained for the fair.

"They say that they respect Kithian as a glaive of the Master-smith, but they can't let us leave until their own master comes. Their master is a good man, they say, and they can't shirk their duty to him."

"Just what we need," Zinder said. "Dogs with principles."

Though they might not have been ready to perform at a fair, it seemed that they were well-trained animals in a different fashion.

"We'll wait until he comes," Kion said, his eyes flashing

impatiently.

The curious, high-pitched bleating from earlier grew louder and more frequent as they waited. Tiryn tried to get Kion to ask the dogs a few questions, but he was in no mood for it and so she hummed a little tune to pass the time away. The dogs stared up at her intently and she fancied that they enjoyed her little melody. It took a good deal longer than any of them would have liked, but the master of the hounds eventually arrived. His unique manner of dress caught the eye at once. A tasseled shawl covered his shoulders. Like the rest of his outfit, it was tinted with rustic browns and shot through with dark red stripes. A cone-shaped hat, a little crumpled at the tip, crowned his head. A black scarf concealed his nose and mouth. Back in Casting Selvedge he would have been taken for a bandit, but the dutiful longhounds had made it clear that he was an honorable man. In the stranger's wake trailed a great heard of beasts as odd and as strange as his dress. Though vaguely resembling sheep, their heads were raised up upon long, thick necks that came up to the man's shoulders. Dusty brown wool covered all but their faces and hooves. The nearest thing they brought to mind was sheep crossed with horses, though they were about the size of mules.

The man pulled down his scarf and graced them with a generous, yellow-toothed smile.

"Greetings, wanderers. I am Haiza. I see that you have already met my hounds. I am impressed that you were able to calm them down. They do not usually treat strangers so kindly. Tell me, what brings you to the Yemmel Grove so early in the morning?"

His accent made his words sound stiff, though his tone was friendly enough.

"We journey overland," Kion said. "Our apologies. We did not know these woods belonged to anyone."

Haiza chuckled, causing the tassels of his shawl to shake. "Own the Yemmel Grove? No, no one owns this place. A man might as well claim ownership of the sky. I can tell by your voice, if not from your look, that you are not from these lands. By thunder, is that a nyn in the back of your cart?"

"Pleased to make your acquaintance, fellow wanderer." Zinder managed a stiff, yet dignified, bow. "These are my two wards, and as he said, we are in the midst of a rather long journey, somewhere between here and there. You spoke true when you said that we're not from these lands; though, as we've only just met, and times being what they are, I'm afraid that's all we can afford to say."

Haiza tapped his chin curiously. "Ah, yes, that is understandable. I meet many who flee the chieftains in these days. Our rulers have grown hard in these dark times, deaf to the cries of the people. I don't mind telling you, I'm not a man for the chieftains myself. Not many shepherds are."

Kion responded with pleasant surprise. "You're a shepherd? But these aren't sheep. What are they?"

"Bresca. Sheep do not do as well in these lands. The bresca can travel greater distances and are heartier creatures. Their rugged nature helps the shepherds stay free of the chieftains' whips."

Bresca. What elegant necks and pleasant coats they had. Tiryn found herself wishing they would venture a little closer so that she could feel their wool. They gazed upon her with heavy-lidded eyes and the subdued interest which most tame animals show toward humans.

"It sounds as if you're no more for this war than we are, then," Zinder said. "If that's so, perhaps you might offer some guidance to those new to these lands."

"Common decency demands nothing less. You have lost your way, perhaps?"

"Close enough. We're headed to Tinesplitter Isle. We have a map, but it's hardly one I'd stake my life upon. If you know the best path from here, we'd be ever so grateful to hear it."

Haiza's face stormed over. "Tinesplitter? Oh, for certain you are not from here if you seek that cursed place. It takes one both foolish and brave to seek those darkened shores. I would not venture there for all the bresca in Noath. Nor would I advise you to seek it either."

If Haiza's face had grown grim, Kion's sparked all the more passionately. "We don't care about the legends. We have to go there. Someone very dear to us is trapped there. And to abandon her would be a fate worse than death. Surely you can understand that."

"She would have to be very dear indeed to risk such peril."

"It's my mother, if you want to know. Mine and my sister here."

A regrettable note sounded deep in Haiza's chest. He considered his response for a long while before giving it. "I can see the truth of what you speak in your eyes. You are not a deaf man like the chieftains. You have ears and a heart. If you must go, then this advice I will give to you. There is said to be a village somewhere upon the shores to the west, though it may only be a rumor, or a place haunted by ghosts. Sometimes desperate men are said to seek it, those who have the chieftains' hands heavy upon them and have no other hope of escaping their wrath. If the rumors are true, the entrance to this place is found in a narrow gap in a line of hills. Seek for that pass and whatever help you may find beyond it. For if you do not find help, my friends, I fear you will not return from that place alive."

The words sent an unseasonable chill across Tiryn's skin. Aonar was not the only one who believed that the island was cursed. Her brother might give little credence to such stories, but there must be some truth to them if they had been repeated by two such very different sources. Tiryn's intuition told her that something awful awaited them down this bleak path. If not for Mother, she would have begged Kion to turn back. Instead, she slipped her arm around his waist. They had to go on. No rumor or curse was dark or perilous enough to keep them from their search. Not when Mother's very life depended upon it. And yet, the grim warning in Haiza's eyes stayed with Tiryn long after the cart had left the Yemmel Grove.

Chapter 23

THE CURSED LAND

A crisp wind blew in from the north as they left the Yemmel Grove behind. Kion pressed the horses as much as he dared across the broken, trackless land. He could not believe that he had slept in that morning. Perhaps he could have made the excuse that he had barely slept the two days before, but he was not willing to forgive himself so easily. Strom, in his journal, had told of marching for days on end with little to no sleep and then fighting in a battle. Kion needed to be strong like that, to push past his own limitations. He could not afford to let sleep or pain or anything else stand in the way, not now that they were so close to the end of their journey, so close to finding Mother.

"Be gentle with the horses. A journey does not consist only in the going, but also in the returning. You will need them then as you do now." Kithian's voice came with its usual blend of gentle firmness.

"Can they not rest when we reach the shore?" It was unlikely they would find a boat big enough to take the horses, unless that rumor of a village turned out to be true.

"Yes, they can rest there. Only be sure that you do not take their service lightly. There is a difference between what a beast can be made to do and what is best for it."

Kion eased off the reins. As a shepherd, he knew not to push his animals so far that they could not recover, but this knowledge did nothing to appease his own inner beasts, which hounded his thoughts, and harried him at each delay.

"You're right, Kithian. So where were we with my lessons?" That, at least, would take his mind off all the setbacks. He had found it easier to understand the beast speech ever since the battle at Dunach. Perhaps something of the terror and his great need to connect with his steed during that fateful encounter had launched him suddenly into a deeper understanding. But his connection to his glaive also had a great deal to do with it. Learning from Kithian was not like learning in other ways. It was less like learning and more like being reminded of things he already knew and he absorbed more and more of Kithian's knowledge with each passing day.

"You were trying to learn the words associated with families and other relationships. Those are some of the most important in all of their language."

And so the lessons resumed. While they did not abolish his doubts and worries, Kion plunged himself into the strange words as the miles rumbled on, the cart listing and bouncing over the uneven ground. They were drifting into lowlands now, where little grew beyond creeping vines and thorn-infested bracken. To the northwest, the horizon loomed still and stagnant, a gray mass of ambiguity. The air turned curiously cooler as the day rolled on. By late afternoon, the sun had abandoned them altogether behind a bank of grizzled clouds. Of the few creatures they saw, most were cranes, gulls, sparrows, and other, smaller birds.

"Have you noticed," Tiryn said, looking up from the scribbles she'd been making in her journal, "that none of the birds are flying north? It's early summer. There should still be at least a few migrating flocks. I saw some heading north before we reached the grove, but none since."

That was Tiryn, always noticing things. "Perhaps it's the dreadful curse of the Furious Fowler, hunting every bird that comes in sight of his all-seeing eyes," Kion said with a little laugh.

She swatted him with her pencil. "I was being serious, Kion.

Aren't you at least a little worried about what awaits us along the coast?"

"It'll take more than whispered legends to trouble my thoughts. The only thing I'm worried about is not reaching the shore by dark."

Zinder leaned in between and whispered in low, overly dramatic tones, "You know, dreadwulfs aren't the only monsters that wander the dark places of the world. They say that in places where the wind won't stir, where the light won't come, and where no track of man has ever been, lie the corrupted creatures that got changed by wandering too long out in the dark."

The effect of Zinder's words was enhanced by the tendrils of fog which had mysteriously crept in across the land during the last hour. A billowing bank of mist obscured the way ahead.

Tiryn looked back at him, the whites of her eyes glowing ghostly under the ashen sky.

"Zinder, you know I don't like your scary stories. I have too much imagination for that sort of thing."

"What can I say? Sometimes the mood just comes upon me."

"Zinder speaks in jest, but his words are closer to the truth than he knows. Ask him where he heard such tales," Kithian said.

Kion passed the question on, leaving off the part about them perhaps being true.

"Oh, back in Lowerwyn, mostly. Why? Would your sword like to hear some of my monster stories? Because I know one that'll curdle your—"

"Zinder, please," Tiryn said. "I want to sleep tonight. Besides, we don't want to miss that gap in the hills Haiza told us about."

"Oh, all right. I really didn't mean to frighten you. Well, not much, anyway."

"So, they are only tales to him. That is well. Perhaps the dim-touched have died out over the years."

"The dim—?" Kion started to ask but held his tongue again for Tiryn's sake. The last thing she needed was confirmation that some of her worst fears were true. But even if such creatures existed in other parts of the world, that did not mean that they were here. "Never mind, Tiryn's right. We should keep our eyes out for that gap. In this fog it may come upon us at any moment."

The rickety wheels and clinking harness were the only sounds now. The terrain grew sandier and wetter. The horses had to work harder to plow through the mire. The fog lingered on mile after mile, at times swirling and sinister. The cool of the afternoon gave way to an unwelcome chill. After a few more miles, Tiryn was shivering. Zinder handed her a blanket and soon had one wrapped around his own shoulders as well.

"Blast this weather! I've never seen such sunblinked nonsense. Summer could use a good scolding right about now. If this is what the weather's like up here, I can see why folk would call it cursed."

"It would be just our luck to wander into another hail storm," Kion said.

"Kion, put on this blanket. You must be freezing," Tiryn said.

"I'm fine." He wasn't, but he didn't want to have to fiddle with a blanket and the reins.

"I think I can see my breath," Zinder said. "Or is it the fog? I can't tell."

"I'm sure we'll be out of this soon enough. Let me know the moment you spot the gap."

Not a minute later, the hills Haiza had told them of bloomed through the fog, a line of dark mounds stretching off into the unknown.

"I see the hills. We're right on top of them. But I don't see any gap," Tiryn said.

Zinder stood in the back and strained his eyes up and down the line. "There. Off to the right. I th-think I s-see an opening." His teeth chattered in an uneven rhythm. If this cold snap didn't leave off soon, they'd be forced to stop and make a fire. They had not brought clothes for this kind of weather.

"You are cold. Let go of the reins and let me guide the horses for you, at least for a while until you can warm yourself again."

Kion had hoped to hold out a little longer, but the tips of his fingers were starting to sting from the sudden chill.

"Fine, but don't slow the pace. Hopefully, it will be warmer on the other side of these hills." He had no reason to think that, but it helped to say it.

The blanket Zinder handed him was coarse and stiff, already half-frozen itself, but it grew supple with his body's heat and it kept the cold from sinking further in.

They passed beneath the shadowy gap, two walls of steel-gray rock rising on either side, severe and forbidding. The fog veiled whatever lay at the end of the pass. The strange conditions and the unnatural thickness and persistence of these mists were no doubt playing right into Tiryn's belief in the curse. They had not been long in the gap when an odd crunching sounded beneath the wheels. Soon, the noise was constant, but the ground yielded no clues, for it was coated in fog. The path was a featureless white track as far as they could see, lined on either side by boulder-filled slopes, which were covered here and there with small patches of white sand.

"Zinder, what is this strange soil we're traveling through? I feel as though I should know it, but it's shrouded in all this fog."

Zinder dangled himself out the back of the cart, reaching down with his cane. Tiryn scolded him for being so reckless, but Zinder paid no heed. "Shar's dome! It's snow. We're riding over snow!"

"Snow? In the month of Lockwin?"

Now that he said it, Kion saw that the white on the rocks must be snow, too, not sand.

"How can this be?" Kithian said. His voice was the only thing warm in all that frozen pass.

"I don't know. But we're coming up on the end of the gap. Once we're through, perhaps we can pull over and—"

"Kion, there are men lying hidden among the rocks!"

But Kithian's warning came too late. The air filled with corded mesh, rough and strong and constricting. Weighted nets rained down upon them and harsh cries burst from the rocks. The horses and cart were trapped a few yards from the end of the pass.

Kion thrust his legs against the floorboards, desperate to stand and free himself, but the cords kept him pinned.

"Tiryn!" he called out as men in shaggy coats swarmed in from the boulders and pulled her from the cart. Kion dove toward her—as if he could have done anything to save her—but all he did was crash his head against the seat. Powerful hands grabbed him and pulled him and Tiryn onto the snow-packed ground.

"Lad, no!"

Men descended onto the back of the cart, lifting Zinder out to join his friends. A heavy boot on Kion's back kept him face down in the powdery snow, but he could still crane his neck to watch the men seize control of the cart and take his place behind the reins.

His only chance was Truesilver. Kion could call the sword to his hand—if only he had a hand to call it to. His limbs were mashed together inside the tangled netting.

"Kithian! Help—"

The boot stamped down, knocking the rest of Kion's words back down his throat.

A man's face, shadowy and indecipherable, hovered next to Kion. "Enough out of you, boy. You're in the Frostkeld, now. And here you don't speak unless you're told."

"Do not lose hope, Kion. I cannot reach you from where I am, but I am still here and we will endure this dark night together."

Kithian's voice brought little comfort. For though Truesilver's fire would have torn through these nets in a flash, the cords were impervious to words of hope. And Kion's fears fanned a lightless flame that burned inside him cold and empty.

Chapter 24

WHITEWIND

More than warmth or sleep or anything else, Kion wanted to speak, to cry out for answers, but his captors had made it clear there would be no talking, a rule they were not above following themselves, communicating with each other entirely through the use of strange signals with their hands. Not one word was spoken as they lashed the prisoners onto wicker sleds and set off upon a snowy trek that lasted far into the night. A world of hushed whiteness swept by as the band of fur-coated men pushed the three of them through the desolate tundra. Mounds of powder piled ever higher as they went, glowing softly under a frosty moon. The farther they traveled, the more empty and frozen the world became. Not even on the darkest winter night of the Tors had Kion known such cold. If their captors had not blanketed them with thick furs before strapping them to the sleds, they might not have survived to see the warmth of another sun.

The tinkle of the harness and the crunching of the wheels upon the snow told that the cart kept pace somewhere toward the rear of the train. Two men took turns trundling behind each of the sleds holding the prisoners while another ran alongside. From his place in the line, Kion could see Tiryn, or at least the men propelling her sled. They were close enough that their muffled footsteps threw occasional dustings of snow onto his legs.

Though he could not see his glaive, Kithian's ancient, unwavering voice was a flame in the darkness on that lonely, frost-bound road. Though the snow dampened all other noises, it could not silence his.

"Legends always have some truth. Some turn out to be truer than others. This unnatural winter surely appears to be a part of some curse, but we cannot yet be sure. Though things seem dire, we do have cause for hope. For I feared the dim-touched had taken up dwelling here, but instead you find yourself confronted by ordinary men. As such, they may be moved by reason or pity to release you. Though your first encounter with them has proven ill-fated, it may be that these people belong to the village the brescan shepherd spoke of. I believe we shall discover soon enough what their purpose is for capturing you. But whatever happens, after they've taken us to where they intend to, be encouraged in this: we are heading north. And that means that once we find our way to freedom, you will be that much closer to finding your mother."

Kithian ought to have said "if we find our way to freedom," but he was never one for doubt or doomsaying. In his mind, a swordspeaker could not be held for long against his will. Kion wished he could share in that confidence, but if these men were going to a camp or a village, there would certainly be even more of them. Kion could fight off half an army if he could get Truesilver back, but even if he won his way to freedom through force of arms and rescued the others, until the snow melted and this strange winter fled, they were as likely to die out in the open from the cold as at the hands of their captors.

"We are on this path for a reason. It is not the path we chose, but it is the path our choices have led us to. Beyond the rising and setting of the sun, rarely can we say what a day will bring, even in the surest of times. But we can be sure of one thing. Nothing ever happens by chance."

Despite the grimness of their prospects for escape, and despite the unending snow and the unnerving silence of their captors, Kion clung to the words of his glaive even though he was not sure that he fully believed them. More than the words themselves, he clung to the wisdom and warmth of Kithian's voice. It was that voice which, more than anything, kept him from giving in to despair.

Many hours later, they passed into a snow-covered stand of houses, and the sleds slowed. The buildings here were bulky wooden constructions with triangular framed roofs, the eaves brushing the heaps of snow that surrounded them. By now, the drifts crested the shoulders of most of the men, though the snow had been cleared near the doors of the houses and along the paths that ran between them. The buildings had a stark beauty and undeniable craftsmanship, but in the darkness of the night they conjured up images of giant tombstones. None had windows, and the way the roofs ran straight into the snow made it look as if they were indeed monuments which sprang out of the ground. Also, like a graveyard, not a single living soul could be seen. For all Kion knew, the little village was deserted. Specks of white, often catching the moonlight in dazzling fashion, floated to the ground with soundless grace, but their beauty could not remove the frozen dread which gripped the village.

The train of sleds stopped in front of the largest building yet, a great hall, three stories high, its thatched roof gray with age. The prisoners were untied and prodded inside. A single, massive room comprised the whole of the structure. Poled torches flickered with amber light and gave off a small but much-needed amount of warmth. Thick beams lined the steep roof, meeting in the lofty pinnacle.

The men left their prisoners to stand in the center of a ringed theater of aged tree stumps, several rows deep. Three of their captors left while the others bound the prisoners' hands and feet. With the furs removed, the cruel cold rushed in, even inside the hall. Kion, Tiryn, and Zinder huddled close together to keep as warm as they could.

"They may take me far enough away that you will no longer be able to hear my voice, but if you search for me you will be able to sense when I am near," Kithian said. *"We will find a way to escape this village.*

Even if you can no longer hear my voice, you are still a swordspeaker. And our bond cannot fail."

Kithian's voice went silent and the cold deepened all the more within the hollow hall. The captors ventured over to an immense hearth at the far end. Within minutes they had kindled a robust fire. The trickle of heat could not come fast enough for Kion's frozen body. One of the men crossed his arms high on his chest and approached. This was the first time Kion had a good look at these people. They had long, dour faces with flat cheeks and compressed noses. Most were Kion's height or taller, though their frames were stockier than the Noathryn Kion had seen marching near on the plains. Their hair ran in shades of black to dark brown with the former predominating. Their coats were of wolf pelts and their pants of padded buckram, worn, but sturdy. They stood still as statues, their eyes fixed on the prisoners in silent scrutiny.

"You are in the village of Whitewind, home of the Frindalian people," the man said. He was not the tallest of their captors, but he might have been the most grave. His slate-gray eyes had the look of unpolished steel and his jaw looked hard enough to be made of the same. "The Frin have no warmth in their hearts for trespassers from the Summerlands. Kalvar Chaw will decide your fate. You will not speak until he addresses you. If you do," —he hefted an iron-studded club—"we will teach you silence."

Zinder, who looked none the worse for wear apart from his leg, wrinkled his nose in wordless defiance. The man either did not notice or chose to overlook it. Tiryn's eyes locked with Kion's, her terror reflected in the torchlight. "I told you the curse was real," her wide eyes whispered.

A puff of cold announced the arrival of several people into the hall. They seated themselves upon the stumps, greeting one another with fierce embraces, but no smiles or words. They had the same long faces as the others, though most were shorter and older. Many gray heads were among them. More and more poured in and still no one said a word.

Kion was half ready to side with Tiryn, but even if there was no curse, it was unsettling to be in a room with so many people without hearing a single word. He would have preferred the farmers' jeers and mocking to this unnatural silence.

The last person to enter was a great, bristling bear of a man. He was not as tall as a haukmar, but was just as broad. His legs pounded the floor in mallet strokes as he traversed the room. He plodded his way through the midst of the crowd, every head bowing as he passed. Stalking his way to the stone slab before the hearth, he anchored himself on the largest stump in the room. With a hard stare he assessed the prisoners, his penetrating eyes set amidst bushels of beard and eyebrows. Kion knew without being told that this was Kalvar Chaw. If nothing else, the perceptiveness in the man's expression set him apart from the others. But he did not enter alone. A scruffy, middle-aged man entered along with him. Unruly patches of hair broke out around the edges of his gaunt face. Physically, he was no more substantial than the kalvar's shadow, but he exhibited more energy and movement than the rest of the room combined —close to fifty people by now. He was the only one who did not take a seat, but stood beside Kalvar Chaw, shifting from one leg to the other, as if warming up for a race.

The Frin who had spoken to them before rose and bowed on one knee before the giant figure.

"Honored Kalvar, we captured these strangers at Winter's Gap. They came with horses and much baggage, including weapons and armor, attempting to sneak into our lands under cover of night, and so we brought them to you to seek your judgment upon them." At a gesture from the kalvar he returned to his seat.

The kalvar stood and spoke with a voice as large as his frame, his words thrumming with authority. "It has been many years since anyone has dared pass through the Gap into our lands. You should count yourselves fortunate that you do not appear to be Noathryn, otherwise Dunwik and the other watchers would not have let you live. Yet you are a puzzle. Though you come ready for battle, you are ill-prepared for travel among our lands and you are only three. Stranger still, you have a nyn among your number, which is something no Frindalian has seen since before the Longwinter came to be."

The kalvar strode around the inner circle of stumps, pacing out his thoughts. The jittery figure followed, peering around the sides of his master, eyeing both the crowd and the prisoners with seemingly the same level of suspicion. Zinder offered him a scowl. Kion didn't like the look of the fellow either.

"Whatever they are, they are spies, Kalvar, spies," said the flitting shadow.

"It is possible. Perhaps the Noathryn hired them, but I doubt they would place their trust in such as these to do their work. The one is barely more than a boy and the other two are a nyn and a girl. No, I would say there must be a better explanation."

Zinder shook, bottled words inside him threatening to spill over, but through sheer determination, he kept them inside.

"They must be thieves, Kalvar, come to steal what few goods we have left," the smaller man said, twiddling the tips of his reedy fingers.

"That may be so, but if they knew of our village, how did they not also know of the curse of winter that lies upon us? See how they are dressed."

"Oh, but they did, Kalvar, they must have. Perhaps they carry a charm against the cold. Perhaps they are sorcerers." The kalvar's brow drew taut as the other continued. "Yes, sorcerers. Perhaps they are sorcerers. Recall how the legends say that the nyn served the wizenthall long ago. Perhaps this one is schooling these two children in the dark arts."

At last Zinder burst out, words erupting from him in a fountain of sputtering syllables. "Humming horn toads, I'm not a sorcerer! Why don't you ask us why we're here for fane's sake? You can't expect to find out anything by just staring at us!"

That was all he got out before a club came flying at him from one of the Frin. Zinder, tied up and gimped as he was, hopped to the side, dodging the blow. Frustrated, the Frin raised his weapon for another strike.

Tiryn screamed, "Stop!" as Kion jumped in front of his friend, ready to receive the next blow.

"Please, don't hurt him," Kion said.

The Frin would have gladly beaten Kion to get to the nyn, but Kalvar Chaw raised his mighty voice.

"Enough." He waved the man to stand down. "It is clear that these strangers do not know our laws. Until we know their purpose, we must overlook their offenses."

"The kalvar is great and merciful," said the flitting man.

Kalvar Chaw assumed his seat once more and now addressed the prisoners directly.

"In Whitewind, order is the highest good. Only by strict discipline are we able to maintain our fragile hold on these, our ancestral lands. Those on the outside, those who have forgotten us, might wonder why it is that we do not leave this place. But home is more than comfort, and loyalty seldom goes by gentle roads. Our commitment to the ancient laws makes us strong, for only the hardiest among us can endure the Ice Maid's curse."

The expression of the Frin, even that of the flitting man, hardened at the kalvar's speech. Not a few—mostly the older ones—nodded in silent assent, their eyes trapped in some timeless rehearsal of ancient traditions which could only be guessed at. Mention of the Ice Maid toppled the last barriers Kion held against believing in the curse. It appeared that Aonar and Haiza's rumors were correct. He dreaded to think what this would mean for his mother.

"I'm sorry, but we're not—" Kion began, but the kalvar's raised hand warned him back to silence.

"As prisoners, you may speak only when you are told, either by myself, the watchers, or my advisor, Eska, the seer of Whitewind." He nodded towards the skittering man, whose eyebrows jiggled with delight at hearing the sound of his own name.

"And don't count on that, sorcerers. Eska wants nothing to do with you." He crouched behind the kalvar as Zinder leveled a needle-sharp glare his way.

Kalvar Chaw cleared his throat, a cavernous rumbling that could be felt in the floorboards. "Very well. Now that you understand us better, tell me. Why is it that you have come to these lands? Do not weary me with long answers. Words are precious. Use those allotted to you wisely."

Zinder opened his mouth to reply, but Kion cut him off. If words were limited, Zinder was not the one to be doing the talking.

"We seek my mother. We believe she's being held prisoner by the Noathryn somewhere on Tinesplitter Isle."

A rustling drifted through the gathering, accompanied by dark expressions and more jitters from Eska. But Kalvar Chaw said nothing and so Kion deemed it safe to continue.

"We did not know that it was winter here. We've never been to Noath before, much less the northern coast. We are from Inris. And in case you didn't know, Inris is at war with Noath, for they are in league with the haukmarn, our true enemies."

More dark looks worked their way through the seated gathering.

"Haukmarn? Tell me of these haukmarn you speak of."

"You do not know of them?" Kion found this hard to believe but decided to take the kalvar at his word. "They are gray-skinned giants, two heads taller than anyone in this room. They seek to conquer our lands and after that, Verisward as well. They are the greatest threat to the Four Wards that exists."

Kalvar Chaw's eyes lit up and Eska stopped his jittering. "The Four Wards? Do they still exist? The legends say that they were shattered long ago."

"Only two wards remain, Veris and Inris, but the hope still

lives in some that the other two may be rediscovered one day, or rebuilt."

"So the fires of hope yet burn in the lands beyond the Frostkeld." The words were the quietest ones the kalvar had yet spoken.

A calm settled upon the room. Kalvar Chaw sat deep in thought. Only the shuffling, shifting, and scuttling of Eska disturbed the peace. Zinder had nearly chewed his lip off by the time the kalvar spoke again.

"I do not believe they are sorcerers, Eska. They lack the guile that students of the wizenthall would have. And yet, I perceive a strange destiny lies upon this boy. He has been touched by the Spark in some way, only how I cannot say. I require some time to think upon these things. I will delay my judgment until tomorrow. For now, Dunwik, take them to one of the empty houses and unbind them, but set a watch. They are to be treated as neither friend nor foe."

Zinder scooted his hand out from behind his back, fluttering his fingers in an effort to gain the kalvar's attention.

"Yes, nyn?"

"Do you really mean to punish us if we talk? Because that will be awfully hard, you know. We have a great many important matters to discuss and I really don't think—"

The kalvar's raised hand ended Zinder's sentence. "The prohibition against speech does not extend to the home or the market. For now, you may consider the place Dunwik will take you to as your home and speak freely while you are there."

Zinder wiped his brow in relief. "Oh, well, thank the forge. Any longer and I might have exploded into gibbering nonsense. A nyn can only keep quiet for so long."

Chapter 25

TRAPPED

Tiryn started awake in the dark, cold air rushing in and out of her lungs.

Trapped. Something was trapped in the ice and wanting to get out. She didn't know why, but she was terrified by it. It needed to stay inside. It needed to stay there forever. She pulled the heavy wool blanket up tight around her neck as though the extra bit of warmth might protect her from her lingering dream.

"It wasn't a vision. It was just a dream this time. Just a dream," she told herself. It was just her mind working through the fear and helplessness she felt. Tiryn, Kion, and Zinder were the ones that were trapped, not in ice, but inside a small house in the midst of a frozen village, a village that in its own way was trapped and isolated from the outside world as well.

A deep knock resonated through the thick black door to her room.

"Tiryn, are you awake?" Kion said. It was good to hear his voice again. It helped her cast off the last shackles of the dream.

"Yes, I'll be right out."

"Good. The watchers are waiting for us outside."

Tiryn pulled the covers close one last time. Crawling out from under them would mean stepping out into the sharp air pinching at her nose. Worse than the cold, the kalvar's judgment awaited outside the covers. But she could no more avoid that judgment than she could bring her mother safely home by wishing. She flung aside the blanket and shivered from the biting chill. Quick as she could, she lit the candle beside her bed and wiggled her way into the strange, old-fashioned clothes they'd brought to her the night before. Knotted stitching ran down the front and along the legs and sleeves, but the rest of the outfit was simple as could be. Both the wool sweater and buckram pants were a little too snug, but the warmth more than made up for the imperfect fit.

The house where they'd spent the night had dark oak framing its blunt doors and angled ceilings. The same wood covered the floor. The dusky beams stood out sharply against the stark white walls. Besides the bed, night table, and rounded chest with her clothes, her room lacked any other furnishings. The main room down the hall was just as bare. It contained a single chest and a low, walnut table with four lacquered stumps set around it. All of these sat on a woven rug of thick fibers. A tiny hearth of dun-colored brick sat in the corner, even smaller than the one in their own cottage. The sparse nature of the house was understandable since it had been empty for many years, but it added to the ghostly feel of the village. It was as if the three of them had wandered through some hidden veil into a place beyond time and memory. A place where no one spoke without permission and there were whispers of an Ice Maid who had brought an eternal winter. A curse did indeed lie upon this land, and it could be felt in every silent and frigid breath.

Tiryn found Kion and Zinder in the main room, speaking in low voices. They were dressed in woolen clothing similar to hers, only Zinder's had clearly been made for a child, with playful green designs around the edges and flaps and pockets in unnecessary places. His boots had little white balls on the tips of the toes and his ivy-green mittens had large white snowflake patterns woven onto the back of the hand. The sour expression on Zinder's face showed what he thought of his attire.

Kion pointed to a coat draped over the top of one of the stumps.

"There's yours. Put it on and let's go face the kalvar."

Tiryn's coat was the same as Kion's. It had a hood and was made of furs and thick wool padding. Zinder's coat was similar, but it lacked the hood and so he was forced to wear a round, bushy cap that looked like a larger version of the fuzzy balls on his toes.

"I fear the punishments have already been handed out," he said. "And mine is having to wear these clothes. I'd rather be tarred and feathered."

"Be careful what you wish for," Kion said. "These people have no love for outsiders."

"Kion, what are we going to do if they don't let us go?" Tiryn said. The kalvar was not a harsh man. She could tell that from his eyes—so penetrating and yet so burdened by the invisible weight of leading his people. Surely he would not be severe in his decision. But that did not mean that he'd just send them on their way. All that talk of traditions and order had ominous undertones.

"I'll find Truesilver and fight my way out if I have to."

"Let's hope it doesn't come to that," Zinder said.

The front door to the little house slid open and Dunwik, accompanied by other watchers, beckoned them out into the freezing air.

Though it was still early morning, the light from the sun was nearly blinding in contrast to the dim interior of the triangular frame house. Dunwik and his companions led them across a circular courtyard ringed by seven other houses identical to theirs. The roofs were encrusted in ice and snow. The courtyard was the only thing that had been cleared, though even there, white powder dusted the cracks between the smooth paving stones.

Kalvar Chaw, Eska, and more than a hundred Frindalians had gathered, a few of them mere children dressed in outfits similar to Zinder's. As with the night before, their unnatural silence put Tiryn on edge. It reminded her of her friend Lina's funeral, but at least then there had been tears and muted sobbing. Here, it was the crowd itself that was dead. If their sullen faces were any indication, the village had already condemned them. But Kalvar Chaw's judgment was all that mattered. His expression was harder to read. He brooded in enigmatic silence, showing neither disapproval nor acceptance. He stood with a great staff in one hand, the top of which was carved to resemble the antlers of a stag. Strings of ceramic beads and balls of fur hung from the tines on leather strands, shifting softly in a faint wind.

"My people. I fear some doom may be close at hand. If these three strangers are to be believed, they come from faraway lands, fleeing enemies we have not known, claiming that the Four Wards yet exist beyond the Longwinter's grasp. They bring with them a nyn, which is an ill omen, for the ancient histories say that the nyn helped the wizenthall in his treachery. And yet, it may be that the old legends have passed into fable and memory, for the wizenthall was defeated long ago. If so, then who am I to punish them for events in which they played no part?"

Eska glowered at them, his head swaying side to side in serpentine fashion. Tiryn averted her eyes and attempted to focus on the kalvar, but it was rather difficult when Eska was the only person moving among the crowd. Strangely, she noticed that he pointedly avoided looking at her. His contempt was reserved solely for Kion and Zinder. If anything, he seemed to pretend that she did not exist.

The kalvar continued, "Therefore, I pronounce this judgment upon these strangers. Instead of putting them to death, as we have with those Noathryn foolish enough to stray into our lands, I shall allow them to stay in the Tathak house for one month to prove their worthiness. During this time, they are to be treated as guests, allowed to speak in the marketplace, and taught our ways and laws. The boy will be required to accompany the hunters on their expeditions. After one month, if they have proven themselves worthy, they shall be accepted as full members into our village. I, Kalvar Chaw, have spoken."

Everyone replied in unison, "So be it." The sound fell upon the courtyard like the closing of a cage. It was just as Tiryn had feared. They were trapped. Though Kalvar Chaw had spared their lives, he may as well have condemned her mother to death. With Kion, Tiryn, and Zinder held in this eternal winter, there would be no one to come and save her now.

Kion's eyes blazed in unspoken defiance. He cast his gaze to the houses around the circle as though searching for a way out. Knowing him, he would either challenge the kalvar's ruling or take off running in search of Truesilver. Perhaps the glaive was speaking to him even now.

Zinder waved his hands wildly. "Excuse me, sir, may I speak? Is it safe to speak now?"

Kalvar Chaw extended his staff, the fur and beads swinging beneath, the carved antlers pointing toward the nyn's chest.

"What is it that you wish to say?"

"Ah, yes, well..." Zinder smoothed his childish coat and straightened himself as tall as he possibly could, but all it did was give him the appearance of a stunted dandelion with that fuzzy hat of his. Still, he launched gamely into his speech, the confidence in his voice making it obvious that he believed he could talk his way out of this predicament. "I am sure that your offer seems rather magnanimous according to your own standards and so forth, but—and I mean this with the profoundest respect—you don't seem to have much taken into account our thoughts on the matter. You see, as Kion told you last night, we did not come here looking for a new home. In fact, we're on a rather tight schedule—"

"My mother could be dying as we speak—" Kion jumped in. Tiryn grabbed his shoulder and he paused, struggling to master himself before he said—or did—something rash.

"As the boy says," Zinder went on, doing his best to downplay Kion's outburst. "We came this way to find his mother. Surely you don't mean to keep us here while she suffers at the hands of Noathryn slavers—people you don't seem to care a great deal about from the sound of things."

The kalvar held up his staff.

"Silence," Eska said, darting in front of his leader just long enough to say the word before slinking back to his side.

"I weigh all things, as a leader should. I must seek the good of my people above all. And it is forbidden for anyone to leave our lands. If the outside world knew of us, they would come and ravage our homes as they did in times past. Only recently, our brothers in Regnir suffered just this fate for disregarding the laws of our people. It is because of this that we have no mercy on the Noathryn who test our borders. Their hatred of us and desire for conquest are too strong even for the Ice Maid's curse to repel. But Whitewind remains yet hidden, and I will do nothing to risk exposing it to those who dwell in the Summerlands."

Zinder tensed, preparing to continue his case when Kion launched himself forward.

"No, you have to let us go, please don't keep us here, my mother—"

Dunwik and half a dozen watchers rushed in and grabbed hold of him before he could get close to the kalvar.

"Speak again out of turn and you'll spend a night on the judgment post," Kalvar Chaw said firmly, without malice or anger, stating it merely as a matter of fact.

Eska's face squirmed into a smug grin and he clicked his heels and shimmied about, doing a frantic little jig. "You'll regret your untamed tongue. The cold will teach you. The Ice Maid's touch is too much for one like you."

Kion struggled against the Frin, but there were too many. His eyes, though, still burned hot as flaming arrows strung taut on the bow, waiting to be fired.

Tiryn had to do something. Both her brother and her mother were in danger. Though her mind spun from a hundred overlapping fears, her feet made the decision for her. She stepped forward and bowed with such an elegant fashion, she commanded the attention of all present. Even Eska stopped his antics. More importantly, Kion ceased his struggles, shocked by the unexpected boldness of her gesture.

Tiryn remained bent over as silence gripped the circle.

"You may rise and speak your mind, daughter of the Summerlands." Kalvar Chaw motioned with his staff.

"Please, kalvar, forgive my brother. His love for our mother made him speak out of turn. He did not mean to disregard your laws."

Kalvar Chaw clenched his staff. His face was still as stone, but his eyes were soft and thoughtful. "I will consider it."

Hearing the sympathy in his tone, she risked saying what she truly wanted to say.

"We mean you no harm. Your secret is safe with us. We will not tell anyone, we promise. Only, please…" Here Tiryn faltered. She had defused the situation with Kion—or so she hoped. Did she dare ask for more? She had to. Her love for her mother compelled her. "Please let us go and find our mother. I beg you, Kalvar. My brother was not lying. Her life may be in your hands."

Eska resumed his fretful flitting, but he continued to avoid looking at Tiryn, as if he feared her in some way, or perhaps he was worried the kalvar would grant her request.

Kalvar Chaw's foggy breath puffed in and out, over and over, the distillation of his clouded thoughts. Each exhale threatened to either seal their doom or grant their freedom. Tiryn never looked away from his gaze, not once, though the effort drained her will so near the breaking point she feared she might pass out.

The clack of Kalvar Chaw's mighty staff on the pavement ended the silence.

"I must seek the good of my people above all. For that reason, my decision stands, though I am sorry for your mother." The sorrow in his eyes showed that though his pronouncement was cruel, the man who made it was not, and rather than heartbreak or anger, his words drove Tiryn to pity instead.

But not Kion.

"No! Let me go or I'll—" he shouted.

The watchers did not let him finish. They clamped their hands over his mouth and wrestled him face down onto the pavement. Kion kept struggling even then, but it was useless. He was defeated. Worse, in the eyes of the Frin, he was disgraced. The expressions of those gathered turned to scorn, except for the children, who looked on in wonder at this brave fool who would defy the mighty kalvar.

The kalvar's staff slammed against the stones.

"You were warned, outsider. Now you will suffer the just punishment for your actions. You will spend a night at the judgment post to teach you the meaning of order and respect for our ways."

The watchers dragged him off, writhing and wild-eyed, wrangling him like a captured beast. Eska chased after, whirling gleefully.

Zinder stood there, quivering, his hands over his mouth, whatever words he wanted to say frozen in his mouth from fear and disbelief.

And now Tiryn's heart did break. Not only for her mother but for her brother who would have to suffer a night out in this terrible cold. An awful premonition arose within her. Kion would not survive this night. She felt it with a terrible certainty.

A tear slid from her eye, but it froze halfway down her cheek.

Chapter 26

OF FROXES

Two of Whitewind's watchers stood guard before the only exit from the Feasting Hall, a structure nearly identical to the one where Tiryn, Kion, and Zinder had first met the kalvar the night before; only this building was full of oak tables and long rugged benches fashioned from a single tree trunk split down the middle. At the far end of the room, the hearth blazed with such sparks and fury that none of the Frin present—all women and children—sat near it. They huddled at the other end of the room, gulping down soup and tearing through chunks of rye with the same eagerness they devoted to their boisterous conversations. The mood was entirely unlike anything the Frin had shown themselves capable of up to that point. Tiryn would have enjoyed the change some other day, but at the moment she could feel nothing beyond a sickening dread. Kion had been led off to some other part of the village—where, no one would say. A long, agonizing day lay before her, and after that an even more agonizing night. The thought of Kion tied to a post, exposed and freezing, utterly alone and unprotected, sapped her appetite entirely. The bowl of mushy brown liquid before her had as much appeal as a mud puddle. It remained untouched, its heat rapidly dissipating in steamy tendrils.

She would have sat away from the others, except that the waves of heat from the hearth gave her and Zinder little choice but to join them.

The boy sitting to her left, with hair so blonde it was almost white and a squirrelly face that looked prone to exaggerated expressions, leaned over and said in an unusually loud voice for someone who was trying to whisper, "If you don't plan on eating that soup, I know a poor, starving soul who could use it." He seemed earnest enough, perhaps a little too earnest. His wry mouth and freckles fit well with the impish sparkle in his eyes. From his height, he must have been close to Tiryn in age, but the guileless way he carried himself made him seem much younger.

Tiryn stared at him, stunned that he had invaded her private despair. Blinking in sudden awareness of her surroundings, she looked about and saw that several of the younger children and not a few of the older women looked like they could certainly use an extra meal or two.

"Please, take it. I'm not hungry," she said.

The boy slid her bowl over in front of him, licking his lips.

"Why, thank you. That was most kind of you."

Before he could devour his newfound bounty, the rusty-headed boy next to him slapped his hand.

"Trik, you'd better not eat that girl's food. She might have cursed it, did you ever think about that?"

The other boy, apart from his hair color and a scar on the bridge of his nose, was the exact image of the first—twins.

"Are you sure she's a sorcerer? Her eyes aren't glowing and I haven't seen her do anything…sorcerous."

"Look at her, she's got a nyn with her. You know what the stories say about nyn—they're all tainted by dark magic." The boy came off as quite convincing, even though Tiryn knew it was all nonsense.

Zinder jerked forward. "We don't use magic, boy. It's just good old-fashioned ingenuity and hard work. Something you know precious little about, judging by the look of you."

Trik barely heeded the interjection. "How do you know it's cursed? It looks perfectly good to me—perfectly." He clamped his hands around the bowl as if he meant to drink it down rather than use a spoon.

"Of course it would. That's the way they fool you into eating it. You wouldn't eat it if it was full of worms and smelled like dead muskrat. Have you wondered why she isn't eating it if it's so perfectly good? It's because they're sorcerers—the kalvar all but said so."

Trik's head hung low, clearly deflated. Zinder dismissed them both with an angry wave.

Trik met Tiryn's eyes with a look of genuine regret. He pushed the bowl slowly back to her. "I'm sorry, but it looks like I can't eat your soup after all. I'm afraid you'll have to find somebody else to poison."

"I'm not a sorcerer, you know. Just a girl, no different from any of the others in your village."

Trik looked to his brother for support. His own reasoning skills did not seem to be up to the task.

His brother picked up his empty bowl and hefted a small bag over his shoulder. "Of course she'd say that. That's just what a sorcerer *would* say. Now come on before you fall under her spell. We've got work to do." He gave both Tiryn and Zinder a wary look.

The bewildered Trik shrugged weakly as his brother pulled him to his feet. "Maybe next time you can give me your food when Trak's not around," he said in his too-loud whisper as Trak yanked him toward the door. "Just leave out the poison next time!"

The two boys bounded outside and into the swirling snow, the door slamming shut behind them.

Zinder shoved his bowl away. "Well, at least we're rid of those two. It's bad enough that Kion's under lock and key and we're trapped inside this eternal winter. I don't need ignorant boys dragging the reputation of my people through the mud, especially if the mud's frozen, which no doubt it is, like everything else about this place."

"I don't think they said it to be mean. They just don't know any better."

"Ah, lass, there goes that heart of yours again. Soft as a

kitten, but blind as a bat. Let's be off. With Kion gone and everything that's happened since we came here, I don't have much of an appetite—something I never thought I'd say."

Tiryn gathered up her bowl and set it in front of an old woman on her way out.

"Here, I'm not hungry, please have this."

The woman pulled away from her at first, but with trembling hands, took it in the end.

"These poor people," Tiryn thought. "They live in such crippling fear." But considering it more deeply, living under the mysterious curse they spoke of, it was understandable why they feared sorcery and magic. They were caught in a never-ending winter. And now its icy chains had lashed themselves around Tiryn, binding her to that same frozen fate.

At home in Furrow, meat was reserved for special occasions. Even then, most of the time it was so old and tough, it was only fit for stew. But though Tiryn enjoyed the taste of it, she'd never been fond of preparing it. The slick texture and iron scent of the blood made her skin crawl. She found preparing fish hardly any better. Though there was almost no blood, the fish in Whitewind were so frozen that scaling and gutting them was more like carving a block of ice. And though the smell was barely noticeable, it was hardly pleasant. Poor Zinder, who had an overly sensitive nose, had no stomach for it. The greenish cast to his face showed that he was on the verge of spilling his morning soup at any moment. It was a wonder he made it long enough for the matron in charge to let their little team of workers outside for a break and some fresh air.

"I will never eat fish again," Zinder said as they strode outside, taking in great gulps of icy air and fanning himself like it was a sweltering summer day. But summer was little more than a memory in that place. Though the sun had made a cautious appearance overhead, its light was so diffused it did little more than touch the courtyard with a feeble glow. At least the cold did not knife through the skin the way it had when they first arrived. The fur coats were a welcome kindness, though little else about the Frin could be said to be either welcoming or kind. Oh, how were they ever going to get out of this place?

"I don't think I'll be able to anything until Kion's back," Tiryn said.

The fish house rested on the edge of a circular courtyard exactly like the one where Kion had received the kalvar's terrible judgment. The other houses ringing the plaza had ice-encrusted signs indicating their function. Though the writing on the signs was indecipherable beneath the ice, the watcher who had escorted them here had indicated what the buildings were: the weaver's house, the butchery, the tannery, the potter's house, the bakery, the woodshop, and the smithy. Zinder had offered to work in the last one, but Eska, who had authority over their placement, had said that such work was far too important to be trusted to a "sorcerer."

Every other building let out at the same time as the fish house and the courtyard quickly filled with noise. Most of the workers present were men, though a handful of women and a few older children were present as well. Several weren't workers at all, but armed watchers with clubs dangling from their belts and sharp eyes roving the yard. The two watchers assigned to Tiryn and Zinder allowed them to mix with the crowd, but always kept within a few paces.

Enthusiastic chatter filled the plaza. Eska traipsed about the middle of it, eyeing everyone as though he was just waiting for someone to break some rule. He talked to no one and no one talked to him. Whatever his purpose, his movements never ceased to be unsettling.

"These people talk a great deal when given the chance," Tiryn said. There had been little talking while she and Zinder had been gutting and preparing the fish all morning, just enough to explain what needed to be done.

"Well, you can hardly blame them. It's like they've been holding their breath all day and finally get to let it out."

Tiryn caught the old woman she'd given her soup to that morning staring at her from across the plaza, near the weaver's house, but she turned pale and looked away when Tiryn waved at her. A few of the others who'd dined with them were gathered around either the potter's or the weaver's houses.

In one corner of the plaza, several children played keep-away with a chunk of ice they kicked across the pavement. Their rosy cheeks and tinkling laughter were almost enough to make the place seem like a normal village, but the watchers shadowing her, and her own dark fears about Kion's fate, were grim reminders of the true nature of this place. The day was half over and the thing she feared most, Kion's night at the judgment post, was swiftly approaching. A chill seeped into her skin at the mere thought of it.

"Look over there—it's our two tormentors from this morning," Zinder said.

At the edge of the ice-kicking game, Trik tossed a stick as far as he could down an empty street. A fox with fur so white it might have just hopped out of a snowbank, whisked away after the stick as the twins cheered the animal on. The creature flew over the pavement, a wintry blur. As it caught the stick, its eyes flashed a brilliant blue, then quickly faded to their natural black. The diamond ears, sleek snout, and downy fur so captivated Tiryn that for a moment she forgot all about the cursed village and the terrible punishment awaiting Kion. Her love of all things living melted the icy chill from her embattled heart.

"Oh, Zinder, isn't that fox the loveliest creature you've ever seen? Can we go see it? Perhaps they'll let me pet it."

Zinder huffed out a glacial cloud. "Oh dear, I should never have pointed them out. You know they'll only call us sorcerers and spout nonsense."

"They're nice boys. I know they are. They have to be to have tamed a pet like that."

The fox came racing back with the half-frozen sprig of wood. Trak took a turn and flicked it away, tossing it even farther than his brother. The fox flew down the street again, snatching it and sprinting back, as fresh as could be and ready for another toss. The twins repeated this four more times before Tiryn could convince Zinder to venture over and talk with them.

Trak nudged his brother at their approach. "Careful, Trik. Remember what I told you."

Despite the warning, Trik couldn't keep himself from giving a friendly bob of the head at their approach.

"Hello again," Tiryn said. "We just want to…" As much as she longed to, she couldn't bring herself to say what she'd been meaning to. Her timid tongue froze inside her mouth.

"She wants to pet your fox." Zinder uttered the words for her. Good old Zinder, stepping in even though he hadn't wanted to come.

Trak knelt and gave the fox a scratch as if to show that the creature had no need of petting from strangers.

"Trak, I know you're smarter than I am, but I don't think they're here to turn us into icicles. They don't look like the icicle sort."

"Snowmen, then," Trak said, pulling the fox close. The beast nuzzled the boy's face and he giggled, momentarily dropping his sour demeanor.

An idea lit up Trik's normally distracted face. He bounded over and handed Tiryn the stick. "Here. Let's let Scriff decide. She'll throw it and if he brings it back to her, it will mean she's not a sorcerer."

"Trik, don't you ever listen?"

"You know how razor-smart froxes are, Trak. This will settle it once and for all. Scriff won't let us down. A frox knows best."

"Excuse me, did you say 'frox'?" Tiryn said.

"Yes. He's a frost fox, actually. But me and Trak call him a frox for short." Trik patted his chest in pride over his linguistic genius.

"Well, I'd love to try if it means I have a chance at petting him. He's such a beautiful animal."

Trak wavered, rising at last, shoving his hands into his coat pockets. "All right, fine. But if anything happens to Scriff, it's on your head."

"See? See? I thought of an idea for once!" Trik bounced on the paving stones in obvious delight.

Scriff stared up at Tiryn, his eyes locked on the stick. She had spent many an afternoon skipping rocks across the silvery streams of the Tors and so had a rather good aim. She put it right in the middle of the street. Though her aim was true, the distance left something to be desired—there was a headwind, after all. Scriff caught the stick after the first bounce. Without stopping, he swiveled his hindquarters and reversed course. Snow dust flew from his paws as he darted back down the street, straight for Tiryn. He dropped the stick into her hand and gave her cheek a lick, as enthusiastically as if he'd known her his whole life. Though the greeting was warm in terms of affection, the tongue was icy cold, and Tiryn shivered and gave a nervous laugh at the unexpected sensation.

"Will you look at that?" Zinder planted his hands on his hips. "I guess we're not sorcerers after all. Frox knows best."

Tiryn took off one glove and ran her fingers through the frox's fur. It was even more soft and airy than she'd imagined. The sheer loveliness of it danced across her skin.

Trik and Trak gaped, eyes unblinking.

"Scriff's never taken to anyone like that before," Trak said.

"I knew she wasn't the sorcerous sort," Trik said. Tiryn noted that he did not include Zinder in that statement.

"He's so playful," Tiryn said. "You're so lucky to have him."

"He's awfully big for a fox," Zinder said, still giving a frosty eye to the twins.

Scriff's nose brushed against Tiryn's hand—it was as cold as his tongue. "Do any other villagers have them as pets? I haven't seen any."

"No, we're the only ones. Froxes are pretty rare. They only live out on Tinesplitter Isle," Trak said.

"You've been to Tinesplitter?" Zinder said, momentarily forgetting his dislike of the boys.

"Well, yes, when we were younger, before Regnir got captured by the Noathryn, but it's forbidden to go there now." Trik looked about nervously and lowered his voice, but his attempt at whispering was hardly different from his normal tone. "We sort of snuck out one night, though, and rescued Scriff from drowning in the bay."

Trak swatted his brother in the arm. "Shh! Someone might hear."

Trik leaned in closer, cupping his hand on one side of his mouth. "We're not supposed to go beyond the shore except for fishing."

"So you two have a boat?" Zinder said.

"Oh no." Trik laughed off the idea. "The bay's frozen solid, from here all the way to Tinesplitter and beyond."

"Ice fishing," Trak said. "He meant ice fishing."

"I see." Zinder smoothed down his already perfect mustache. Tiryn wondered what plan he was cooking up in that sharp mind of his.

"Well, whatever the rules are, it was brave of you to risk your lives saving Scriff," Tiryn said. "I'm so glad you did. He's simply wonderful."

"Kalvar Chaw didn't want to let us keep it, but we convinced him in the end," Trak said. "Do you know how froxes capture their food? They freeze it. They can breathe a small burst of ice fog when they want to and it'll freeze anything caught inside it quick as a wink."

"How strange." Tiryn took a closer look at Scriff's maw. His gums were bright blue and his teeth were coated in a thin layer of ice. "I imagine it's a challenge feeding him."

Bells sounded in the courtyard, small and brittle, like clinking glass. Eska bore tiny ones in each hand and shook them for all they were worth, though the snow deadened the sound. He kept ringing them over and over as he waltzed in his curious way towards the woodshop. Everyone drifted back towards the various houses from which they'd come.

"Do you two work in one of these places?" Tiryn asked as they strolled towards the center of the courtyard.

"We're stacking wood today," Trak said, hanging his head. "We usually go out trapping."

"We're expert trappers—and trackers," Trik said.

"But we got in trouble and so we have to stack wood. Only for two more days, though."

"Well, I hope to see you two—and Scriff—again soon."

"Yes, I'd like to ask you a few more questions about the bay," Zinder said in a low voice.

"Perhaps," Trak said, nodding sagely, as though he were far older.

"I'm glad we're friends," Trik said, waving enthusiastically. "And I do hope you find your mother, no matter what the kalvar's punishment says." The last was added in his boisterous whisper, which earned him a slap on the arm from Trak.

"Shh!" Trak ordered. "Watch what you say."

The bells pealed on with plinking persistence as the two parties took their leave. Trik and Trak scurried towards the woodshop where a red-faced Eska stamped and skittered. Whatever he said to the twins was indecipherable across the square, but the tone was far from pleasant. At one point, he lunged at poor Trik, frightening him so badly that he tumbled into a large stack of wood. He hit it just right and half the logs rolled off in a wooden cascade. Trik, Trak, and Scriff deftly avoided the clunking onslaught, but Eska danced right into the oncoming wave of timber. The stream of logs tripped him up and sent him flailing, but he "fell up," as Zinder put it afterward, and landed in Trik and Trak's arms rather than on the ground, avoiding the wayward wood.

By then, Zinder and Tiryn had arrived at the fish house. The fish matron stood outside, wearing a scowl fierce enough to smoke trout, and fuming wintry wisps from her nostrils.

"You two quit your gawking and get back to work," she said, then added, under her breath, "Those two boys'll be the death of us all."

Tiryn risked one last glance before going inside. Trik and Trak were dusting Eska off and offering endless, if less-than-convincing apologies, for they were unable to keep a straight look on their faces. Eska was having none of it. He whirled away from them, his face burning red as a sunset. A few innocent chuckles escaped from Trik. The display of mirth, so foreign and unexpected in this gloomy village, struck a chord in Tiryn's memory. Scenes of Kion laughing at her expense rose to the surface of her troubled thoughts. All those times he had been there when she tripped or tumbled or went sprawling to the ground. She had hardly appreciated his laughter then, because it had so often been at her expense. But looking back on it now, his mirth had helped her to laugh at her own clumsiness and make it less embarrassing than it otherwise would have been. And it gave them a shared memory they could both look back upon and laugh about together. Perhaps making her brother laugh had been worth a few skinned knees and a little wounded pride.

But when would she hear his laughter again? If only she could find out where he was and rescue him somehow. Together they could find Mother and go back to their bright sunny little farm in Furrow and make new memories to laugh over. But the farm lay abandoned, Mother was gone, and Kion's laughter had been swallowed up by the judgment of cruel men.

She followed Zinder back into the dank, tomb-like silence of the fish house, misery and dread once again taking hold. She feared laughter would be hard to come by in the days ahead.

Chapter 27

THE JUDGMENT POST

Kion's prison was a decrepit old shed that leaned hard to one side. Four more miserable walls could not be found in all the land. The pine slats surrounding him were so thin and full of gaps he might as well have passed the day outside. The wind poured through them like a sieve. Despite his coat and boots, he was already shivering by the time the door swung open that night. Though two watchers had stood guard outside all day, Kion had not said a word since Chaw had sentenced him to this fate. He had learned that much. Anything he said would only make things worse. In Whitewind, words were rare as gold and hoarded just as much. Only the kalvar and Eska, that unsettling fool who pranced around him, seemed to be exempt from the laws of silence. And it was Eska who stood now at the door, his eyes gloating.

"Time for your punishment, summerlander. Are you ready? Do you like the cold? Will winter be your friend? Hmm? No, I don't think so. I don't think you're strong enough to last the night. The Maid of Ice will not treat you kindly. She has eyes only for one. Will she take your life? Will she pick the flesh from your bones? We'll have to wait until the morning to find out!" He twisted his fingers into a knot of anticipation.

Eska's taunting had no effect upon Kion. He knew how to handle taunts. He'd been picked on by farmers all his life. No, the taunts he could handle. He wasn't even worried about the cold all that much, either, for he was already freezing, though that might change after the sun had been down a few more hours. What bothered him most, what crushed him on the inside, was knowing that he had let his mother down. If only he'd kept quiet, if only he hadn't let his temper trick him into rash words, he could have been sleeping tonight with Tiryn and Zinder, plotting a way to get out of this village. His father had never allowed his anger to best him like that. Kion had failed him as well. Perhaps if Kithian had been there, he could have calmed Kion down and helped him hold his tongue. But would Kion have listened? He wasn't sure.

But he held his tongue now. He would not make the same mistake again. The kalvar's advisor went on for several minutes, bouncing and flitting the entire time. Kion wondered if he ever stopped shaking, even in his sleep. Something was clearly wrong with him, but the rest of the village acted as if it was none of their concern. Maybe if Kion started acting like a madman they'd let him talk as well, but he doubted that.

"You think you can be happy just because you have a sister?" Eska said, jabbing all five fingers toward Kion in a strange gesture. He had mentioned the fact that Kion had a sister several times, as if that were part of his offense as well. "You summer-landers are all the same. Living in your bright world of innocence and light, but you'll know suffering before the day is over. Oh, yes, you will! And your sister will know sorrow the same way I—the same way we—know sorrow."

When Kion failed to respond to Eska's jibes, the advisor eventually grew weary and left, sauntering away in graceless gyrations, muttering to himself. He decided not to come to the pole with the watchers once it became clear that Kion wouldn't prove to be any sport. It was already well below freezing by then, and Eska no doubt had warmer places to be.

The four watchers who tied him to the pole did so with none of the delight Eska had displayed. Neither sympathy nor scorn touched their grim faces. They had a duty to perform, no more, no less.

"We'll come for you at dawn," one of them said after they'd

fastened the shackles on his wrists. They stalked away, their boots thumping against the pavement of the plaza. Kion watched them go through the one clear path leading out of the circular courtyard, fading into the blur of darkness.

The judgment post was now his sole companion. It was so old and weathered it was difficult to tell what kind of wood it was made of. Ice filled its cracks like frozen sap exuding from its frosty heart. The indifferent pole rose ten feet above the pavement. Kion had to crane his neck to see the top. Two chains stretched from his wrists upwards, keeping his arms extended above his head and forcing him to stand. The metal shackles bit through his gloves, chilling his wrists to the bone. As time went on, the chill only deepened and spread.

Restless currents flicked snow dust from the rooftops of the surrounding houses. Other currents caught the crystals up in a swirling, moonlight glitter. It would have been enchanting if seen from a distance, from somewhere warm and safe from the elements.

He listened for any sounds from the village, but it was still as the grave. These people cared nothing for him, but that was to be expected. What he struggled to endure was the loss of Kithian. Kion had not heard his voice since the night before. The glaive's absence left an ever-widening pit gaping inside. The loss drained his will and made the cold that much harder to bear. Without his glaive, a part of him was missing. With Truesilver, Kion could face any enemy, even this Maid of Ice they kept mentioning, if she were even real. Without his glaive, he was nothing but a shepherd far from home, in trouble far deeper even than the snow drifts which mounted steadily against the sides of the houses.

"If ever I needed your voice, it is now, Kithian," he said.

Tiryn and Zinder had been taken from him, too. No one would be coming to free him from this terrible post. Could he get through this on his own? He wished he could fall asleep and wake up in some warm bed and this terrible night would be over, but he could ill afford the luxury of sleep tonight. He would need to keep his feet moving to stave off the cold. No, any sleep in a cold like this would be the sleep of death. He forced himself to shuffle from side to side, for he was unable to move more than half a step away from the pole.

The wind rasped and hissed, soon stirring more than just dust. As time dragged on, large, papery snowflakes whisked in to blanket the courtyard. The snow covered his shoulders and the tops of his legs and landed like pinpricks on his face. With his hands tethered above him, he could not easily brush it off. He closed his eyes, keeping his head tucked between his arms so that his limbs bore the brunt of the powdery assault, but it did little good. He shuffled some more, to keep his feet from going numb, but it was a battle against an implacable foe.

Hordes of snowflakes whipped past him, an endless rush of tiny soldiers seizing the courtyard and trampling underfoot all that was there. The dark houses standing vigil around the courtyard slowly went under, shrouded by the blinding barrage. Kion's fingers turned into blocks of ice fastened to the ends of his arms. The frozen pavement stabbed at him through his boots. His breath came in trembles and shakes. His shackles were now frozen to his gloves, the icy metal burning through the wool as if it weren't there. The air hurt to breathe. The burning frost poured down his throat and into his nostrils. His teeth felt like they would snap in two. Worst of all were his eyes. The wind seemed to throw its iciest darts straight into them. The freezing barbs buried themselves deep, plunging into his skull. And still the storm flailed on. It was unnatural in its fury—as if it possessed a will of its own, a will bent on the destruction of all that was living.

He wondered again about the Maid of Ice. Was it just a figure of speech or an old legend? Could it be that some invisible being was slowly squeezing the life out of him with her wintry embrace? Kion searched for some phantom, some power behind the pelting flakes, but saw nothing beyond the surging storm.

"Kithian, where are you?" he said, but his words were snatched away by the wind as soon as they left his frost-coated lips. A shivering chill grabbed hold of him, wrapping itself around his bones, slowly transforming his skin from flesh to ice. His face grew hard as wood. He could no longer feel his lips. His mind began to fog. Sights and sounds dimmed and deadened. His thoughts grew numb along with his body. He came to question the most basic things. Where was he? Why was he here? He fought and scraped for some snatch of memory. The Maid of Ice. It had something to do with the Maid of Ice…

No, that wasn't it. It was…Mother. Yes, his mother was… lost…somewhere out in this storm. But where were Tiryn and Zinder? Why had everyone abandoned him?

"No—stop it, Kion. They're here," he told himself. "Tiryn and Zinder are here. And so is Kithian. We're prisoners, trapped by the…the…was it the Noathryn or someone else?"

A faint memory flitted by and he latched onto it—the first time he held Truesilver in his hand. Such warmth, such comfort and peace. It was as if he had touched the living heart of another. The veil of this world had been lifted and the hidden light obscured by form and appearance had broken through. Wonder and awe had visited him in that moment and he would never be the same.

But the memory turned to mist and scattered amidst the torrents of snow lashing his body. Kion could no longer feel his feet. He willed his legs to keep moving, but could not tell whether or not they obeyed. The seething waves of white surrounding him swallowed everything. This was more than just a storm. A mountain of frost had been hurled upon him and he was being buried alive.

"You're too weak," he heard Kithian's voice say. "You're not strong enough to survive this. Look at me. You think the cold bothers me? I am a glaive, made from living metal. The cold means nothing to me. You are frail and helpless. You are not worthy to wield a blade such as myself. One day you will die—

perhaps tonight—but I will live on. I will know other sword-speakers and fight other battles. I will endure, but you, you shall be carried away by this storm, never to be heard from again."

Hearing Kithian's condemnation hit with greater force than even the wind. Kion needed his glaive to bring him hope, but instead, Kithian had mocked his weakness, like one of the farmers from Furrow. The betrayal stung, but it hurt all the more because Kithian was right. Who was Kion to wield a glaive anyway? He was nothing but a foolish shepherd, too weak to protect his own mother.

"That's right. You're just a shepherd. Woolhead. Sheepstink." The voice had changed into the surly speech of Dougan Shaw. "You can't fight. Give up that sword and go back to your cudgel, woolly. Your father's a coward, just like you. You don't deserve to be in the ring with me..."

"Why couldn't you hold your tongue?" It was Tiryn's voice now. "Why couldn't you keep quiet and obey the kalvar's law? You always have to have your own way, don't you? Your foolishness will cost Mother her life..."

"What a disappointment you turned out to be, lad," Zinder said. "What would your father say if he could see you now? You were ready to abandon me at Dunach. What kind of friend would do that? Oh, lad, you're hopeless, just hopeless..."

Kion's head dropped to his chest. The voices were right. Kion was a miserable failure and the proof of it was that his foolishness and brashness had led him here. He couldn't recall exactly what he had done to deserve being cast out into this storm, but he was certain that he must deserve it.

But even as despair rose to master him, a golden light sparked amidst the blinding white. At first, he could hardly make it out, for the snow was all-consuming and the light flickered no more brightly than a dying candle. But the longer he stared at it, the brighter it grew until he could see that this golden dash of color came from a small animal that had emerged from the snow. If he could have trusted his snowblind eyes he would have said it was a squirrel, and yet this animal was as large as a small dog. The color of its fur was unnaturally bright —it shone like the finest gold, as if the animal were fashioned of precious metal and not of flesh. What in the Four Wards could it be? Zinder had spoken of golden animals before, and they'd even seen one streaking across their path once, though that had been a hare and not a squirrel. Were there golden beasts of other kinds as well? Or were they just another one of Zinder's tales? He blinked away the ice crusting on his eyelashes to make certain he was seeing clearly, but when he looked again the squirrel was gone.

He strained to find it again, but the creature was nowhere to be seen. It must have been swallowed up by the storm, along with everything else in the courtyard. Or perhaps it had never been there at all, a mere trick of his slowly dimming perception. A sense of loss settled upon him, as if that animal had been his one source of hope in all this bitter, raging cold, and, now that it was gone, the storm would claim his life.

Kion struggled to recall his thoughts before the beast had appeared. Someone had been telling him something, but he could not recall the words. Perhaps he had imagined that as well. He had the impression that whatever it was—imagined or not—it had been hard to take. An awful truth that could only be seen when looking in the face of death. But didn't Kithian say that the truth was hard? Kion strained to hear anything beyond the howling storm. Above all, he longed to hear the voice of Kithian, that ancient voice as bright and sure as the rising sun. If he could but catch a few words from his glaive it might stir the fire inside of him and sustain him through this awful night.

A warmth emanated deep inside of him at these thoughts, drawing him into a secret inner haven, lit with flickering flames upon a blazing hearth. In this hidden refuge at last he found shelter from the cold. He could rest from the storm here and wait for Kithian to speak to him and tell him what he should do. Kithian's wisdom never failed. Nor would it fail to come to him now. Holding tightly to that hope, his strength flowed gradually from his frozen body into his spirit. He no longer bothered stamping his feet and fighting to stay awake. Far better to take refuge in this warm, expectant place inside himself, the place where Kithian had always met him before. Kithian must not be far off now. He would come and light a way out of this darkness. Perhaps Tiryn would bring his blade to him. Kion would feel it once again in his hand and the cold would melt away.

Kion would sleep, just for a little while, until Tiryn came.

Sleep. If only for a moment. Rest. His glaive would find a way to him while he slept. Kithian had never failed him before. Surely, he would not fail him now.

Chapter 28

TIRYN'S LAMENT

Tiryn met the watchers at the door. She had not slept all that long and fearful night. If she had not made Zinder drink some sourberry tea he would not have slept either.

Her breath caught in her throat when she saw Kion's frost-encrusted body. His skin was pale blue, as cold and lifeless as the fish she'd spent the day preparing. Sheets of frozen snow covered his coat and pants. His black hair was caked in ice crystals, turning it a leaden gray. They laid his body on the floor. He did not move and was not breathing.

"I am sorry." Dunwik, who was among the watchers, dropped his usual stern mask and spoke with genuine remorse. "Last night a storm came through, the worst one Whitewind has seen in a generation. The Maid of Ice took your brother."

She looked from Dunwik's face to Kion's, refusing to believe the watcher's words. In desperation, she grasped his hands. They were as cold and unyielding as if they'd been sculpted from ice. "No. No, he just passed out. He can't be dead. He's too strong, too young. He's…he's my brother."

Dunwik's head bowed in silence. For that is what death is: silence. The end of words, the end of laughter, the end of hope, the end of dreams. Cold, black silence. And it swept the room.

Tiryn drew her arms around her brother and pulled him into her lap. The chill burned through her, but she welcomed the pain. It kept the sorrow from breaking in and overwhelming her in its depths. Kion's eyes were sealed, his eyelashes coated in a layer of tiny icicles. His hair was stiff and broom-like. She tried to smooth it, but it would not move. It was as if he had been turned to stone. A cold, lifeless statue.

"We brought him here so that you could say good-bye. Take as long as you wish," Dunwik said.

She buried her head in Kion's ice-blue neck and tears poured from her eyes. She clung to her brother's frozen frame, her knuckles as white as his coat. "Oh, Kion, no. Please. You can't leave me. You can't leave your sister all alone. You said you wouldn't leave me this time. You promised. Don't leave me, Kion. I need you. Please don't go away. Please…"

Tiryn's voice was swallowed by terrified heaves. She struggled to breathe. First her father, and now her brother. The two men she loved most in all the world were gone. Kion was courageous and noble and handsome and kind. He was the closest thing to a father she had left. How would she ever survive without her brother to protect her in a world so full of hatred and death? If only Mother were here. She would know what to do. She would know what to say. But Mother was lost as well, and without Kion there was no hope of ever seeing her again. Tiryn's body convulsed with the depth of her loss and the injustice of it all.

These cold, cruel men! Why had they done this to her brother? What had he done to deserve this? Why, oh why, did life cut down all the people she loved most? Her eyes rose in accusation against the watchers who had borne her brother's body to her like this, battered and broken. Did they see the bitterness of what they had wrought? Did they know the needless, senseless pain they had caused? If they did, they said nothing, but looked away, unwilling to face this slight young girl whose heart they had shattered beyond hope of repair.

Her tears rained down upon Kion's neck and face. They formed small puddles on his forehead and cheeks, tiny havens of warmth that erased some of the icy mask, but they were mere droplets on the surface of a frozen sea. Not even the hottest fire could melt that ocean of death and bring him back to her now.

Or could it?

An impossible thought tore through her mind, a single spark in a great void of nothingness. Kion had told her once that in bonding with his glaive, he'd felt as if a part of him had passed into the weapon and that a part of Kithian had passed into him. He said that the two of them were stronger together than they were apart.

Tiryn swallowed several times before she could get enough air to speak. It was a wild, outlandish hope, but it was hope all the same.

"Watcher Dunwik."

"Yes, young one?" He met her eyes and she thought she could see some of her own pain reflected there.

"Please bring me my brother's sword." Just speaking the words filled her with an unexpected strength. Her tears ceased to flow and her breathing eased back to normal.

"Excuse me?"

Half-frozen tears fell like scales from her cheeks as she brushed them away. "I asked you to please bring me my brother's sword."

Dunwik knelt on one knee, as he had before the kalvar. "We will bury it with him if that is what you wish."

"No. I need you to bring it here. To this house. At once."

"You are overcome with grief. That is understandable. But bringing your brother's sword—"

"Please. I need you to bring it. It is a special sword." She did not bother finishing the thought. No amount of explanation would make him understand and she was probably wrong anyway. "Please bring it to me. Once I have it, you may take him away."

Dunwik cast a doubtful glance at the others, who only dropped their heads in dismay. "Very well. I will honor your wish. I will return with it as quickly as I can." He and one of the other watchers departed.

Tiryn began to shiver, half from her impossible hope and half because Kion's body was so terribly cold. But she would not let go. Not until Truesilver was here. Not until she knew, one way or the other, if her desperate idea was something more than a foolish delusion.

Dunwik returned at length with the sword. The beautiful, golden hilt and sparkling gems glowed as if they possessed the light of the sun condensed into tiny points. When Dunwik placed it in her hand, it was surprisingly cold. Her hopes fell. She'd never held Truesilver before, having no skill with a blade. But the warmth would come when it touched Kion's hand. It had to. She scrambled to pull the unwieldy blade out of the sheath, desperation driving her on.

The watchers stared at the scene, puzzled by the presence of the blade, but also in pity for the grief-stricken maiden. She twisted and yanked and tore at one of Kion's gloves until it came off at last. Feeling more tears welling up inside her, she hurried on, staving off a rising sense of despair. She wedged Truesilver's hilt into Kion's stony hand, forcing his fingers around the supple leather.

Nothing happened. The blade's magnificent hilt shone with a generous light, but that was all. No change came to her lifeless brother.

She dropped her head in defeat. The tears surged up and spilled out once more. Sorrow rushed in, twice as bitter and poisonous as before. She chided herself for her vain belief. What a foolish little girl she had been to hope…

One of the watchers gasped…

Like a drop of dye into a glass of water, a tiny fleck of color appeared on Kion's palm. It radiated out across his hand wherever his skin touched the blade. The color rose up his arm, absolving even his coat sleeve of its frosty tinge. The heat bloomed up his shoulder and spread to his head and chest at the same time. When it reached his heart, Kion gave a start and took in a sudden breath.

Tiryn's hand went to her mouth, too startled to speak.

Kion's eyes opened and met hers. Silence once more ruled the chamber, but this time it was not the silence of death, but of joy and wonder.

"I'm back," he said. Those intense, blazing eyes of his had never looked so beautiful.

"Oh, Kion." She flung her arms around him. His flesh felt like Old Slick Rock on a sunny afternoon, hard and cool beneath, but warm and sunny on the surface.

"It's all right, Tiryn. Kithian's here and we're together and everything will be all right now." His voice was weak, but he was alive. Somehow, beyond all reason, he was alive.

"It is as Eska said. They are sorcerers," said one of the watchers, recoiling in fear. The words struck Tiryn like a blow. All her joy teetered on the edge of a new-formed, yawning abyss.

Dunwik gripped the man's shoulder. "No, have you not listened when the kalvar recites the legends? This blade is one of the glaives of old. And that boy…that boy is a swordspeaker."

Dunwik and another watcher went for Kalvar Chaw and Eska at once while the others stayed, regarding Kion and Truesilver in terrified awe. The next moment Zinder rushed in, still dressed in his nightclothes. He stumbled over the edge of the rug, not at all his usual self, and more or less fell on the floor beside Kion and Tiryn.

"Oh, lad, look what they've done to you. And me asleep and warm like a mangy old dog in my bed. Some friend I turned out to be! Tiryn, why didn't you wake me?"

"It's all right, Zinder," Kion said, his voice a quiet rasp. "Just seeing you is enough. I thought I might never get to again."

Tiryn laid her hand upon his chest. "Hold off on speaking for now, Kion, if you can. Let me bring you some water." She rose and went to the hearth to stoke the fire. She placed a battered kettle on the top plate and soon it was sputtering, fumes spurting from the spout.

"You're even worse off than you look, judging by the tone in Tiryn's voice. Not to mention the strange looks on the watchers' faces. They couldn't be paler if they'd seen a ghost. Why, your face is downright rosy compared to theirs. What in the Four Wards is going on?"

Tiryn poured Kion a mug of tepid water, stirring in dark shavings of tea. A rosy pungent smell filled the room. "There you go. Not too hot, not too cold." She and Zinder propped Kion against one of the stumps and then she tipped the mug so that Kion could take a few sips. "Zinder, Kion didn't make it through the night. When they brought him here he wasn't breathing."

"Wasn't breathing? But how—? You're a fine healer, Tiryn, but last I knew there was no cure for that. Surely you were mistaken."

"I don't understand it either, but when they brought Truesilver in, he came back to life."

"Came back to life?" Zinder's hands pressed against the sides of his head, as if he had to keep his good sense from flying into the air.

The tea lent greater strength to Kion's voice. "Kithian says that I was not truly dead. Somehow, I was put into a sort of enchanted sleep that protected me through the night. Even so, I should have died, and would have died, if Tiryn had delayed much longer in bringing Truesilver to me."

"Enchanted sleep?" Zinder eyed the two watchers warily. "You might not want to say that too loud in a place like this. But what's that even supposed to mean?"

"It was the Spark. It quickens both mind and heart, but it can also work in the reverse, to slow and protect. It works upon us in ways that even Kithian does not fully understand. Someone put me to sleep by means of the Spark, by casting me into a sleep that allowed me to survive the storm."

"Well, that sounds like a bowl of cracklenuts if I ever heard of one. Who would do something like that? You're sure it wasn't the sword?"

"No. Kithian isn't sure who did it. But I've only been awake for a short time. Perhaps he can tell me more once we've had a chance to discuss it further." Kion took another long sip of tea, his eyes half-lidded from exhaustion.

"Could it be this Ice Maid they keep whispering about? This village has more secrets than a nynnian attic."

Tiryn patted Zinder on the shoulder. "When he gets his strength back perhaps he can tell us more, but the kalvar is on his way right now so you might want to change your clothes."

"Oh my." Zinder's cheeks flushed apple-red as he looked down at his clothes in horror. "All this dying and coming back to life made me forget where I was." He bumbled his way back out of the room, his voice echoing down the hall. "A nyn in his knickers, what a scandal!"

"I've never seen Zinder lose his sense of fashion that way," Kion said, ruminating behind the steaming cup of tea, the old spark of mischief twinkling in his eyes. "Do you have any medicine for that?"

"Shh. Try not to talk so much. It's more than just his clothes, you know. He almost lost his dearest friend. You're worth far more to him than the finest hat in all the land."

Kalvar Chaw and Eska returned with Dunwik while Zinder was still getting dressed.

Kion struggled to rise, but Tiryn would have none of it and laid two firm hands on his shoulders to keep him down. It was the only time she could remember when she was actually stronger than her brother.

The kalvar's frame seemed to fill half the room. He stood over Tiryn and Kion, a great dark hill of a man.

"It is good to see that you survived the night. Though it

passes reason how any man could endure such a night as that. The streets are covered in snow up to my chest and an ice fog still lingers north of the village." His words were tinged with regret, but also amazement. Eska clucked beside him, swiveling with great agitation. "Dunwik tells me that it was not your strength alone that carried you through the storm, however. He says that the blade you bear may be one of the glaives of old. Is that so? Are you indeed a swordspeaker?"

"Yes, Kalvar, I am," Kion said, grasping the sword that lay beside him. "I can see you are as surprised as I was when I first found Truesilver, but I give you my word that it is so."

"Truesilver. Greatest of the Mastersmith's glaives," Kalvar Chaw said in quiet astonishment.

Eska cringed, refusing to look at the blade. Its soft glow and unequaled craftsmanship were unnatural and threatening to his fearful eyes.

"How is it that you know of the glaives?" Kion said. "They have been lost for an age." His body shook with a ragged cough. Tiryn grimaced at the sound, wishing he could speak to the kalvar after he'd had some rest, but there was little she could do. This was the kalvar's domain, not hers.

"In the Frostkeld the legends have not died. When the Longwinter came and trapped our lands, our ancestors made a pledge to preserve our history. The ice has frozen not just our land, but also our memories, after a fashion. For us, the world is unchanged from a thousand years ago. That is how we have kept alive the knowledge of the Noathryn campaigns to wipe us from our lands and of the wizenthall's curse upon the Four Wards. And we also know of the glaives the Mastersmith sent to stop him. Knowledge of the past is the only remedy against the decay of truth."

Kion was wracked with a bout of deep-chested coughing, but he suppressed it with some effort. His eyes grew distant as the fit subsided and Truesilver's voice captured him for several moments.

"Kalvar, Truesilver tells me that the one you call the wizenthall is named Talinyon. Do you know what happened to him after he was defeated? Or what happened to the other glaives besides Truesilver? They were lost shortly after Talinyon disappeared and passed out of all knowing."

Eska pointed accusingly. "Surely, kalvar, we don't believe this sorcerer just because he claims that, that...that that *blade* is a glaive. How can that be? Do not the legends say that all the blades were lost? He lies! I am sure of it."

"So the legends say. But how many swords do you know that can bring a man back from the dead?"

"A trick. He was only pretending. He's a clever one, yes. Quite clever for his age, but he doesn't fool me. I see the truth. I have the sight. I speak of things before they come to pass. And I say that this boy is no swordspeaker, but a charlatan and a fool!"

Kalvar Chaw ruffled his immense nest of a beard, pondering his advisor's words.

"Dunwik, you are certain that he was dead?"

"His breath had left him. I do not believe that any man could have survived that storm, not even the hardiest of my men."

Eska glared at the watcher, fidgeting inside his cloak as if he had a sudden itch. "No, no, no. I am a seer. And I say he is a sorcerer. He has beguiled you. Yes, surely he has beguiled you, great kalvar."

Tiryn started forward, stifling a squeak. It was one of the few times in her life she could barely hold in her words, but she remembered the kalvar's prohibition against speaking without permission.

"Yes, young one? You have something to say?" Kalvar Chaw said.

"If it pleases you, kalvar. I only wanted to say that yesterday —in the courtyard outside the fish house—when we were not working—I met two boys named Trik and Trak." A troubled line traced Chaw's brow and Eska sneered. Tiryn worried that she might end up doing more harm than good if the twins were somehow out of favor with the kalvar and his advisor, but she pressed on. "And they had a frost fox, or, as they called it, a frox."

"Troublesome beast," Eska muttered.

"They said a frox could tell if someone was a sorcerer or not. And they put Zinder and me to the test and the animal showed no fear of either of us. If you want to be sure that Kion is no sorcerer, why don't you send for the frox and see how it treats him."

Eska scowled, but the kalvar nodded thoughtfully. "What you say is true. I had forgotten the old tales about the frost foxes. It is said that they can sense the Spark as well as the sorcerous perversions of it. Their eyes glow if they draw near to it. But as there have been no such things in an age, some wonder if they have lost the talent. I am surprised Trik and Trak remembered this. Perhaps they are better listeners to the old tales than I had thought."

Eska raised his twitching chin imperiously. "Very well. Bring the animal if you wish. It will only prove that either the boy has you under his spell, kalvar, or that frost foxes no longer have the power to sense either Spark or sorcery."

Tiryn clutched Kion's arm, wondering if anything would sway this bitter man who seemed to hate them so.

Chapter 29

ESKA'S TEST

Eska did not wish to bring Scriff into the house, but Tiryn's insistence that Kion not be exposed to the cold won out.

It was odd. Every time the kalvar allowed her to speak, Eska grew quiet and withdrew, as if he wished to avoid her at all costs. She could not think why this would be. She'd never said or done anything to offend him as far as she knew. Then again, little that Eska did made sense.

In short order, the kalvar, Eska, and Dunwik returned with Trik, Trak, and their pet. The other three watchers, wary of Eska's talk of sorcery, were more than happy to leave when Scriff arrived. Even so, there was hardly room for so many people in the little room, and they had to move Kion onto one of the stumps in a corner so that they could all fit. Kion's voice had lost its rasp, but he was still weak. Tiryn could see that she was going to have a rough time nursing him back to health if he kept pushing himself and insisting that he was fine.

"I wish Mother were here," she thought for the thousandth time. Kion would listen to her.

Trik and Trak entered the house with broad grins, pleased to have gotten the attention of the kalvar, and even more pleased that their frox had been called upon to show off his talents.

Scriff was remarkably well-behaved inside the house. Trak had him on a leash, but he made no effort to strain against it.

"You see? You see?" Trik said the moment they passed

through the door. "Scriff's eyes—just look at 'em! They're blue as sapphires!"

It was true. The frox's eyes had been glowing since it entered and the nearer to Kion the frox got, the brighter they became.

"The blue was faint outside," Trak said. "But it started out beyond the courtyard, didn't it?"

"Sure enough. It's like Trak and me always say. 'A frox knows best.'" He crossed his arms, gloating, but it was more comical than conceited.

Eska pushed his way to stand before Kion.

"Look at those eyes. It is as I told you, Kalvar. He is a sorcerer. The frost fox has proven it once and for all. This boy is a red-blooded disciple of the wizenthall if ever I saw one. I foresaw his coming in my dreams, and that he would deceive even the strongest among us. But at the last I am vindicated. He must be taken to the bay and thrown beneath the ice before he beguiles us all."

Zinder bit his finger and stifled an outbreak. Kion was too weak to allow Eska's accusations to rattle him, but Tiryn's heart ran red-hot inside her. She pleaded with her eyes for the kalvar to let her speak, but he was not looking at her. His eyes were fixed on Kion.

"It would seem Eska's vision has proved true once more. I should not have doubted it. What do you have to say for yourself?"

Eska laid a hand on his leader's arm. "Best not to let him speak, kalvar. He may entrance you with his voice."

"The law demands that he be given a chance to prove himself."

Dismayed, Eska snapped his fingers rapidly and tapped one leg fast as a woodpecker against the floor. "Very well, speak. Kalvar Chaw is far too just for his own good, but beware, sorcerer, your spells have no power over one such as me."

Perhaps it was the weakness stemming from his brush with

death, but Tiryn had never seen her brother more calm or even-spoken.

"Thank you. Kalvar, did you not say that the fox could sense the Spark as well as sorcery?"

"I did."

"Then should not the sword lying at my feet possess more Spark than that fox has ever seen in its life? Allow my sister to take the sword outside and see what happens to the fox's eyes."

Horrified, Eska's eyes bounced between the sword and the door. But his mouth could manage no more than incoherent stuttering. "B-b-buh-buh…"

The kalvar studied Kion while the light from the frox's eyes shimmered across his face.

"Accompany the girl outside with the sword, as the boy says," he ordered Dunwik.

The watcher waited for her at the door.

Tiryn reached down and hefted the sword. It was so heavy and long she didn't see how she'd get it outside without slicing herself or someone else unless she dragged it along the floor and she dared not do that. In the end, Zinder helped her sheathe it and she donned her coat and a pair of gloves to protect against the cold; then she was able to hold it with both hands along the length of the blade.

Outside, the morning air was still and expectant. A nebulous gray mantle, glittering with falling snow, hung over the village. Never had Tiryn been out in such bitter cold. A path had been cleared by the watchers through shoulder-high heaps of white across the courtyard. Everywhere she looked the blizzard from the night before held the village of Whitewind fast within its grasp. Tiryn and Dunwik had not gone far when Eska ran screaming from the house, shouting "No! No! Noooooo!" He collided against the door frame and tore past Tiryn and Dunwik, kicking up snow as he went.

The two of them rushed back to find the kalvar slowly shaking his head. A deep sadness echoed at the back of his voice.

"It is as you said, Kion. I knew the blade for a glaive the moment I saw it. It is just as the legends describe. But I refused to see the truth. Please forgive a foolish man if he chose to believe his friend of many years over whispered legends from long ago. Eska was once a brilliant advisor, and I—I was not willing to allow my friend's failings to keep him from the high place he has held in our village. But ever since his daughter's death on Tinesplitter, Eska has not been the same. When his decisions affected only disputes between villagers over petty grievances or the rationing of resources when the hunts and traps came back empty, it mattered less. But your coming has forced me to see what I could not before. To think that in my blindness I almost killed a swordspeaker. That would have brought everlasting shame to my people."

Trembling from the effort, Kion dropped to one knee before the kalvar.

"You may have preferred to choose friendship, but you did not forsake your commitment to the truth. You allowed Tiryn to leave with the sword, even when you thought I was using sorcery against you. Your desire for truth and justice may have been overshadowed by your love for your friend, but it was not lost altogether. You did the honorable thing in the end. And for that, I thank you. You will find no bitterness on my part."

Kalvar Chaw's downcast expression softened. Scriff frisked excitedly, his eyes once again gleaming ice-cold blue.

"You have no need to bow to me, swordspeaker. Rather, it is I who should bow to you." Chaw lifted Kion to his feet and then his great bulk sank to the floor with a shuddering thud. Even kneeling, he was still almost as tall as Tiryn. The gesture took everyone aback, especially Trik, Trak, and Dunwik. "A swordspeaker is above the authority of a kalvar, above a margrave, above even that of the fane. If only you had told me your true identity before. But no, I would not have listened. Yet I am listening now. And I pledge what support to you that I can spare in these shattered days. My people are few, but hardy. Ask of me what you will. For I am yours to command."

Tiryn moved beside Kion and clasped his hand. Her brother could have lashed out at the kalvar for nearly costing him his life. Instead, he had borne the ill-treatment with humility. Kion looked to Tiryn and Zinder, half dazed from his ordeal and half in shock at how quickly everything had turned in their favor. One minute he was to be killed as a sorcerer, and the next the kalvar was bowing before him.

"My first request is for you to rise to your feet. You are far too great a leader to bow to anyone, least of all me. You've kept your people alive in this wintry desolation and for that you have my respect. I would urge you to leave this land, but I fear that in the days ahead, the perpetual winter of the Frostkeld may prove your only protection from the coming threat. The second thing I would ask of you is to release me and my friends to find my mother. And—" he added, reconsidering, "for guidance and direction as to how to reach Tinesplitter Isle."

Chaw and Dunwik exchanged dark looks, but Trik and Trak danced in place.

"Oh, please, Uncle, let us guide them," Trik said. "We're excellent pathfinders and we traveled there many times when we were young. We know the way."

Kalvar Chaw shambled to his feet and swiftly resumed his air of command. "Firstly, though you have seen me bow, it was not to you, Trik O'Trannon. Kion may be a swordspeaker, but you two are still under the kalvar's authority. And secondly, nephew of mine though you be, you shall address me by my proper title when in public—that goes for both of you."

"Yes, sir," the twins said in unison.

"Finally, the last time you two went to Tinesplitter you were five years old. Do you honestly expect me to believe that you would be of any use as guides?"

"But we've got him." Trak reached down and held Scriff up by the belly with his four paws dangling. The frox panted excitedly. "And he knows the way. He used to live on Tinesplitter, remember? He knows it better than anyone in the village."

"And what makes you think your animal will show you the way? Or have you trained the fox so well that you've taught it to speak?"

"He knows how to play fetch," Trik said with a hopeful shrug.

Kion gave a small cough. "Actually, it may prove to be of some use. I do not know how versed you are in the lore of the glaives, kalvar, but they are able to speak to animals as well as to their glaivebonds. I am still learning the skill myself, but if this fox truly does know the island, he might prove more valuable than any human guide."

Chaw's brow remained as rigid as stone.

"We know what it's like to be without a mother, Kalvar," Trik said.

"That's right. We can't get ours back, so let us help them get theirs," Trak said.

The kalvar's face loosened, giving way for the first time to the face of an uncle instead. "Very well. Though I question the wisdom of sending you on such an important task, I will allow you to go in honor of my dear sister. But I would be abandoning my duty to her if I allowed you to go alone. I will also send some of the watchers with you."

Dunwik stepped forward. "I will go with them. It will help me atone for the dishonor I have shown the swordspeaker in not treating him with the respect he deserved. And I know the way to Regnir. I was last there but a year before it was conquered."

"Much could have changed since then," the kalvar said.

"Which is why you'll need Scriff," Trik said. "And us, his official handlers."

Kalvar Chaw brooded a great while. "Very well. Dunwik, I leave it to you to outfit the party and choose whichever watchers you deem worthy to accompany the swordspeaker."

Zinder's hand shot up. "Excuse me, it seems we're all on

speaking terms now—yes? Because if so, I have a comment—or two, or three—to make."

"Of course, Master Nyn. As the swordspeaker's companions, you are no longer bound to the customs and laws of Whitewind. You march under the Mastersmith's banner, and that is an authority no human ruler may gainsay."

"Oh, well, that's quite nice, then, isn't it? The Mastersmith's banner. I'm pleased to see that you have such respect for smiths in this village. But as to what I wanted to say; I am most grateful for your sudden change of heart towards us and all of these offers of help, but before we run off with half your village, I think you should know that this is meant to be a stealthy affair. We need to catch the Noathryn unawares, if you see what I mean. And so it won't do to arrive with a great band of warriors, handy as that might be. I should think three or four guides would be more than enough. Not that we don't appreciate the help, mind you, but we need to keep our party rather on the small side, you see."

"It is well spoken. If circumstances allow, Kion Sword-speaker, when you return I should very much like to understand how you won one of the nyn to your side. For most of them served on the side of the wizenthall in the last great war."

Now it was Zinder's turn to cough, and far more forcibly than Kion. "Yes, well, as you said, your information is hardly up to date here. You may grant that in eight hundred years a thing or two may have changed. I can assure you that no nyn living today would have done such a thing. But enough of that, back to the matter at hand," he hurried on. "If you think these three are good enough to serve as our guides then I think that will do."

Kion nodded in support of his friend's suggestion.

Kalvar Chaw placed his slab-like hands upon the shoulders of his nephews and drew them close. "It is settled then. You shall have the services of Dunwik, one of my finest watchers, and Trik, and Trak, my two dear nephews. If their mother were still alive, I believe that she would want them to go. For they are young and eager to prove themselves."

"Did he just call us 'dear'? Does that mean we're not on his bad side anymore?" Trik asked his brother in a noisy whisper.

Trak hushed him with a finger to the lips. "We'll make you proud, Unc—I mean, Kalvar. The swordspeaker and his friends will be safe with us."

Neither Kion nor Kalvar Chaw looked convinced, but Zinder clapped his hands together as if he had just finished a day at the smithy.

"All right, then. That's settled. Now may we please see about getting some breakfast? If we're setting off for some frozen island, and with the swordspeaker only just come back from the dead, he'll need all the fat on his bones he can get."

"How kind of you to think of me, Zinder," Kion said, and it did Tiryn's heart good to see the smirk on his face. "I'm sure it had nothing to do with your rumbling stomach."

"Oh, you heard that, did you? Well, at least your brush with death didn't have any effect on your hearing."

Kion would have laughed at that some other day, but all he could manage was to turn his smirk into a grin.

That night, the Feasting House resounded with rowdy talk and cheer. Bowls and plates overflowed, and this time not with mush. Pickled vegetables, fresh-baked loaves of sourdough, slabs of butter, golden squash soup, and oven-smoked fish lit up Tiryn's senses with rich, tingling smells. Zinder forgot his rash oath against the consumption of aquatic creatures and was on his second luskan bass before Tiryn had finished half of her first.

A merry fire licked the sides of the hearth, and with so many people packed in around the tables, Tiryn actually had to unbutton her collar for a bit of relief. The warmth, good food, and pleasant conversation did wonders for Kion. His color had returned and he moved and spoke as though his ordeal at the post was long past. Villagers came to interrupt his meal every few minutes, asking how he'd found his glaive, what wars he'd fought in, what monsters he'd slain, and what great feats he planned to accomplish after he drove the Noathryn from Tinesplitter Isle.

Truesilver lay upon the mantel above the hearth for all to see, the unsheathed blade captivating and magnificent with its bright amber sheen. Though no one touched it, the villagers stood as close as they dared, whispering in reverent tones—telling how they would never forget this day, the day they'd set their eyes upon one of the legendary weapons of old.

The interest did not stop with Kion and his sword. Dunwik, who sat with his wife, two young boys, and little girl, received nearly as much attention, greeted by wide-eyed questions and congratulatory claps on the shoulder. Zinder was given a more tepid reception. The curiosity amongst the people of Whitewind was high, but so was their concern. Tiryn did not understand their fear of him—he was the gentlest, most harmless person she knew—but the murmurings of the supposed nynnian betrayal in the great war of the Shattering still weighed heavily on a people so steeped in tradition.

Trik and Trak, who sat across from Tiryn, were afforded even less respect and attention than Zinder. The older villagers, and even a few of the younger ones, shook their heads at the twins' boisterous antics. When Trik was not trying to beg off more food from those around him, he was attempting to balance his fork on his nose and Trak took up the challenge to catch it each time it fell. Their laughter rose above all others, and when they slapped the table in the throes of yet another horrible joke or foolish stunt, they shivered the place settings four seats down.

Eska was the only sullen spirit that remained. He made his appearance halfway through the meal, and had to be dragged to his spot beside Kalvar Chaw. Grumbling protests about his unworthiness to serve the kalvar or even sit beside him were dismissed with a glare from the Frindalian leader.

"This is no hour for self-pity, my friend," the kalvar told Eska. "We have been spared a great tragedy. Take of my table and of my goodwill. The heart may lead us to error, but we need not follow when its counsel proves false." He said this with no ill intent, but Eska was incapable of accepting the wisdom of his friend.

The dismayed seer sat with his hands in his lap, not speaking a word. Something between a scowl and a look of profound shame plagued his face. Strangest of all, he did not move. His body appeared to be an empty husk while his spirit wandered in gray lands past the edge of thought.

Well after everyone had taken their fill and the laughter and fine talk had at last begun to die, Kalvar Chaw rose upon the small step surrounding the hearth.

"People of Whitewind, hear the voice of your leader." It took only a moment for the raucous hall to grow silent. "This day marks a new beginning for the Frindalian people. Two days ago we lived under the long shadow of the past. We knew the legends were true, and yet none among us had ever seen them with our living eyes. And then we were visited by the swordspeaker. Though we did not know him at first for who he was; and through my folly, he was nearly taken by the Maid of Ice; by an unlooked-for grace he was rescued from my hand."

Mugs and forks pounded the tables and applause spilled across the room.

"For a swordspeaker is not easily defeated, even by the Maid of Ice, and Kion's glaive roused him to life again. Dunwik, Torvid, Yorvin, and Pakar were there. They saw it for themselves."

Dunwik and the other watchers nodded, their normally hard eyes touched with astonishment at the memory.

"Even our forefathers, noble and wise as they were, never laid eyes upon a true glaive. And this is Truesilver, no less, first of the Mastersmith's glaives. Look upon it and never forget what majesty has graced this hall."

Long moments of silence passed as hundreds of keen eyes gazed upon the masterful blade, each person caught somewhere between the present moment and whispered legends from long ago.

Kion rose amidst the stillness. "Truesilver thanks you for the kindness you have shown us this night. It pleases him to know that in Whitewind the old legends are not forgotten, and that here the Mastersmith's name is still afforded the honor it is due."

The people's eyes glinted with wonder at being addressed by one of the glaives of old. Young folk pointed with eagerness and old folk nodded approvingly. One gray-haired fellow in the back wrote furiously with ink and quill inside a tattered ancient book, recording the events of this night for the Frin and others yet to be born.

As Kion took his seat once more, Kalvar Chaw resumed. "Sadly, a pressing need drives them on, and tomorrow they must leave us for Tinesplitter Isle. No doubt, great deeds await them across the frozen waters, but they have promised to return once their task is complete. We await the day when Dunwik and my own dear nephews, Trik and Trak, will regale us with new tales to deepen the ones that came before. It may be that one day we shall look back upon this time and say, 'That was the hour when the Four Wards began anew.' That is our hope and prayer. May it be so."

Hearty voices roared their approval of the kalvar's words. All minds and hearts were knit together in that moment, bound by their shared suffering in the Frostkeld and their shared hope in the old legends and the restoration of the old order. Tiryn did not know how much truth there was to the legends of the Four Wards, but like everyone else in Inris, she had heard songs and tales which spoke of the golden age when the Four Wards stood as one. And for that brief moment on that one night, she could almost believe it was possible that the old tales could spring to life and come true once again.

As in all that had preceded, Eska's dour countenance was the sole detraction. But unexpectedly he looked up and his eyes met Tiryn's. His scowl dissolved into a pool of agony and he looked away at once, but Tiryn had seen enough in that brief moment to know the sad state of Eska's heart. The dreams that danced in the minds of everyone else held no sway over him. He was too lonely, too lost in his own sorrows to see the wonder of the moment or any hope in days to come.

Her feet struggled to find the floor, but she forced herself up from her chair and caught the kalvar's eye.

"Yes, sister of the swordspeaker? What is it that you have to say?"

"Only that…that the hour is growing late and that Kion, and I'm sure the others as well, will need as much rest as they can for tomorrow's journey. But before we go, I was wondering if…if I might sing a song for everyone. It's one that we sing in Inris when saying our good-byes."

"I can think of no better way to finish the evening," Chaw said.

Though Tiryn stood on trembling legs, her voice rang out strong and true.

The evening dark makes swift approach
I must up and away
For though it breaks my heart to leave
I know I cannot stay

These moments, words, and memories
The laughter that we've shared
Shall comfort me on my dark road
Should I grow lost or scared

How fast the hours have passed us by
How vaporous the day
But know that I shall hold you dear
Each step along the way

For though the miles may come between
And journeys bear me far
Just speak these words and think of me
And I'll be where you are

As the fading strains of her voice drifted toward the ceiling, the dew of quiet tears graced the cheeks of many gathered. Nowhere was this more so than on the face of Eska, the broken sage and seer of Whitewind. He sat beside the kalvar and sobbed, rocking back and forth, his frame wracked with shuddering sorrow. His mind was gripped by memories of a beautiful little girl whose life was cut short on the frozen ground of Tinesplitter Isle. And somewhere deep inside that memory, Tiryn's song, or more likely it was simply Tiryn herself, unlocked a latch and he began to be free.

Chapter 30

THE CROSSING

The abandoned docks of Whitewind lay in the grip of centuries of ice and snow. If Kion had not been told what they were, he would have thought them no more than curious fingers of land jutting out from the shore. Between the low mounds and out beyond them, the snow ran smooth and level for as far as the eye could see. The only signs marking the ice beneath were several holes bored into the surface where the Frindalians did their fishing. Vague lines in the vast field of white marked the paths their sleds had taken. They were only just visible, having been almost entirely covered by the storm from the night before; but an unchecked wind blustered across the bay, sweeping much of the snow off the surface of the frozen water.

The whole of the village rose to see the travelers off, though the light was so feeble it was difficult to tell how many had gathered. Dunwik embraced his wife and three young children, a boy and two girls, the oldest not even coming up to his waist. The twins said their good-byes to Kalvar Chaw, who had many stern words of advice to give them, admonishing them to not do anything foolish, but also telling them that their mother and father would have been proud.

Scriff frisked about Tiryn's legs, his blue eyes alight from the presence of the sword. He was the most energetic of them all, as if sensing that he would soon return to his homeland. The rest of the villagers stood in silence, taking in their last moments with the swordspeaker and his companions in a quiet vigil of awe, believing that the legends of old had returned and that new ones were now unfolding before their eyes.

The wind bit into Kion's eyes and forehead, evoking a shudder at the memory of his night at the judgment post. His bones still ached and he had slept little during the night, but he dared not tell Tiryn. She would make them stay another day—perhaps even longer—and they could not afford any more delays. Kithian had told him that the soreness and the weakness in his limbs would pass in time. For now, Kion busied himself with helping Zinder tie down their gear to the two sleds they would take across the ice. They'd brought food enough for an eight-mark and plenty of oil for Truesilver's fire, along with two tents, a small bundle of firewood, several hunting knives, and plenty of rope and tools for climbing.

Truesilver was the last to be strapped down, though Kion fastened it in such a way that the blade could easily be drawn from the scabbard at need. Zinder's large crossbow topped the other sled. Dunwik carried his own weapon, a tall spear, by his side. It would serve as a walking stick and to sound the ice, as well as a weapon.

Smokewind and Cyprian were given over to the care of Kalvar Chaw. He promised to house them in his own stable, safe from the wind and snow, and to care for them as if they were his very own. And though if all went well, they'd see the horses in a four-mark, Tiryn wished aloud that she could have seen them one last time before they set out. They also left behind things they would not need like their summer clothing, Zinder's stash of extra hats, Tiryn's pipes, Strom's journal, and the letter Kion's father had written to him before going off to war. These last two Kion was not willing to risk losing amidst the snow and ice and other dangers they might face on Tinesplitter Isle.

Kion and the others said farewell to Kalvar Chaw, waved to those gathered, and at last pushed the sleds out onto the slope leading down to the ice. They guided the stiff, angular frames loaded with baggage until they reached the edge of the bay.

Walking across the frozen bay was hardly different than walking on land, for it was wholly blanketed in snow. Only the unending flatness and the absence of all trees and growing things told them that they now stood upon the great waters of Tinesplitter Bay. As the sleds came to a halt, Kion and Dunwik fastened themselves with harnesses and ropes, each to the front of a different sled. The travelers turned to the blurred figures on the shore and gave them one last wave before setting off across the frozen bay. Kalvar Chaw's hulking form was the only one recognizable among the others.

"So begins the final part of our journey." Kithian's voice was weighed with some unspoken concern.

"Yes. It will all be over soon." Kion said the words as much to himself as to Kithian. They were not fifty paces from the shore and already he could feel the sled's weight taxing his strength. Dunwik pulled his sled easily, following one of the old tracks. Neither sled was overly laden, and Kion's was the lighter of the two, but he could already see that a long day of toil awaited him.

"And yet, often the end we find is not the one we saw from the beginning. I worry that your sorrows are not yet over, swordspeaker."

Kion knew Kithian spoke only out of concern, but he refused to consider the possibility that his mother was not on Tinesplitter, or that she would not survive until their arrival.

"I can face whatever awaits, so long as I have you at my side."

Tiryn, who walked beside him, measured his condition with every step. "You have to get to the island first," she said. "I know Mother is in danger, but I wish you'd waited one more day."

"So I hear. How many times do I have to tell you? I'm fine."

"You think I don't know you? I know you're just putting on a show of it. You need rest."

"Perhaps. I may not be at full strength now, but I will be by the time we get to Regnir. Zinder healed up just fine on the journey. And if someone as weak and frail as him can recover that quickly, I should be able—"

"I heard that," Zinder said, moving nimbly across the snow on the opposite side of Tiryn. He'd managed to secure a new set of clothing without the fuzzy balls and stitched snowflakes. He looked more like a regular Frin now, though his cap was rather unique, made from deerskin lined with wool as white as snow. "These flaps on my hat can't stop the ears of a nyn." If Zinder's fur hat did not impede his hearing, Kion didn't know what could. It was so thick, a pillow strapped to his head would have been little better. Where he'd gotten it, Kion had no idea, but Zinder found hats wherever he went.

The light banter failed to diminish Tiryn's worries. "Well, at least promise me you'll let me pull the sled if you get too tired."

"We can help, too, Tiryn. We can take over for Kion, or even Dunwik, when they get tired," Trak said. He and Trik traveled on either side of Kion's sled in order to "guard the swordspeaker." They carried long, smooth walking sticks, but no real weapons beyond the hunting knives strapped to their chests, so it was not clear how much protection they could actually offer.

"Remember, we're young and strong and we didn't almost die yesterday," Trik added.

Dunwik shot them a stony look. "I don't trust either of you with the sleds. The last time you went out on the ice you took off running when that fox of yours saw a rabbit. It took the rest of the day to find you and the hunt was ruined. If Kion needs the rest, we will all halt together, but as for me, I will require no help in pulling my sled on this journey." His manner was not unkind, merely direct—like something Fielder Lorris might have said back in Furrow when he caught someone breaking a rule. Trik and Trak gave deflated frowns but had enough sense not to question the watcher. After that, the enduring quiet of the lake descended upon the little band of six and their fox. The wind dropped down to a mild flutter and the sun rose to cast hazy shadows before them as they trekked out across the invisible sea. Well before the first hour had passed, the sled tracks ended and the shadows, now more compact, shifted as they turned to a more northerly course. They passed around one last arm of land before finding themselves out in the wide-open bay.

They took no rest until the coastline was little more than a smudged line behind them. When they did pause for water and a bit of rye bread, Kion leaned against the pile of gear on his sled, grateful for the rest, but aware now more than ever that this journey might be more than he could bear. Weariness burrowed deep into his bones. Too late he saw how brash he'd been to think that he was ready for such a trip. But he could not turn his back on his mother. He would march until he dropped, and then crawl on after that. What was it Strom had said as he died? "When strength fades, the will grows stronger." Very well. Then so be it.

"No dweller of Whitewind has passed beyond this point since the fall of Regnir, eight years ago," Dunwik said, staring off into the endless white. Now that the sun was hitting the bay more directly, Kion had to squint to look at it. "The last time I set foot on Tinesplitter Isle, I was near your age. Who knows how the Ice Maid's storms may have shifted the land since then. There is little chance the old path to Regnir still stands. And we dare not go along the coast, for we would easily be seen coming from that direction. Unless we can go in under cover of a storm, our only approach lies in passing through the hills west of Regnir and coming in from the north, through the Standing Cliffs. That is our best chance at entering the town unseen, though it has perils of its own."

"Have you traveled through the Cliffs before?" Trak asked.

"No, even when Regnir stood no one with any sense would go there, for there are strange creatures that lurk among those hills. This is where your fox may prove useful, for frost foxes have a way of sensing danger and sniffing out safe paths."

"Hmm, well, I actually know another way," Trik said. "Uncle Ch—" Trak elbowed his brother in the ribs. "Kalvar Chaw told us once of a secret way into the mines that he found when he was young."

"And the mines are just north of Regnir," Trak said.

Trik waved his hand between himself and his brother. "Trak and I were talking about it last night. It's a smart plan, isn't it? A secret entrance to the mines! The Noathryn will never see us coming."

"Trik does occasionally have a good idea," Trak said.

Dunwik only gave the suggestion a stiff shrug and began harnessing himself back onto his sled.

"The swordspeaker will have the final say, but we can discuss these things along the way. We should get going."

As grateful as Kion had been for the rest, the longer they went without moving, the more aware of his weakness he became. Starting up again would not take it away, but it would at least take his mind off of it.

Tiryn put her arm around her brother. "Let me take a turn. You can walk with Zinder and the others for a bit."

"I know you mean well, but I can go a little longer." Though every muscle in his body screamed for rest, he could not bring himself to let Tiryn bear his responsibilities. He was the older brother. It was his job to take care of her, not the other way around.

Tiryn gave in as she always did. He hefted the harness back over his shoulders, secured it around his waist, and in a short time they were back underway.

"Did Kalvar Chaw tell you where this secret entrance was?" Kion said after a time.

"Not exactly," Trik said. "But we could hunt for it. Trak and I are champions at that sort of thing. We can find a sunbeam in a snowstorm."

"No." Dunwik was quick to cut him off. "If you do not know how to find it, then we do not have time to go hunting for some hidden entrance that may or may not be there. The hills and the cliffs offer a surer path. After we cross them, we will sneak into the town under cover of night and pray the Mastersmith's hand is with us."

Trik pointed to the frox. The creature trotted spryly beside Tiryn, staring up at her as if it were waiting for her to give it some command.

"Scriff can find it. He can find anything!"

"And if he cannot? What then? Our supplies are limited. The longer we spend there, the greater chance that we will all die on that island. Do you understand?"

The twins gave dejected nods.

"There, there, lads," Zinder said. "Your little Scruff will have his time to shine sooner or later. We can't always pick our moments of glory."

"His name's Scriff," Trak said.

"With an *i* as in 'icicle,'" Trik said a bit haughtily. The twins still regarded Zinder with suspicion, as if he might breathe fire or call down a curse upon them when they least expected it.

"Oh, Scriff, is it? Well, Scruff is a much better name. It's got that rascally quality to it that would make him the envy of all the other foxes. But since I wouldn't want to offend your dear fox." He offered the slightest of bows to the creature. "Please forgive me."

This satisfied the brothers, who treated their fox in many ways as if he were an actual person.

"Say, Kion," Trik said.

"You should probably call him Swordspeaker," Trak said.

"Right, Swordspeaker, I was wondering if you could ask Truesilver to tell us what Scriff is thinking."

Kion's head dropped in weary assent. "Certainly. And you can call me Kion."

"Oh, right," Trik said, his eyes dancing in anticipation.

"So, what does Scriff think of the pen we made him back in Whitewind?" Trak said.

"And what was he yipping about two nights ago?" Trik said.

"Also, tell him we can't eat those frozen rabbits that he keeps bringing us."

"Our teeth aren't really made for eating through solid ice."

"Kithian, did you get all those questions?" Kion said.

"Yes, but before I ask them, the fox wanted me to tell them that his true name is Gim-dor-ren. I spoke with him briefly this morning while you were preparing the sleds."

Kion repeated Kithian's words.

"Gwin-dor…what?" Trik said.

"Glimdren?" Trak said.

"Gim-dor-ren." Kion had to repeat the name five times before they could say it correctly. In the process of attempting to correct their tripping tongues, he managed to trip over his own feet. He found the snow harder than it looked when he hit the ground.

"Perhaps it would be best not to distract you from your present task just now," Kithian said.

"Kion, are you all right?" Tiryn was at his side at once.

"I'm fine." He dusted off his legs and forced himself back up, hurrying to catch up to Dunwik and ignoring Tiryn's show of concern.

"Her worry for you is not without cause. Do you not think it better to rest during this part of the journey? If you do not wish for Tiryn to shoulder your burdens, you might at least allow one of the boys to pull your sled for a time."

"It was just one little fall. I'll be fine." The words fell as flat as the frozen bay. He might be able to feign strength to his sister, but he could not pretend with his glaive. Kithian could tell when lies were spoken, after all.

Pulling the sled through unspoiled snow was far more grueling than he'd thought it would be. During the last mile before the rest, it was all he could do to keep putting one foot in front of the other. Even then, his feet dragged, leaving long tracks of their own. Before this fall, he'd already stumbled half a dozen times. The clear, still skies and glittering sun were the only mercies afforded him. If the weather had been against them in the slightest, he would have collapsed long ago.

Kion whistled for a halt and waved Trak over.

"Here." He offered him the harness. "My sister thinks I need a little rest. Would you mind taking over for a little while so that I can keep her quiet?"

"Yes, Swordspeaker, of course!" Trak fairly jumped into the harness. Trik's face glowed with pride as he helped fasten his brother into the straps.

"Carrying the swordspeaker's burdens...Wait until Uncle Ch —wait until the kalvar hears about this!"

As the journey resumed, Kion, no longer burdened by the weight of the sled, felt as if he were waking from a dream. For the first time that day, he saw the world around him as more than just an obstacle to be overcome. The air was clear and clean and he took pleasure just in breathing it, cold as it was. The wind had blown the snow into little swirls and swells, in some ways resembling a sea of frozen ripples, as if the icy waters had poked through. The snow crystals sparkled like diamonds strewn over white sand. The serenity of that long, lonely expanse stretched out into eternity. And somewhere at the end of that eternity, his mother awaited him.

An hour after midday, a bluish shadow rose in the distance. Zinder spotted it first, but soon all of them could make it out. Spying the misty shape rising above the flatness sent a twitch of anticipation down Kion's back. Had they reached the end of eternity so soon?

"That is Tinesplitter," Dunwik said.

"Is it really blue? Or is that a reflection of some sort?"

"No, that is its true color. The ice and snow there have always been that way."

"Tinesplitter blue," Trak murmured.

"It's our favorite color," Trik said.

"The same color as Scriff's eyes when he's near the sword."

A soundless chuckle trickled into Kion's throat. Those two were fourteen, but they acted like they were half that. Tiryn seemed as old as Mother by comparison.

"Mother." Kion breathed the word into the crisp air. She was closer than ever.

The winds were picking up again. He needed a drink of water. His throat was far too dry. He waved Tiryn over, mouthing the word "water," and pointing to his lips.

The liquid seared his throat as it went down so he only took a little. He handed the waterskin back to her, or rather, he tried to. A wind flew up without warning and his feet skated out from under him. His head slammed into the ground and he was slow to get up. What little strength he had left seemed to have been knocked out of him.

"I'm fine, I'm fine," he protested, but for once Tiryn's will held sway. The twins did not dare question the swordspeaker's strength, but Dunwik and Zinder both agreed that Kion was not fit to keep going on foot. He protested stubbornly as they carried him over to Dunwik's sled and made room for him to lie upon it, but he was too weak to put up a serious fight. They fastened him in, covering him with an extra blanket for good measure.

They were so close to the end of their journey. Kion only needed to hold out for another day or two. He couldn't fail now.

"When strength fails, the will grows stronger," he said to himself. But at that moment they were no more than empty words.

Chapter 31

SHARDS FROM THE SKY

Kithian's voice flickered in the dark corners of Kion's thoughts.

"Awake, Glaivebond, awake. Your companions have need of you!"

The fiery voice had been pressing in on him for some time, but the sudden urgency caused it to flare and penetrate the cloud of weakness fogging his senses.

Kion opened his eyes to a world of half-light, battered by swirling flurries of powdered blue. He lay on the back of one of the sleds. Dunwik stood in front of it, but he had stopped pulling. The twins, along with Tiryn and Zinder, were staring at the ground before them. Dozens of icicles jutted from the frozen blue snow, some as thick as Kion's forearm. No one noticed that he was awake. He struggled to sit up. His limbs and back were stiff as boards. His arms moved like he was underwater.

"These spikes are not natural," Dunwik said.

Trik and Trak exchanged fearful glances.

"They appear very recent," the watcher added.

"What's so unusual about—" Scriff's yipping cut Tiryn off. The frox leapt at her, knocking her back so that she went down and slid across the frozen ground. Before Kion could gain his feet and chastise the unruly beast, a shower of ice crashed onto the ground where Tiryn had been, leaving another swath of icy shards piercing the snow.

There was no time to praise the intrepid frox for saving Tiryn's life, for Zinder's shout drew everyone's eyes skyward.

"There! By the forge light, it's a mountain on wings!"

The words were close to the truth. A great winged beast soared above them. Cloaked by swirling snow, all that came through were glimpses of a large hooked head and shiny wings coated in ice. There was something primeval about its presence. A terrible peril sounded in the great *whoosh* of its lumbering wings. One thing was clear, even from the creature's shadowy outline: it was the largest living thing Kion had ever seen.

"It's a dragon!" Trik cried.

"It's spotted us!" Trak said in a panic. "What do we do?"

"That's no dragon. It's an izzinchard," Dunwik said. "Stay on guard and dodge its attacks. It can only launch its shards for so long before its feathers will need to freeze over and it will have to withdraw or swoop low and try its talons. If it gets close enough, we may be able to strike it with bolt or spear."

"Right, I'll ready my crossbow," Zinder said, his bright eyes roaming the skies.

Kion lurched his way out of the sled, staring back at the jagged fingers of ice that had just fallen from the sky. Any one of them would have thrust Tiryn straight through.

"Kion! You're awake!" Tiryn scrambled toward him over the strangely colored snow.

"Kind of you to join us!" Zinder shouted over his shoulder as he ran to the other sled.

"It's gone now," Trik said.

Indeed, the creature had vanished into the freezing clouds above, but the deep thrum of its massive wings could still be heard above the wind.

"Do not be so sure," Dunwik said, hastily freeing himself of his harness and taking up his spear. "Once an izzinchard spots its prey, it rarely leaves off."

By now, Zinder had unstrapped his coalwood crossbow from the gear and readied a bolt.

"Draw your sword, if you have the strength, lad. I'm sure that thing can't do much against fire."

"Watch out!" Trak shouted. Dunwik barreled into Kion and swept him off his feet. The man's hardened frame hit like a sack of stones. The two of them went flying across the icy snow.

Another hail of jagged barbs shredded the ground where Kion had stood.

"Thank you, Dunwik. You—you saved my life." Kion's chest throbbed from the impact, but his gratitude overshadowed the pain. That was twice in the span of two days that his life had been spared.

"Horn toads! I missed," Zinder shouted. "Are you two all right?" He was already arming his crossbow with another bolt.

Dunwik sprang to his feet and took up his spear once more, surveying the skies.

"The swordspeaker is safe. Trik and Trak, keep your eyes locked on the sky."

The izzinchard reappeared, gliding lower this time to avoid the blinding snow higher up, and revealing the full extent of its dreadful form. The creature resembled a giant buzzard with shards of ice for feathers. The eyes were hollows of darkness, skull-like and terrible. Its massive wingspan would have stretched the length of Whitewind's great hall. It seemed impossible a thing of that size could stay aloft amidst the whirling winds. The izzinchard's horn-like beak opened in a shattering wail that could be felt in the bones as it wheeled toward them.

"It's coming around for another pass," Dunwik cried.

Kion staggered to his feet and ran toward the sled where his blade was stowed away. If he could get close enough with Truesilver, he would give the beast a mouthful of glaivefire.

"Aim for the spot under the wing where it meets the body," Trak said, pointing.

"Yes, Kion, come. This is one of the wizenthall's abominations of old. Unsheathe me and together we shall bring down this fiend of ice and winter."

The stiffness in Kion's legs made covering the short distance feel as though he'd traveled a league, but he made it to his sword just as the creature swept in low, its wings snapping together in great, chilling wafts. A hail of spikes lanced toward Zinder and Dunwik as they raced to close the distance. Zinder was too quick for the enormous bird. He dodged to the side, rolling to his feet past the danger. Dunwik fended off a large chunk of ice with his spear, but several smaller shards fell into the snow around him and shattered in a spray of tiny daggers. A few grazed his face, leaving half a dozen small gashes, but he avoided the worst of it.

"Dunwik, are you all right?" Trak said, running up, but before Dunwik could answer, Tiryn shouted.

"Trik, behind you!"

The izzinchard swooped past the forward group and let fly another wave of ice as its wings beat toward the sky once again. Trik turned in time to face the spray, but not in time to escape it. The ice came down along his side, piercing his hip and leg and pinning him to the ground.

"Ah! No!" Trik wailed in shock and pain, writhing in the snow. Tiryn ran to help.

But the bird paid for its attack.

Zinder buried a bolt where the left wing joined to the body. The izzinchard screeched and contorted awkwardly. Its ascent stalled and the creature plummeted, bottoming out into a bank of snow.

Everyone but Tiryn and Trik rushed toward the downed beast. Kion drew Truesilver, summoning every last bit of strength he had. For a few moments he led the others, but Dunwik and Zinder swiftly overtook him.

"Hurry, glaivebond. The beast has foundered, but it is still strong. One shot will not slay a creature of that size," Kithian said.

Kion listed badly as he ran. He feared he would not come within reach for the glaivefire to land before the beast recovered and rose back into the skies.

The izzinchard shrieked and sent another barrage of spikes at Dunwik and Zinder as it struggled to right itself.

Zinder, by the luck of the nyn, ran through the icy teeth of the onslaught without a scratch, cocking his crossbow for another bolt as he went. Dunwik was not so fortunate. Spikes pierced his arm and shoulder. He roared, but from rage, not pain, as he hurled his spear. It buried itself deep into the beast's chest. The wings flinched and blue ichor poured from the wound, yet the bird struck the air with its wings once more and a shower of ice went flying toward Kion as it leapt aloft.

The icy barrage was ill-prepared and went clean over his head. The wounded beast was slow to ascend. Sprinting forward in a last desperate burst, Kion thrust Truesilver forward in a flash of red, crying, "Glaivefire!"

Bright, swirling flames leapt from the sword, catching just enough of the creature to lick its feet and belly with the deadly fire. The great monstrosity shuddered. It hung in the air for the longest time, writhing and fighting to stay aloft, but in the end, the flames won out. They spread to its wings, engulfing the pale white body until it plunged back into the snow. There it contorted in upon itself in a great heap of char and cinder and melted ice, a broken mound in the sky-blue snow. It convulsed briefly, gave one last strangled cry that sounded startlingly like a curse, and was still.

Kion collapsed almost as gracelessly as the izzinchard. He could not have swung his blade one more time or run one more step.

Dunwik stared at him in concentrated awe. "You truly are a swordspeaker. If I did not know it before, I know it now."

Looking over at Trik, still fallen in the snow, Kion took little pleasure in the watcher's words. "I should have struck sooner. Maybe we could have slain the beast before it got to Trik."

"You came when you could," Kithian said. *"In your weakened state you could have done nothing more."*

That may have been true, and yet it did not ease the weight of sadness and regret pressing down upon his heart. Tiryn was right. He was too weak. He should have waited. Perhaps if they had come tomorrow the izzinchard would not have seen them, or perhaps Kion would have been stronger and quicker to the fight. But he had to put that aside. This was no time to wallow in his failure. Dunwik was wounded and Trik might be dying, if he was not already gone.

"It's all right, Trik. If you'll just hold still so I can get a look at your wounds," Tiryn said, probing the area around the shards of ice with a light touch.

"No, leave me, Tiryn. It's all over for me. I…tell Trak I love him, and that I'm sorry I sold his favorite snowshoes for some peppermint pie."

Trak came running up just then. "I'm here, Trik—wait, what did you say?"

Tiryn grasped the shard near his hip with both hands and pulled.

"No, ow! What are you doing? My hip!" Trik howled.

But Tiryn slid the icy spear out and held it up to him. "This went through your coat, Trik, not your hip. It didn't miss by much. Just close enough to scare you out of your wits from what I can see." She smashed the icicle into the other one in his leg, shattering both. "The one through your pant leg missed too. You haven't been hurt at all."

"Oh," Trik said, his lips shriveling into an embarrassed pucker. "I thought, well, it *felt* like I was wounded."

Trak buffeted him across the top of his head. "You squirrel brain. You had me scared to death! Well, I'm glad you're alive, but I can't believe you sold my snowshoes!"

"Tiryn," Zinder said. "Come see to Dunwik. His wounds are not imaginary."

Tiryn abandoned the skittish boy and hurried over to the watcher's side. Dunwik was standing, but blood seeped into the snow along his left side.

"Oh, Dunwik."

"I've been hurt worse," he said, forcing the words through gritted teeth.

"Here, you need to sit down at least." She eased him onto the snow.

Kion, whose strength was slowly ebbing back, lumbered across the snow toward his sister as she examined the four shards impaled in Dunwik's shoulder and arm. The largest was as wide as a coin. Dunwik bore Tiryn's ministrations in grim silence, breathing quietly, bearing the pain with steely calm.

"I don't want to pull those out," Tiryn said. "You might bleed out, but I'm afraid I'll have to. I'll wait a moment until they melt a little. Zinder, bring me some cloth and the cleansing tonic."

Zinder scampered off to the sled.

"Touch my blade to the ice," Kithian said.

"But your fire would be too much. I don't want to burn him," Kion said.

"No, my fire is not needed here. But I can warm the ice enough with my blade alone to hasten the melting so that your sister may more swiftly bind the wounds."

Kion explained to Tiryn what Kithian intended.

"Yes, that might work. Only be careful not to move the shards," she said.

Zinder arrived with the cloth as Kion set to work. Scriff stared at all the commotion with curious eyes, but something about the way he held himself, tight and alert, showed that he understood what was happening in his own way.

Kion touched the ice shards as lightly as possible. The only noticeable change in Truesilver's blade was that it glowed with a more intense light than usual. The first spike shrank quickly and Tiryn eased it out and onto the snow, hurriedly binding the open wound.

"Thank you, Tiryn." Dunwik gave her a rare smile and squeezed her hand. "And thank you, Swordspeaker, for slaying the beast."

"You and Zinder brought it down. It took all of us to defeat it," Kion said. And though he had managed to reach the izzinchard with Truesilver's fire, looking at Dunwik's wounds and the blood on the snow, the empty void inside him made it feel as though he had done nothing at all.

Chapter 32

FROXHOLE

The weary band plodded onward until just before dark, when they began looking for a place to make camp. The snow was coming down thick and heavy by then, but there was no shelter in sight. High and forbidding cliffs rose in a great icy eruption to the north, sheer walls of midnight blue. The snow-covered ground below them bore a more celestial hue. Walking upon it was like walking upon a great mirror reflecting the sky. No path penetrated the frozen barricades before them, and climbing them appeared all but impossible. But that obstacle could wait until tomorrow. The pressing need now was finding someplace safe and warm. The freezing wind fought with them at every step, spitting sapphire flakes and cloaking most of the island from view.

"This snow is so strange," Kion said. "What could have turned it this shade?"

"It is the work of the Maid of Ice," Dunwik said.

"I have seen ice of this color before, but never in such vast amounts." Kithian's voice hinted at some troubling memory.

"Are you sure about that?" Zinder said, eyeing Dunwik. "The izzinchard we slew was able to produce ice of its own. You told us that there were strange beasts roaming this island. Could it not be a pack of ice dragons or snow worms or some other monstrosities?"

"No, it is the Maid. She it is who makes it always winter and she it is who makes the snow and ice on this island into Tinesplitter blue."

"This ice troubles me for other reasons," Kithian said. *"If there were not so much of this strange snow and ice, I would swear it was the work of Rimewinter."*

"Rimewinter? What is that?" Kion said.

"Eh? Is that from something the sword said?" Zinder said.

"Oh, he's talking to it again," Trik said, drawing nearer to Kion and raising the tip of his ear.

"Rimewinter, what a beautiful name," Trak said.

Kion related Kithian's words. The wind was so loud he had to raise his voice, and even then he needed to repeat it several times. But no matter how great the noise around them, glaive and swordspeaker could always hear one another if they were near.

"Rimewinter was one of the Mastersmith's glaives, one of many lost at the end of the last age. But this is far too much frost for any glaive to bring forth. Unless...but no, it is better not to consider that."

"Unless what?"

"Unless Rimewinter fell and became corrupted. But I will choose to think there is some other force at work here before I think of that."

"You're saying that there's another glaive somewhere on Tinesplitter Isle?" Trak said.

Kion shook his head vigorously. "That's not what Truesilver meant."

But by the dreamlike look in his eye, Trak didn't hear him. "Another glaive...think of that, Trik."

The same faraway look was mirrored in Trik's gaze. "It would be a wonder to behold..."

Another glaive. Kion had known that there had been others in the past, but he always imagined that Truesilver was the only one left. Did that mean that there were other swordspeakers also? Perhaps not. A glaive still had to send forth its call for a swordspeaker to arise. Truesilver had lain dormant for hundreds of years before seeking out Kion, passed down as an ordinary weapon of the bladewardens, its origins lost to time. It might be many more years before another swordspeaker was called again.

Kion would deal with that if and when another glaive was found. For now, their most pressing concern was surviving a night in this snowstorm. Kion was too weak to last through another night like this and Dunwik needed to rest and heal as much as he could.

They trudged east along the wintry shore, the cliffs to one side, the frozen waters of the bay on the other. The snow was glazed over with ice here so that Trik and Trak had to punch holes in the thin crust with their walking sticks. Their trail-blazing made an unsettling shattering sound with each step, but the ground beneath was firm and even. The wind and cold grew more furious as the darkness deepened, until Dunwik called for a halt.

"The caves I had hoped to find are no longer here. Covered in ice and snow, most likely. And there is little chance of finding new ones in the dark. We must find shelter soon. The tents will not hold against this wind. The Maid of Ice will batter them to shreds. Another storm is coming."

"You mean this isn't a storm already?" Zinder said, waving his hands at the blasts of snow stinging their faces from every direction.

"Nothing like what is to come."

Kion strained his eyes against the impervious night. There had to be more than ice and snow and cliffs on this cursed island.

"What about those mounds of snow up ahead? Could we dig one out and take shelter in one of them?"

"It would take too long," Dunwik said. "We are all weary from the journey, and would likely freeze to death before we carved one of sufficient size."

"What if we didn't have to dig? Truesilver, could your fire make us a cave in those mounds?"

"Yes, that would not be difficult, but the snow would melt so quickly you would be standing in water."

"True. We couldn't sleep until the water froze back over."

"I've got an idea," Trik said. "If Truesilver can make us a cave, Scriff can freeze it back up again."

Trak's face lit up with pride. "Trik, you're brilliant!"

"That idea's not half bad," Zinder said, openly surprised.

"What do you think, Truesilver?"

"That should work as long as the fox has enough frost inside of him. What do you say, Gim-dor-ren? Could you freeze over a snow cave if I made one for us?"

Several yips affirmed Scriff's consent and what Kion thought he heard was, *"my pleasure,"* or perhaps *"my duty"*: they seemed to be the same word in the beast speech. *"We do the same when we make our dens,"* Scriff added, hopping about on the ice-coated snow, prancing like he'd just caught the scent of a rabbit.

The plan was swiftly put into action. Trik and Trak stood amazed once again to see Truesilver's thick red fire licking up the snow with ease. In little time, a space was carved into the great blue mound and Kion emerged, stamping out of the slosh. Scriff padded in and all that could be seen for several minutes were clouds of milky air, billowing out from the horseshoe-shaped opening.

At last, Scriff emerged with something close to a grin on his face, his radiant blue eyes brimming with satisfaction.

The space Truesilver had opened up was large enough to slide both sleds inside with room for the six of them to lay down in the middle. It was so big that at first Kion wondered whether the roof would hold, but Scriff had frozen it to solid ice and the fox assured them that he had made dens far larger. The walls, floor, and ceiling blended so seamlessly together, it looked like the work of a master stonemason. The top was a bit low, though, so that only Zinder could stand up straight. Pushing the sleds off to the side, they situated themselves within as best they could. They were touching elbows by the time they got everyone in, but they were out of the howling wrath of the storm.

"It's so beautiful," Tiryn said, touching the deep blue walls. "And it blocks out most of the wind. I can barely hear it now."

"More importantly, we can barely feel it." Zinder shook the snow from his clothing, spraying Trik and Trak, who shrank away from him as if he'd coated them with some sorcerous dust. Zinder snorted and shook his head. "Though we'll need to seal up the opening."

Dunwik unbundled some of their gear and produced two short-hafted shovels and handed them to the twins.

"You've aided us greatly by manning one of the sleds for the last leg of the journey and forging a path for us along the shore. Now it's time for you to further earn your keep."

"Yes, sir!" the twins said in unison. Their faces were still red from the day's trek, but they jolted up at Dunwik's words and snatched the tools from his hands. Of all of them, Trik and Trak were the least weary from the day's journey. They set to work at once shoring up the entrance against the elements. Zinder and Tiryn pitched in using a cup and the frying pan; but the entrance was so narrow that it was hard for so many to work at once and the twins ended up doing the bulk of the labor.

A small opening near the ceiling was left to bring in fresh air and allow for the smoke from a small fire to escape. The wind grew distant and remote, as if it had been banished to some far stretch of land beyond the mighty cliffs.

"Now that we're out of the storm," Kion said. "I wanted to thank you again, Dunwik, for saving my life—and to thank Scriff for saving Tiryn's."

Dunwik said nothing, but tipped his head quietly from where he sat against the sled, his shoulder wrapped in the cloth bandages Tiryn had fashioned for him from a rag.

"We told you Scriff would come in handy," Trak said.

"Frox knows best." The smug look on Trik's face was so guileless it was impossible to take offense.

Zinder gave the fox a little bow. "Yes, in addition to his heroics with that ice vulture, Scruff's quite the architect when it comes to building snow caves."

"Well, his name's Scriff, but thank you," Trak said.

Tiryn gave each of the twins a heartfelt embrace. "You've both proven yourselves twice over and we haven't even reached Regnir."

"Indeed, you did well today," Dunwik said.

Trik and Trak looked as if they wanted to burst into a jig, but they settled for bumping shoulders in the cramped quarters in celebration of all the unexpected attention.

"I only wish I had Trik's ability to recover so quickly from a mortal wound," Kion added.

Tiryn stifled her giggles with her hand, but Zinder was not so well-mannered.

Enough blood rushed to Trik's cheeks for several mortal wounds. "Oh, um, well, I was hoping you would forget about that."

"I'm afraid I shall never forget it if I live to be a hundred!" Zinder said amidst his bubbling laughter. And the snow cave grew all the warmer.

All the next day a wintry tempest railed against Tinesplitter Isle, battering the protective mound of snow where the little band huddled inside. For once, Kion did not resent the delay. Though he longed to find his mother as much as ever, yesterday's journey had taught him how desperately he needed rest. Under Tiryn's watchful eye and through the use of her blood root and some sourberry tea, both he and Dunwik grew stronger by the hour as the day drew on. As for Zinder, his legs were now as sprightly as they ever had been before his injuries at Dunach.

They spoke of many things during their long hours together. Tiryn was curious to know about Trik and Trak's parents. Their mother had died during childbirth, but everyone remembered her as a kind-hearted woman who went out of her way to help others, particularly widows and the sick.

"She sounds a lot like our mother," Tiryn said.

"All the more reason for us to help you find her," Trak said.

"It will be just as if we'd found our own mother—in a way," Trik said.

"And what about your father?" Kion said.

"He was killed when wolves attacked the village," Trak said.

"We were only three, so we don't remember him much, but everyone says he was a great hunter," Trik said. Though they showed no great sadness when discussing their parents, they did grow noticeably more serious than usual. Kion could tell they were at peace with the loss.

"Your father was a great man," Dunwik said. "He was twice the hunter I am. It is a shame he did not live to pass on his skills to the two of you." There was silence for some time after that. Kion found thoughts of his own father returning. He had traveled much when he was younger. Though he seldom spoke of those travels, Kion was certain he had never come to the Frostkeld, but if he had, he would have enjoyed the company of these simple and straightforward people. Once you got past their strict traditions and taciturn ways, they were as warm and giving as any people Kion had ever met.

When the talk resumed, it turned to the lands beyond the Frostkeld. Trik and Trak were anxious for news of the world, and Kion, Tiryn, and Zinder—but mostly Zinder—were more than happy to tell them all that they knew, especially concerning the haukmarn and the current war.

"It's a dangerous world, the Summerlands," said Trak, growing serious again after Zinder told of the attacks on Roving, Charring, Fennigar, and Grettling.

"Maybe living in the Frostkeld isn't half bad," Trik said.

"Oh, for certain," Zinder said, rubbing his hands over the small fire in the center of the cave. Its flickering light wove feathery patterns upon the walls and upon their faces. "If you don't mind the giant ice buzzards and storms that will freeze the life out of you and never seeing green meadows or fields of daisies or listening to a gurgling stream on a spring day after the rains have swollen it to bursting."

"I suppose it is a little lacking when you put it like that," Trik said.

"Yes, a sky free of izzinchards would certainly be nice. Then again, that's the first one Trik and I have ever seen," Trak said.

Tiryn finished changing out Dunwik's bandages for a fresh set and wedged herself beside Kion in front of the fire. "About that creature, are there many of them here? I've read stories of monsters in books, but never anything like that."

"Yes, there are others," Dunwik said. "I knew the way to the cliffs would be dangerous, though I did not expect to face an izzinchard before we even reached them. No one has seen such a creature and lived to tell of it since before I was born."

"They were known as icewings of old. One of the many dim-touched unleashed upon the world during the Shattering by Talinyon; though he could have done none of his evil without the guidance, and some say the dominance, of his glaive, Malix, or as it later came to be known, Shadowriven. Together, they used the Spark to twist and maim the form and nature of many beasts, for Talinyon's own armies were small and unable to stand on their own against the united might of the Four Wards," Kithian said.

"So his evil spread beyond just his betrayal of his people. How did he create these dim-touched creatures?" Kion said.

"Talinyon created nothing. Evil's power lies in its ability to twist and mock that which already is, never to create. Through twisted means he brought forth a menagerie of monsters too many to count. We can only hope that in the many intervening years most of them died away. For brave men of old took up weapons to hunt them down, along with the solif sent by the Mastersmith."

"The solif? What are they?"

"They are living sparks which fly from the Mastersmith's hammer as it strikes the anvil. The golden or bright ones, they are also called, and the forge-touched and the everborn. They are those who wander the night skies, facing evils even beyond those known in this mortal realm.

Yet from time to time when the need is great, they descend from on high and dwell within the Wards for a season. Then they take the form of beasts, or rarely, of great and powerful beings like unto men. They are silent hunters who have mended much that is broken, though they most often work in the shadows, for light shines brightest where the night is darkest."

"The golden animals…" Tiryn said in a breathless voice after listening to Kion's recitation.

"We saw one, didn't we, lad? On the road to Roving."

"Yes, and that wasn't the only time. I forgot to tell you, but I saw another one while I was at the judgment post, or at least I think I did. It was a squirrel, I think, with fur as bright as the fane's own gold."

"You saw one and never told me? And you saw them twice?" Tiryn leaned back, her head bumping one of the sleds and bouncing a waterskin off the top. It would have landed square in her lap if Zinder hadn't snatched it out of the air. He popped the lid, and took a swig in the same motion. Tiryn failed to notice, but the twins sat up in a mixture of admiration and suspicion.

"Sorry, I didn't think it was all that important at the time. We were so busy planning the journey to Tinesplitter that I forgot all about it."

"Never take lightly a visit from a solif. I have little doubt that it was by this solif's craft that you were put into the sleep which protected you through the night. If you ever doubted the Mastersmith's hand was upon you, swordspeaker, you surely should know it now."

Kion hardly knew what to make of this, but he had rarely heard Kithian speak with such wonder and awe. It was hard to understand how any animal, even a golden one, could invoke such respect in a glaive. First the dim-touched and now the solif. Knowing that such creatures wandered the world made the Four Wards into something more akin to a dream. Or perhaps it was the old days of Furrow and farmers and sheep that were the true dream and he was just now waking up to the true world.

The talk moved on to other matters from there, for Kithian

knew only a little of the solif and their secretive ways. The conversation turned instead toward Rimewinter, and the twins were especially keen to know more about the missing glaive. When Kithian told them that Rimewinter was only a dagger they were at first disappointed, but they were so taken with the thought that they, too, might become swordspeakers that eventually they warmed to the idea of a smaller blade.

"Trik and I have fought with daggers since we were old enough to spit in the wind," Trak said.

"We spar all the time with wooden ones," Trik said.

"Every chance we get."

"I once killed a wolf with a dagger."

"You did not." Trak snorted in disbelief.

"Well, it was a large dog at least."

"Rubbish."

"Fine, it was a rabbit. But that's not easy to do with a weapon that small and a creature that quick."

"You knocked it out when the pommel hit its head. And it was pure luck and you know it. Who throws a dagger at a rabbit and expects to kill it?"

"Well, you've never killed a rabbit with a knife."

"You mean dagger."

"Right, dagger. My point is, I'm quite handy with one in a pinch."

Trak leaned over to whisper in Kion's ear. "He hasn't beaten me in the last forty-one tries."

"I heard that, Trak—"

"Trik and Trak, stop arguing and patch up the door," Dunwik said, handing them back their shovels.

The little wall at the entrance Trik and Trak had put in place the night before had slowly worn down from the top where they'd left the slit for air. The storm had doubled the size of it since they'd last patched it up. The twins quickly rebuilt the door back up to where it had been.

"It's not showing any signs of letting up out there," Trik said as they finished.

"I wonder what we've done to stir up the Maid's anger," Trak said.

Dunwik stared at the slit where snow flew by in a powdery blur. "Two storms of this strength in three days. It is a bad omen."

"So tell us of this Maid of Ice you speak of," Tiryn said. "Is she truly real?"

Trik's eyebrows raised in alarm. "Of course she's real." With his noisy whisper he added, "Don't talk of her as if she isn't. She might get even angrier."

"She could probably blow this cave down in a single puff if she wanted to," Trak said.

The twins and Dunwik were serious. But Kion was dismayed to see Tiryn and Zinder nodding along as if they believed as well.

"If she's real, what does she look like, and where does her power come from? Have you ever seen her?"

"No one's ever seen the Maid of Ice," Trik said.

"Of course not. Except her victims," Trak added.

"And they can't tell about her for obvious reasons," Trik said.

"Ah, I see. And Dunwik, you believe this as well?"

"Yes, Swordspeaker. Her legend goes as far back as the time after the War of the Shattering. The same tales and songs that tell of Truesilver also tell of her."

Zinder tugged at Kion's elbow. "Like *The Lay of the Glaives.*"

This reminder gave Kion pause. He wouldn't have believed the glaives existed either, or that the *Lay* was true, before he found Truesilver. And he'd been unconvinced about the curse of Longwinter until he experienced that as well.

"Is it true, Kithian?" he said. "Do you know about the Maid of Ice?"

"I once knew someone who went by that name, but I have no idea if she is in some way connected to the legends of the Frin. In any case, it

would be wise to listen to what these people have to say. Every legend has some truth to it, for those wise enough to see."

Kion fixed the twins with his gaze. "Very well, then. What do the legends say?"

"We can sing them the song," Trik said.

"Yes, we'll sing you the song," Trak said.

They rose, their faces taking on a ruddy hue as their high voices bathed the cave with a haunting rhythm.

The Maid of Ice sometime appears
Her face a-glitter with diamond tears
To mourn the one that she has lost
Beneath the hoary frozen frost

There are no tracks upon the snow
That tell the tale of grief and woe
The bitter, grave, and awful price
Paid by the girl now made of ice

She drifts amidst the howling gales
Unleashing tearful cries and wails
Her wintry robes of blinding white
Are thick with sorrow's chilling blight

The Maid of Ice sometime appears
Her face a-glitter with diamond tears
For should she ever cease to cry
Her heart would melt and she would die

As they sang, the twins' faces had looked older than they ever had before, but as the last notes drifted to silence the youthful gleam of their faces returned. Tiryn had listened hunkered over, her chin resting on her clasped hands, her mind carried away by the words and melody.

"So the snow and ice are from her grief. How terribly sad," she said.

"Yes," Dunwik said. "Other stories say that once the Maid's grief passes, these lands will return to what they once were. It is for that day that we in Whitewind wait and hold out. The day when our homes and lands will be restored to the springtime beauty they once knew."

"It is a curious tale," Kithian said.

"In Inris, we have similar hopes for the Four Wards. I understand, perhaps, why your people have not left," Kion said. He was still not sure the Maid of Ice was real, but the Frin's desire for release from the Longwinter was something he could believe in. No people could be free while the lands they loved were held in bondage, whether from ice and snow or an invading army.

A somber air settled inside the little cave, but nowhere more so than upon Tiryn. Her thoughtful expression made it clear that for her, the legend of the Maid was more than just a tale.

Chapter 33

THE STANDING CLIFFS

Tiryn fumbled for her charcoal pencil and journal, moving whisper-quiet in the glimmering dark. At last her fingers found what she sought within her pack and, struggling to calm her breathing, she began to write by the fading embers of the fire.

22nd of Lockwin

The others have yet to wake. I must write down what I saw in my dream before they do. It may have been a vision but I do not think it will come again. I do not want it to come again, and yet, if it turns out to be true, I dare not forget, awful and terrible as it was.

I dreamed of the Maid of Ice. At least, I thought it was her until right up to the very end of the dream. Now, I'm not sure.

I was speeding above the ice, floating upon swift and wild winds. I was being pulled against my will and could not turn back for all I tried, bound by an invisible thread to the figure that went before me, tall and stiff and devastatingly lovely, like a force of untamed nature. Her skin and dress were all of one color, a shroud-like, blistering white. I saw only the back of her, but something in the way she held her head, high and graceful as a statue, seemed familiar. A sense that I should know those movements nagged my thoughts, but at last it came to me—this must be the Maid of Ice.

As the Maid rushed headlong through the night, she wailed in grief. Her cries summoned forth storms of frost and fury. I could feel the anger in her vengeful dirge as if it were my own. The longer I listened, the more drawn into her plight I became until it seemed to me that her anger was justified. For there is righteous anger as well as the false and foolish kind. And it seemed to me that her wrath served some greater purpose.

The Maid of Ice flew onward, laying waste to the ground beneath her, shackling it with frozen chains. When I looked down I saw why the chains were needed. Beneath the ice, a slumbering darkness threatened to stir. Cruel as the ice was, it held back another, even greater source of hate than the one that burned inside the Maid. Something lay buried within that icebound tomb. Something shadowy, something that flitted at the edge of my vision, shifting and moving ever so subtly, waiting patiently for its moment to strike. A great, lurking presence brooded in those depths, one that could not escape—must not escape—for the whole world would be imprisoned once it broke free. And the Maid's thoughts were ever upon that thing, whatever it was.

On the Maid floated, drawn by her inner fire of wrath, and the doom of that unending frozen road. But the presence beneath the ice swelled and grew until the ice could scarce stand against it. Just when I was certain that the shadow would burst forth and smother us both, the Maid stopped and raised her hand. She held something inside it, but I could not tell what it was. The mysterious object began to glow. The brightness and the blue of it was hauntingly beautiful, as though light and water had melded into one. The light spread up the arm of the Maid and into her throat, filling it with brilliance and woe. And I saw that it was not the Maid from whence the ice and frost came but from the light within her hand.

The Maid thrust the object into the ground. The shadows swirled and shrank and slunk back into the dark from which they came and for the first time I felt safe, though the storm still raged on around me.

Then the Maid of Ice turned, and though the light burned and was painful to look upon, I could not look away. Amidst that chilling, glorious light I saw plainly what I should have known all along. At last I saw the Maid of Ice for who she was. But oh, how terrible and unforgettable that sight was. That is the worst part of visions and dreams, the knowing what you ought not to know. For that face was the most beautiful one I have ever seen, the face I have loved above all others since I was a child. It was the face of Mother, though it looked both simultaneously older and younger than it should have been. The face itself was smooth and devoid of care as Mother must have been in her youth, yet it was drained of color and absent all the marks of life and of wisdom that should have been there, making it look older than any person I have ever met. It was the face of a woman in death and yet somehow still alive.

Oh, please, let this be just a dream. Please let this vision die upon this page and never see the light of the waking world.

Someone is stirring. I must go.

Tiryn could not have craned her neck back any further without falling over. The ice wall towering above their party disappeared into chalky mists. The ebony blue mass had the all imposing beauty of a frozen waterfall. Its chiseled facets were long and severe and relentless, as if the ice had kept this shape for hundreds of years. The walls were as impregnable as a fortress. It was not hard to imagine some powerful ruler dwelling beyond them, immune to all assault from his enemies. Perhaps that ruler was the Maid of Ice herself.

"She's not my mother," Tiryn told herself. "It was just a dream." She'd been telling herself that all morning, but it didn't seem to be working. The harrowing image of Mother's lifeless face refused to leave her thoughts.

"I've never seen the like," Zinder said. He walked up and felt the wall, running his hands along the icy surface.

"You're sure there's no other way to Regnir?" Kion said, looking in both directions along the base of the cliffs. All that could be seen were drifts of sky-blue snow butting up against the dark barrier.

"Not if we want to avoid being seen," Dunwik said.

"Don't worry," Trak said. "Every Frin knows how to climb, and Dunwik is the best of us all."

Dunwik gave little heed to the boy's praise but continued to unpack the climbing gear. Ropes, pitons, two clawed metal frames, and two hook-like axes were soon laid out on the snow. The rest of the gear had been left in the snow cave, along with the sleds.

Zinder watched with particular interest as Dunwik strapped the two frames of metallic teeth onto the bottom of his boots. In addition to the triangular teeth along the iron rims, they had a thick spike thrusting outward from the toes. He plodded to the base of the wall in these strange under-shoes and struck at the ice with the toe spike. Shards and shavings fell like frosted sparks. In four kicks he had a foothold. With two strokes of his axe, the needle-like head sunk in. He repeated the process with his left side, kicking and pounding until he was just off the ground. Alternating back and forth with the axes and clawed feet, he rose more quickly than Tiryn would have thought possible. He was soon above Kion's head.

"I've always fancied myself a decent climber," Zinder said. "But that fellow might as well have wings."

Dunwik ascended with little effort, as though he were climbing a ladder and not pulling himself up a bulwark of sheer ice.

"What if he falls?" Tiryn said, shivering partly from the cold, but mostly out of fear for Dunwik. Her shivering grew worse once he disappeared into the mists. The only sign of him then was the sharp *thricckkk* of his axes and climbing shoes and the chips of ice hurtling down.

"He won't fall," Trak said.

"Frin learn to climb before they learn to crawl," Trik said.

Tiryn certainly hoped that was true.

"I'd feel better if he used a rope."

"And slow himself down?" Trak said.

Tiryn grimaced and tore her eyes from the mist. She couldn't look anymore.

Then came a scream from above.

She nearly jumped out of her boots. Her gaze darted skyward, expecting to see Dunwik's body plummeting down.

"I've reached the top," Dunwik shouted. It hadn't been a scream, just a way to let them know he was safe. Intense worry and an over-active imagination did not make good friends.

Trak muffled his laughter into one of his gloves. Trik did the same, but his was too loud to be contained that way.

"Are all summerlanders as jumpy as you, Tiryn? You should have seen your face! It went as white as the Maid of Ice."

"How do you know her face is white?" Tiryn wanted to say, but she bottled up the thought before it could go any further. It was just a dream. After her heart dropped back down into her chest, she allowed herself a nervous chuckle.

"Well, I'm glad I could at least offer you two a little enjoyment."

Zinder's chuckling was far more reserved, though an abundance of mirth bubbled in his eyes.

"That's the spirit, lass," he said. "We need all the laughter we can get in a place like this."

Kion was the only one unaffected by the lightened mood. He pressed his lips together in the barest echo of a smile. Other matters swirled behind those dark eyes. With each day that had passed since he'd found Truesilver, he became more and more swordspeaker and less and less her brother, even more so since his night at the judgment post. It was as though a part of him had been lost during his wanderings upon the edge of death. Perhaps once they found Mother, his old joy would return. Yet another reason to press on and find her as soon as they could.

Tiryn kept her eyes locked onto the ice wall during the whole of the ascent. Though they had her tied up in six different ways to the rope, she could not bear to look either up or down. She did not want to allow her mind any chance to acknowledge the dizzying ascent into the mist. Only when she reached the jagged summit did she risk a glance back into the churning fog she had just passed through. Her head swam at the sight and just as quickly she flicked her eyes away. It looked too much like clouds, and clouds were not meant to be seen from above.

The mist and flurries pelting the Standing Cliffs certainly would cloak their approach to Regnir. But how they would ever find a path across these barren heights was a question as daunting as the ascent. The land atop the Cliffs was full of angular thrusts of ice, as if an izzinchard ten times the size of the one they'd slain had rained down shard after shard for years upon end. The only advantage the terrain above had over the sides of the cliffs was that the ice was not sheer. But a slip might be just as deadly, for it could easily send a person sliding over the edge.

"I'd see clearer if I stuck my head in an oven," Zinder said, staring into the waves of falling snow.

"An oven sounds nice about now. How will we be able to walk across this without slipping?" Tiryn said.

"The Cliffs are locked in ice here, but there may be other places where the underlying rocks are exposed," Dunwik said. "If we can find such a path, we will be able to travel more safely. Here is where we must rely on the fox to be our guide. Swordspeaker, please instruct Scriff to find us a safe path."

Kion's eyes glittered with the light from Truesilver's citrine gems as he listened to the voice of his glaive.

In response to Kithian's requests, Scriff let out several quick screeches and squeals. Trik and Trak's faces glowed, soaking up every word as Kion relayed the animal's reply.

"Scriff says he's never been this way before, but there are always paths for those clever enough to find them."

After a few more yips and yelps, Scriff went off by himself to see what he could find. No one spoke as they stared into the chalky blue shroud into which the frox had gone. The wait for his return, sitting in silence on the cold, unforgiving ice, dragged on and on until Trik and Trak began to wonder whether or not they should go after their pet.

"You will not risk yourselves for a beast," Dunwik said. "Have patience. A frost fox knows how to take care of itself in a place like this."

Tiryn sympathized with the twins' fear. She had not known Scriff long but had already come to love his quiet obedience, intelligent eyes, and stunning white fur. The thought of a lovely creature like that lying broken and lifeless at the bottom of some cliff, or carried off in the beak of another izzinchard, sent a quiver through her heart. But she had a selfish reason to hope for his safety as well. The loss of Scriff might mean an end to their chance at finding Mother. They would be forced to retreat back down the cliff and seek some other, more exposed path to Regnir, and perhaps end up captured and imprisoned alongside her.

When Scriff's yips finally came across the windy heights,

they were as heart-warming as any song Tiryn had ever heard. A few moments later, the frox came padding out of the snowy mist.

"Scriff!" The twins smothered him in their arms.

"He's found a way," Kion said, his voice infused with some of its old warmth.

"I never thought I'd follow a fox, much less trust one with my life," Zinder said, half-jokingly, though he shared in the others' elation. "But when you're lost on top of the world, I suppose you must take any guide you can get."

Scriff escaped the twins' embrace and trotted over to Tiryn for more adulation, which she was happy to supply. "You did it, boy. I knew you could." She gave him a good solid rubbing down, which the animal thoroughly enjoyed. Kion came and joined in the indulgence of the astute little fox as he yipped out answers to Kithian's questions.

"He says there's an exposed spine of rock about four hundred 'jaunts' away, as he calls them, northeast. A jaunt seems to be about one of his strides, so that puts it at less than a quarter of a mile. He's not sure how far it goes, but he followed it for a while and never came to the end of it."

Dunwik produced a long, thin rope, different from the one they had used to pull the party up the cliff. "Very well. We rope ourselves together until we reach the spine. Even then, we will go with the utmost care. Do not be brash simply because we have the rope. It's only meant to serve as a last resort." He leveled his gaze at the twins. "Mind where you walk and be careful to speak quietly. It is mostly only ice here, but there is snow as well and we do not want to risk an avalanche."

Zinder threw up his hands. "It seems only fitting we're to be tied to a leash, doesn't it? If we're to be led by a beast, we might as well be treated like one too."

They tied themselves about two paces apart. Tiryn's fingers were so numb she'd never have managed to get the knots tied right if Dunwik and the twins had not helped.

Once they set off, Tiryn, above all the others, was the most cautious. She surely held back the pace, but she couldn't keep from calculating every step. Back in the Tors she had taken tumbles in the flattest and fairest of meadows. If she could fall there, how much more in a place like this? If her clumsiness reared its nettlesome head here, it might be the death of them all.

By care and patience, small steps, and great mercy, they made their way to the exposed rocks. The stone was dark and rugged and the path Scriff had found was little more than a gash in the surrounding ice. It was webbed with frost in spots, but it was a thousand times more sure than the great sheets of ice surrounding it.

They stopped to take a quick meal before setting out once more. Half-frozen biscuits and ice-water were all that could be managed, but it staved off their hunger. When the journey resumed, the ropes were no longer needed, for the path took them into a small channel with two shoulder-height walls protecting either side. Still, they kept themselves fastened together, for it would only slow them down to untie themselves and put the ropes back on again later. They traveled a long cold mile in the channel before it ended at the base of a small cliff. The deep blue swath of ice rose up before them, blocking the way.

"Time for Scriff to find another path," Kion said. Not even Dunwik suggested climbing in the fiendish winds which held sway atop the Standing Cliffs.

Scriff yelped back his reply and snuck off once again into the chilling mist, skirting the base of the cliff. They did not have to wait nearly as long for his return this time.

"Scriff found some snow-covered hills to the south. It will be more slippery than the rock, but it will be better than walking on ice."

They set off down the icy slope, determined to follow Scriff's advice, for no other choice remained save to turn back and abandon the cliffs altogether. Everyone—not just Tiryn—had to measure their steps now. The pace slowed to a crawl, but at last they hit a stretch where the flurries cleared enough for them to see the snowy ground ahead. It stretched off to the east until it disappeared into the mist a few hundred paces away. Near where the ice turned to snow, the ground plunged into a yawning chasm. Perhaps the sight of the snow, and their eagerness to edge away from the deadly drop-off, allowed their pace to quicken without them realizing it, or perhaps it was just that Trik hit an invisible patch of ice without knowing it, but not ten steps after they'd spotted the snowy path, he slipped and fell.

He slid away from Dunwik, who was walking in the lead, and pulled Trak and Zinder down after him.

"Help!" Zinder shouted.

Tiryn's body slapped the ice a moment later. Her mind went into a spin. It was worse than falling into the current of a raging river for at least with that there was a chance to swim. She could do nothing here to avoid sliding off the edge.

Her scream cut itself short when something tugged at her hood, yanking her back before she could be swept away with Trik and the others. Scriff had her coat in his jaws. Though the beast weighed less than she did, its claws dug hard into the ice. Scriff's quick reaction allowed Kion to keep his balance at the anchor of the line. For all that, Scriff 's heroics might have been for naught if Dunwik had followed Trik down toward the chasm. He did hit the ground, but before he'd gone anywhere, he buried an axehead into the rock. Trik's rope went taut and Trak grabbed hold of his brother's boots and stopped sliding, though for a moment it looked like he might pull Trik's boots clean off and keep going. Without the twins dragging him away, Zinder bounced to his feet and skidded to a stop.

"I—I'm still alive," Trik said, his mouth a frosty chimney, billowing clouds of panic. Everyone but Dunwik was panting from the near miss. The edge of the cliff was not ten paces away from where Trak dangled.

"Yes, lad, by the forge light and a dog's leash, we're all still alive."

Trik was close to tears. "I'm so sorry. I should have been more careful. I could have killed us all."

"It wasn't your fault," Dunwik said. "It could have happened to any of us." And those few words, from that somber voice, might have been the kindest he had ever spoken to the poor addled boy. At that moment, they were exactly the words Trik needed to hear.

Chapter 34

WHAT THE SKIMMERS BROUGHT

Twice more Scriff led them across the treacherous ice of the Standing Cliffs before the day ended. They slowed their pace and doubled the caution with which they went and kept clear of any further falls.

"You have our thanks, Gim-dor-ren, for your guidance over these perilous heights," Kithian told the fox once it grew too dark to continue.

"He says it was no less than his duty to the Mastersmith and the young men who saved him from the ice," Kithian reported.

Scriff had impressed Kion from the first with the thoughtfulness of his responses. The horses had been kind and noble, but there was an intelligence in the fox that was surprising among animals. Whether that was something common to all frost foxes or was particular to this one, he couldn't say. It was likely that different kinds of animals had different levels of intelligence, even though they shared a common language. From his experiences before he could talk to animals that certainly seemed true, and sheep would certainly have to come in near the bottom of any such estimation. He loved them dearly, but they could be utterly thick-skulled about most things.

The party ended their journey that day near a high stand of rocks. The rocks rose boldly into the air, thick fingers of stone jutting from the surrounding snow. The high formation gave them relief from the battering wind, which otherwise ran uncontested across the heights.

Kion did his best to help Tiryn and Zinder set up the tent the three of them would share, but he was spent from the grueling trek. As soon as the tent went up, he crawled inside and slipped into his bedroll, descending so rapidly into sleep that the words of Kithian came to him only in his dreams.

"Sleep well, swordspeaker," Kithian said in his thoughtful, comforting way, and yet there was a hardness to it as well. *"For tomorrow may bring the answer to many questions and questions to many answers."*

The fabric of the tents was stiff as six-day-old bread when Kion crawled out of his tent the next morning. It took a good deal of pounding, shaking, and wrangling to get the contraption rolled back up and packed. Most of the work had to be done with bare hands, so that by the time they'd bundled everything up, Kion's fingers were stinging and bright red from the cold. After he finished packing and blowing on his fingers until they could move again, he took breakfast with the others. It was an unappealing meal of biscuits and pickled fish, but it was enough to ready them for the last push through the Standing Cliffs. If Scriff's judgment was correct—and the fox had not failed them yet—they would be within sight of Regnir by early afternoon.

They set off in a pre-dawn glimmer in which light and expectation melded into one. When the sun finally appeared, it shone in a pale blue circle through a haze of clouds, struggling to overcome the horrible ice and frost which entombed the island. Through the cold they marched, seven solitary figures toiling on the lonely heights where few if any had ever trod.

Strength seeped into Kion's body, slow and steady as the warmth of the sun. Like the day's sun, he was not as strong as he could be, but he was strong enough. He had to be. For today would be the day that he found his mother. That ought to have made him nervous or hopeful, but it was hard to feel anything when he was so numb and weary. He tried to muster up the intensity and conviction that had carried him through so many dangers and obstacles, but all he had left now was the raw will to press on. The emotions would come later, when he saw his mother's face. Until then, all that mattered was the next breath, the next step, the next patch of ice or rock.

The final part of their journey through the cliffs led them over a long, snowy ascent and then down a crumbling escarpment of loose stone peppered with patches of dark ice, which at times was nearly invisible against the coal-colored rock. Spitting snow kept them from seeing much beyond a few dozen paces in any direction.

Scriff trotted gamely beside Tiryn, his keen blue eyes always on the hunt for hidden threats. Trik and Trak lamented over how their pet had "abandoned them for a pretty young maiden," and they were half serious.

"I'm sorry," Tiryn said. "I'm not trying to keep him from you. He probably just knows that I need some extra protection while you two are more than able to hold your own in a place like this."

That placated them and quieted their grumbling.

Just after the sun had climbed to its noonday heights, they emerged onto the cliffs overlooking Regnir. Though a few flurries still drifted by like wayward tufts of wool, the snowfall had mostly ceased and they had a clear view of the town from their lofty perch more than a hundred feet above the valley below. The town of Regnir lay half a mile to the southeast, wedged between a low glacial formation to the south and a run of snow-capped hills to the north. The settlement ended on the far side in an ice-locked harbor, which arose beyond the snow-covered shore. Heaps of snow enveloped the buildings and streets, as though the whole town was an assortment of frosty blue cushions. Snow-rounded roofs ran in circular patterns around little clearings, creating a well-ordered tapestry, serene and still and beautiful.

"It's so quiet, as if the whole village were asleep," Tiryn said softly, as though she feared to wake the slumbering town. But she needn't have spoken so quietly. Regnir was too far away for anyone to hear, and there was no danger of an avalanche where they lay hiding, for it was mostly ice and rock. Off to the south, though, where the cliffs ran closer to the town, great mounds of snow towered above the shore, holding their breath, waiting to sweep down onto the land below.

"It's not as beautiful as Whitewind, but it is pretty," Trak said.

"Like the Maid of Ice, I suppose. Frosty, but beautiful," Trik said.

Tiryn's brow shadowed over at those words, but she made no reply.

The six of them crept to the edge of the precipice and stretched themselves flat on the ground with only their heads peeking above the clifftop. A thin, meandering path dribbled out from the town, leading north. But the best approach would be the uneven hills which bordered that road.

Zinder pulled out his spyglass. Dunwik marveled at the craftsmanship, though Trik and Trak pulled away from it, afraid it might be some sorcerous device.

"Those are the strangest ships I've ever seen," Zinder said.

"Ice skimmers," Dunwik said. "No other ships can reach Regnir. The ice runs out for half a league until it gives way to open water."

Zinder finished his survey and passed the glass to Kion. The metal rim was so cold it singed the skin around his eye, but he hardly cared. His mother might be down in that village. He would give anything just for a glimpse of her.

Kion trained the glass first upon the ships Zinder had spotted. They had sharp, spear-like prows, a single large mast, and three enormous curved beams underneath the hull. The beams ended in long metal runners like skates and propped the ship up well above the icy ground. Surely these were the same kind of ship the Noathryn had used to bring his mother to this accursed place. How satisfying it would be to set them alight with Truesilver's fire and reduce them to piles of ash.

Kion turned the glass upon the other parts of the city, amazed by the amount of detail the powerful lens afforded. People, windows, doors, even beards and footprints began to emerge. The city was far less serene than it appeared to the naked eye.

"It is significantly larger than Whitewind," Kithian said, sharing Kion's sight through the glass. *"The few people moving along the streets are clearly Noathryn from their long, loping strides, like those we saw marching past the pond. Several of the larger buildings could hold prisoners, but none walk the streets who might be taken for Inrisians. The Noathryn may have their slaves working elsewhere, or we may see them if we wait. If we have not seen any soon, we may need to use stealth to enter the town to find out where they are being held."*

Kion shared Truesilver's observations with the others.

"Some of the prisoners would be working the mines," Dunwik said. "Though they likely have the women and children working elsewhere—if the Noathryn have not lost all sense of honor." The disdain upon his face showed that he had little faith in that holding true.

"So the Noathryn are here for the mines?" Kion said.

"Yes," Dunwik said. "The mines hold rich veins of silver and some iron as well. The kalvars of Regnir amassed great wealth over the years. The last kalvar, Hildal, began to openly question the Law of the Frin which kept our people hidden from the outside world. He desired to trade for the fine things made in the Summerlands and to use his hordes of silver to acquire them. The Noathryn still trouble us in Whitewind from time to time, but the Frin of Regnir had seen no intruders in centuries. They forgot the reason the Law was put in place."

"Ah, I see how it is," Zinder said. "Once the Noathryn got a taste of the silver, they eventually sought its source, here on this island. That's the problem with wealth. It leaves a scent for the greedy to follow. Not even eternal winter will keep thieves away."

The mines. Kion grew hot inside his coat thinking of his mother working in a place like that. Perhaps it was true, as most believed, that Noath had once been part of Inris and that the two peoples had lived as one, but if so, that bond had been severed long ago. The Noathryn were now no better than haukmarn if they could treat their Inrisian prisoners like that.

He passed the spyglass off to Dunwik. The watcher regarded the device warily and took some time before he ventured to put it to his eye.

"This is a marvel. It gives one the eyes of a hawk. I would think it sorcery if you had not used it yourself, Swordspeaker. Ah, look, I see a new skimmer is gliding into the harbor. It is crewed by several dozen men."

"May I see?" Kion said. Dunwik handed him the glass and Kion focused it in upon the sleek skimmer sliding to a stop at the docks. On the deck, several dark figures moved to lower the gangplank onto the pier. "Those aren't men, they're—"

"Haukmarn," Zinder said in a low growl.

"Yes. A small group of Noathryn is piloting the ship, but most of the others are haukmarn. They're beginning to disembark. The haukmarn are the first ones off, but here come several men…Oh no…one of them looks like…"

A sharp chill ran up the back of his neck, cold as his night on the judgment post.

"Ilk."

"Ilk? Here? In Regnir?" Zinder's voice was shrill as a sparrow.

"Oh, I hope you're wrong," Tiryn said.

"Impossible. He should be in prison. Let me have a look." Zinder snatched the glass and pressed it to his eye. His rosy cheeks swelled in disgust. "That's him all right. The traitorous rotter."

"Is this the one who tried to trick the glaive from you? May I see again? I would look upon his face," Dunwik said. Zinder, grinding his teeth like mill flour, passed him the spyglass. "He has the look of a wolf about him, though one so old and frail its teeth have lost their bite."

"It's not him we have to fear, but the pack he runs with," Zinder said.

"You're sure it's him?" Tiryn said, her face pinched and pensive.

"The glass is all too clear," Kion said.

Dunwik offered the spyglass to her, but she would not take it.

"No, I trust you. And I'd rather not see his face again if I don't have to," she said.

The spyglass made its way back to Kion instead. He watched Ilk shuffle from the docks to a large building in the center of town. It was larger than the great hall of Whitewind, with the same severe roof lancing skyward. Just before Ilk passed inside he looked up and for a shivering second, Kion imagined those conniving eyes looked into his. It was impossible that Ilk could have seen him. Even the eyes of a nyn would not have known him from so far away. And yet, when Ilk disappeared into the longhouse, Kion lowered the glass and said:

"He knows we're here. Ilk knows we're here."

Zinder's eyebrows tightened into a stitch. "He can't know that, not for certain."

"He was the one who told us Mother was here. Could that have just been a trap for him to lure us here and capture Truesilver? Does he want the sword that badly?" Tiryn said.

"It's not Ilk who wants Truesilver. It's Vayd. He wants Truesilver's fire for himself. I could see it in his eyes at Charring. He doesn't know that only a swordspeaker can truly wield a glaive."

"His folly is equal to his pride. We must be cautious. Ilk knows more than he let on when we questioned him in the stable."

"The haukmarn must have captured Fennigar and freed him," Zinder said. "This puts a nick in our gears for certain."

"If he is as treacherous as you say, we will have to take that into account when making our plans. You must think like a wolf to defeat one," Dunwik said.

Kion pressed his eyes shut, trying to make sense of this terrible turn. Ilk's presence was unsettling for many reasons, but it did tell him one thing. His mother was here. Ilk would not have sent them to such a remote place if he merely wanted to set a trap. That he intended to use Kion's mother as bait there could be little doubt, but perhaps there was a way to get to her before Ilk's schemes set in motion.

"Dunwik, we have to get down there now. We have to act before Ilk does."

"Are you certain, Swordspeaker? I was hoping to send one or two of us to scout the town first."

"We don't have time for scouting. We have to find her now before it's too late. If I have to fight the whole town, so be it. That's what I did at Charring."

"Yes, but never count on the same trick twice," Zinder said. "The conditions are hardly ideal for the kind of firestorm you made there."

"Truesilver's fire can burn through the swamp and snow. He doesn't need ideal conditions."

"That is true, but these buildings are not likely to be deserted the way those in Charring were. And some of them may hold prisoners, perhaps even your mother. We dare not set the city ablaze until we know more."

"You're going to burn Regnir down?" Tiryn's voice was tight and anxious. She looked as though Kion had just told her he planned to burn down their own cottage.

"There are innocent people within the town," Dunwik said. "I do not doubt the greatness of Truesilver's fire, but I doubt the wisdom of using it in such a way."

"Listen to the counsel of your friends. Do not rush into battle without knowing your aim. We still do not know where your mother is. But wherever she may be, an attack now may place her in even greater danger."

Kion pushed himself to his feet and wandered away from the edge of the cliff. The old fire was stirring inside him once again and his weariness burned away at this unexpected challenge. The only problem was the one Kithian had spoken of: there was no way to know exactly where his mother was. But this much they did know: she had to be in either the town or the mines if she was here at all.

The wind pressed relentlessly across the packed snow as Kion paced out his thoughts. His friends followed him down the little slope leading away from the lip of the cliff but said nothing. He was the swordspeaker. This was his decision to make. But his thoughts, like the unforgiving land around him, offered no clear path. He would need the cunning of a frost fox to see his way through.

"Trik, didn't you say that there was a secret entrance to the mines somewhere?"

Trik bobbed his head in excitement. "Sure as snowfall. Is that the plan then? We search for the secret entrance?"

"Me and Trik'll find it, just you watch!" Trak said.

Dunwik stepped forward. "Swordspeaker, if we are pressed for time, that hardly seems the best way to spend it—hunting for an unknown path which may not even exist."

Kion turned to the others. "Zinder? Tiryn? What do you think? If we could find the secret entrance, we could get into the mines now. Something tells me the Noathryn have her there. Though I worry that if we're wrong and she's in Regnir, we'll never get the chance to save her."

"I don't know, Kion. It doesn't seem like much of a chance either way. But I'm with you whatever you choose," Tiryn said. Her plain words brought a quiet and yet steady peace. If Tiryn was behind him, that was all he needed. Ever since she had saved his life in Whitewind, he no longer doubted his decision to bring her along, but he was never more glad for her presence than at that moment.

Zinder smoothed his well-groomed mustache. "Like Tiryn

says, I'm with you no matter the road, but I don't put much stock in us finding this secret way either—and I'm not so sure Annira isn't somewhere in the town. But there's one thing I'm wondering about. Have you asked Truesilver? I should think if anyone had a better plan, or could spot something we've missed, it would be the sword."

"Yes. He told me to listen to my friends. He said that it was not good to act until we know where Mother is, and that the wrong decision could put her in greater danger. "

"Wise words," Dunwik said. "I shall follow whatever decision you make as well, Swordspeaker, but it seems to me that if you wish to pursue the path to the mines we could divide our company and search in two directions at once."

"What?" Trak said. "Split the group?"

"But Trik and I would stay together, right? And we pledged to guard you until the end, Swordspeaker. We won't abandon you now."

Kion stood long in silence, considering the words of his companions.

"I still feel that she must be in the mines."

"I have the same feeling," Tiryn said.

"But if we're wrong and she's not there, we'll have lost half a day, and Ilk will be that much further ahead of us," Kion said.

Zinder set his chin like flint. "It's settled then. I'll go into the town. Someone has to go there and I'm the stealthiest among us. It will be a blow parting ways, but if that's what we have to do to snatch your mother from Ilk's claws, then I'm willing to risk it."

"I can't ask you to go into the city alone. What if you get caught?" Yet even as he said it, he saw no other way to head off whatever Ilk had planned.

"Ah, now, lad. Do you really think so little of my talents? No one notices a nyn unless he wants them to. I came through in Charring, I'll do the same here."

"And he will not be alone," Dunwik said. "I will go with him.

I am a watcher and not unskilled in the ways of stealth, especially in the snow."

"So we're splitting up after all," Trak said. "Well, that means that we'll be left to guide the swordspeaker to the mines."

"Don't worry, Dunwik, we'll take care of him," Trik said, his face beaming with confidence.

Yet doubt rose within Kion and he wavered. "If only we had more time—"

"Every moment we stand here blathering gives Ilk another chance to do his mischief," Zinder said.

"Oh, Zinder," Tiryn said. "You're the dearest friend our family has ever had."

"She's right." Kion stepped over and offered his hand first to Zinder, and then to Dunwik. "And you, watcher, are one of the finest men I have ever met. Thank you for your kindness both to me and to my sister."

Necessity drove their emotions quickly away. There was no time to think or feel now, only to act. Dunwik gathered up the climbing gear and headed for the edge of the cliff. The others followed in his wake. An iron certainty settled upon them. It may not have been the ideal plan, but once decided, there was nothing to do but to follow through.

As Dunwik anchored the rope into the rock, Zinder poked Kion in the ribs.

"So, Swordspeaker, are you glad you didn't leave me behind at Dunach, now?"

"You're the Hammer of the North, Zinder. I expected nothing less." Then Kion turned serious. "In all honesty, though, my father knew what he was doing when he chose you to watch over me. And I'll always be grateful for that—and not only that, but that you chose to be more than just my guardian. You chose to be my friend."

For once, Zinder was at a loss for words. All he managed was a muffled sniffle, and it wasn't because of the cold.

Chapter 35

HOLLOW IN THE ICE

One by one they came down the cliffside, lowered by Dunwik and wrapped in dark blankets which disguised them from any curious eyes that might stray north from Regnir. The plan was far from perfect. Spotting Ilk had been a stroke of luck, but his presence on Tinesplitter cast a pall of doubt over everything. He was here to trap Kion and take Truesilver; there could be no other reason for his presence. And if Ilk was expecting them, not only might it no longer be possible to save Kion's mother, he might lose Truesilver as well. They were sliding toward the edge of another precipice now, one far more dangerous than those of the Standing Cliffs, and all they could do was scramble and claw and hope to find their feet before plummeting over the edge.

They now parted ways. Kion, Tiryn, the twins, and Scriff turned and made their way west along the cliffside toward the mines. As they went, Kion's eyes followed Dunwik and Zinder south as they dissolved into two faint spots against the blue snow. They were more than able to take care of themselves, but his heart quivered with the thought that he might not see them ever again.

The twins took the lead. Scriff, sensing their urgency, kept trying to push the pace, but even Trik and Trak, who were more used to the snow, could not keep up. They had to call him back time and again. Tiryn followed behind the two brothers and Kion brought up the rear.

"Tell me if you spot anything with your glaivesight," Kion

told Kithian. "I'm not sure, though, what we're even looking for. Some secret tunnel hidden in the cliff wall perhaps."

"Very well. I leave it to you, then, to survey the sunlit world. I will be blind to it while not looking through your eyes."

The snow soon gave way to solid ice along the base of the cliffs. Though this forced them to be more wary of their footing, it was the most direct path to the mines. The cliff walls aided their balance. Keeping one hand against them, they steadied themselves as they went.

"Has Scriff been here before? Does he know anything about a secret entrance to the mines?" Trak said.

Kion passed the question on through Kithian and the fox was quick with his reply.

"My brothers used to play and hunt here, but they are all gone now. There is the smell of death at the foot of the tall rocks. We travel here at great peril. And I know of no opening into the rock," Gim-dor-ren said, and Kion was pleased to discover that he understood every word, though less pleased with the fox's actual reply.

"The smell of death? Is he telling us that we should seek a safer path?" Tiryn said.

"I fear no path will be safe between here and the mines," Kithian said.

"This is the fastest way. We have no choice," Kion said.

"Scriff will see us through, won't you, boy?" Trik said.

"Of course," the fox yipped, though it was doubtful that Scriff actually understood his master's exhortation.

A narrow track ran from the village to the cliffs, half a mile or so long. Up ahead it disappeared into a small outcropping of rock. Though from their position they could not see any opening, a faint glimmer of yellow light told them that this must be the entrance to the mines. They crept forward, tensing whenever their boots scuffed the ice or their hands brushed frozen chips from the cliff-rock. If anyone came along the road, they'd be spotted for sure.

They were almost to the mines now and had yet to see any

sign of a secret entrance. They couldn't just sneak in through the front. It was sure to be guarded and Kithian had warned Kion to avoid any fighting until he knew for certain where his mother was.

Scriff stopped still as a stone, ears pointing to the sky.

"What is it, boy?" Trak said.

No one moved for a handful of quick, anxious moments. Scriff kept so still he might have been made of ice. His head twitched to the left.

"There!" Trak pointed in the direction Scriff was looking.

The others saw it at once. A line was moving along the top of a large swath of snow off to their left. It ran in subtle curves, leaving a powdered trail. Whatever was making that line was coming their way, and quickly.

"Kithian, what is that?"

"It is one of the dim-touched. Talinyon warped birds of the air as well as creatures of the ground. But they all have this in common: they were bred to hate all living things. We must face it with my fire."

Kion dropped his pack and unsheathed Truesilver, dropping his baldric onto the ice. Glaivefire was the only way to turn back such a beast in a place like this. The ground was far too slippery for any bladework.

Scriff gave three quick yelps. *"It's a snowwinder. Be ready to dive out of the way when it opens its mouth."*

The rumbling line would soon reach the end of the snow, which gave way to the ice some fifty paces from the edge of the cliffs.

"Ready the fire!" Kithian said.

Kion swung his sword toward the burrowing line.

"Glaivefire!"

Truesilver's red flames danced along the blade, dazzling the ice around them in rippling reflections. At the snow's edge, the ground erupted in a shower of wintry blue. An enormous white head thrust from below, rearing high above them. Its features were serpentine, with a sleek nose and large, fan-like folds of skin stretching out on either side at the base of the head. The maw was large enough to swallow a nyn whole, perhaps even Tiryn. Its eyes were black and lifeless, unnatural pools of hopelessness and fear that threatened to paralyze any who gazed upon them for too long. The sinuous body was covered in supple scales. The snowwinder did not wait for the rest of its body to emerge before opening its mouth wide. A bulbous chunk of ice the size of a pumpkin burst from inside its cobalt-colored throat, streaking towards Trik.

With a swipe of his sword, Kion sent a jet of flame to intercept the projectile. The ice shrank and sizzled into harmless shards in midair.

The giant snake let out a screeching hiss, and came on with fresh fury, its frosty scales sliding out from the snow yard by yard. It launched another projectile of ice towards the party, followed by another. With two strokes from Truesilver, Kion dissolved them both, but still the snake came.

"Quick, everyone come to me. Trak, throw down your walking stick in front of us."

Trak hurled it down and Kion lit it with fire. It wasn't much extra flame, but it would do.

"Kithian, make a wall to protect them while you and I go out to face this beast."

The flames rose up in a bright red sheet before them, just wide enough to shield them from the snake's view. But the fox did not stay behind the protective curtain with its masters.

"Scriff, no!" Trik shouted. "Come back!"

Scriff charged off around the flames in the direction of the snake, yipping defiantly.

"Don't worry, Trik, I'll make sure he doesn't get hurt. The rest of you stay—" Kion had taken his first step away from the others when a loud snapping sound cut off the rest of his words. An ominous rumbling shook the ground. Cracks lanced through the ice beneath the fire.

"What was—?" Tiryn said. "Kion, look!" She pointed beneath their feet to where the cracks expanded in a shattering web.

"Hold still, Trik," Trak said, reaching out in warning to his brother.

The ice buckled and Tiryn nearly lost her footing.

"Kithian, stop the fire! It's melting the ice!" Kion shouted.

But it was too late. The world fell down and the darkness came up. The ground disappeared in a rain of crystal and shards, of wrenching pops and grinding clicks. It happened so fast no one even had time to scream.

Scriff yelped off in the distance and a great hiss came in answer, but those sounds were the only thing that followed them through the broken ice and into the unknown.

"Kion!" Kithian's voice burst into Kion's ears. That was the last thing he heard as faint streaks of light hurtled past and something hard as iron slammed into him and all thought and perception fled away.

"Kion, it is time you returned. You have wandered too long in the dark." As it had other times before, Kithian's voice pulled Kion back into the waking world. Kion had blacked out, but memories of the cracking ice and his helpless fall rushed back the moment he opened his eyes.

He lay propped against a smooth wall. The chamber around him was mostly made up of the hauntingly beautiful ice of the Tinesplitter hue. It swirled and twisted in turbulent patterns like frozen taffy, covering not only the floor and the sides of the cavity, but the ceiling as well. The ice was especially thick above him, but along the sides, it was thin enough that dark patches of something beyond—most likely rock—shone through. The cavern would have been wholly dark but for the gentle glow from Truesilver's unsheathed blade and the motes glittering within its amber gems. The glaive lay beside him on the right and Tiryn lay, unmoving, on his left. Trik and Trak stared at him from nearby, their lips colorless, their eyes moist with tears, and their faces pale with dread.

"Swordspeaker, you're alive. Thank goodness!" Trak said.

Trik wiped away his tears with the back of his glove. "But poor Tiryn won't wake up."

Kion bent over her. Her skin was ghost-white and he could not feel or hear her breathing.

"Tiryn, can you hear me?" he said. He shook her gently but she failed to stir.

He yanked off his gloves and touched her neck, her forehead, her fingers. All were gripped by a frightening chill. A wild panic knifed through him.

"Kithian, tell me, is she still alive?"

"I can no longer sense her mind as I can with you and the twins. But that may only mean that she is unconscious."

Kion held fast to those words as he would to a branch on a cliff. He had been knocked out from the fall. Tiryn must have suffered the same fate and, like him, would soon awake.

"Why did I have to make that wall of fire?" he said under his breath. "Right where the ice would break and send us down here."

"The fire belongs to both of us. And neither you nor I could have known the ice was thin enough there to bring us down into this hidden cave. All of our attention was upon the snake."

"I suppose...but that doesn't change what happened to Tiryn."

"I'm sorry, Swordspeaker..." Trik's mournful voice dwindled in upon itself. His face had lost all traces of that undisciplined but infectious joy that was its defining characteristic. He was a hollow version of the spry, irrepressible boy he once had been.

"Don't worry, Trik. She's not dead. Truesilver says she's just unconscious."

Trik's head dropped forward and he hid his face in his hands, shaking his head in doubt. For once, he refused to believe the swordspeaker's words.

Trak put his arm around his brother. "The swordspeaker woke up, Trik. We woke up. We just have to wait."

But Trik buried his head deeper and bawled like a child into the crook of his elbow.

"He'll be fine, Trak," Kion said. "Let him be for now. It's so cold down here. We've got to do what we can to keep Tiryn warm."

Kion's face felt as stiff and brittle as glass. He knew this feeling; he had felt the chill of death before. Grasping Truesilver's handle, a tingle of warmth seeped into his hands. Slight though it was, compared to the frozen air, it may as well have been a bonfire. But that warmth wouldn't help the others. He had to warm the rest of the cave.

"How long have we been down here?"

"We've been awake for a few minutes," Trak said.

"You've been unconscious for more than half an hour."

"Fire and ice. We'll freeze if we stay down here much longer." He looked above him. The cliffs and the opening they'd fallen through were nowhere in sight. All was ice and rock. They were trapped in the bowels of an underground hollow. The only way out was a chute of ice above, far beyond the reach of anything save a rope. They must all have slid down through that hole. The sides of the cavity were rounded, as if they had landed in an icy bubble. There was no chance to climb out, even if they'd had Dunwik's hammers and claws.

"We have to find a way out of here. That hole up there is the only way I can see. Do you think it's safe to move Tiryn?" Kion glanced at Trak for an answer, but Trik was the one who spoke.

"What if she broke something?" he said miserably.

"I do not believe there is any danger in moving her, but the opening above extends beyond what I can see. Even if you can reach it, it may not lead to freedom."

Freedom. The word mocked him in a place like this. Here

there was no freedom, no warmth, no hope. His sister lay within an inch of death. His Mother was in chains. Somewhere far to the east, Inris was falling to the haukmar axes and Noathryn spears. Failure upon failure upon failure. But looking at Trik, Kion steeled himself against the rising swell of despair. If he allowed their plight to pull him under he would be no good to anyone. He had to think of Tiryn and the twins. Kion had survived the judgment post. He would make it through this as well.

"Trak—your rope. Do you think you could get it all the way up to that chute?"

Trak gave it a long, dubious look. "I don't know, Swordspeaker. I can't even see the top of it."

"You have to try. We have to get out of here."

"I'll try if you think it will help."

"Good. You get to work with tying the hook to the rope. I'll see about warming this place up a bit."

"Swordspeaker, what about Scriff?" Trik asked. "What happened to him?"

"Kithian, do you know?"

"No. I think he meant to draw the snake away. But he knows the ways of this wintry land and how to evade such creatures. I would not worry on account of him."

Trik pitched onto his side at this news, curling up on the icy floor. "Even if Scriff survived, we'll freeze before we ever see him again." He folded his face back into his hands, his shoulders twitching to the rhythm of his muffled sobs. Trak gave Kion a despondent look. He was ready to give up as well.

Sorrow and fear were sapping their will. Kion darted forward and yanked Trik upright by the front of his coat and gave him a good shake. "No one is going to die, Trik. I'll protect you. I'll keep us safe. But we need to take action right now. We've got to get Tiryn back and find my mother. Are you with me? The swordspeaker needs you. Can he count on you?"

Something flickered in Trik's watery eyes, if only faintly. His head buoyed up and he blinked away the icy tears hardening around his eyes.

"Yes, Swordspeaker. What do you want me to do?"

"Shield Tiryn while Trak throws the rope. Make sure she doesn't get hit by the hook if it comes back down."

Trik slid over and crouched beside her. When he looked at her, his face contorted into the beginnings of another bout of tears, but he looked away and nodded fiercely. "All right."

Trak had the hardest time tying off the hook with his frozen fingers, but Kion's words had restored some of his spirits as well and he labored fiercely, muttering under his breath for the frigid rope to cooperate.

Kion stepped away from the others and held out his blade.

"Glaivefire." He held the sword in such a way that his body shielded them from the full force of the flames. Some of the fire licked his hair, but it caused not so much as a tendril of smoke.

"Wonder of the ages…" Trak said.

"It never gets old, does it, Trak? It's hotter than the forge, even from here," Trik said. "Are you sure you're not getting burned, Swordspeaker?"

"I am protected from Truesilver's fire while I hold the blade. Tell me if it grows too hot."

"It's fine for now—more than fine. I can feel my fingers coming to life already," Trak said. A moment later he announced that he had finished the knot.

"Good. Now let's hope your aim is true and that the rope can go far enough to latch onto something."

Kion tried twisting his neck around to watch, but he couldn't see Trak without turning his body and he did not want to risk exposing the others to too much heat. The clink and clatter and scrape of the hook as it went up into the chute, or perhaps collided with the ceiling, did not sound promising. The metal clunked as it landed back on the floor.

The sounds repeated over and over, though once the hook thudded into Trik's coat.

"I'm all right, I'm all right," he said.

While the heat from Truesilver's flames did not affect Kion, neither did it dispel the cold from his long time in the hollow. The only warmth he had was the subtle heat that came through Truesilver's grip, which was no longer as intense as it had seemed at first. If Trak didn't snag something in the next few tries they were going to have to think of something else.

Kion's foot slipped, though he had not moved.

"Still the flames a moment, Kithian." With the fire gone, he could better see his surroundings. A small puddle had formed around his feet, making the ice beneath all the more slippery.

"Trik—look out, that water's running toward Tiryn. Don't let her get wet," Trak said.

Trik and Trak gathered up Tiryn as a tiny stream dribbled its way from the puddle around Kion's feet.

"Look at the size of that hole, Swordspeaker," Trik said. "Truesilver's fire is hotter than a forge, just like I said."

At first Kion didn't know what he meant, but then he followed Trik's eyes to a hole nearly the size of Kion's body in the ice wall. It glistened from the runoff which continued to pool onto the ground. The flames had been so close that he hadn't noticed the effect it was having on the nearby ice. And all this during the time it had taken for Trak to get off a half dozen or so throws. Kion stared at the concave space for the longest time. At last, a door opened in his mind.

"Truesilver, what lies beyond this hollow? Is it solid ice or rock?"

"Mostly rock, though some of the ice runs out beyond to the edge of my vision. But I see the thought behind your question. If we could venture through the ice far enough, we might perhaps find another cavity more favorable to our escape."

It was a better chance than trusting to Trak's aim and figuring out a way to haul Tiryn up through that tiny hole.

"Trak, forget the rope. We're going to see what's on the other side of this ice."

"We're going to what?" Trik said.

"Just stand back and keep my sister off the ground." Kion stepped closer to the freshly carved hole in the ice and gave word to Kithian to renew his flames.

Trik and Trak retreated with Tiryn as far back as they could.

Kion placed Truesilver's blade directly against the ice. Water poured away from the surface as pure and fresh as the Tumbling Spring where he used to water his flock in the Tors.

"I'd like to see what the Maid of Ice would say to that," Trik said.

"So would I, Trik. I'm guessing she'd be none too pleased!"

Chapter 36

THE SILENT MINES

"Swordspeaker, look!" Trak exclaimed.

A wisp of stagnant air breathed through the crack in the wall. If it could even be called a crack. It was more like a faint discoloration in the rock. Kithian had told them there was a passage on the other side, but they'd had no hope of getting through until now.

"The secret door!" Kion exclaimed. "Well done, Trak."

The twins bounced with anticipation, full of energy even after the long, arduous trek through the bowels of Tinesplitter, burrowing through twists and turns in the rock that had led them at last to this long and clearly man-made passage. Though old and weathered and crudely fashioned, the tunnel was too uniform to be natural. By the time they reached it, Truesilver had burned through an entire round of oil and had to be replenished. This was the last flask, but now that they'd found the door, Kion hoped they would no longer need the glaivefire.

"I wonder how we open it," Kion said. The crack ran from the floor to just above Kion's head, then cut across the bedrock and back down, making it roughly square in shape.

Trik pulled off one glove and ran his fingers up and down the crack.

"How did Uncle Chaw say he did it? Think, Trik, think!"

"It had something to do with rocks," Trak said.

"Of course it had something to do with rocks. The door is made of rock. Anybody can see that."

"I can see the mechanism inside the door," Kithian said, *"but not the manner of triggering it."*

Truesilver lay propped against the wall to give them light. Kion held Tiryn in his arms to keep her off the cold stone floor and to give Trik some relief, though she seemed to weigh barely more than her clothes. The underground journey had brought no change in her appearance. Her skin was still frozen to the touch and she was pale as a sheet. But Kion refused to believe that she was gone. "Soon," he whispered in her ear. "We're close to finding Mother. If you're not awake by then, she'll know what to do. Hold on a little longer, Tiryn. I need you to be strong and fight." Despite his words, Kion wrestled with doubt every time he looked at her corpse-like face. She could not hold on much longer.

Trak took off one of his gloves too and was tapping on the wall with his knuckles. It made a dull plunking sound near the crack and a more solid, thumping noise everywhere else, but this did nothing to tell them how to open it.

"Hmm…maybe Uncle meant that the key was hidden in a nearby rock. Look, there's some rubble in the corners. Let's search through it," Trak said.

"But there's no keyhole," Trik said.

"Well, search anyway. Unless you have a better idea."

They rummaged about in the rocks for some time before giving up.

"Nothing, Swordspeaker," Trik said, plopping down into a defeated heap in front of the hidden door. "We've come all this way and we're as trapped as we were back in that hollow. Why does the underground have to be so full of rocks?"

Trak turned one of the rocks he'd found over in his hand. "Hmm…this is an odd rock. It's smooth—not like the others. It doesn't look like it belongs here."

"Maybe someone left it here to mark the entrance."

"That's it! I remember now. Uncle Chaw said he used a special rock to open the door. If you tapped it with that rock in just the right spot he said it would set off a vibration that would trigger the door to open. Something like that anyway."

Trik leapt to his feet and Trak tapped furiously all up and down the surface of the door. The clicks and clacks sounded like a small hail storm had erupted underground. Kion squeezed Tiryn a little tighter. "Soon," he whispered again to her.

"I found it!" Trak said.

"Oh, Trak, I hope it's true!" Trik said.

Trak rapped the stone against a spot in the middle of the door. When nothing happened, he did it again, a little harder. The door still failed to move. He tapped it again. And again. Each time a little harder. At last, he tapped it so hard the door made a *thwick* sound and gave a shudder. A popping sound followed and then a rush of warm, dusty air as the thick stone door eased open on one side.

"You're brilliant, Trak!" Kion said. "You, too, Trik. Your persistence paid off."

"Trak's the one who figured it all out, but I gave him moral support, right, Trak?"

"I couldn't have done it without you," Trak said genuinely.

Trik strained to get the door open until it was wide enough to walk through.

"My, this is heavy. And it wants to close back up. I'll hold it open while you two get inside."

Kion passed Tiryn into Trak's arms and recovered Truesilver. He went through first, followed by Trak and then Trik. The door clicked shut after Trik came through.

"I can't see a way of opening it on this side," Trik said.

"We'll deal with that on the way back," Trak said.

A noticeable increase in the warmth of the air raised Kion's spirits. It was still bitterly cold by normal standards, but any heat was welcome.

"There is reason for hope in that we have made it this far, but you must keep silent from here on," Kithian said. *"We do not know whom we shall meet in these tunnels, but if these are the mines and the slaves*

are here there will be guards and overseers as well. We may need to capture one of them to find out if your mother is here, but only if we can do so without raising an alarm."

Kion shared Kithian's advice, urging the twins to silence.

"Are you sure the Noathryn would tell us the truth if we captured one?" Trak said.

"They're about as true as spoiled milk," Trik said.

"I've got Truesilver. He can tell when someone is lying."

"Truly?" Trak said.

"My nose is three feet long," Trik said. "Could it tell that that was a lie?"

"You don't need one of the ancient glaives for that," Trak said.

"Well, it's hard to think of a good one. I'm not used to lying."

"That would be a lie as well."

"Truesilver thinks you're not being truthful."

"He's right! You told a lie last week when you told Old Lady Yanna she forgot to give you soup. You got seconds when she thought she was giving you firsts. You know she can hardly remember her own name."

"Oh, I forgot about that. So Truesilver knew? Oh dear. I'll have to watch myself. I do sometimes stretch the truth, but they're honest lies. Sometimes I don't even realize I'm telling them."

The twins stared at the blade with the kind of respect they might have given to a trained bear. Kithian was good, but he was still dangerous. The more Kion told them about the glaive, the more strange and astonishing they found it.

"Enough about your fibbing habits. Forward now," Kion said. "And no more talking unless I tell you."

The tunnel they passed into could fit two abreast, but not comfortably, so they went single-file with Kion in the lead. Dark, rough stone wreathed the edges of the passage. Dust coated the uneven floor. It was clear that no one had taken this route for many years. They stole down the length of it until it dog-legged, and then did so again. Not long after that, it ended, plugged up with rubble.

"The rubble is not thick and another passage runs past on the other side. You should be able to clear a way through without much trouble."

Trak and Kion pulled down the rocks as quietly as they could, though with the natural shifting that occurred, it was impossible to avoid all noise as rocks broke free and tumbled down the heap. Once they could feel the fresher, cooler air drifting in from the other side, they pressed on faster, pulling rocks down more carelessly until they had an opening large enough to pass through.

They had a difficult time passing Tiryn through the hole they'd made. Her clothes kept snagging on the edges of the rocks and they had to take extra care not to injure her. They did not bother filling the hole once they were through. There wasn't time and they might need to pass this way again in a hurry.

The newly revealed tunnel dead-ended on the right, but to the left it delved through the rock for a good distance. A glow beckoned to them from some point far down its length.

"Truesilver, douse your light. There may be someone up ahead."

Utter black enveloped the tunnel. As they shuffled along its length, using the walls to guide them, Kion's hand touched several patches of ice, but it was mostly rough stone.

They drew closer to the light. Pebbles and rocks scudded beneath their feet. There was no way to stay completely silent, but they did the best they could, being careful not to drag their feet and taking their time. Eventually, the ice patches on the walls grew so common, there was hardly any rock. And of course, along with the ice, the air grew ever colder.

By now, they were close enough to see the source of the light. The stub of a candle sat on the ground, surrounded by dribbles of wax. It sputtered and hissed, the flame close to guttering. Beside it worked two boys, younger even than Trik and Trak. Their compact noses and squat frames were the same as the Frin children of Whitewind. One of the boys looked a year or two older than the other. They wore tattered coats that barely kept out the cold. Dust caked their matted hair. They worked indifferently with picks against the sides of the tunnel, their blows landing with little effect, barely strong enough to wrest a few shavings from the rock with each stroke. Judging by the empty wooden bucket between them, they had little to show for their efforts.

Kion paused, considering his words, and then strode forward as unthreateningly as he could, his hands held up and empty.

The boys stopped working and took a step back, frightened looks on their faces. Kion's thick coat and relatively clean appearance—not to mention the sword on his back—gave him away as not being a miner, but he had no way to hide these things.

"Sorry to bother you," he said. Trik and Trak came with him into the light. "We're looking for a woman named Annira. Do you know where she is?"

The boys shook their heads with some vigor and waved them on. When Kion didn't leave, the older one raised his pick and made to return to his work.

"Please, my sister needs a healer. Annira can help her. Have you at least heard of her?"

The older boy kept his eyes pegged on Kion and the twins the whole time, but resumed striking the wall as if they weren't there. The younger one stared anxiously at Tiryn, unsure of himself.

"You're Frin, aren't you?" Trak said. "Why won't you talk? Are you afraid we'll hurt you?"

The younger one looked hard at his brother, who shook his head so that dust flew from it. The gray motes hung suspended in the candlelight.

The little boy dropped his head, bowing to his brother's authority. He took up his pick and joined him once more in chipping away at the rock.

"They must have their reasons," Kion told the twins. "We'll just have to keep searching. Maybe we can find others who will tell us." He moved on, trying to act indifferently, but inside, their silence troubled him. No guards or overseers were nearby. The boys had no one to fear. Why wouldn't they speak?

The passage remained empty and dark for a while until another warm glow appeared farther down, at what looked like an intersection.

"Those boys were hiding something. Be wary," Kithian said. Kion wanted to ask him to elaborate but held his tongue for fear that his voice might carry in these tunnels.

They pressed on to the next light. When they reached it, it proved to be a battered and rusty lantern, hanging from a hook in the ceiling. No one worked here and the path forked in two directions, both of which led to faint lights down other passages and the sounds of miners chipping away in the dark.

The sounds were louder down the passage on the right, so Kion chose that way. The more miners, the more chances that one of them would know about his mother. Patches of ice were few down this new passage. A good way down its length, two women, an older man, and three boys about Trik and Trak's age labored around a lantern on the floor. Though they had two buckets between them, each was no more full than the last one. The workers stopped their mining and regarded the newcomers with the same troubled stares the two boys had given.

"Greetings," Kion said, not liking his chances already. "We're looking for Annira Bray. We need her to heal my sister. Do any of you know where she is?"

The miners exchanged narrow-eyed looks.

"They are under orders not to speak."

Was that a general rule, or was this part of Ilk's plan? He wished Kithian would elaborate, but he did not want to unsettle them even more by addressing someone they could not see.

"Listen." Kion stepped toward them. "As you can see, I have

a weapon. If you help me, I can try to free you from this place. Won't you please tell me where she is?"

They bowed their heads or looked away, unable to shake off whatever compulsion lay upon them. They turned their backs and resumed their labors.

Kion and the twins waited a moment longer in disbelief before hurrying on. They had not expected the slaves to treat them as enemies, but there was no time to stop and unravel the mystery. Kion had to find out if his mother was here or not. It was looking, though, like they would have to take Kithian's suggestion and capture one of the guards, only there didn't seem to be any guards in this part of the mine.

The miners cast furtive looks at them as they left, sorrow and fear written upon their dust-caked faces.

"I know why it is that they do not speak. If they told us anything, I would know whether or not it was true. Ilk has ordered them not to speak to anyone who is not a fellow slave. He is the only one who would know of my gifts."

"If Ilk knows we're in the mines, then we have no hope of finding Mother, even if she's here."

"We can still outsmart him, though. He's only got one brain and we've got three," Trik said. He looked wistfully at Tiryn in his arms. "Hopefully four soon."

"I'm not so sure. Truesilver says that's why the miners aren't talking to us, because Ilk warned them about us."

"Oh my," Trak said. "What do we do now?"

"Folk from Whitewind have far better manners," Trik said.

The passage sloped down toward another intersection with another lantern. Two side passages led away on either side, but they were dark and narrow. The tunnel walls closed in around them, oppressive and unyielding. The stale, unmoving air grew heavy and threatening, as if the three boys had just woken up inside a tomb and realized that they had no way out. Finding Kion's mother seemed impossible now. After all they had been through, it looked as though they were walking into a trap.

Would they fail so close to the end? And yet, what choice did they have but to press forward?

"Oh, Tiryn," Kion whispered. "Please wake up. Tell me what to do."

"We have set our hand to this task. We must continue on until we find your mother or it becomes clear what our enemy has planned. Just because someone sets a trap it does not mean you have to fall in."

Kion looked back at Tiryn, motionless and half-frozen. He was a swordspeaker. He was supposed to be able to protect his sister and save his mother. He did not fear the haukmarn or the Noathryn, but Ilk was another matter. Against his cleverness, Kion had no answer. He was as helpless as one of Farmer Jeslan's pigs, prodded to the slaughterhouse.

"We can't go back the way we came," Kion said. There seemed little point in keeping silent now that the miners, and most likely Ilk himself, knew that they were here.

Dreading each step, he plodded on. They passed three more groups of workers with their miserable, fearful stares, and unbreakable silence, and still they met no guards. The sense that his mother was not here grew the longer they went on. Their hopes lay more and more with Dunwik and Zinder. The mines had yielded nothing. The best they could hope for now was to find a way out of this place as quickly as possible.

The air grew even colder as they went. Trik and Trak's faces had started turning blue again. Kion's frozen cheeks felt hard as metal. If they didn't find a way out soon, he would have to risk using glaivefire to keep them from succumbing to the cold.

They wandered into a great chamber covered in ice so blue it mimicked a twilit sky. The ceiling rose two stories above them, filled with massive hanging icicles. It looked like a great frozen forest turned upside-down. Two lanterns hanging atop poles lit the center of the room. Between them, a large metal cage dominated the cavern. Its wrought-iron bars were thick and many, but it was completely empty. Shadows hid whatever lay on the far side of the cavern, as well as down the five tunnels leading out of it.

Thirty paces away, in front of the cage, sat a woman tied to a chair, her arms wrapped around behind it. A dark hood shrouded her face. From the position of her head, she was either asleep or unconscious. A few stray locks of wavy black hair escaped the darkened cowl. None of the Frin Kion had seen had hair like that. Even in Furrow none of the villagers had such hair. Only his mother. Hope burned anew inside his chest.

"Mother?" he said. Forgetting all else, he broke into a run.

"Are you sure it is her? It could be a trap."

Kion pulled up and drew Truesilver from its sheath. He studied the exits, but they were riddled with darkness. He had to hurry. Tiryn was dying. Mother would know how to help her. But what if that wasn't her?

"Stay where you are, you two," he told the twins. "I need a moment to think. Kithian, tell me what to do."

"Whoever that is, she is alive. But there is no way to tell if it is your mother without removing her hood. It might be an ambush, but none lurk within the passages that I can see. On second thought, Ilk knows what you did in Charring. He would not count on an ambush. You would likely defeat however many he sent at you, especially in an open area like this. I'm afraid the only way to find out the truth is to unmask that woman. But, Kion, keep your eyes sharp. Ilk is a clever foe."

Kion crept forward, step by step, his eyes flitting from one exit to the other. He even glanced above but saw no danger there beyond the looming icicles. That cage roused his suspicions, but with no guards to force him into it, he didn't see how it could threaten him.

He reached the chair and knelt beside the woman. Her skin was as pale as a frozen lake. She must have been freezing in that thin dress. Laying his sword upon the ice, he reached for her hood. Her chest rose and fell quickly with a sharp intake of breath. Oh, how desperately he longed for this to be his mother.

He raised the hood. The lock of hair rose with it.

It had been pinned to the fabric.

"I'm sorry," the woman said, trembling. Her straight brown hair and long, fearful face bore all the features of the Frin.

Glass shattered behind the chair. Green smoke billowed swiftly up from the ground, engulfing the both of them. It had a faint, tangy smell to it. A strange shock ran up Kion's neck. Weakness poured down from his head.

"Kion, no! How did I miss the vial? I should have seen it…"

Clever. Ilk was so terribly clever.

The world spun in ever-widening circles until all was black and nothing more.

Chapter 37

CHAINS

Freezing cold air stung Kion's lungs. He felt the absence at once, the shrunken emptiness inside of him. He did not have to open his eyes to know that Truesilver was gone. But he opened them all the same.

He was sitting with his back against thick iron bars. Trik and Trak sat on the opposite side of the cage, Tiryn spread across their laps, pale and motionless as ever. For a brief moment Kion envied her, for she did not have to face the bitter knowledge that their search for Mother had failed. Ilk had set his trap and Kion had walked right into it.

They were still in the chamber of ice, but the woman and the chair were gone. The iron cage rose above them, an invulnerable reminder of Kion's failure. As had happened so many times of late, his instincts had betrayed him. He had almost traded Truesilver for his mother at Fennigar. He'd tried to abandon those who loved him at Dunach. At Whitewind he'd nearly gotten himself killed trying to impose his will on Chaw and an entire village. Now this, his final failure. If he had fashioned the iron bars himself it could not have been more fitting. He should have known Ilk would never just leave his mother tied up alone, unguarded. His foolishness had doomed his mother's life as surely as it had doomed his own.

His one hope now was to at least see her again, even if it was as a fellow slave. That lock of hair had been hers. He was sure of it. She was somewhere on Tinesplitter. Somewhere close.

"Swordspeaker, you're awake!" Trik said.

"I'm sorry," Trak said. "We tried to save you, but the guards rushed in before we could. Some of them had disguised themselves as the miners we passed. They must have followed us after we passed them by."

"And the woman? What happened to her?"

"She left with some of the guards. She was crying when they took her away, Swordspeaker," Trak said. "I think she was forced to trick you."

Kion gazed around the room. Torches now lined the walls, dispelling the shadows from the edges of the chamber and giving reflective life to the icy surfaces. A dozen Noathryn, dressed in thick furs and holding long, leaf-headed spears, stood guard a good distance from the cage. Each of their faces was carved from the same cruel stone. And yet, fear glimmered at the back of their eyes. Twelve warriors to guard three boys and a dying girl locked in a cage and yet still they feared them.

"Has Tiryn shown any sign of recovering?"

Kion leaned across the cage to feel her skin. But he did not go far before his arms were yanked back. Chains rattled behind him. His wrists were shackled so tightly his movements caused the metal to bite through his sleeve.

"You weren't shackled?" Kion said.

"No, what threat are we? They know who the real danger is," Trak said.

"We're just a couple of tag-alongs," Trik mumbled.

"Don't say that. We couldn't have crossed the bay without you, or found the secret door, or carried Tiryn this far. And now that they have Truesilver, I'm no more dangerous than those slaves we passed in the tunnels."

Trik and Trak dismissed his words with wrinkled brows. To them, he was still the swordspeaker, even if he no longer had his sword.

"You'll get us out of this," Trak said. "It's Tiryn I'm worried about now."

Echoing footfalls interspersed with a sharp clicking silenced their talk. The noises grew louder and multiplied as they listened. Soon, they were strong enough to recognize, for Kion had heard pounding boots like that before: haukmarn. A large number of them marched into the chamber. The mysterious clicking noise continued behind them, its source yet to be revealed. Off in the tunnels, a pick struck against a wall several times, but the din of the haukmarn swallowed it up.

The gray-skinned brutes filed in quickly, fully dressed out for battle, axes and armor and all. They were forced to crouch as they passed through the entrance. They spread out on either side of the exit, forming loose ranks, some twenty harriers in all. Trik and Trak stared at them in undisguised terror, having never seen the monstrous giants before.

And last came Ilk, shuffling, ambling, and laboring forward with the assistance of a metal cane that clicked against the floor with every other step. He had no need to hunch to enter the room, yet he hunched all the same, for his body was old and bent, the same as his mind. The pleasure of victory danced in his eyes. He was genuinely elated, though his happiness could not mask the withered quality of his skin nor the sunken weariness that pooled about his eyes.

But Ilk did not enter alone.

Beside him, less massive and yet far more intimidating than all the other haukmarn put together, marched Vayd Mokán. Like the rest of the haukmarn, plates of armor covered his legs and gut. He wore iron gauntlets as well, and a thick leather jerkin. Though a long wolfskin cape covered his back, his arms were bare, but he showed no sign of being cold. Nor did he give any indication that he still suffered from the injuries he had received at Kion's hands during their battle in Charring. And yet the hatred seething in his eyes told that he remembered every moment of that fateful meeting.

Kion's courage would have shattered at that moment, but for one thing: Vayd carried Truesilver in his hand. It did not matter that his enemy now possessed his glaive. The sword belonged to

Kion, and always would. Vayd could no more harm him with it than he could force Kion's own hands to rise up against him. Hope glimmered in the sheen of that marvelous blade, for Vayd carried the means of his own downfall into the chamber with him.

"Greetings, glaivebond. Though it pains me to see you shackled, you will not be so for long. Only have patience and seize your moment when it comes."

At those words, the bars and chains holding Kion melted away. Strength flowed through his limbs. His invisible bond with his glaive was renewed. He was no longer a prisoner. He was a swordspeaker. And that was something to be reckoned with.

"Kion Bray." Vayd's voice rumbled throughout the chamber. "A treacherous foe you proved to be in Charring. Long have I sought you and your blade. And now I have both."

Valor from the presence of his glaive filled Kion's heart with fire. All Vayd had were empty words. He would never know the bond Kion shared with his ancient weapon, nor the quickening that came when he held it in his hand, nor the wisdom to be found in its immortal voice.

"We have a saying back in the Tors: 'One person can no more own another than he can grasp the wind.' And that is all you have now, Vayd, a fistful of wind. You've won nothing."

The confidence in Kion's words passed to Trik and Trak, kindling a hopeful light on their bedraggled faces.

"Watch your tongue, boy, or Vayd will cut it out," Ilk said, relishing Vayd's anger as he stamped toward Kion, bellowing incoherently. With his free hand, Vayd shook the cage so that it slid across the icy floor. The bars banged into Kion's back and he pitched to the side, nearly hitting his head on the ground. Trik and Trak spilled over Tiryn, but scrambled to pick her back up once the cage had settled.

"I did not sail through sea and ice to listen to the boasting of some foolish whelp. You are nothing without your sword. You never would have defeated me without it."

The other haukmarn echoed the howling rage of their leader, their booming cries filling the icy cavern. The Noathryn guards cast unsettled glances among themselves. Whatever the terms of their alliance with these gray monstrosities, it was uneasy at best. They may have feared the haukmarn, but Vayd did not have their trust.

Kion's eyes lingered on Truesilver. His blade was so close. He could call it to his hand in an instant. Yet he could not fight with his arms in chains. Summoning it now would only bring trouble. As Kithian had said, he needed to have patience.

"If you unlock this cage, I will fight you again with whatever weapon you choose."

Vayd gave the cage another shake. "You think I'm witless simply because I am a haukmar? I saw how you made the blade fly into your hand. No, little worm, I did not come to fight you this time. Why would I? You're already beaten. I came to learn the secret of your weapon's fire. You will tell it to me now. Ilk says there is a special word, a command needed to invoke the fire. Tell it to me and I will let you and your companions go. If not, your friends will suffer and die before your eyes."

"Ilk has studied much of the glaives. He may even know about the reagent. But he does not understand that the bonding between a glaive and his swordspeaker are needed to unlock its gifts." Kithian spoke with quiet assurance, as though Vayd were the one in the cage and not Kion.

Vayd's great frame blocked the light coming from that side of the cage. His features dwindled in shadow, but insatiable desire burned in his eyes, the desire for power. Truesilver was a means to that power and he would not be denied its secrets.

"The longer you try me in this, the more pain awaits those you care for." Vayd's gaze lingered over Tiryn and the twins. "And if there is one thing the haukmarn know, it is how to inflict pain."

There was no reason to answer. Provoking Vayd again would only cause him to shake the cage even harder, or perhaps do something worse. But his words had their effect on Trik and Trak. They huddled closer to Tiryn, casting anxious glances at Kion, pleading silently for him to stop the haukmar leader before he did something terrible.

Vayd tossed the sword from one hand to the other, his gaze fixed upon Kion. But when Kion didn't answer, the mighty haukmar stomped his foot so hard the cage rattled. Growling, he turned away.

"Ilk told me you would say nothing. Humans have no understanding of power unless it is learned through suffering. Very well, Ilk, have your turn."

Ilk hobbled forward, his clicking cane plotting a course to the side of the giant haukmar. He stood in Vayd's shadow, a shriveled mockery of the haukmar leader's strength and prowess—but the same twisted spark flickered in both their eyes.

"I agree, he is wasting your time. Very well, boy. You think this a game? You think you can have your way with us? You shall soon learn to esteem the zaron's time better." Ilk clapped his hands, a weak, flaccid sound reminiscent of dripping water. Two Noathryn guards left the chamber, retreating down a tunnel on Kion's left. "You came all this way in search of your mother, did you not? I'm sorry I had to disappoint you with that other slave."

A wave of helplessness threatened to swallow Kion's courage. His mother was his one weakness. Ilk knew this. He was playing Kion now as Tiryn played her pipes. If Kion's hands had been free he would have come at the traitor and rattled the cage himself. Vayd looked on, pleased to see the rage boiling inside his adversary.

"Steady, swordspeaker. Do not let anger blind you to your chance when it comes."

Kion forced himself to speak calmly. "Where is she, Ilk? Where is my mother?"

"Oh, you want to see her? I knew you would. That is why I've already sent for her. You see, I'm not so heartless as you suppose. Though I expect payment for my kindness. That's reasonable, wouldn't you agree?" Ilk's eyes gleamed with a hollow light.

Kion and the twins stared at the exit where the guards had disappeared. Shuffling footsteps mixed with regular ones came from down the tunnel. The passing of time turned into an ache. The waiting bound him as tightly as his chains. Was it truly her? Or another of Ilk's tricks? What would Kion say when he saw her? Would they be allowed to speak at all? A thousand thoughts crashed against each other in his head. The thumping and shuffling grew louder and louder until at last they grew into sights and not just sounds.

Two guards dragged in a woman, slumped and haggard, barely able to walk. Dirt mottled her hands, her dress hung in tatters, cords bound her hands behind her back, and a rag stretched tightly around her eyes. She swayed uneasily, barely able to stand. Her skin was pasty and dirty and her breathing came in constant sighs, heavy and burdensome. In all this she might have been any other poor and wretched slave like the ones they had passed in the mines—even the one Ilk had used to fool Kion—but for her hair. The wavy strands were marred and matted and far longer than his mother had worn them in years, but they signified the beauty of the one beneath the dirt, the rags, and the bonds.

"Mother." Kion's voice was little more than air, but the word echoed in his ears as clearly as a trumpet call. He had found her at last.

If only Tiryn were awake to see this moment. Now that Mother was here, she would bring Tiryn back. They just had to find a way to break out of the bars and bindings that still held them apart. Mother would make everything better, just the way she always had.

His mother's head rose at the sound of his voice. Her covered eyes searching this way and that. The skin around her mouth was scabbed and flaking. She made a mangled sound, a half-cry from a voice made dry and inarticulate from thirst and disuse. But at long last she found her words.

"Kion, my son. My dear, beloved boy. How I've missed you. How I've longed to hear your deep and beautiful voice again—"

"Enough, woman," Ilk cut her off. "This is no time for tiresome treacle. Silence, while your ill-gotten progeny decides your fate."

Vayd swept Truesilver through the air, pointing it at Kion's mother, who stood half a dozen paces away.

"You came all this way for that? A frail female with no skill in battle? You waste your time saving one life when you could have saved whole cities and routed whole armies with this blade? This is why your people are weak and deserve to die. This is why the haukmarn are the true heirs of Terroc, the rightful rulers of the Four Wards. We know how to weigh the value of a life. It is meaningless unless it serves the purposes of claw and clan."

The words battered Kion more brutally than anything Vayd could have done to his body. They struck to the marrow of Kion's deepest doubts. Had he abandoned his people by this long, arduous quest to find his mother?

The memory of Kithian's words returned to him now. *"You are the Four Wards' best hope for ending this war. And the longer you avoid taking up that mantle, the harder it will be to defeat the enemy when you do."*

He had been willing to pay any cost to see his mother safe, but he had pushed out of his mind the cost that others might have paid for his choices. How many had died because Truesilver was in this icy cave and not defending the cities of Inris? The image of Endrith, riding from the smoking city of Grettling, struck him to the quick. How many had fallen because he had not been there to save them? His mother meant everything to him, yes, but had his love for her blinded him to his true calling? He'd given all he had to find her. It had nearly cost him his life.

It might have cost the life of his sister. And seeing his mother now, pale and weak and broken as she was, he wondered if all his sacrifice had been in vain. Had it been worth all the toil and struggle only to share in her chains, to watch her tottering on her feet, hardly able to stand? Even if he vanquished every enemy in these mines, she might not survive. She walked on the very edge of death. It would almost have been easier if she had already died. Seeing her suffer like this was beyond what he could bear.

"Kion, do not give in to despair. This road has been a hard one for you to travel. And the light has grown dim for you at the end. But all is not lost. Your mother yet lives. Whatever happens, hold onto that. While life endures, there is always hope. She needs your strength now more than ever. And might it not be that your presence will prove just the thing which gives her the will to fight on? Do not waver, not now when you are so close to what you have sought."

Kion, roused to life by the words of his glaive, rose to his feet, his chains scraping against the bars as they slid upwards.

"I cannot give you what you want, Vayd," Kion said, fighting the great sorrow bearing down upon him and clinging desperately to Kithian's words. He had to be strong. He had to hold on a little longer until he saw his chance to break free.

Vayd pointed the sword at him. "You can and you will. Tell me the incantations to release the sword's fire—now! Tell me, if you want this woman to live."

"Oh, please, just let me hold him," Mother said, moisture seeping out from the cruel rag that hid her eyes. "Let me embrace him one last time." She struggled against the grip of her captors, but her efforts gave her guards little trouble. Slipping from their grasp was beyond her power. The woman who had worked every day from sunrise to sundown on the farm in Furrow was only a memory. Her strength was gone. Only a shadow of herself remained.

Though the guards held her easily, one of them looked off to the side, and Kion thought he caught a pained look in his eyes, though his face remained a grave mask.

"Oh, Mother. Don't worry. Everything will be fine. We're together, and—and Tiryn is here too, only she's asleep right now."

"Tiryn? Oh, please could I see her? Would you please let me see my son and my daughter?"

Kion turned to Ilk. "Please, sir. I beg you. At least let us see each other. Can you not at least grant us that?"

But it was Vayd who answered. "Are all humans as weak-willed as you? Listen, whelp, tell me the words or watch me cut her head from her body with your own blade. That is the last time I will ask." The uncaring monster stepped toward her. Kion strained against his chains. He had no way to save his mother. Even if he commanded Truesilver to erupt in flames and the heat seared Vayd's flesh, he would only succeed in fanning the haukmar's wrath.

The chipping sound of metal on rock halted Vayd's steps. Everyone in the room turned to look off down the passage Kion had traveled to reach here. The next moment a muffled thunder sounded from down the same corridor. The icicles above the cavern shook, tinkling like glass, but the shuddering passed as quickly as it came.

"What was that?" Vayd said.

Ilk gave a petulant sneer. "A cave-in, perhaps, caused by some reckless slaves. Do not worry, zaron. It is nothing that will not be quickly remedied." He glowered at the Noathryn guards. "I told the overseers to move the slaves to work off in another part of the mine. Go, see what that is about."

Two guards near the exit peeled away to obey Ilk's command.

"No—not the disturbance in the mines, the voice—did you not hear it?" Vayd said.

Ilk paused, sucking in his lips until they disappeared, which was not difficult since he barely had any to begin with.

"What voice, my lord?"

Vayd's head swiveled in a new direction.

"What? What do you want from me? Who are you?" he said, his voice dark and threatening.

The harriers behind him looked more empty-headed than usual. They shifted and glanced about, suspecting some hidden threat lurking within the cavern, but it was far too open and well-lit for anyone to have entered undetected.

"My lord? I'm not certain I—" Ilk said.

"Shh! Quiet, you chittering rat. The voice is speaking again..." Vayd sized up each of the guards and his own harriers before turning his glare on the prisoners in the cage.

Trik and Trak withered under his gaze and turned away, but Kion met the haukmar's burning eyes as they fixed upon him.

"What game is this, whelp? How are you whispering into my head like this? Is this another power of the blades Ilk did not tell me of?"

Whispering...into his head...was Vayd telling the truth? If so, it could only be...

"Another glaive calls out to him," Kithian said. *"I can see the truth of it in his eyes."*

Even the torch flames ceased to flutter as every eye turned to Vayd, most suspecting madness, but Kion fearing something far more terrible.

"No, it cannot be," he said.

"It is Rimewinter. What other glaive could it be amidst all of this ice? Oh, my friend, have you truly fallen so far?"

Fallen? Kithian had warned as much before. Surely no true glaive would call to one such as Vayd.

The haukmar leader's expression grew more sinister. "Show yourself, invisible one. If power is what you offer, I will hear your words."

Trak leaned forward. "Is it...is he a...?"

"No, they only call the good and the pure-hearted," Trik said.

Ilk tapped his cane on the ice, shifting his feet in a half-circle of worry. "Oh my, I don't know what the meaning of this is, but could we not discuss it after we've dealt with the boy and his blade? The soldiers are beginning to—"

"Silence, cling-cloak." Vayd waved Truesilver in Ilk's direction, causing him to jump, though the blade did not come close to touching him. "What do you mean you are about to be freed?" Vayd addressed the unheard voice once more.

Another distant roar rippled down the same tunnel as before.

"Another cave in?" Trak said in a hushed voice.

Moments later, the ground shook. The cage slid along the ice. The guards and harriers threw out their hands to hold their balance. Ilk dug into the ground with his cane and only just managed to avoid a fall. The ceiling danced in a deadly wave, an invisible current running through the spiked tapestry. A great snapping broke through the highest parts of the cavern and a barrage of icicles as tall as Ilk crashed onto the open floor near Kion's mother and the two guards. All three lurched forward and his mother hit the ground. Kion fought against his chains, pulling uselessly against them. Was this his moment? Should he take advantage of the confusion to call Truesilver to him?

Vayd dropped the sword and it clattered on the stone.

"I have no more need of this useless toy, Ilk. I go to seek a weapon of true power. Dispose of this rabble and I will meet you back in Regnir."

A stunned Ilk watched as Vayd Mokán, leader of the haukmarn, marched from the room.

"What about the glaive? You can't just leave now, zaron. After all I plotted and planned to bring it into your hands?"

Vayd cut him off with a look—the wild, cunning look of a beast on the scent of its prey. "Silence. I have spoken."

Though Vayd's orders could not have been more clear, no guard or harrier moved to slay the prisoners. For at that moment the cavern came falling down around them. Their only thought was to save their own lives. Vayd passed through the deluge half aware, caught in a trance by the voice inside his head.

The twins pulled Tiryn to the center of the cage to avoid the splintering shards crashing in through the bars. The noise and rumble of rock and ice exploded in every corner of the cavern. The terror of the collapsing mine gripped both guard and prisoner alike.

"Now, Kion, call to me now, before I am buried in this ice."

"Truesilver—to me!" Kion shouted.

The blade whipped off the ground, darting perfectly through the bars and into Kion's shackled hand.

"No—the glaive!" Ilk cursed and turned to go back, but another cascade of falling ice fell before him, obscuring him from view.

Kion's mother had worked her blindfold loose by rubbing it against the floor. Her eyes found Kion's through the dust and debris. And that one look into those eyes, so full of love and kindness, of gentleness and understanding, was worth all the suffering, all the struggle, all the long, exhausting miles to reach this place. He and his mother embraced in that moment in a way no distance or time could hold back. And he knew, somehow he knew, that even if this cave fell down around them, or the haukmarn carried them a thousand leagues away, or even if her broken body failed and she passed beyond the veil of this world, still they would find each other again one day.

But the look lasted only a moment. In the midst of the ominous shattering and quaking, a heap of crumbling rock fell between Kion and his mother, cutting them off from each other. Kion thrashed against his chains.

"Mother!"

The cage quivered from the battering of falling ice. Terrified feet pounded out of the room as the guards fled to save their lives. A grinding, groaning, clattering, bellowing cacophony of pain and destruction filled the room, but one sound rose above them all.

"Kion! My son! I love you! Tell Tiryn I love her!"

"I love you, Mother!" Kion cried back.

And then came a terrible scream.

"No!" Kion's throat erupted in a wail of pain. A torrent of inarticulate sound poured from deep within. It was the sound of a great fortress of memory and tenderness and hope crashing down around him. He clenched Truesilver so tightly he felt his fingers would burst, but there was nothing he could do. Not even the most magnificent blade in the Four Wards could save his mother. His body shook uncontrollably, but not from the tremors which gripped the cavern. No, his body convulsed from the horrifying, crushing weight of knowing that his mother was dead.

Chapter 38

A SPARK IN THE DARKNESS

The only comfort Kithian could offer his glaivebond at that moment was the gentle warmth of his grip. No words could console a grief so fresh, so stunning. All the long journey had been for nothing, all had been for naught. In the end, Kion was left to watch, chained and caged and helpless, while his mother died. Her voice, so tender, so gracious, so constant in life, had been strained into one final loving exclamation and then snuffed out, consumed in a clarion of death. Those two sounds were inseparable in his memory. The love and the suffering. Both were fused together. For to love was to risk suffering and never had Kion suffered more, nor loved his mother more, than in that moment.

The cage shook violently. Kion didn't care. Let the whole mine fall down on top of him now. Let him be buried alongside his mother. The ice and the rocks would numb and crush him until he shared her fate.

"Kion, I know your pain runs deep, far deeper than I can know, but you must gather yourself as best you can for this place is not safe. See, even now help comes in ways unlooked for."

It was all Kion could do to open his eyes, but what he saw nearly shocked his heart back to life. Zinder, his pointed nose and cheeks red as ribbons, was jostling the door with his lockpick. "Hullo there, lad! Awfully sorry I'm late," he said amidst his grunting and squirming as he labored to spring open the door.

"Zinder? How—how did you get here?"

"That'll have to wait." Zinder made a stubborn face. He was all business, though his eyes were moist from recent tears. "It's hard enough picking locks under normal circumstances, but when your feet keep sliding this way and that…and the door's bouncing and you're dodging spears of ice…you need all…the…concentration…you can…get!"

With a high-pitched shout, he triumphantly kicked in the door and jumped inside, just in time to avoid a glistening shower of debris.

"Zinder, you little spark!" Trik said.

"Are you a ghost or a dream?" Trak said.

"Neither—yet. But if we don't get out of this mine, we might all end up being one or the other—or both." He cast a fretful glance back at the door where huge mounds of ice now blocked the exit. Shards of it spilled into the cage through the opening. "Keep that shut, lads. We don't want any more spilling inside if we can avoid it."

The twins cleared away enough ice to be able to force the door shut. Trak stayed with his back up against it while Trik went back to keep Tiryn from sliding about. Buckets of ice had already filtered in through the gaps between the bars, with more coming in by the moment. The floor was already ankle-deep in crushed chips.

Kion pitched onto the frozen shards, welcoming the sting of the cold—any pain was better than the hollow emptiness that raged inside him.

"I failed, Zinder. I couldn't save her…"

"Oh dear, lad, everything's gone wrong, hasn't it? I am so terribly sorry about your mother. It's the worst thing we could have imagined…I saw when they brought her in, those savages —" Zinder's breath caught and he looked away. The grief welled up in Kion afresh, a stinging, drowning flood that washed over him and choked his will to live. Zinder, seeing Kion's tears, righted himself and touched Kion under the chin. "I'm sorry you couldn't save her, lad. You did everything you could. No mother could have asked for more from her son. I can't imagine the burden you're bearing, but I'm afraid we've no time for grief. I need to loose you from those chains and we must leave before we're buried alive and—oh my, what happened to Tiryn?"

"Tiryn..." Kion had utterly forgotten his sister in his blinding grief. "She fell and hit her head and hasn't woken up. She may be, well, we're not sure if she's..." The rest of his words were swallowed up by another inrush of sadness. Everything. He was losing everything that mattered to him. First his home and flock, then his mother, and soon his sister. What did it matter if Inris or even the whole of the Four Wards were overrun? There was nothing left to return to anyway, nothing left worth fighting for.

"Oh, dear. Just hold still, then, while I fiddle with these shackles." Zinder twisted a needle into the lock clamping Kion's right hand, but it kept on popping out from all the shifting of the cage and the ice pouring in. But none of that could stop a determined nyn. "There! That's one. Good thing these are the usual shoddy human craftsmanship. Worse than usual, actually." He jiggled his tool inside the other shackle a few times before it clicked open as well.

As Kion's bonds fell onto the crushed ice beneath them, unexpectedly, the tremors stilled.

"Well, all that hurry for nothing," Zinder said, stowing his tool in a little pouch he had on his belt.

"Not to my way of thinking," Kion said, still waiting for another tremor. "You arrived just in time."

"Just in time to get trapped in the cage with us," Trak said. "Look at this place."

Trik had been forced to bring Tiryn into the middle of the cage where the ice was thinnest. He stood with her in his arms, bouncing slightly to keep both her and himself warm. Ice mixed with rubble was piled so high it went knee-deep around the edges. Outside, the destruction ran all the way to the ceiling in many places. It had blocked off their view of the tunnels exiting the cavern.

"Truesilver can get us out, though, right, Swordspeaker?" Trik said.

Kion thought long before he answered. He wanted to say no. He couldn't save his mother. How could he promise to save them, knowing he might fail them too? And yet, it wasn't right to simply leave them to find a way out on their own, to abandon them because of his own private devastation. His mother would not have done that. She had always sacrificed herself for the sake of others. But he was not her. He was not that strong.

"I…I don't know. I need some time to think…to…" His voice died away. What was he supposed to do now? How could he go on in the face of his mother's death? The tide of his mother's loss swept over him, making the cage around him seem dream-like and insubstantial. How he longed to turn back to the past to dwell in, to cling to, instead of this dark and cruel cave of ice and ruin. He wanted to go back, back to where everything had been whole and good, back to where it had just been he and Tiryn and Mother and the little cottage. Nothing else mattered anymore.

"I know your heart is broken, lad. Mine's smashed to pieces, too. But you'll pull through. We all will. I found you in the midst of all this madness and sorrow, you know. That must count for something. It means there's still hope. That life won't always kick you in the teeth. Don't give up, lad. We need you."

"Yes, Swordspeaker, all of us," Trak said.

Trik set Tiryn gently down on the ice and the twins came over and each wrapped an arm around Kion.

"We're sorry you lost your mother," Trak added.

"I could tell she was a wonderful lady," Trik said. "Even in just those few moments."

Kion felt faint. He wanted to double over and cry until his tears ran dry, until he froze along with the surrounding ice, but he knew that if he fully gave in to his grief, he might never move again.

"Thank you, both," Kion said, forcing the words out. "And thank you, Zinder. I—I just need a moment."

The presence of his bright-eyed and faithful friends brought some measure of comfort. They brought him back from the edge of the swirling sea. And yet, Kion still found himself unable to move, unable to take up his sword and lead his friends to safety.

"He just needs to rest a little; isn't that right, Swordspeaker?" Trik said, bending down to lift Tiryn back into his arms.

"Right. That's all he needs, a little rest," Trak said.

Kion nodded and the cloud of grief returned. How could he find rest with his mother lying dead a few paces away?

Zinder and the twins shared several worried, scattered looks. They had no answers either. But it was not long before Trik broke the silence.

"How did you find us, Zinder?" Trik said, uncomfortable with the eerie quiet of the cavern and needing to fill it was some sort of sound. "Seems like a smashing stroke of luck that you're here."

"It wasn't luck, I can assure you," Zinder said. "For there's no such thing. Just good old-fashioned quick thinking and common sense. 'Follow your nose and you'll never get lost,' as we nyn say. Here's what happened after I left you. We didn't spend long in Regnir, you see, before we came across one of the Noathryn going out alone for firewood. Dunwik knocked him into the nethers and we dragged him outside the town. I would not want to be on the bad side of that watcher in a fight. He knows his business. The Noathryn told us that all the prisoners old enough to carry a pick and a bucket went to the mines every day. We'd just finished tying him up and were preparing to head off to the mines when Scriff came flying across the snow, excited as a hornet's nest. He led us to the hole and we climbed down after you. Of course, we had to leave him at the top. We didn't think it would be safe for the little fellow in the bowels of the underworld."

"Scriff's safe! Thank goodness! And you even remembered his name," Trak said.

"So I did. And I don't expect I'll forget it again. He's quite the creature, that fox of yours."

"He survived the snake, then. Was he all right when you left him? Was he injured at all?" Trik said.

"I don't know anything about a snake, but he was as healthy as a frost fox can be when we left him. Don't you worry. Scriff'll find us again once we get out of this pit."

A bit of color returned to the twins' faces.

"But how did you find us once you got down the hole?" Trak said.

"We followed your trail to the secret entrance. It wasn't hard. Those melted tunnels Truesilver made were rather obvious."

"What about the secret door?" Trik said. "How did you get through that? Trak and I never would have gotten through it if our uncle hadn't told us how."

"Ah, the vibration trigger is an old time-honored mechanism. It's quite clever but so common in Lowerwyn that any nyn worth his spark knows how to trigger it."

"But wait," Kion said. "You said that you and Dunwik came together through the tunnels. Where is he now?"

Zinder grew quiet and gave the back of his head a good long scratch. His voice turned solemn, which was not a good sign, for he almost never struck that tone.

"Yes, that's a hard one to explain. You see, not long after we got into the mines he said he heard a voice. I couldn't hear it, though, and the more he went on about it, the clearer it became that he was going through what you did, Kion, back in Roving. 'The Call' was the way you described it, I believe. Well, Dunwik was convinced the voice came from a glaive. He deeply regretted that he couldn't go on, but said it would be wrong to deny it, and that it might even turn out for the better if he could return with a glaive of his own. He seemed a bit uncertain about the whole business—but he promised he'd meet me as soon as he found the glaive that was calling to him."

Another call? The troubling memory of Vayd's departure

snapped Kion temporarily out of his grief. Were Vayd and Dunwik both meant to be swordspeakers? Was there another glaive besides Rimewinter on Tinesplitter? Or had the same glaive called to them both? "Kithian, how can this be?"

"If both were called, it would have to have been from two different glaives. No glaive, no matter how corrupt, can put out more than one call at a time. And yet there are other things that may call to men in other ways. It could have been one of the dim-touched creatures, for they have ways of luring men to their deaths. Even so, we cannot rule out the possibility that a second glaive lies somewhere within these tunnels."

"Can each swordspeaker only hear the call of his own glaive?"

"Yes, until the glaivebonding. Once that is complete, the glaive fully awakens and its voice may be heard by any swordspeaker."

So not only Vayd, but Dunwik was a swordspeaker as well. Kion was no longer the only one. He wondered what it all meant, especially if one or both of the other glaives had fallen into corruption. If a glaive was truly calling Vayd, he did not see how it could be any other way. With Dunwik, he could at least hope that was not the case.

"Something strange is happening, Zinder. Vayd may have been called by a glaive as well."

"I can think of no other explanation for what has been happening. After the War of the Shattering, all the weapons that had betrayed the Mastersmith were thought to have been lost or destroyed, but perhaps we were mistaken. That was so very long ago. Many things may have changed since then."

"Vayd, a swordspeaker?" Zinder made a face like he'd sat on a pin. "Horn toads! Tell me you've got that wrong."

"I wish it were so. He left this cavern claiming to hear a voice no one else could. It was at the same time the tremors began. I wonder if they are connected in some way?" Thoughts swirled inside Kion, mixing with his grief, but not taking it away. If anything it blackened his mood all the more for doubt now ran together with sorrow.

Trik kicked at a pile of ice. "Why don't Trak or I get called to be swordspeakers? Seems like we're the only ones down here that didn't. Except you, Zinder, but you're a nyn so you don't count."

Zinder gave Trik a glare that made him bite his lip, but now was not the time to argue. "This will all sort itself out, but I don't see there's much we can do about it now," Zinder said. "Right now what we need to worry about is escaping this frozen mine."

The cold was creeping in. They could not survive long in this frozen cage. But Kion was not ready to leave. He turned to where he had last seen his mother. If only he could see her one last time, even in death. The thought of her buried on this cursed island, so far from the sun and the green turf of the Tors and the land she loved so well turned another knot in his mangled heart.

"Kithian, can you see where my mother's body is buried?" he said.

"It is beyond my vision. I know you must wish to see her, but I cannot help you in this and for that I am sorry."

"Perhaps it's better that way. Seeing her dead might be too much for me to bear. A part of me died here, though. In some ways, I wish that all of me had. I know none of you want to hear that, but it's true. I don't want to go on without her. She was my light after the darkness of my father's death. She gave everything she had for me and Tiryn. It's so hard to abandon her…all the more because we came so far…"

"Kion, is that you?"

The voice did not belong to Zinder or the twins.

Kion turned slowly, the whole of his body tingling with awe and dread. His mind told him that in his grief he must have only imagined his sister's voice. For that was the only thing that could staunch the wound of his mother's loss: knowing that his sister still lived.

Tiryn's head rose from where Trik cradled her in his arms. She stared at Kion with eyes that echoed the beauty of their fallen mother. In those eyes, Annira lived on. Those kind, soft, precious eyes were a glimmer, however small and fleeting, that life would go on, that bitter tears would not always be his drink, and that the sun would rise again no matter how unyielding the night.

"Please tell me you're not just another dream," Tiryn said.

Kion let Truesilver fall to the ice.

"No, it's not a dream. It's real. All of the horrible things and all of the good things, too."

If his words did not convince her of his reality, his blanketing embrace surely did.

Chapter 39

THE MAID AND THE MIRROR

From the moment she fell through the ice, Tiryn had been running. Running from a vision she did not want to see. But once we close our eyes to sleep, we open them to dream, and we do not close them again until the dream is over. To dream is to see. Yet there are some things better left unseen.

A living shadow dwelt in that frozen husk of the world she dreamed, malevolent and cunning, patient and ageless. It brooded beneath the ice-covered land, searching, seeking, spying out for some crack in the surface to free itself and rise again into the lighted world above. It was a voracious thing that once freed would swallow all that it touched. It slid and shifted beneath the land, following Tiryn's fleeing feet. Long she ran from it, but always it remained near. She could no more escape it than she could sprout wings and fly, and yet she ran on, hoping to find a place of safety, somewhere the shadow could not reach.

But it was more than just the shadow that sought her in this place. The world above the ice had terrors of its own. Swirling, sleeting winds hounded her every step. More troubling than the winds and their piercing chill was the knife-like voice that came upon them.

"Come, child, come." The voice spoke with an urgent edge. "Come and be one with the ice. Only through your sacrifice may the darkness be kept at bay."

It was a cutting voice, a cold voice. It was the voice of the Maid of Ice, that deceitful creature who had worn the face of

Tiryn's mother. But the voice was far too unnatural, far too primal to belong to her mother. It sounded more akin to the rasping, raging wind than anything human.

"Only you can stem the swelling dark and hold it fast within its icy prison. The power to bind the shadow runs through your blood, power to entomb our ancient enemy for all of time... Come now, come give yourself up to save this world, to remove the shadow's blight from the lands and people you hold dear."

They were lies, all lies, just like the Maid's false face. Each time Tiryn heard the voice, or sensed the shadow draw close, she ran harder. Through white forests and frozen plains she ran, her feet barely sinking into the snow, so swift was her flight. If she slowed, one of her enemies would surely overtake her, the shadow or the Maid. Tiryn had to find a way out of this frost-bound land before one of them found her.

Everywhere she ran, inescapable winter engulfed her. She passed league upon league of ice-encrusted valleys and glens, meadows and meres, all frozen and dark, all lifeless and sullen. No sun found its way into that world. No day ever dawned. It was a land of eternal, frozen night.

But Tiryn could not run forever. Her breathless flight sapped her strength. Her will to press on, to be free of these two terrible threats, kept her going long beyond her natural endurance, but even so, it was not enough. As her pace flagged and her steps faltered, she discovered the cruel truth of that land. Through some awful trick, all her running had only brought her back to where she began. She had gone in a circle. There was no way out. No matter how far she ran she would never escape. And with that revelation, a choice was thrust upon her. She could run until her strength failed utterly and wait for whichever power came first to claim her, be it frost or shadow. Or she could stop of her own accord and choose which master to serve.

As if reading her thoughts, the Maid of Ice spoke once more. "I offer you the honor of a noble death, a sacrifice that will not be in vain. If we do not stop it, the shadow will take you into itself.

You will not die, but neither will you live. You will exist within its ashen folds, a faded memory of yourself. Only a mockery will remain. But if you help me fight, if you give your life to push the shadow into its prison once more, your death will have purpose, and honor shall sing your praises. There is no other way." The words were blindingly clear. Tiryn was an instrument to the Maid, a piece in some larger plan, nothing more.

Tiryn staggered and fell to her knees in the snow, overwhelmed by the weight of the decision before her. The Maid of Ice was a deceiver. Tiryn could not trust her words. And yet Tiryn feared what would happen if what the Maid said of the looming shadow proved true. Its evil was palpable. She trembled each time she contemplated that unbearable nothingness. If she did not take the Maid's offer it would swallow her up. But what the Maid of Ice asked was too much. She was asking Tiryn to give up her life. Neither choice held any hope. Her life as she knew it would end one way or the other. She cast herself upon the snow. It was an impossible choice. And in the end Tiryn surrendered to whichever power would come and claim her first. She could run no longer.

But it was neither the shadow nor the Maid who came out of the tempestuous storm to claim her. It was her brother. Kion came bounding to her out of the blinding snow, his hands outstretched.

"Tiryn! I found you! Quickly, I need your help—"

Before he could reach her, his body jerked backward and he nearly fell to the ground. Two enormous chains held him fast. They stretched from his arms far into the pelting snow. He had run to the end of them and could go no farther.

Tiryn ran to meet him, flinging her arms around him.

"Kion, you came just when I needed you. I'm being chased by—"

"I know, a shadow lurks below. It is bound by the ice and snow for now, but if it gets loose, it will consume the world in its hunger. I need your help to stop it. That's why I came. I can't do it on my own." Truesilver was in his hands, though it had not been there a moment before. Kion pushed her away. "The shadow is coming. Can you feel it, Tiryn? Truesilver's fire can hold it at bay, but only for a little while." The sword burst into flames. Tiryn shrank back and hid her face from the light. She had been so long in the night that it hurt to look upon.

"It's not only the shadow that's coming, it's the Maid of Ice as well. She's the one who made this unending winter. She wants me to sacrifice myself to fight the darkness. She says that if I give myself to her that together we can stop it, or keep it imprisoned somehow. But I don't want to die, Kion. I'm so afraid. I don't know what to do."

Kion's chains shook as he strained against them. "If the Maid of Ice has set herself against the shadow, perhaps she can help us."

"Kion, did you hear what I said? She wants to kill me. She wants to sacrifice my life to imprison the shadow."

"Tiryn, our lives don't matter. All that matters is holding back the shadow. If we don't do that, all of us will die. We must fight against it, whatever the cost. I would give my life willingly if it would stop this shadow."

The scarlet flames cast Kion's face in wild, shifting shapes. Passion lit up his eyes, as all-encompassing as the darkness he sought to oppose.

"Kion, how can you say that? Don't you care about me? I thought you would protect me. I thought you would fight for me."

A harsh wind gusted across the icy ground where she and Kion stood. The shadow was coming, and so was the cold, a cold more bitter than what the winds alone could account for. This was something else. It was the chilling presence of the Maid, sweeping in from behind her.

"It is time for you to choose. You must give up your life, or all is lost," said the Maid, her voice cold as winter, sharp as a dagger, and closer than ever.

Tiryn would have clung to her brother, but the heat from Truesilver was too great. Still, she refused to turn and face the Maid. She could not bear to see the frozen mockery of her mother stitched onto that withered, emaciated frame.

Tiryn cried out to Kion, "You heard what she said. I have to choose between her and the darkness. Don't be fooled by her face, Kion. It's only a mask. She may look like Mother, but it's someone else. Mother would never seek to take my life."

"Where, Tiryn? Where is she? I can't see anything in this storm. They tied me to the judgment post, remember?"

Kion's mind must have been slipping from exhaustion or the cold. There was no judgment post. The chains were there, but whatever they were fastened to remained infinitely far away. But the Maid of Ice was right behind her. Tiryn could feel her deadly chill. How could Kion not see her?

Stinging clouds of frost billowed past. A web of ice formed upon Tiryn's hair.

"Your brother cannot help you until you give in to my call."

"No! I will not serve you. You want to kill me. You said so yourself. Kion, why won't you help me?"

"Tiryn, stop raving and find a way to free me from these chains." She gazed along the length of the chains, looking for some weakness or a way to undo them, but they were hard and thick and she had no way to break them and no key to unlock them. What Kion was asking her was impossible.

"I can't, Kion. The chains are too strong."

The ground shifted and she nearly slipped. The snow had begun to melt. More than that, the frosty ground was turning the color of ash. The world shook again beneath her. From close by came the snapping and cracking of ice. Like some black geyser, the infernal shadow burst free. It roiled and thundered and the land buckled beneath their feet.

Tiryn fought to pull air into her panicked lungs. Kion was the only one who could fight the shadow, but he was bound by his chains.

The Maid of Ice drew near, her frozen breath blasting Tiryn's cheeks from behind.

"There is no time. If you want to save your brother you must heed the call. Come to me. Embrace the cold and give yourself over to it. It is the only way to break his chains and push back the shadow."

Kion's chains went taut as the swelling shadow spilled across the land. It hesitated at Truesilver's flame, but all around Kion and Tiryn it gathered itself, growing thicker and thicker until no light could escape its darkness. Kion struggled and strained against his chains, but slowly they pulled him back, dragging the light and the fire away. His feet gouged long furrows in the snow.

"The fire isn't enough," Kion shouted. "You have to help me fight the shadow. Only together do we have a chance."

"How, Kion? How can I fight something like that? It's pure darkness."

"Seek the help of the Maid," Kion said. "Her cold has held the shadow back all this time. Please, Tiryn, I cannot defeat it alone."

Ice crept down Tiryn's arms. It encircled her neck and seeped into her shoulders. Perhaps Kion was right. Perhaps giving in to the Maid was the only way to stop the shadow. But no, there had to be another way. She could not allow herself to be bound to this frozen fate, to sacrifice herself for the Maid's heartless designs. She couldn't. Her life was too precious to simply throw away.

A great wind blasted the ground beneath them, carrying away the snow and revealing a silvery mirror of ice under their feet. In it she saw a pale face, frozen in sadness, diamond tears glittering down its cheeks.

And in that mirror a terrible truth overtook her. For though at first the face appeared to be the same as before—the face of her mother, though frozen and white—the face mimicked her own movements and expressions. And Tiryn was forced to see that it was not the face of her mother at all.

It was her own.

"No!" she screamed. "No, no, no! It can't be. It's a lie, a trick." And yet she could feel the cold grabbing hold of her, burrowing down into the depths of her flesh and she knew that what she saw must be true.

Tiryn flailed aimlessly. She could not accept this fate. She would not become like the Maid. She would not give her life over to this deadly cold. With her fists she pounded against the icy mirror—over and over again. The ice cracked. Tiryn beat against it all the harder. She struck and struck until at last the mirror shattered. The shadow howled with delight and Kion screamed.

"Tiryn, no! We failed—" he cried as the chains jerked him off his feet and he went flying into the surrounding shadow. It was so black by now that not even Truesilver's fire could stand against it. The red flame disappeared into the swirling darkness along with Kion.

The ground below Tiryn split into ten thousand pieces and in a flurry of shards and blinding motion, Tiryn disappeared into unending darkness.

Her eyes opened at last.

Chapter 40

AWAKE AT LAST

Tiryn cast the dream aside, burying it deep, never to be remembered again if that were possible. She told herself, as she had done so many times before, "It was only a dream…" Fleeing what she had seen, she threw herself headlong into the waking world. There was much to take in as Trik eased her onto her feet: the iron bars holding mounds of ice and rubble at bay, the astonished expressions of Trik and Trak, the kindly gaze of Zinder—struggling to conceal his emotions in the dim light of Truesilver's blade—and the inscrutable face of Kion, the face she knew best of all, careening somewhere between utmost joy and unspeakable sorrow.

"Where am I?" she said.

A heaviness fell upon her companions.

"I'll tell her lad, to spare you the pain," Zinder said.

"No. I should be the one," Kion said. He reached out and held her hands. Their warmth brought life to her frozen body, but the bitterness of his eyes was cold as death. "We're in the mines. Ilk captured me and the twins and then Vayd came."

"The leader of the haukmarn?" No wonder Kion looked shaken. She studied him for any wounds, but if they had fought, there was no sign of it. There was hesitation on his lips, though. He was holding something back.

"He wanted to know how to unlock the secrets of Truesilver's fire. Of course, I couldn't tell him. The gifts of a glaive are only for its glaivebond. And then…" He stared her full in the face. Tears broke out from the corners of his eyes. Kion, who never cried. "Oh, Tiryn…"

"Mother," Tiryn said. Kion's face was no longer a mystery. She understood now the battle of sorrow and joy warring there. Joy at seeing Tiryn, sorrow at… "Oh, no, Kion, she didn't…She's gone, isn't she?"

A swift and plunging sorrow cleaved her heart. The chamber grew strangely dark. She pitched forward into Kion's arms and was overcome by bitter, searing tears. She wept in voiceless torment. All faithfulness was faithless in that hour. All hope for the old enchanted life failed. She would never work in the garden pulling weeds, never go dancing on the heath and be called in for supper, never watch the new lambs come, never play a song before the glowing hearth of the cottage. Memories cascaded over her in an endless roar of foaming grief. All lost, all carried away by this thoughtless, indifferent world. Not her mother. Not her dear mother.

"Where…where is she? What happened to her?" she said.

"She is over there, buried under the rock and ice. The cave came down on top of her."

Tiryn looked, but there was nothing to see. No indication that the loveliest woman in all the Four Wards had met her end in this place. All was ice and rubble, chaos and destruction. She felt so very small in that moment, so helpless and fragile, like her limbs might crack if the slightest pressure were applied.

"I didn't get to see her. Did you see her, Kion? Did you get to speak to her?"

"She…yes. She said—her last words were—'tell Tiryn I love her.'" After that he could say no more. But that was enough. Those words were a gift beyond price. But, oh, how dearly they had been bought!

The five of them stayed huddled together long in that constricting cage of loss and lament. They stood and shivered from the cold, but it did not matter. No one dared move or say a thing, for the wounds were too deep, the despair too heavy. The grief was an almost physical thing that pressed down upon them, as if they too had been buried under mountains of rubble.

And in the midst of all that grief and hopeless silence, Tiryn heard a voice.

"I am here, dear one…Awake after all this time and all the woe that I have caused. I have been given a second chance. I know not what vision has led you here. I fear it may have been twisted by the dark paths which I have wandered. But you have not come all this way for naught. Heed my call and come. Come and let us walk a new path together."

The voice ran like icy fingers across her skin. A sorrow far different from Tiryn's, though in its own way as wounded and bitter, saturated every word the voice said.

Tiryn looked up, but no one stood outside the cage. How could there be anyone there? It was surrounded by ice. Of course, it had not come from inside the cage either. Was she having another vision? Was this another dream? There was something familiar about this voice…Flashes from her vision returned and a horrifying suspicion seized her, for the voice was the very mirror of the one belonging to the Maid of Ice.

"What is it, Tiryn? Is something the matter?" Kion said.

Zinder shared Kion's look of concern. When Tiryn did not answer, he tapped Kion on the shoulder. "We should let her be for now, lad. But if we stay here much longer I fear we'll never leave. It's time to light up that sword of yours and carve us a way out of this icebox and give us a little warmth besides."

Tiryn did her best to pretend she had only imagined the voice. She told herself that it must have been some unexpected response to her mother's death, her mind inventing some reason to distract her from the pain of her loss.

"Yes…I don't much feel like going on, but Zinder's right. It's terribly cold here. And even if it wasn't, I don't want to be here anymore. I want to leave this place forever and forget that we ever came." She grasped Kion's hand. "Lead us out of here."

"I...don't know if I can. I failed to protect her, Tiryn. I failed to save her when it mattered. All I could do was stand and watch her die." Kion kicked at a mound of ice and sent it spraying across the cage.

Her brother's pained expression galvanized Tiryn's will against both the shock of the voice and the bitterness of her mother's death. She could do nothing to erase her own pain, but she could rise to comfort her brother's.

"You were there. That's all that matters. That's what she needed—to know that you would come for her. You can't protect her now but I'm still here. Zinder and the twins—we're all still here. And we need you to keep going, to press on and not give up."

Her words came out more forcefully than she could have ever expected, but they were born as much from panic as from love for her brother. She had to leave this place—escape the Maid of Ice and escape the vision and escape this horrid cavern that had killed her mother.

The words struck home, awakening Kion to many things which his grief and failure had overshadowed. He took up Truesilver and gazed at the singular blade. What words that ancient sword told her brother, Tiryn could not say, but together with the words of his sister, Kion's eyes gained renewed resolve and though the grief was still there, it passed away for now. He spoke the blade's fire back to life. The heat and light swept over her, and she was struck once more by how beautiful and intense that fire was, something no honest person could look upon and fail to be amazed.

"Let us be free of these caves of death," Kion said, and the red-flamed sword bathed his face in a blistering glow, accentuating the terrible sorrow engraved there. Seeing her brother's plight, she clenched her lips and gathered her shattered will as best she could and met his eyes with all the love she had left. If he could go on, then so could she. Her pity for him outweighed even her own grief and though words failed her, with her eyes she told him, "Together we must go on. For Mother."

Kion gave her a nod that told her he understood. The bond between them as brother and sister had never been deeper. No matter how painful and piercing their loss, they would walk the path of grief together. And that was enough. If they had nothing left, at least they had that.

Kion opened the cage door and loads of ice poured in, burying him almost to the waist. Plunging his sword into the frozen barrier, the loose chunks vanished quickly under the unquenchable heat. Water ran along the floor so that there was no way to avoid stepping in it. It sparkled in the red sword light as if it were pools of blood. Tiryn shuddered at the sight. She wished Scriff were there to ice it back over and restore it to its original blue.

"Where are Dunwik and Scriff? Why is Zinder here and not them?" Tiryn said.

"Scriff is somewhere out on Tinesplitter, and Dunwik left to…" Zinder's face clouded over. "He went to follow the call of a glaive."

"A glaive?"

"Yes, that is what it seems," Kion said. "Or it may have been one of the dim-touched. But Kithian says that once a swordspeaker bonds with his glaive, he can hear the voices of other glaives nearby. If Dunwik's call was from a glaive, perhaps we can find each other again, as long as his glaive is not corrupted."

"Wait," Zinder said. "Then won't Vayd be able to hear you as well?"

"Vayd heard the call too?" Tiryn said, only half understanding what all of this meant.

"We think so. But as far as Vayd hearing Truesilver, he won't be able to do that unless he is close. Corrupted glaives lose some of their ability to communicate with any beyond those they enthrall except for the dim-touched, who can hear them at great distances. That is one of the prices the glaives pay for forsaking their maker and their true purpose."

"So, one glaive called Dunwik and another called Vayd?" Tiryn said.

"Sure seems that way," Trik said. "And it also seems like not all glaives serve the Mastersmith."

"That's in the legends too, come to think of it," Trak said. "Though they were always a bit vague on those parts."

"Hurry, while there is yet time." The voice of the Maid sounded again in Tiryn's hearing. The words set her teeth on edge. *"The prison has been broken. The ice is melting. Come, before these caverns fall down around me and seal me away forever."*

Tiryn pressed closer to Zinder, as if that would somehow protect her from the Maid's voice. He was walking behind Kion as he forged a path through the ice. She tugged at his coat from behind.

"Zinder?"

"Yes, lass?"

She could see in his face that he had not heard the voice. Glancing back at the twins, she could tell the same.

"Never mind." She was too terrified to tell them. If she did, it would be admitting that the voice was real.

Kion knifed through the heaps of ice crowding the cavern. Above them, a few scattered icicles hung ominously, bulbous drops of blue water dripping down from the tips. Most of the cavern roof was covered by dark rock riven with spidery cracks. It was hard to imagine a force powerful enough to splinter the cavern in that way. The sight only intensified Tiryn's desire to flee this awful place.

"This is far easier than it was on our way here," Kion said as the shimmering piles sloughed off to either side and the water soaked his boots up past the ankles. "It's not just that the ice is already broken up. Look up there." He pointed toward the glistening spears of ice which still clung to the ceiling. "It looks as though it may be melting on its own."

A small quake shook the room. Weak as it was, with the slippery stream of water running along the bottom of their makeshift tunnel, Trik nearly slipped and fell.

"I can sense you drawing closer. You are following the proper path. Soon you shall know more of me than just my voice." The Maid spoke with greater force this time. A presence, like a soundless echo, loomed ahead in the direction they were moving. If the voice and the presence were one and the same, that meant they were heading toward the Maid of Ice. Tiryn thought about asking to go in a different direction, but her mind went numb when trying to come up with an excuse. What if the Maid could hear her? Would she try to stop Tiryn if she fled? There was a terrible urgency to the voice's words. Perhaps it did not matter whether or not she fled. Perhaps the Maid would come for her no matter what path she took. And yet, it sounded like the Maid was waiting for Tiryn to come. Was the Maid truly in danger or was it some kind of trick?

As Tiryn struggled to make sense of what she'd heard, Kion brought them out of the chamber and into an open tunnel carved through the rock. There he dismissed Truesilver's fire.

"We do not have much oil left for glaivefire. I do not know the way out, but this was the clearest tunnel Kithian could see. Let's hope it stays this way."

Tiryn opened her mouth to speak, but once again the words froze on her tongue. She could not ask Kion to waste Truesilver's fire and risk their lives over imagined voices that only she could hear, however convincing they might be.

The chiseled rock was dusty gray with sparkling crystals flung all through it. Pockets of ice endured here and there, but for the most part it was clear. The going was far easier without having to splash through melted ice. They rushed down the new tunnel, passing fallen rock and glistening veins. Picks and buckets lay abandoned here and there as they went.

"I hope the miners all got out," Trik said. A tremor ran

through the rock, sending down a shower of dust and ice crystals up ahead. They covered their mouths and plowed through the haze, finding the air clearer on the other side. Tiryn recalled the Maid of Ice's words, *"Come, before these caverns fall down around me and seal me away forever…"* Would this place claim more lives this day beyond her mother's? Would it claim the Maid's? Would it claim Tiryn's as well?

The tunnel carried them through the mine for a good while without incident. They passed several unpromising offshoots, all smaller than the one they were in. Eventually the passage began to slope downward. Ice coated the majority of the walls and ceiling, growing thicker the farther down they went. Before they knew it, the tunnel had turned solid blue. Even the ground was hidden by ice, though a thin sheen of water revealed that it was melting, making the way forward all the more unsure. Dripping sounds now played a constant rhythm, gaining cadence as they went. The passage narrowed so that Tiryn could almost touch both sides with her elbows. Traversing the treacherous slope, Tiryn fell several times, too distracted by the growing sense of the Maid's presence to pay attention to her footing. Surely all of this ice heralded the nearness of the Maid. This could not be the way out. They were headed to a trap. She had to warn—

"Hold up, what's this?" Zinder's voice burst into her thoughts. The party came to a halt before a pile of ice shards. A sharp whistle pushed through Zinder's teeth. "Do you see that sheet of metal embedded in the ice? It's far too low quality to be anything but haukmarn make. They make their armor thick like that as well. Looks like it came off a gauntlet. I'd wager my anvil —if I still had one—that Vayd came this way, too. He probably bashed through a sheet of ice blocking this passage."

Tiryn might be wrong about the Maid of Ice, but Vayd was very real. He had nearly beaten Kion the last time they fought even though Kion had a glaive and Vayd did not. If he had somehow found one of his own…

"What will we do if that big brute's found his own glaive?" Trak echoed Tiryn's thoughts.

"Vayd set out long before we did," Kion said, speaking to their fears. "And he will not stay in these tunnels once he finds what he is looking for. It's too dangerous. He would look for a way out, the same as us."

"I hope you're right, lad. In any case, there's nothing we can do about it now. Let's continue on with our parade, then. At the rate this ice is melting, we'll have to swim out if we don't hurry," Zinder said.

"You are close now, very close. Even so, time slips away. You must free me before it is too late. It is no longer safe here. Hurry!" The voice came with fresh intensity. The urgency of the words would have tempted Tiryn to pity had she not known the truth of the one behind them. The Maid sought her life. She had said so in the vision. And yet, what did it mean that Tiryn had seen her own reflection in the mirror, wearing the dress of the Maid? Was the Maid a ghost who sought to possess her body? Was the mirror a trick? None of it made any sense. Whatever it meant, the burden of the vision and the chilling voice had grown too great. She could keep it to herself no longer.

"Kion, wait," Tiryn called out, pressing past Zinder in the narrow passage. "Kion, I have something I need to tell you. I... I've been hearing voices. Well, a single voice, anyway. It's telling me to come and it's telling me that I'm getting closer."

"A voice? Are you sure? What does it sound like?" His eyes flared with intensity.

Did he believe her? She dared to hope.

"I know this will sound strange, but it's a cold voice. And I don't mean cruel or uncaring, I mean cold like frost. Just hearing it makes my skin prickle. I can't explain how. But I think the source is not far away."

Kion stopped to listen to Truesilver's voice. When he finished he took her gloved hand in his. His eyes were softer than usual. Understanding shone within.

"Tiryn, listen to me. Both Vayd and Dunwik said they heard a voice. They thought it was from a glaive. Kithian thinks that Vayd's call was real, but with Dunwik, we don't truly know. It seems hard to believe that there would be two glaives in one place, much less three. But Kithian says that there are other things in this world—the dim-touched creatures—that can play with people's thoughts and lure them to their death. It may be that the voice you're hearing is from one of them."

She pulled him close and clung to his lanky frame. "Thank you, Kion, I just wanted you to believe me, that's all. I'll do whatever you say, just so long as I know you don't think I've lost my mind. But could it be the Maid of Ice? Does Kithian think she exists?"

A violent tumult rattled the right-hand wall. A crack buckled out from the ice, spraying shards and knocking both Trik and Trak off their feet. But the movement receded as quickly as it came and the twins hopped up and brushed themselves off, pale-cheeked from shock, nothing more.

"Not my fault that time," Trik said.

"We need to keep moving," Kion said. "Somehow I don't think that will be the last of the tremors."

"But what about the Maid of Ice? Is she real? Or is my mind playing tricks on me?"

Kion paused a moment to consult his glaive once more.

"Kithian does not believe the Maid of Ice is an actual being. Long ago there was a warrior who was called the Maid of Ice. He thinks the legend must have grown up around her, though she was nothing like what the Frin say about her. I believe you are hearing something, Tiryn, I do. But whatever it is, you don't need to fear. I'll protect you—whatever it turns out to be."

So the Maid of Ice was real, or had been once. Could it be her ghost, then, that was calling out to Tiryn? Or was it some insidious monster, one of these dim-touched creatures Kithian had told them about? Or perhaps the dreams were taking over her mind so that she could no longer tell what was real and what was a vision. If only Mother were here. But she was gone. Gone forever. And yet, she still had Kion.

She let go and moved back behind Zinder. She still had no answer why she was hearing what she was hearing, but at least Kion believed her. And if the Maid of Ice did indeed lie in wait somewhere close, Tiryn knew that he would keep her safe.

Chapter 41

RIVER OF NO RETURN

Though the others voiced their dismay and frustration, Tiryn was grateful when the passage came to an end. A mass of ice shards blocked the way forward, a sparkling blue barrier that would require Truesilver's fire to pass through. But the glaive's oil was running low, and Tiryn wondered if perhaps they might turn back and take one of the other tunnels they had passed and free her from having to face the presence that was calling her.

"What does Truesilver say, Swordspeaker? Is there a path on the other side?" Trak said.

"Yes, a passage and something more. Listen. Do you hear that?" Kion said.

The low sigh of rushing water whispered from beyond the twinkling ice before them.

"Are you sure it's safe, lad? You won't be bringing down a river on top of us?" Zinder said.

"Kithian says the river flows in a channel of its own for now. It may not stay that way if things keep melting the way they've been. The ice blocking the passage goes on for no more than a dozen paces. If we pass through now, we should reach the river before it overflows its bounds."

By the time Truesilver had melted an opening through the blockade, the sound of the river had gone from a whisper to a roar. A burgeoning stream, rimmed by icy ledges, raced swiftly into the dark, the sound of its rushing amplified by the stone cavern around it. High above, long dripping fingers of ice hung like a crowd of bats waiting to take flight. Drops fell onto the river and rocks below in sputtering, irregular bursts. On the far side of the river and off to the right, a single opening pierced a large, ice-coated wall. It was too high for anyone to reach without climbing and looked barely large enough for a single person to crawl through, but it was the only way forward. Within the opening glowed the light of the sun, feeble, and yet to eyes that had so long labored under the subdued emanations of Truesilver's blade, it was bright as an open meadow on a cloudless day. The light played upon the glistening, melting walls of the chamber, draping it in a thousand splashes of dappled radiance. The sight of that underground chamber, after so much pain and despair, stirred the little company with fresh hope. Not only did it tell them that beauty might be found in the grimmest and darkest of places, but it also meant that a world beyond this crumbling prison awaited, a world of unbridled sunlight and crisp air and endless sky.

"Now there's something to write a song about, eh, Tiryn?" Zinder said.

"You are close now. Do not fear. All will be made clear when you find me." The chill voice hounded her to the last, stealing the wonder of the moment, splashing ice water in her face. It was more undeniable than ever. There could be no doubt that the voice came from the other side of that opening.

"Yes, I'd say it is," Tiryn said in a toneless voice. She dreaded what lay beyond that opening, sunlight or no. And yet, the hole was so high up, there seemed to be no way to reach it. Again, she nursed a private hope that they would be forced to find another way.

"Sweet, blessed sunlight," Trak said. "We've only been in these tunnels for a few hours, but I was starting to think we might never see it again."

"Hear, hear! Three cheers for the sun!" Trik said.

But Zinder turned serious. "Dunwik had the climbing gear. It will be a bit of a dodge getting all the way up, but I have tools of my own. I'll find a way."

"I see no other way out. I'm confident that you'll make it, though," Kion said.

A hollow dread gripped Tiryn's throat. Was it the way out, or the end for them all?

"Kion, the voice I heard—it's coming from that lighted opening. I'm afraid of what we'll find if we go through."

"We have no choice, Tiryn," Kion said. "There is light there, so it has to be close to the outside. And with all these tremors, we dare not risk going back to look for some other way."

Tiryn stared into where the river disappeared into the darkness, willing her eyes to penetrate its mysteries. "What about this stream? It might let us out of this place." It was a foolish idea, she knew, but any danger was worth facing if it kept her from confronting the Maid of Ice.

"There's no telling where that might take us. It will pull us under and drown us, most likely, if it doesn't freeze us first," Zinder said. "Kion is right. That opening is the only way."

"Everything will be fine." Kion gave her a look he had given her countless times before. Once, when they'd gotten lost in the Tors and had to spend the night out in a rainstorm, Kion had somehow found a cave for them to take refuge in. But before that, when the lightning was still flashing and the thunder so loud it shook her bones, he had given her that same look and it had filled her with the courage to keep going. "Trust me," it said.

Yes, she could trust him with her life. Yes, he would protect her. She knew that. But who would protect him if the Maid of Ice was beyond that opening?

"We're ready to face anything," Trak said, patting the knife he wore strapped to his chest.

Trik imitated his brother, adding, "And evil doesn't like the light as far as the tales go. So I don't think whatever is up there could be all that bad."

Zinder pressed his hand into hers, a steely light in his eyes.

"I'd burn every hat I own before I saw something bad happen to you, lass. You've just got to trust us."

Tiryn looked at each one of them in turn. They were all in their own way so very noble, brave, and sincere. Her very own troop of soldiers every bit as worthy as Roardin or Aonar or the bladewarden himself as far as she was concerned. Perhaps that was enough. Perhaps her visions and fears were not as strong as the four people who stood beside her.

"Come along now. That river's swelling by the moment," Zinder said. "Kion, do you think you can make the jump?"

The stream was no more than five or six paces across, but it ran dark and swift. If someone fell in, they would be carried away before anyone could pull them out.

"I'm not sure. The ice will make it hard to get up enough speed, but I'll try."

"Aren't nyn supposed to be fantastic leapers?" Trik said. "Maybe you should go first, Zinder."

"Well, I'm glad you think nyn are good for something. But while we nyn are impressive jumpers for our size, I can't outdo Kion unless I grab hold of a kite in a strong wind."

Kion took off his baldric and entrusted it to Trak. "Take care of Truesilver," he said.

Trak's eyes bulged at the unexpected request. His hands trembled visibly. "Oh, yes, Swordspeaker, I will. I promise. I'll guard it with my life." Trak squeezed the scabbard tight to keep from losing his grip. He held the blade before him, taking in every detail of the gilded hilt with its radiant gems, the stylized golden flames on the guards, and the rich, dark leather of the handle.

Trik stared at his brother, mystified, as though Trak was already halfway to becoming a swordspeaker.

Kion patted them both on the shoulder with quiet assurance and withdrew to the edge of the tunnel. He took a running start, his great loping stride sending him across the damp stone with the speed and grace of a fawn. Though he slipped as he planted his foot to launch, he extended his legs at the end and went skidding across the floor on the opposite bank. He tore through the knee of his pants, but it looked to be no more than a grazing cut.

"Send over the rope," he said, not bothering about his knee.

Zinder tied a hammer and spike to one end of a rope and tossed it over the water. Kion pounded the spike into the ice on the far side. After the hammer was tossed back, Zinder did the same on his side, tying the rope as tight as he could so that it stretched above the river in a taut line.

Trik ventured across first, going arm over arm with his legs scissored together securely around the rope. He had a rough moment when he looked down in the middle and it looked like he might slip into the water from sheer terror, but Trak warned him that if he fell he'd never see Scriff again and that seemed to restore his courage enough to make it the rest of the way.

Tiryn was made to go next. She tried her best to put on a brave face but would have rather grabbed the blade of a knife with bare hands than touch that rope. It was not the rope that she feared, though, but what the rope would bring her to.

"Be strong, Tiryn," Kion said. "Don't think too much about it. It's better if you just go over as quickly as you can."

Though every bone and sinew in her body wanted to pull her in the opposite direction, she had to press on. "Fight, Tiryn," she told herself. "Fight like Mother would." But, oh, it was so hard going on without her. She tried to press the wave of grief back down inside her, but a rebel tear squeaked out from one eye. Tiryn brushed it away before anyone could notice and set her gaze on Kion, once again borrowing strength from her brother. She fought through the bout of despair and grabbed hold of the rope. She might never wake from this nightmare, but that did not mean she had to surrender to it. She was Annira Bray's daughter, and she had to keep going, even if it meant the Maid of Ice or some other dark power waited ahead.

Tiryn made it across the river by the combined strategy of never once opening her eyes and holding on as tightly as she could. She ended up taking much longer than Trik, but she made it without stopping.

"Well done," Kion said. "I knew you could do it."

She embraced him as he helped her feet find solid ground once again. Though her legs were still weak with fear, she tottered over and sat down against the far wall. The effort had taken more out of her than she realized.

The ceiling quivered with a great clack and clatter, as though hammers were pounding against it. Ice shards dislodged and came shattering down, accompanied by a shower of pebbles. A long crack opened in the ceiling, deep and black and foreboding, but the cavern held together.

"Hurry, Zinder, you're next," Kion said, flicking his hand to beckon him over, but Zinder needed no encouragement. He shimmied across with the speed of a mouse scurrying to its hole.

Trak was last to go. His crossing was nowhere near as fast as Zinder's but he was carrying Truesilver on his back so it was understandable that he would take extra care.

"This chamber will not hold forever. The ice melts swiftly now. I need you. Hasten to me while you still can." The frantic tone of the voice startled Tiryn. It sounded genuinely afraid. Could it be the Maid was not wholly evil? There had been no talk of sacrifice or of imprisoning the shadow as there had in her vision. A spark of hope flickered inside her. Perhaps this voice was not the Maid from her vision, but something else, something that did not mean her harm but truly needed her in some pressing way.

Trak handed Kion back his sword with great reverence and solemnity. The seriousness came off as overly dramatic, though that certainly wasn't Trak's intention. If Tiryn had been capable of laughter, it surely would have come. As it was, her heart went out to these two dear boys who had done so much for them and come so far and been so faithful. They may have been young and even a little foolish at times, but they had courage to outmatch many a grown man.

Zinder unfastened the rope and together the company approached the great wall of stone and ice.

"Look." Zinder pointed upward. "Those gouges in the rock were made by Dunwik's axe. He must have come this way."

"That's a good sign. Perhaps we'll find him soon—wait." Kion turned his head to the side, gazing back along the wall and taking in Truesilver's words. "Kithian says there is another pathway through the rock in that corner, behind that outcrop. It may not lead anywhere, but we should take a closer look."

Zinder hurried toward the shadowy section of the wall. When the light from Truesilver's blade came close enough, it revealed a passage roughly the size of the one they had just come through. It had been hidden before by an outcrop of rock that kept it shrouded in darkness. As with many of the other tunnels, icy debris littered the floor all down its length.

"Shar's dome, how did I miss this? That sword's eyes—or whatever it uses to see—are sharper than a nyn's."

"I hope it's safe," Trak said.

"Nothing's safe down here," Trik said.

"True enough. Let's be going before this cavern decides to have another hiccup," Zinder said.

They set off down the hidden passage. The tunnel, while melting like the others, had smooth, rounded walls that looked almost sculpted, though here and there cracks marred the perfect surface.

"This looks like one of the tunnels Truesilver might have made with its glaivefire," Kion said.

"It's not natural, that's for certain. A hundred nyn couldn't have made one better," Zinder said.

Tiryn hesitated at the lip of the tunnel. Her limbs seized with fear.

"Tiryn?" Kion pulled up and looked back. "Is something wrong?"

"Heed the call," the voice said. *"You will know no peace until you do. It is pointless to resist the doom that has been laid upon you."*

The voice spoke the truth. Her resistance only delayed the inevitable. Tiryn had no choice but to travel this path. She could no more avoid it than if she had fallen into the river and been swept away into the darkness. Yet even so, every step she took was harder than the one before.

Chapter 42

RIMEWINTER

A relentless and unyielding cold knifed into Tiryn's flesh the moment she stepped into the new cavern. Her coat may as well have been made of paper. The chill pierced through skin, bone, marrow, and all. Its invisible tendrils wrapped themselves around her joints, tightening their grip with every frosty breath.

"I am going to die in this room," she thought. If not from the Maid then from the cold.

Frost crystals formed on her gloves and sleeves before her very eyes. Her shoes kept wanting to meld with the ice-coated floor. Thick and impenetrable walls of ice rose around her until they ran out of sight. Instead of a roof, they tapered closer and closer together into a narrow cone until disappearing in a tiny spark of sunlight far above. Icicles nestled along the slanting walls. Their tips glinted expectantly, a thousand frozen eyes peering down from the heights. The light from above bounced between innumerable facets along the walls, lighting the chamber and amplifying itself in a treasury of wintry jewels. There was piercing beauty no matter where Tiryn looked. And yet it was a beauty too keen to be endured. No living thing could survive long in such a place.

There were gaps, though, amongst the jewels of the icy chandelier overhead. And the fate of the missing icicles could clearly be seen in the shattered heaps of frozen debris below. Of the icicles still intact, several rattled and clinked as another weak tremor passed through the cavern.

One of the walls jutted strangely out into the middle of the room. It was more rounded than the others. It seemed to grow out of the right side of the cavern, an immense build-up of ice far thicker than that which covered the rest of the walls. A long crack ran down the center of the bulge and a great heap of ice shards lay before it.

In the corner opposite from where they entered, the hole they had seen from the river cavern opened some three stories above the floor. A small ledge lay beneath it, large enough for two or three people, before ending in a sheer drop to the floor below.

Not one soul disturbed the frozen stillness. The Maid of Ice was nowhere to be seen, neither was Vayd or Dunwik or any dim-touched creature. And yet, Tiryn sensed the Maid closer than ever, only she could not say where in the room she was. Could it be that she was in some way hidden from mortal eyes?

"I never thought I would experience worse cold than my night on the post, but this is unbearable," Kion said, though he was the only one not shivering, for he held Truesilver in his hand.

"You s-s-said that right," Trik managed through chattering teeth.

"Th-this must b-be what it's like g-getting eaten by a f-f-frost fox," Zinder said.

Kion paused, held again by Truesilver's voice, while the others kept moving to avoid being frozen in place. They could not go far before piles of ice blocked their way. A few topped even Kion's height.

"We c-can't stay in h-here," Trak said. "Let's h-hope th-there's an exit on th-the other s-side of these m-m-mounds of ice."

"S-s-swordspeaker, p-perhaps a little f-fire would help?" Trik said.

Kion turned away and gave the command. A welcome heat washed over Tiryn, giving new life to her half-frozen body. "Kithian says that this is no ordinary cold. Such cold can only come from one source: Rimewinter. The glaive must be here, either inside the walls or somewhere among these piles of ice."

A different kind of chill, one that came from inside, ran through Tiryn's body at these words. So there was a second glaive here after all.

"Can't Truesilver see through the ice to find her?" Zinder said.

"Unfortunately, no. Though the rest of the ice in these mines came in some way from Rimewinter as well, the ice here is different. It comes directly from the blade itself, pure and unmingled with other elements, and no glaive may see through it. The ice piles will melt away easily enough, though. It won't take long to bring them down."

As Kion swept his blade over the mounds of shards before him, two voices spoke at once.

Zinder pointed at the bulging wall and said, "Ho, lad, what's that?"

The other voice only Tiryn could hear.

"You have brought friends, one of them as old as I, though I wonder if he would consider me a friend if he knew what I have done." The voice rushed through Tiryn's ears with greater force than ever before. It was so clear now, Tiryn could hardly believe no one else heard it.

She had no time for what Zinder saw, though he rattled on about a "frozen tomb." The voice was so close she had to believe that whoever it belonged to could hear her if she spoke. But did she dare? Truesilver's warnings lingered at the back of her thoughts. What if this voice did not belong to the Maid of Ice, but to the glaive Truesilver had spoken of? And what if that glaive had become corrupted? Tiryn stumbled forward, her fear-crippled mind lost in a storm of uncertainty. Her lips trembled. She dreaded what might happen if she answered the voice and yet the mystery of it all was greater than her fears.

"Who are you?" Tiryn said. It was time. She had to know the

truth. For good or ill, she had to face whoever was behind the voice.

Zinder and the twins turned from their study of a barely visible figure bound inside the rounded wall to regard Tiryn with puzzled expressions.

"I'm fairly certain that fellow won't be answering your questions," Zinder said.

"Did you not hear the words of Truesilver's glaivebond? Do you have the gift of Sight, but not of hearing? I am Rimewinter, child. And I am meant for you and you alone." The cold clarity of the voice snapped something inside of Tiryn. The meaning of the words was undeniable, but rather than calming her fears they had the opposite effect. The voice belonged to Rimewinter, but it might still be corrupted. If so, Tiryn, and perhaps the others as well, could be in terrible danger. And yet, how would she know? *"Even now you do not believe. But you shall see me soon enough. Then you shall know the truth. Then your doubts will melt as easily as the ice disappears from Truesilver's flames."*

The pile of ice that stood before the crack in the wall had receded to the point that a shadowy figure could be glimpsed within. The fingers of the right hand were extended beyond the ice and the skin was slate gray and withered. The rest of the body could only just be made out within the opaque bulge. Whoever it belonged to was long dead, though the ice had preserved the corpse remarkably well.

"It may have been some miner who got trapped down here long ago," Kion said. "Best to leave him undisturbed." He moved to spread Truesilver's fire to other parts of the room.

"Poor fellow," Zinder said. "That crack in the ice looks recent, though. If it hadn't freed his hand loose I would have missed it. I fear we might be joining him if we don't find the way out of this place. That patch of sunlight is far too high to reach, even for someone like Dunwik."

The presence of the entrapped corpse pressed itself into Tiryn's awareness. If the voice belonged to Rimewinter, had the blade's ice been responsible for his death? The idea of Rimewinter's corruption gained force in her thoughts. The glaive's ice was cold as the grave. Tiryn had felt it. If not for Truesilver's flames, she might already have succumbed to it.

The heat from Kion's flickering red sword wafted to the icicles above. Several fell, bursting with a crash or a tinkle depending on where they landed and how big they were. The glaivefire melted those that would have fallen on Kion. The others took shelter in a cramped nook where no icicles loomed above.

"Where are you?" Tiryn asked the voice, studying the melting piles for signs of glinting steel.

"Is something the matter, lass? Your eyes look a bit hazy," Zinder said, but his words came to her ears as a far-off echo. Tiryn was too captivated by her search for Rimewinter to pay much heed to his words. She tried to recall if Truesilver had given a description of the glaive, but her memory stubbornly refused to dredge up any details.

Under Truesilver's withering fire, water sloughed off the piles of ice at a terrific pace, the ice melt flowing into sapphire pools at Kion's feet. A dark sliver of metal floated out on one of the rivulets. It was small and cross-shaped, no longer than Tiryn's forearm from end to end. It looked old and ancient and dull as rust, but when Tiryn saw it, she knew. The voice she had been hearing all this time had come from that small, unimpressive piece of metal. This was Rimewinter.

"Kion, stop the fire," Tiryn said, fearing the flames would engulf the weapon. Though reason might have told her that a metal weapon could not be destroyed by Truesilver's blaze, she knew little of weapons, much less of glaives. All she knew was that this was indeed a glaive and that the voice belonged to it. She still did not know if she could trust it, though. That was not yet clear. But she was surprised to find herself hoping that she could.

"It is time, dear one. Take me up and let me show you what true Sight is."

"What? Is something the—?" Kion did not finish. He, too, had spotted the dagger. The surface was pitted and the handle worn away, leaving nothing but the raw metal of the tang. Parts of the blade were chipped. It looked to all appearances like a dagger that had been left out in the elements for an age or more. "What is this?" He reached down to pick up the battered weapon.

Tiryn wondered if he should, but Rimewinter's voice remained silent and the flames were too hot for her to approach.

"What have you found, Swordspeaker?" Trak said.

"That weapon looks older than the moon," Trik said. "I wonder how it got here?"

Kion turned the blade over in his hands, brushing off the ice and melted water. He studied it long.

"It's a glaive," Tiryn said. "And its name is Rimewinter."

"Rimewinter!" the twins exclaimed.

A look of understanding passed then between Tiryn and Kion. He had as many questions and doubts as she did, but one thing was clear: he knew that she spoke the truth, and he feared what it might mean for his sister.

"This is the voice you were hearing, wasn't it?"

Tiryn gave a nod, her lips trembling. Should she do this? What would it even mean if she did? What would it mean if she refused?

Kion quenched Truesilver's fire. Though the cold returned at once, it was not as sharp and unbearable as before, for Truesilver's heat still lingered. "Before I give it to you, there's something I want you to know. You do not have to do this, Tiryn. Kithian is sure that Rimewinter caused all of this ice somehow. This whole wintry curse is most likely the fault of this glaive. Fallen blades have a way of bending those who answer their call to their will. He fears what might happen if you take hold of it, and so do I."

Trak stepped up. "If the dagger is evil don't give it to her, Kion. You don't want to have to fight your own sister."

"Let one of us try instead," Trik said, as serious as he had ever been. "I'll take the weapon. If it takes me over, it would be better for you to kill me than your own flesh and blood."

"Oh, Tiryn..." Kion's eyes fell to his glaive, searching for answers even as he harkened to its words.

"So, your name is Tiryn," came the voice, soft as the wind and yet biting all the same. *"It is a pleasant name. And the swordspeaker is your brother. I must be honest with you, young one. The path of the swordspeaker is no easy one. And yours may be harder than most. Truesilver is right to suspect me. I did stray from the path of wisdom in calling down this curse. Though I meant it for good, it was wrong in the end. So I have come to learn after all these long and bitter years. For no good can be found outside the Mastersmith's will, however much the wisdom of the world may call it good, and however much we may think and wish that it is what he would want. But the Mastersmith has awakened me once more. He has given me a second chance. Now our moment comes. It will be a bit frightening, but the fear will pass soon enough. And you will see that my steel shall once again ring true."*

Tiryn gazed at the weathered blade. The voice had struck a new tone—wise and understanding—reminiscent of the tone so often used by her mother. Tiryn wanted to believe the words, but it was impossible to know if they told the truth. Yet there was an even greater reason she hesitated to answer this call. For even if Rimewinter was not corrupted, Tiryn had no desire to wield a glaive. She did not want to be a swordspeaker. It would have been better if Rimewinter had chosen Trik or Trak. They were the ones who were fascinated by such things. Even Zinder, with his love of swords and smithing, would have been a better choice. Instead, the awful burden had fallen to her.

"I don't know what to do, Kion. Rimewinter is calling me to take up the glaive and become a swordspeaker. I can feel its pull even when the voice is silent. But I don't know if the glaive is corrupted. I had a vision after I fell. And though this is nothing like it, I can't help but think that what's happening now is somehow connected to it."

"What was the vision like?"

"I was in a frozen land. The Maid of Ice was there and she wanted me to sacrifice myself, to give myself to her. It was the only way, she said, that we could stop a shadowy presence that was trapped within the ice. You were in the vision too. You said I should give in to the Maid so that we could fight the dark together. But in the end, I couldn't do it. I rejected the Maid's call and you were lost. I failed you in that vision. Oh, Kion, tell me what to do. Tell me like you did in the vision. And this time I'll listen. I'll do whatever you say. Should I accept this call? Should I become a swordspeaker like you?"

Kion looked away, giving his attention to Truesilver's voice. As he listened his brow tightened and his eyes grew dark with worry.

"This shadowy presence you saw is troubling. Truesilver thinks it may be something very real, but he's not sure."

"It is, Tiryn." Rimewinter's voice brushed her ears once more. *"Though much of what you saw was false or only half-true, that much at least you saw rightly. For it is Shadowriven that you have seen in your vision and he has been freed. You must fight him, along with your brother. With me in your hand you shall take up the mantle of the Maid of Ice and she will walk the land once more. Be not afraid to become what you were meant to be. The Mastersmith's wisdom is deep beyond all knowing, but it is always for good to those who choose to listen. And if you do not embrace it, your brother may have to face Shadowriven alone, and without your help, it may be that he will fail."*

"The Maid of Ice?" So it was true after all. That was what she had seen in the mirror. That was who she would become. And yet for all the wisdom and certainty in Rimewinter's words, Tiryn could not see how this could possibly be the correct path.

"But I don't know how to fight. I'm no warrior."

Kion took hold of her hand. In the absence of Truesilver's flames, the stinging cold was seeping back into the room, making her decision all the more urgent. "Whatever the glaive is telling you and whatever vision you had, it doesn't have to come true. You still have a choice. Remember what you told me back in Dunach? We can change our dreams. You changed the vision you had then. You can change this one too. But whatever you choose, know this. I will stand beside you. Truesilver and I will make sure that no harm comes to you." Kion's face softened in a way that it rarely ever did. Echoes of Mother's kindness arose in that look. Tiryn's fears seemed small and momentary in the light of that face she loved so well.

"I see now that your Sight has been dimmed by the curse surrounding this place. Its influence has twisted my call and given you false visions of this Maid of Ice of which you speak. The Maid of Ice is the name that was given to my glaivebond, Sable. I do not know how she appeared to you in that vision, but the true Sable is long gone. Once you take me into your hand I will help you see through the phantoms and falsehoods. It may be difficult for you, but you must trust me, young Tiryn. I have learned from my folly. I will not stray from the Mastersmith's path again. Take me up, and you shall see that faithfulness and honor pulse anew within my blade."

"The glaive spoke to you again, didn't it?" Kion said. "I can't tell you what you must do. I don't know if Rimewinter is corrupted or not. Even Kithian doesn't know. But remember, I'll be here for you, whatever Rimewinter turns out to be. I lost Mother—I won't lose you too."

Kion was right. She had to make the decision. Not Kion or anyone else. Not even Mother could have made it for her had she still been alive. And the words of Rimewinter had cut through the last vestiges of her doubts and fears. The Maid of Ice was not some tortured spirit or malevolent power which sought to end her life. The Maid was a legend that had come to represent the curse that held this land in eternal winter. What Tiryn had seen in that mirror was a sliver of truth that had penetrated her enigmatic vision. Tiryn was meant to be the new Maid of Ice. Not the frozen figure of legend, but a swordspeaker who would once more wield the glaive known as Rimewinter.

Tiryn stepped before Kion and put out her hand.

The twins drew their knives, their faces gray with dread. Zinder's head hung low. "Dear little Tiryn? A swordspeaker? What's the world coming to?"

"No matter what happens, remember that I love you," Kion said.

"I love you, too."

Tiryn removed her glove. She wanted—and knew somehow that she needed—to touch the metal with her hand, however cold it might be.

Kion let the battered weapon fall into her hand. And everything changed.

A shimmering blue light fell from the hole above. It hummed throughout the chamber, engulfing the walls, the floor, and everything in between. It splintered off the faces of her companions, zigzagging in a latticework of cold blue beams, wrapping them in a web of angular light. A vibration thrummed inside Tiryn, rising up from the floor through her feet, coursing through her heart, and erupting at last from her throat in a crescendo of light and sound, pouring toward the ceiling and back through the opening above, returning to the sky from whence it came. And just as quickly as it manifested itself, the vibrant shower of incandescent blue faded and silence took hold of the room once more.

The weapon in Tiryn's hand was wholly different from the one Kion had given her. It had shed its weathered shell and now shone bright and masterful, as if it had been fashioned that very hour. The narrow blade gleamed with a sharp, faintly aquatic tint to the metal. Three glorious gems exuded an ethereal blue glow. Two of them were fanned out to form part of the guard and give it a wing-like shape. The third stone served as the pommel, deep aqua in color like the others, with large facets. The grip had dark, smooth leather that fit naturally in her hand. And where the hilt met the blade, a metallic snowflake of ingenious design pulsed with the same inner light as the gems.

The deadly chill of the chamber vanished for Tiryn. The only cold now came from the handle of the blade itself, but it was a coolness that was not at all unpleasant. It was like the touch of fresh water on the skin after waking from a night of wearying dreams.

The beauty and quality of the blade were undeniable, even to Tiryn's untrained eye. But its appearance mattered less than the spirit bound within. And even before the glaive ever spoke a word, Tiryn sensed the deep, contemplative character of the blade she held in her hand.

"I am Nurien the Wanderer, least of all the Mastersmith's glaives, but in those songs that have not forgotten me, I am also known as Rimewinter."

The voice was crisp and fresh and no longer blasted Tiryn with chilling force. Best of all, it had that quality she cherished most in any that she had ever called friends, that of humility. Tiryn did not make friends easily, nor did she open her heart to just anyone, yet even now the blade had captured her affections in a way few others had, and she knew that bond would only deepen with time. A tear streaked down her cheek. What would Mother have said if she could see her now? Her daughter, the swordspeaker.

"Rimewinter, my name is Kion, and I am the glaivebond of Truesilver. We greet you in the hope of friendship."

"Indeed, Nurien, I hope that despite the dark paths that have led you here, wisdom has brought you back to the light. I do not know what led you to lock this whole isle and the coast beyond it in winter for a full age of men, but if you would be true once more and walk by the light of the great forge, know that I stand willing to forgive you, and more than that, to name you Friend, as of old, when we served our master together in the dark days of the Shattering."

Tiryn held up the dagger in a fresh wave of wonder. "Wait, Kion, you can hear Rimewinter? And did I—did I just hear Truesilver's voice?" It was even more warm and sage-like than she had imagined. This was something she had not expected.

"You did, Tiryn. You are a swordspeaker now. And I can't help but think it's going to be a lot harder for me to protect you. Or perhaps you won't need any protecting at all. We'll see. But either way, it was your decision to make, and though it may still be too early to say, I think you made the right one."

"I will do my best to prove that to all of you. I hope that with time I can win your trust, Kion, and regain yours, Kithian. My gifts and wisdom I pledge to your cause. The future is never certain, but I look to it now with hope."

Chapter 43

A FROZEN TOMB

An endless flood of questions poured through Tiryn's mind. Why was Rimewinter here? What gifts did it have? How had it brought about this curse of endless winter? And what was Nurien's relationship to Kithian?—for clearly they knew each other. But all of that would have to wait. Another rumble stirred off in the distance and a wave of ice cascaded from above, mixed with large splashes of water from the melting surfaces.

"My power over this land has ended. The long winter is no more," Nurien said.

"The curse is over? So summer will return?" Kion said.

"Yes, and it will come swiftly."

Trik and Trak stared at Kion, their mouths unable to form any words for several long moments. A light danced on their faces as if the sliver of sun streaming down from above was the first drop of a great sea of warmth and goodness to come. The joy of it all leapt into Tiryn's heart as well. No more winter. No more cold. No more curse. A longing to see the land renewed welled up within her.

"So Whitewind will be free of the snow and ice?" The words burst from Trik's lips at last.

"And the streams will melt and we won't have to bundle up all the time and we'll be able to plant gardens and feel the warmth of the sun on our faces?" Trak said.

"Yes, the land will be restored. Which I'm sure will be a sight to behold. But if we don't find a way out of here we'll never see it. The melting ice is causing some of the tunnels to collapse," Kion said.

"It is more than just the melting ice," Kithian said. *"The rock itself has also been weakened."*

"All the more reason for us to leave this place before it comes crashing down around us," Kion said.

"Wait, does all this mean that Rimewinter isn't corrupted?" Trak said.

"And that we don't have to fight Tiryn?" Trik said tentatively. Both twins lowered their knives ever so slightly.

"As far as Truesilver and I can tell, Rimewinter is to be trusted for now. The ending of the curse is an important sign. A corrupted glaive would not so easily surrender its power. And beyond that, I think I would know my sister well enough to tell if the glaive was trying to influence her toward evil ends."

Trik puffed away a lock of hair that had fallen over his eyes. "Well, am I glad to hear that! Fighting Tiryn would have scarred me for life."

"Same with me," Trak said.

"You realize what this means, Trak? It means that even though we're not swordspeakers—which is an awful knock for sure—we got to see the birth of the newest swordspeaker of all!"

"You're right, Trik. That's not so bad when you think about it, is it?"

Trik hooked his brother's elbow in his and together they did a little jig, nearly taking a spill on the ice in their excitement.

"Just think, when we get back home, this will be added to the legends—and our names will be part of it." Trak swept his arms before him and plunged his voice as deep as it would go. "'And they were led to the glaive by their faithful guides, Trik and Trak,' it will say."

"Yes! Uncle Chaw is never going to believe we saw the awakening of one of the Mastersmith's glaives. That blue light, the way it zinged about the room. I'll never forget it. Thank you,

Tiryn, for allowing us to come on this journey with you. I don't think I'll ever be the same after what I've seen."

A snapping sound cut short the twins' dreams of glory. More icicles rained down from above and sprayed the ground on the far side of the cavern.

"If we don't leave this place soon," Zinder said, "the legends will say that Trik and Trak led the swordspeakers to their deaths! I'd love to stay and get a better look at Tiryn's dagger and hear the tale of how this wintry curse came to be—I'm all for uncovering ancient mysteries—when it's not freezing cold and the roof isn't falling down around my head and the ground melting under my feet—but just now, I'd like to find some place where I'm not in danger of getting my nose clipped off by spears of ice. It's no use crafting legends if you can't live to tell about them."

"Let's hope there's an exit out of here besides the one above," Kion said. "No rope in the Four Wards could reach that and no man or beast could climb something that steep, even if it wasn't melting and threatening to come apart."

"There is a tunnel in the far corner," Nurien said. *"Or at least there was when I came here long ago. But before you seek it, we must gather the other glaives that are here. They were no doubt buried in the icefall along with me."*

"There are other glaives here as well?" Kithian said, his voice full of wonder, yet also troubled.

"Yes. This icy prison was not formed with my power alone. Here lie Gorven and Barazain, brothers in arms, as well as the great Veleros, stout Kelgrist, and Falskein the Keen. There were six of us in all who crafted Shadowriven's bonds."

The light from Truesilver's blade lost some of its luster. Tiryn took it as a sign of grief or foreboding, perhaps both. For Tiryn's part, the news was so unexpected she hardly knew what to think. There were five other glaives in this cave? Just how many glaives had the Mastersmith made?

"What's wrong, Kithian?" Kion said. "Why does this news

trouble you? If there are more glaives here, shouldn't we seek them out as Nurien says?"

"What? More glaives?" Trik said, hope rekindling in both his and his brother's faces that they might have the chance to become swordspeakers after all.

"It is not the presence of the glaives that troubles me. It is the knowledge of what was done in bringing them here. I did not see it before only because such a thing was unthinkable to me. For a curse of such lasting power could only have been forged by that which is forbidden: drawing upon the lifeblood of those we are sworn to protect: our glaivebonds. Nurien, tell me this was not so."

The subtle blue glow from Rimewinter's gems wavered. *"I make no defense of our decision to forge the curse, for none can be made. But you should know that no glaivebond came here unwillingly."*

"Shared folly is no better than folly achieved alone. Tell me, Nurien, what vile lie drove you to forsake your loyalty to the Mastersmith and sacrifice your glaivebonds in this way? I have my suspicions, but I wish to hear it from you."

"Oh, Kithian, folly it was indeed. For I foresaw that Malix the Darksheened had taken refuge in this place after his defeat in the War of the Glaives. And so Sable and the other swordspeakers fled Gilding in secret and confronted him here. Through the deaths of our dear glaivebonds we caused this icy cage to rise up to entomb him for all of time."

"But you failed. Shadowriven is not here or I would have sensed him. For though a dormant glaive would have gone unnoticed, the corrupted ones may resist the Mastersmith's sleep if they so choose and Malix would not have lain idle, imprisoned though he was."

Nurien's voice grew wispy and weak. *"As always, your instincts prove true. Yes, I failed. I believed that this was the only way to stop him, but his power is beyond even what I foresaw. When I awoke, Malix was already gone. That crack in the wall and Gairom's vacant hand tell me that he has been freed. Though the curse kept him bound for a time, Shadowriven's evil is loosed once more upon the world."*

Kithian's citrines flashed with a strangely ominous light, as if in warning or even anger. *"So it is not Talinyon who lies entombed in the ice? But that may be addressed some other time. Malix has found yet another thrall now. And if that one is Vayd, the Four Wards are in greater peril than ever before. For there are only two swordspeakers now to oppose him and in the War of the Shattering it took far more to overcome him and even then we could not fully defeat him. I fear a grim path lies before us. Of all the dark tidings that have come this day, this is the most dire. And yet, surely for this reason the Mastersmith has stirred us from our slumber in this black hour."*

Nearby, perhaps in the cave of the river from which they'd just come, a great crash sounded. A shudder broke through the floor.

"We must hurry," Zinder said.

"Kithian, should we take time to search for the glaives?" Kion said. "Is it worth the risk?"

"If we do not save them now, they may be lost forever, or fall into evil hands," Nurien said.

"Yes, it must be done. Let us move swiftly."

Truesilver's fire flared brightly once more. Nurien directed Kion to an icy heap near where Rimewinter had been found. The glaivefire made quick work of it and soon the blade went cold again and Kion called the others to see the weapons of which Rimewinter had spoken. A small arsenal lay scattered about in a half-circle, all gray and worn, in pools of glistening water, chunks of blue ice floating within. None of them were remarkable. All were in stages of disrepair and decay. Had Nurien not told them that these were glaives, there would have been no reason to recover them.

Each weapon was of a different sort: a great claymore, tall as Kion; a large morningstar; a thick, metal-shod staff; and a curious double-bladed sword. Most of these weapons Tiryn had only ever read about in books. The weapons, though, were not what most caught her attention. For also inside the melted pools lay six skeletons, each resting near one of the weapons, some still holding them in their bony hands. If the weapons were battered and half-broken, the bones were as clean and white as if they'd been coated in paint.

"The glaivebonds," Kion said, his brow darkening.

"It seems wrong to look at the bones of great heroes like that," Trak said. Both brothers cast their eyes at their feet.

"And yet, isn't it odd that the ice did not preserve their bodies the way it did that figure in the wall?" Zinder wondered aloud.

"The curse consumed their flesh to the uttermost," Nurien said, sharp sadness marring her voice.

"I have seen what Malix did to Talinyon in drawing upon his lifeblood, but this is beyond anything which even he has done. Nurien, how could you?"

"I can give no worthy answer for what I have done. My folly is laid bare before you. Sable's sacrifice was in vain. How bitter to know that I, as her glaive, was the one to lead her astray." The light from Rimewinter's blade ebbed to a feeble glow. The pain of the glaive's shame and regret stabbed Tiryn's heart as if it were her own. And she saw that Nurien's loss was in many ways greater than her own. For Tiryn, at least, had not been the cause of her mother's death, but Nurien had sacrificed all these people and watched them die.

A heavy silence fell upon those gathered to witness the open grave. Truesilver's ominous words about "drawing on the lifeblood" haunted Tiryn. It was hard to fathom how her own weapon could have done this to its former glaivebond. And yet, Nurien's sorrow was so deep that Tiryn knew she would never stray down that path again.

"What is past may not be undone," Kithian said wearily, the words coming hard-fought. *"We have had far too much sorrow for one day. Gather the weapons and let us flee this place. And yet, Nurien, you spoke of five other glaives, and but four are scattered here."*

"You are right. Gorven is missing. This is troubling."

More ice and frozen rain hurtled to the ground, spurring them to swiftly gather the weapons from the pools of icy water.

"Let us hope Vayd did not take a second glaive with him when he came for Malix."

"Wait—I have found Gorven. But there is something else as well," Nurien said. *"There, beneath the rubble and ice near Gairom—someone is buried within, and the hammer with him. My thoughts were so fixed upon the other glaives I did not notice it before."*

Another body. The death and the sorrow of this place would not let Tiryn go. How she longed to be free of it. But now a terrible premonition rose up inside her.

"How recently did he die?" she said.

"Not long ago. Less than a day. The body is not encased in ice like the others and shows no sign of decay."

"Is it…one of the Frindalians?"

"Yes, judging by the appearance, he is of that people. You are thinking it is someone you know," Nurien said. Already the connection between Tiryn and her glaive flowed as naturally as one thought to another. Nurien could sense the foreboding welling up inside of Tiryn as easily as Tiryn had felt Nurien's sorrow at the fate of the glaivebonds. *"Would you like me to show you to be sure?"*

"Wait, are you thinking that it's—" Kion said.

"Dunwik. Oh no, it couldn't be…" Zinder said as fallen ice battered the massive pile of debris where every eye was fixed.

"I hope with all my heart that it isn't," Tiryn said.

"I will melt the ice and we'll find out. We have to retrieve the glaive anyway."

"Yes…" Tiryn held the dagger up before her, cradling the razor sharp blade in her gloves. "Only…Nurien, you said that you could show me what lies in the ice. How is that possible when Truesilver said he can't see through the ice here?"

"No other glaive may penetrate my ice, just as I cannot see through Truesilver's fire. But my sight penetrates my own creations. I could share it with you if you wish," Nurien said.

"I would like to see what you see, if only for a moment. Though I fear it will crush my heart to see what lies beneath that ice."

As Kion made his way to the enormous deluge of ice near the great bulge, Nurien said quietly to Tiryn, *"See what lies beneath, dear one."* And then the room was gone. Only it wasn't. It was still there but in a different way. No longer did she see it through her own eyes, but from somewhere above. She could see through the ice and even the rock. Little crystals and irregularities sparkled inside the walls and floor, as if the night sky were trapped within. But stranger still were the forms of the others surrounding her. The outlines of their bodies gave off a subtle light so that looking at them was like looking at a living drawing. She even saw herself in the drawing and thought how small and frail she looked and wondered if the others could see her fear and the way her outline trembled. She saw everything inside the cavern at the same time with unblinking vision. That meant the piles of debris, and more importantly, what was in them. Nothing was hidden from Nurien's sight and Tiryn could not look away. She could not avoid the confirmation of her dark premonitions. For the body of Dunwik lay inside the mound of fallen destruction just as she had feared.

The hopeless anguish of death battered her emotions afresh. The noble-hearted warrior lay in a way he never would have in life. His body was twisted and broken, his stern but honest eyes forever closed in death. Was it not enough to bear her mother's loss? Why did the paths of so many have to end in these cruel caves?

"It's him, isn't it?" Trak said. "You can see Dunwik in there, can't you?"

Tiryn's chin fell to her chest in answer.

"No, no, no..." Trik folded onto his knees and dropped the glaives he had gathered. His head shook in vain denial and the cavern echoed with his tender sobs.

Nothing could keep Tiryn's own tears from flowing as well.

Why did Dunwik come into this cave? Why didn't he stay with Zinder? Better yet, why did he come to this cursed island at all? He had a wife, children. He should have been at home with them, asleep and safe in his own bed. Why had they agreed to let him come? How would they tell his family that their brave and honorable husband and father was gone? Tiryn knew what such loss felt like. She would not wish it on the cruelest person in all the world. She curled into Kion's arms, her head and heart swimming with grief. Nurien's sight faded mercifully and Tiryn could at last shut her eyes to the harsh and unforgiving sight.

"I can't believe he's gone," Kion said, his voice hollow and lost.

"I told him not to go. To wait until we found you first," Zinder mumbled bitterly.

But the falling ice took no pity upon their sadness. A great lance of it plunged and shattered into the ground near Zinder. If not for his nynnian quickness, he surely would have been speared.

"It is a hard loss," Kithian said. His voice was solemn, yet unshaken, recalling the others back from their sorrow. *"But we have tarried far too long."* A thunderous explosion of ice came down upon the entrance, blocking the path from which they'd come and sending the companions scattering. *"Recover the hammer and let us be gone."*

The room was swept into a frenzy of motion. The sudden activity blunted their grief, as did the growing danger from the disintegrating cave. Truesilver's glaivefire winnowed down the ice, but it took far longer than anyone would have liked and they had to endure several more icefalls before the glaive was revealed. The red fire quenched at last and the twins came and together excavated the massive weapon. Though it was decayed like the others, the large, rust-encrusted head was far too large for the average man to wield. Even with the two of them hauling it out they had a hard time of it, for Dunwik's body lay beside it and they cried more tears every time they looked at him. Tiryn could not bring herself to look again for she felt she might collapse from grief and they would have to drag her from the cave. Once the hammer was free, Zinder and Kion did their best to cover Dunwik's body back up with some of the surrounding shards of ice.

With more and more debris falling by the moment, they quickly divided up the weapons. The hammer was given to Trak to carry since he was the strongest besides Kion, and Kion would need to hold Truesilver to light their way. Zinder took the mace, Trik the claymore, Kion held the staff in his free hand, and Tiryn carried the double-bladed sword. She found the weapon unwieldy and would have preferred to hold only Rimewinter, but the dagger could be tied to the strap across her chest, and she had no similar way to stow the larger weapon.

Nurien's tunnel was just where she had said it would be off in the corner, though blocked by a large pile of ice shards. After laying into it with Truesilver's flickering fire, a way was cleared into an open passageway. With one last glimpse at the unraveling chamber, which had become little more than a frozen tomb in Tiryn's mind, the party fled at last. But Tiryn's thoughts tarried there for some time, fixed upon the bitter mound of ice beneath which was buried their dear friend and guide, Dunwik, watcher of Whitewind.

Chapter 44

THE STRENGTH OF ICE AND SNOW

Truesilver's amber light guided them from the front of the line and Rimewinter's powder blue radiated at the back from Tiryn's chest like a frozen heart. Melting ice coated the whole of the passage, forcing the companions to pass over slick, wet ground and slowing their progress. Tiryn dreaded what would happen if she fell while holding the strange two-bladed sword she carried. The metal was blunt and dull enough, but it was jagged in places and far from harmless.

The path turned in many directions, rising and falling many times. But the way was clear. The most difficult stretch came when they passed through a cavern with a large pool on one side. Part of it was still frozen, but in many places, great chunks of ice fell through the thawing surface and opened gaping holes. They had to rush through the chamber, dodging the icy chunks raining down around them. A fist-sized spike grazed Trik in the head and he staggered to the side. He might have stumbled into the pool had Trak not turned back to right his steps and spur him on.

All the while, great rumbling and crashing sounds echoed before and behind them. Tiryn ran as if in a dream, one more bewildering and terrifying even than her visions. For at least those might not come to pass, but this, her present path, was one she could not escape.

Through terror and uncertainty they fled. Stumbling through the falling ice and slippery floors they came at last to the end of the passage. Here Tiryn's hopes dimmed, along with the others', when she saw where all their trouble and torment had led. Another great blue mound barricaded their way, rising from floor to ceiling. It sloped toward them so that it did not fully block the passage until a good twenty paces in, but they would be forced to slow down and lose more time. At first, Tiryn took the blockage for ice, but as they drew close it became clear that it was actually something else.

"Snow!" Trak said. "That must mean we're close to the outside."

"Or that there's another hole in the ceiling like there was back in Rimewinter's cave," Kion said.

"Whichever the case," Zinder said, "it means that we'll be through soon enough. Truesilver can turn snow to water quicker than a nyn can swing a hammer."

"Let's hope this is the end. Truesilver's oil is almost spent," Kion said. He stalked forward, the snow shrinking into a small river before the blade's red blaze. Not long after, he pressed through the blockage and gave a cry of triumph. "Kithian says he can see the other side—and it's open sky!"

Cheers rose down the tunnel at the news. Kion forged through the snow faster than ever, not bothering to avoid the water streaming past him and soaking his sleeves and pants. The packed blue snow dissolved into a gushing flow. Within moments, daylight—precious daylight—pierced the snow, clear and bright and beautiful, and growing stronger by the moment.

They rushed after Kion as he charged into sweet fresh air under a glowing white sun. Though the sun was shrouded by clouds, its rays were more than enough to lift their spirits and warm their hearts. The great light which had so long eluded them had not abandoned them while they toiled among the ice and rock of the constricting mines. All that death and darkness lay behind them. Before them was a world of endless light and freedom to move in any direction they chose. How much more welcoming was this wintry world than when they had left it. What had once seemed harsh and brutal and uninviting now offered hope and comfort and life. It was not nearly as cold as Tiryn remembered it. The more she looked around and thought about it, it *was* warmer than before. The place they had come out was very near to where they had fallen in, but the snow was no longer crusted and hard. It sagged in places, and the ice glistened in the sun.

Rimewinter's words crashed in Tiryn's ears like broken glass, shattering the wonder and the peace of the moment.

"Kion, watch out!"

An image flashed through Tiryn's thoughts even as the glaive's words ripped through her hearing. She saw a torrent of ice and scales burst from beneath Kion and snatch him away in its frozen maw.

Tiryn screamed. But there was nothing she could do to stop the vision from coming true. As Kion turned back with a questioning look, a wave of serpentine flesh swept up from under the snow and he was gone.

A moment of motionless shock followed, as the giant white body rushed past them. But before it could go completely back under, the twins came to themselves, dropped their glaives, and rushed past Zinder, who was unstrapping and arming his crossbow. Trik and Trak pulled out their tiny knives in a foolhardy attempt to wound the giant snake as its body rushed sideways past the entrance. Though it seemed like miles of milky flesh now plunged into the snow, the twins failed to reach it before it disappeared into a yawning hole which instantly collapsed, leaving only a shallow depression to show that the snake had been anything more than a horrible dream.

"Run, Tiryn, your brother needs you." Nurien's voice had the ferocity of a howling wind. The force of it catapulted Tiryn across open snow, running she knew not where.

"What should I do, Nurien? Where is he?"

"Remove the gem from my pommel."

Tiryn's mind went numb. What did that have to do with finding Kion?

"Listen to me now. Remove the gem." Nurien's words came with even greater force, scattering Tiryn's questions and confusion. Her hands moved as if they had a will of their own. She had seen Kion fill Truesilver's pommel with oil. Rimewinter must be asking her to do the same thing.

"But I have no oil," she said, quickly unscrewing the gem and seeing the hollow space in the handle.

"I do not need oil. Fill my handle with water."

"Look, lads, there's Truesilver's fire in the snow. Kion must be close by." Zinder pointed with his crossbow at a red patch upon the blue frost, as if the ground had turned to molten rock beneath the powdery surface.

"Water. Right," Tiryn said, wrenching her waterskin off her shoulder. Whatever it took to save Kion. She flipped it upside down over the dagger's handle. The water poured over her hands, much of it lost, before she cast the skin aside and replaced the pommel gem.

The head of the great snake reared up out of the ground. The black eyes glared like open pits, no light glimmering within. Icy fangs and pallid skin lined its gaping jaws. Zinder lodged a bolt just below the head. The snake gave a screeching hiss and returned the attack with a barrage of its own. Icy globules hurtled from its cavernous throat and Zinder came out the worse in the exchange. Though he dodged several of them, and others missed him entirely, all it took was one to bring him down. A globe of ice caught his legs like a spider webbing a fly. Zinder toppled face down in the snow, his crossbow flying from his hand. The frozen ball bound his legs in icy bonds. With its opponent no longer able to move, the snowwinder pelted him with three more globes in rapid succession, encasing Zinder in ice as fully as the dead man from Rimewinter's cavern.

"Zinder!" Trak shouted. Trik's inarticulate cry followed.

"Foul, dim-touched creature of Malix's twisting. Your gifts are but a mockery of my own," Nurien said.

"Rise up, Kion," Kithian urged. *"Call me to your hand. The others need you."*

If Kion could hear, he gave no reply. Was he buried inside the serpent? Had he fallen into another icy hollow?

Tiryn cried out across the barren snow, adding her voice to Kithian's call. "Kion! Are you there? Can you hear me?"

"He lies near me in the snow," Kithian said. *"The snake cast him from its mouth shortly after it swallowed him up. It could not suffer the glaivefire. Follow the fire and you will find him."*

"We must deal with the snake first or we will all die here," Nurien said.

"Very well, only make haste; my fire keeps the creature at bay, but it wanes by the moment."

Tiryn wanted to challenge Rimewinter's decision. She wanted to follow Kithian's command and protect her brother, but Zinder was in even greater danger and as long as the snake was free none of them would be safe. She tossed her pack to the ground and plowed into the knee-deep snow.

The snake knifed through the melting snow toward Zinder, its supple spine undulating through the sea of blue, while the twins rushed to his defense. As Trik tried hopelessly to chip away at the ice encasing Zinder, Trak picked up the discarded crossbow and let a bolt fly. It went so wide it would have missed a mountain, but it drew the snake's ire. Trak took two icy balls to the chest in return and fell backward onto the ground.

"Trak, get up!" Trik scrambled over to his brother, but an ice globe to the shoulder knocked him prone. In a matter of moments, the snake had covered the pinned brothers in the same icy encasements trapping Zinder.

"The twins. We've got to free them," Tiryn said.

"The snake first. We can do nothing while it rages. Give the command of 'glaivefrost' and point me at the beast." Nurien's words rushed through Tiryn's ears.

Tiryn struggled to swallow back a tightness in her throat. It all struck her as madness. Everyone had fallen and she was listening to voices on the wind. A snake that ran half the length of the Commons was careening toward her and all she had was a small dagger to fight it. But her connection to Rimewinter made her trust in the blade's word. Nurien knew what to do. Tiryn just had to listen and follow as best she could.

"Glaivefrost."

Tiryn rushed forward, right arm extended. A surge of sky-blue ice burst from the dagger's guards and flung itself through the air. The brilliant blue cone crashed into the snake's open jaws. Upon impact it shattered and spread, cutting off the snake's airway. The creature let out a gurgling hiss and flailed about, gagging and sputtering—but only for a moment. With its massive jaws, it crushed the ice and spat it out in a spray of blue shards.

Tiryn kept the dagger before her as she pushed forward through the snow. More and more ice erupted from the blade. The icy darts struck the snake's neck three times, once in its eye, and twice farther down its body. At each place it spread, forming icy shackles which sought to encase the creature in the same way that its ice had bound Zinder and the twins. But the monstrous snake was too large and too accustomed to life in the cold to be held for long. It broke the bonds almost as soon as they formed.

"More. Faster," Nurien said.

Tiryn thrust again. And again. And again. She stabbed the air, filling it with an icy assault. None of the darts landed any serious blow, but the cumulative effect took its toll. The creature's head was soon wrapped in a glittering blue prison. The snake collapsed from the sheer weight of it. It banged its head against the ground in an effort to break free, but the slushy snow blunted its efforts. Suddenly, the snake disappeared, burrowing into the ground. Tiryn, who was beginning to grasp the use of her blade, dared to hope that she might have defeated the giant beast.

"Well done, Tiryn," Kithian said.

Kion rose up out of the snow near the fire. He looked around in bewilderment for a moment, then, seeing Tiryn, he staggered toward her.

"Truesilver, to me," he called out. The blade lifted from the snow and flew to his hand, though its flames died in mid-flight as if snuffed out by some wind. Kion veered back towards the tunnel, shaken and weak. "The fire is gone. But the snake may return. I dropped my pack near the tunnel. I'll get more oil and free the others. You see to it that—"

The great white body of their enemy ejected out of the snow. With the fire gone, the snowwinder knew no fear, for nothing had ever come close to testing it before. Rimewinter's ice had confused it more than anything, for it had never suffered its own attack. But the creature, finding the hard ground below and smashing its head against the stone, had sundered the frozen chains by which Rimewinter had sought to bind it. As it reared up, it took them by surprise. Before Tiryn could react, a hail of icy globes had struck her. The ice landed with the force of bricks, knocking her clean off her feet and spreading swiftly over her body.

"Nurien, what do I do?" Tiryn said. They were the last words she spoke before the ice enveloped her head. She lay in the snow, enveloped in an icy coffin, like Zinder and the others. She wondered how long she could hold her breath.

"Tiryn, hold on! I'm coming!" Kion shouted, but his voice was muffled by the icy barrier surrounding her.

"Stay calm, my child," Nurien said coolly. *"I may not be the strongest of the Mastersmith's glaives, but no power of ice and cold can stand against those under my protection."* Even as she spoke, vibrations crackled through the ice. Shards flaked away and the thick casing surrounding Tiryn's head splintered in two. Cold air rushed into her lungs. It stung bitterly, but the relief of it far surpassed the pain.

"The creature is coming for us. I can feel it tunneling through the snow. My darts are not able to subdue it, so we will use the very snow

against it. Lie still a moment. It is almost upon us. When I tell you, plunge my blade into the snow, as close to its body as you can."

The last of her icy bonds fell away, but Tiryn remained where she was. The snow shifted around her and sounds as of a great rush of water came upon her, growing louder and more terrible by the moment.

"Now! Plunge me into the snow!"

The great bulk of the snowwinder was upon her, barreling down swift as an avalanche. Tiryn flung herself to the side, burying Rimewinter deep in the snow. The snow popped and shook all along the length of the great snake's body as it hurtled past. The blue powder hardened so quickly, the beast could not escape. The white form disappeared beneath a prison of opaque ice. A long, wavy shaft of blue, twice as thick as the snake, had frozen it in the snow. And this time, it could not thrash about to free itself, but lay completely still.

"Will it die inside?" Tiryn said.

"I do not know. If it is accustomed to burrowing, perhaps it can survive without air for some time. The air is growing warmer by the hour, but even so, that ice will take a day or more to thin to the point where the creature can get free. We will be long gone by then."

"Fire and ice! That was something, Tiryn," Kion said. He had pushed his way across the snowy field beyond where Zinder and the twins lay near the tunnel entrance. Tiryn found her feet and hurried after him, as swiftly as the deep, half-melted snow would allow.

"I hardly know what happened. It was all Rimewinter's doing," Tiryn said. "But it won't mean a thing if we can't save Zinder and the twins." She kicked up clumps of snow, her arms windmilling with graceless abandon until she reached Kion's side.

Kion had just finished refilling Truesilver's handle with the last bit of oil from a flask. "Stand back. I'll free them from the ice. I only hope they don't get burned."

"Wait, Kion. We do not need fire to free your friends," Nurien said. *"Hold my blade against the ice and I will break it."*

Tiryn stared at her blade a moment, failing to grasp the meaning of Nurien's words. How could she…Ah! She remembered the way Nurien had cracked the snowwinder's ice around her. She ran to Zinder, slapping the slender blade against the outer coating. The cloudy shell surrounding him shattered to pieces. Zinder took in a great heaving breath of air, sputtering and gasping until he could fully recover. She hurried over to Trik and Trak and moments later they both emerged with the same struggle for air. All of the wheezing and croaking sounded like a herd of dying cattle.

"Remarkable. So you can break the ice as well as create it," Kion said. "Is everyone all right?"

The newly unfrozen companions offered weak waves in reply.

"Saved us you did, Tiryn…" Zinder muttered between gulps of air when at last he could speak. "All by yourself from the looks of it. Gave the snake a sip of its own tea, I'd say. That ice block around the creature is your handiwork, yes?"

Tiryn brushed off his words. "I'm just glad you're all alive."

"Just had the wind knocked out of me…Which is hard to do in a place as windy as this…but we nyn are known for our unusual talents."

"I thought we were gone for sure," Trik said, lying face up in the snow, still too exhausted to rise. "I kept thinking, 'so this is what all those frozen rabbits Scriff brought us felt like before they died.' What an awful way to go."

"I don't think I could have held my breath much longer," Trak said, managing to raise himself up on his elbows.

"Thank you, Tiryn," they both said together.

Kion took Tiryn's hand. His grip was weaker than usual and he had a slight tremble in his fingers. He had a gash on his cheek and his coat was ripped in places but it looked as if the thick furs and Truesilver's fire had largely protected him from the snake's attack.

"Yes, thank you, Tiryn. And thank you, Nurien. You more than proved yourself today."

"It was good to see your glaivefrost come to our aid, as of old," Kithian said.

Nurien said nothing, but the blue light shining from the dagger glowed with greater brightness than before. Tiryn took no small amount of pride in hearing her glaive praised. It had been all Rimewinter's doing, after all. Tiryn had simply followed what she said. Tiryn was good at following. That was something she could do. She and Kion might both be swordspeakers, but his glaive was as different from hers as she was from him. She had never wanted to walk the same path as her brother, especially not when it came to weapons and fighting, but things rarely turn out as we plan. What lay ahead for her on this path she could not say, but she had walked uncertain paths to reach this place, and she would walk this one as best she could. They may have lost Mother on this long terrible journey, and that grief seemed now as if it would never heal, but Kion would not be running off to join the war without her now. For she had a glaive of her own, and she was swept up in this great conflict along with him, whether she wanted it or not. She had answered the swordspeaker's call, and because of that, and because of so much else that had happened on this cursed island, things would never be the same.

Chapter 45

WINTER'S END

The five companions stood staring at the solitary set of tracks in the melting snow. They would have turned back to Whitewind by now but for those troubling impressions. Kion had lost so much on this island: his mother, the brave watcher Dunwik, even Scriff had gone missing. He wanted nothing more than to escape from this isle of death. It mattered little that the ice and frost were in swift retreat. The curse of this place ran far deeper than the unnatural winter. The memories seared into his mind here would follow him all his days. He longed to be free of Tinesplitter Isle, but those large, booted prints kept him tethered to these terrible shores.

"So Vayd survived," Kithian said soberly. *"And there can be little doubt that he is now under Malix's sway."*

"Vayd has an iron will. I do not think he will easily be controlled."

"The path of corruption is subtle at first. The glaive will lure its thrall with promises of what it senses he wants, but all the while it will be working to accomplish its own purposes. And once a thrall gets a taste of the immense power a corrupted glaive has to offer, few are they that can turn back. Talinyon was once a noble man, the greatest and wisest of all children of the first-spark and all who came after. If Malix could break his will, how much more quickly will he break the will of one whose heart is already given over to its own dark designs?"

"We must follow him," Nurien said. Her voice came as a brisk breeze compared to Kithian's intense fire. Both rang with ageless wisdom, but of a different quality. Nurien's had a touch of

remorse to it, and inevitability, while Kithian's was born of the hope and belief that what was right was always best, no matter the cost. *"As great as Malix's power is, this Vayd you speak of has not been in possession of the axe for long. If we can catch him before Malix has the chance to draw him far into his web, we may prevent a second war of the glaives before it begins."*

"War has already begun. Even now Vayd's armies march freely across northern Inris. But I agree, we should do everything we can to stop Vayd before he rejoins the bulk of his forces on the mainland."

"Shadowriven's thrall is a leader in this war?"

"We shall tell you more on the way. We must strike while the trail is fresh."

"Kithian's right. We must find Vayd. We may never have another chance like this."

"That may be so, but that doesn't mean I have to like it," Zinder said. "You only just bested him last time when he *didn't* have one of these fantastic talking weapons at his side. I shudder to think what it will take to bring him down now that he has his own."

"You're forgetting Rimewinter," Kion said.

Tiryn shivered at his words, but kept her thoughts to herself. Though Kion was loathe to bring his sister into danger, he feared he might not be able to defeat Vayd without the help of her glaive. From what he had seen, Rimewinter's ice could be used from a distance, so perhaps he could keep Tiryn out of harm's way. "But we have to find him first, and that may prove even more difficult than defeating him. Haukmarn can move overland at tremendous speed when they want to."

"If only we had Smokewind and Cyprian," Tiryn said in a thin voice.

There was nothing to be done for it but to set out with all haste after the massive footprints. Vayd's strides were considerably longer than Kion's. From the long slide before each print, it was obvious that the haukmar had been running. And yet, from the degraded state of the tracks, it was also clear that he had passed this way several hours ago. There was little hope of catching a haukmarn on the run, but they pursued him all the same.

The tracks veered around the Standing Cliffs back toward Regnir and the main entrance to the mines. But when they rounded the bend to where both of those places should have come into view, all they could see was a vast mound of snow, sloping all the way up to the cliffs. Blue and silent and still, it rose like a newly fashioned ramp butting against the high walls of rock. It took several moments to register that Regnir was gone, buried under an avalanche so immense that it ran all the way out to shore. There it tapered out just before reaching two ice skimmers, the only things that had escaped the town's destruction. Curiously, though the entrance to the mines was also buried under mountains of snow, a large number of tracks appeared some distance away from the enormous slope, coming from the direction of where the opening to the mines would have been.

"Let's hope at least some of the prisoners survived," Zinder said.

"I'm sure they did," Trik said, though his voice had as much doubt as confidence.

The prints were a mixture of haukmar and human-sized boots, but there were shoe prints as well, confirming Zinder's hopes. Vayd's prints eventually joined the other sets, and yet his were still visible even amidst the great exodus, for they were far fresher.

Following the tracks, they arrived at what would have been the docks of Regnir. The tops of a few ill-fated structures poked through the blue snow like pebbles on the edge of a lake, the last sign of the entombed settlement. One of the blades of the two remaining skimmers had begun to sink into a wide crack in the icy harbor. Farther out, more cracks splintered the once smooth surface of the bay.

"There were six ships before," Zinder said. "If those folks

from the mine didn't shove off and sail away after the avalanche hit then I'm a talking snowman."

"Yet Vayd's prints stop here and head south along the shore," Kithian said.

"They left without him?" Kion said.

"They probably thought he died in the mines," Zinder said. "They only just made it out themselves from the looks of it."

"If Vayd didn't emerge until later, they may have given him up for dead," Kion said.

"And they couldn't stay in Regnir," Tiryn said.

"There is hope in this turn of events," came Nurien's windy voice. *"If Vayd is alone, we have a greater chance of defeating him."*

"Eh, what's that over there?" Zinder said, stepping forward.

"What do you see, Zinder?" Kion said.

"There, coming toward us along the shore, a speck of white. If my eyes haven't gone snow blind I'd say it's—"

"Scriff!" Trik shouted. He broke into a run, Trak not far behind, their pumping feet pulverizing the melting snow.

"Hold off, lads," Zinder said. "Let him come to us. The fellow's awfully close to the shore. Walking near the ice may be safe for a fox, but not for you."

Trik kept going despite the warning, but Trak caught him and yanked him by his hood. "Listen to Zinder, rabbit legs. I'm as anxious to see him as you are, but he'll be here soon enough."

Scriff came loping along, his light step skimming across the top of the snow. He raced into the arms of his masters, covering their faces with icy licks from his blue tongue, his eyes aglow with dazzling light, made all the more intense from the presence of two glaives. Tiryn snuck in her share of affection, praising the clever fox for escaping the snowwinder and for finding them again. Zinder sported a wide smile and gave the fox a good rubbing down. Kion held back to let the others have the fox to themselves, but the sight of that faithful creature was as heart-warming to him as anyone. For a moment at least, his looming grief withdrew back to the shadows where it belonged.

"Gim-dor-ren, you are a welcome sight indeed," Kithian said, his voice pleasant and expansive.

"Greetings, Kithian. I see you are joined by another of the Mastersmith's glaives."

"Yes, forgive my manners, this is Nurien."

Rimewinter and the fox exchanged greetings and Kion was once again pleased to find that he understood most all of what the creature said. Kithian had to fill in a few details, but Kion sensed that soon he would no longer need to be told exactly what the fox was saying.

"What adventures have you had while we were gone?" Kithian said.

"Much has happened since you fell through the ice," Scriff said in yips and barks, his fur shaking from joy and excitement. *"I went to find the climber and the small white-haired one and brought them back to where you fell. In truth, I did not have much hope I would ever see my masters again. I am glad that they have evaded death's shadow. I suppose I should not have doubted, for the Mastersmith's touch is upon them."*

"And yet you proved faithful even in the face of doubt. No more could be asked of you. But what of your travels after you left the two companions?"

"That is an even stranger tale. I wandered long, waiting for my masters' return. Then a great rumbling shook the hills, enough for the end of the world. I fled, fearing the shadow of death was upon me as well. The man den by the shore was swallowed whole as the cliffs came down on top of them. Once the sliding snow settled, I returned from hiding. I saw a pack of men making for the water vessels. I followed behind, but none of your pack were among their number. There were pale men and the tall, thick gray ones and many in fetters. They mounted the vessels and fled across the waters."

"I see. But was there another? A large one with a dark glaive who walked alone? Can you tell us of his fate?"

"Wise Kithian sees all. Yes, there was another who came after, holding a great sharp metal instrument that looked as if it could fell a

tree in a single blow. Darkness followed in that one's footsteps so that I withdrew and hid in fear. But not so far that I did not see him leave after a time and head along the shore. The signs of his passing are etched in the snow, so clear that even a cub could follow."

As Kion related Scriff's tale to the others a grim mood fell upon the company. Their pursuit had not ended, for Vayd was headed toward Whitewind. Kion yearned for that place now almost as much as his own home of Furrow. And if Vayd dared threaten it, Kion would do everything to ensure that Whitewind did not suffer the same fate.

"We travel on, then," Kion said. "Our road lies with Vayd. But we are made stronger now that Scriff is by our side again."

With each step along Vayd's trail, the curse of winter released Tinesplitter from its grip. Centuries of snow sank and crumbled along the shore and the sun shone clean and strong for the first time since Trik and Trak could remember. The wind no longer cut the eyes and pierced the skin, but drifted by with a fresh springtime scent. Though they could not yet be seen, aromas whispered that somewhere on the island, flowers had found their way to the new un-cursed light. By evening, they had unfastened their coats and cast off their caps and hoods. Summer was still far from taking hold, but the land was running swiftly into its embrace.

They left the trail at twilight to return to the snow cave, for it was close by and they needed to gather the sleds and the rest of their gear before the return to Whitewind. The roof had opened up and dissolved into puddles on the floor, dark mirrors where spark trails now played. But the supplies had been stowed on their sleds, which rested along the sides of the cave and so everything remained dry. Though lighter than they had been on the journey here, the sleds felt heavier than ever as they pulled them through the melting snow. Seeing the cave brought another kind of heaviness, for the weight of Dunwik's absence lay hard upon their hearts. He should have been with them, harnessed to his sled, but now it was given to Trak while Trik pulled the other. Kion made no show of false strength on this journey as he had before, for sorrow had sapped what little he had left and he did not bother to mask it. His mother's death and Dunwik's both lay in some way at his feet. All he could do was to keep placing one foot in front of the other and try to think of Vayd, to let his anger at the haukmar leader smother the swelling sadness, but he had little success.

"I miss them both, too, lad," Zinder said quietly as they set out from the cave. Good old Zinder. The grief was still too strong and fresh to pass, but it was a comfort to know he did not bear the burden alone.

Just past midnight, the trail ended and they were left staring at their defeat. Vayd's muddy tracks turned at last from the shore into the frozen lake, but they soon saw that not only did the prints fade to nothing, there was no way now to follow Vayd even if they hadn't. For though large sheets of ice still covered most of the bay, it was now too thin to safely travel across.

"How do you think he made it?" Kion said, staring into the flat, glistening gray expanse of the bay. The snow blanketing the ice had all but vanished. Here and there chinks had opened up in the flat surface, but none were big enough to suggest that Vayd might have fallen in.

"He must have come here when it was still solid enough to cross," Zinder said. He picked up a stone and skipped it out along the ice. It gave a hollow, unsettling sound. "There's no way we'll catch him now, if we can cross at all. By tomorrow we'll need a boat to make it or wings to cross without falling in. Unfortunately, there are no boats in sight and I left all my wings back in my shop."

"You have wings? What do they look like?" Trik said.

"He's joking, Trik," Kion said.

"Oh, well, but I bet he could make some if he tried. I hear nyn can make anything."

"Your confidence is flattering, but there are things even a nyn cannot make. Wings are one of them. Boats on the other hand I might manage. But even I can't make a boat without wood and I've not seen one tree in all this snow-blown island."

"We dare not cross the ice in the dark in any case," Kithian said. *"Though there is moonlight to spare, I do not trust the ice to bear our weight. Vayd has eluded us. I fear he may make landfall at Whitewind, if he has not already."*

"As great a warrior as he is, he is alone. I doubt he would last long against the kalvar and his watchers," Kion said, though knowing how he himself had stood against a whole company of haukmarn in Charring, it was more out of hope than true belief that he said it.

"The power of a fallen glaive is a terrible thing," Nurien said in a bitter voice. *"Malix is not limited to the use of a reagent to use his gifts. Even if we overtook him now, we would be hard-pressed to defeat him."*

"But if we can't cross the bay, we won't reach him anyway," Tiryn said. Of all of them, she was the most content to let the search for Vayd end. She had little desire to test her glaive against the haukmarn leader, but Kion did not see how they could just give up the search.

"Overtaking Vayd seems unlikely now," Nurien said. *"But we will cross the bay in the morning and see if we can pick up the trail on the other side. The ice will all be gone by dawn."*

"But you heard Zinder," Kion said. "We have no boat to carry us. Even if we went back to Regnir and took the skimmers, we're too few and too unskilled to man them."

"Perhaps a nyn cannot make a boat out of nothing, but there are other ways to cross water besides a boat."

"What do you have in mind, Nurien?" Tiryn said.

"In the morning you shall see."

. . .

The sun blazed keen and fresh the next day, bringing with it the final assurance that the unnatural winter and cold were but fleeting memories. With the resurgent sun, the ice had passed away, just as Rimewinter had said. Only small floating chunks remained. A great bluish-black sea had arisen to take its place. Now it was time to see what Rimewinter had in store.

"It's called an ice bridge," Nurien said. *"You used my ice to come here. It is only fitting that you use it to return."*

"How does it work? Can you make a bridge that spans the whole bay?" Kion said. Truesilver's fire could never stretch anything close to that far, but then again, water was Rimewinter's reagent and there was an endless supply of it before them.

"If Tiryn places me in the water with the pommel off, I can use my gift without end. I can create a pathway of glaivefrost for you to traverse the bay."

"You can do that? Truly?" Tiryn said. Kion delighted to see her eyes flash to life once again. The same bright spark had shone in his mother's eyes on countless occasions. But the memories turned quickly painful and so he cast them aside. His grief was still too near to dwell upon for long without pulling him under.

"Truly. There are many uses for ice in this world. I may not be as formidable in battle as the other glaives, but battles are not always won through feats of arms."

"Exactly." Zinder flung his arms in the air as if the words came as a great relief. "That's what I've always said. I think I'm going to like this dagger of yours, Tiryn. I do wonder, though, can it make ice cream? I'm not picky, you know, any flavor will do."

"Zinder!" Tiryn's lips showed the faint glimmerings of a smile. "You say the oddest things."

"I, for one, will be happy enough just to have an ice bridge," Kion said.

"Fine. I suppose the ice cream can wait until after we're on the other side." Zinder gave Kion a nudge.

The water ran dark and deep in the early morning light. Here and there little feathers of foam flickered upon the surface like the back of some enormous sleeping bird. Indeed, the great body undulated with life, brooding upon hidden thoughts and restless to break free of its bonds and reclaim the shore for its own. The five companions were mere specks against this vast unsearchable sea.

"I finally got to see the ocean," Tiryn said, the lapping water reflecting in her eyes. "It's more beautiful than I ever imagined. I don't know if I'll ever see it again, but if I don't, this once will have been enough." She locked arms with Kion, the wind rippling through her auburn hair. Kion knew she wanted to say more. "If only Mother could have been here to see it, too." That was what she longed to say. But some words are too costly for the heart to give away. A lone, cruel tear carved its way out from one of Kion's eyes, but he was quick to wipe his cheek dry.

"I think the ocean is just about the prettiest thing I've ever seen," Trik said. "And all the prettier for what lies across it."

"Home," Trak said. He walked over and knelt before Zinder.

"Zinder, before we start back, I would like to apologize for my brother and me, for thinking you were a sorcerer. It's plain to see that the legends got that wrong the same way they got the Maid of Ice wrong. I guess legends aren't always true on every point. I hope you'll forgive us for questioning your word."

Zinder lifted the boy up from the rocky shore. "No harm's done, lad. Though I do admit it would have been useful to have had some sort of magic these last few days. But whatever happened in those legends, these days us nyn have to earn our keep the old-fashioned way. Which is the best way, to my mind. 'Short cuts make for big mistakes,' as we say in Lowerwyn."

"Lowerwyn? Is that where you're from?" Trik said.

But Zinder pretended he didn't hear. Kion didn't know why he ever bothered mentioning the place if he was going to turn around and act like it didn't exist.

"Well, then," Kion said, anxious to be gone once and for all. "It's time we were off. Nurien and Tiryn, lead the way."

Tiryn removed one of her gloves and strode ankle-deep into the water and dipped the dagger in. She nearly slipped on the loose stones of the shore. Her arms flew out and she recovered in time to avoid a fall, though her cheeks wore cherry patches of chagrin for some time after. The air was still unseasonably cold, and near the water it was even colder, but she did not shake or shiver. Kion wondered at this at first, for Tiryn had always gotten a chill when her skin touched the streams of the Tors. Then he remembered that she was protected from the cold as long as she held her glaive, the same way he was protected from fire when holding Truesilver.

A thick plank of diamond-blue ice formed in front of her hand. It grew until it was wide enough for two people to walk abreast. After that, it shot off across the bay. Swift and smooth it ran, floating upon the waters, a shimmering path that soon stretched out of sight.

"It worked!" Trak said.

"Another tale to add to the legends," Trik said, putting his hand to his brow as he gazed out across the shining blue path.

"Nurien, this is wonderful," Tiryn said.

"I cannot extend the bridge across the whole bay at once. We will have to stop once we near the end of this span and extend it farther, but you should be able to travel a good distance on this first section."

"It is well crafted, Nurien," Kithian said. *"The Mastersmith would surely be pleased. It is good to have you back."*

"I am not deserving of your company, Kithian, but I am grateful to have it."

"Forgiveness does not demand worthiness. For then what would there be to forgive? It is enough that you have seen your folly and learned from it. Though I have not your gift of foresight, I believe we shall need you greatly in the coming days."

They struck out once again, pulling the sleds across the ice, though this time they had a fresh, salty breeze blowing in their faces and summer unfurling in splendor all around them. Shocks of white clouds drifted on lofty currents, majestic in size and ponderous in their lazy wanderings. A tapestry of light kissed the tops of gentle waves. And between the fresh light and the easy air and a good night's rest along the shore, Kion felt strength returning to the winter of his own body, though not his heart. Mother was still dead. The return of summer and the end of the curse could not change that. Her memory was a great hollow gaping inside of him. To stand on the edge of that lightless chasm was to risk the ground giving way and sliding into a bottomless nothing. The ache inside him would never know release. The shadow of his failure would hound his every waking moment, lurking, sniffing, howling along his trail. It had taken years to come to peace with his father's death, but this loss…he did not see how it would ever be mended.

But he could not afford to dwell on his own private grief. Shadowriven had returned. Kion stood now on the edge of another, even greater chasm, the one between him and his enemy. Though he still knew little of what it would mean for the Four Wards and the present war, listening to the way Kithian and Nurien spoke of the fallen glaive filled him with mounting dread. Zinder was right. Kion had bested Vayd in their first battle because of Truesilver's fire. Now that Vayd had a glaive of his own, it might be impossible to defeat him. And yet, what choice did they have? As long as Vayd's armies marched upon Warding, Kion would be forced to oppose him however he could.

Though he had left his father's letter back with the horses and the rest of his things in Whitewind, he knew the words by heart. Those words returned to him now, renewing his strength as they so often did:

…I will fight with all that is in me to keep the clouds from you.
I will not falter, however black the storms, nor must you.

Kion had failed to defeat Vayd, as he had in Charring. Even more bitterly, he had failed to save his mother. And beyond those failures, he had left the soldiers of the Four Wards to face the invading hordes on their own. No more. He could no longer save his mother. His path was now clear. From this day forward he would lend his blade wherever he was asked, wherever the fighting was fiercest. Until Vayd was fully and finally defeated and Shadowriven destroyed once and for all, he would not rest. He was a swordspeaker and this was his calling. But looking at his sister striding across the ice beside him, he took heart. For the next time he faced Vayd he would not be alone.

Continue the series

THE SWORDSPEAKER SAGA

GRIMBRIAR

BOOK 3

Also by DJ Edwardson

A hero is measured by the size of his heart.

Every century a motley is born. Though only children, their patchwork skin marks them as dangerous, especially to those who know about the first motley. That one nearly destroyed the world.

But a chance meeting with a simple tailor may hold the key to breaking the curse and saving their world.

Read book 1 in *The Null Stone Trilogy*

The key to the future is unlocking the past.

A man with no memories. A device with the power of time. Is it his salvation or the end of humanity? Read the unique, Grace Award-nominated science fiction series as unpredictable as the future itself.

Read all three volumes in *The Chronotrace Sequence*

About the Author

DJ Edwardson traveled a lot when he was younger. Now he's busy crafting exotic destinations of his own. Although he has written both Science Fiction and Fantasy novels, he likes to say he writes in the "genre of imagination."

He has a degree in English from Cornell College where his emphasis was on the works of Shakespeare. He's tried his hand at both acting and directing in the theater, but these days is happiest with a pen in hand. He lives in Tennessee with his wife and three children.

For more information about DJ Edwardson's writing please visit: *www.djedwardson.com*

www.ingramcontent.com/pod-product-compliance
Lightning Source LLC
Chambersburg PA
CBHW020911310726

48980CB00011B/838/J
9780988508286